"She is, quite simply, one of the best storytellers around."
—Tess Gerritsen

"Lisa Black writes with immediacy and unmatched authenticity."
—Jeff Lindsay

LET JUSTICE DESCEND

"Let Justice Descend is the definition of psychological suspense! Superbly drawn characters, nonstop plotting and a style that's downright lyrical keep us racing through this tale of crime, politics, power and journalism from first page to the last. This is a one-sitting read!"
—Jeffery Deaver, author of *The Bone Collector*

"This latest Gardiner and Renner mystery builds on the personal relationships among the leads while effectively exposing the underbelly of politics on the local and national levels. A high energy narrative with a final twist that will leave readers wanting more."
—Booklist

"An intriguing tale of skullduggery."
—Publishers Weekly

SUFFER THE CHILDREN

"With its solid grounding of information about child development, this fourth entry in the Gardiner and Renner series is instructional as well as being a well-plotted and -paced thriller with a pair of intriguing protagonists."
—Booklist

"A well-crafted thriller. Black keeps the suspense high throughout."
—Publishers Weekly

"In Suffer The Children, Black introduces a difficult topic and makes it come alive through her characters. The suspense builds to a well plotted climax that leaves the reader

"Fast-paced and appealingly written, with a somewhat light, occasionally witty style that *partly* offsets the gruesome subject matter…a good read."
—*PCA/ACA Mystery & Detective Fiction Reading List*

THAT DARKNESS

"Lisa Black always delivers authentic characters in riveting stories. *That Darkness* takes things to a spellbinding new level with a taut and haunting story that will stay with you long after you finish reading it."
—*Jeff Lindsay,* creator of *Dexter*

"Intriguing forensic details help drive the plot to its satisfying conclusion."
—*Publishers Weekly*

"Black is one of the best writers of the world of forensics, and her latest introduces Maggie Gardiner, who works for the Cleveland Police Department. Her relentless pursuit of answers in a dark world of violence is both inspiring and riveting. Readers who enjoy insight into a world from an expert in the field should look no further than Black."
—*RT Book Reviews,* 4 Stars

"The surprising ending is sure to keep readers coming back for more."
—*Booklist*

"Black, a forensics investigator, skillfully portrays the stark realities of homicide cases in her latest thriller. In this series launch, she pairs Maggie with Jack Renner, a determined detective with secrets of his own who has no intention of allowing murderers to evade their punishment. A great choice for readers of psychological suspense, forensic investigations, and mystery."
—*Library Journal*

"A crime thriller with a sharp psychological edge. . . . *That Darkness* left me thinking for days about the intricacies of the plot, the beauty of Lisa Black's writing, and the profound relationship between law and justice. Black, through her incredible characters and narration, has written a book that everyone should read. If you are a lover of mystery and suspense, this is an absolute must read."
—*Suspense Magazine*

Books by Lisa Black

Let Justice Descend

LISA BLACK

KENSINGTON BOOKS
www.kensingtonbooks.com

KENSINGTON BOOKS are published by

Kensington Publishing Corp.
119 West 40th Street
New York, NY 10018

All Kensington titles, imprints, and distributed lines are available at special quantity discounts for bulk purchases for sales promotion, premiums, fund-raising, educational, or institutional use. Special book excerpts or customized printings can also be created to fit specific needs. For details, write or phone the office of the Kensington Special Sales Manager: Attn. Special Sales Department. Kensington Publishing Corp, 119 West 40th Street, New York, NY 10018. Phone: 1-800-221-2647.

Kensington and the K logo Reg. U.S. Pat. & TM Off.

ISBN-13: 978-1-4967-2236-2
ISBN-10: 1-4967-2236-1
First Kensington Hardcover Edition: November 2019
First Kensington Mass Market Printing: July 2020

ISBN-13: 978-1-4967-2237-9 (ebook)
ISBN-10: 1-4967-2237-X (ebook)

10 9 8 7 6 5 4 3 2 1

Printed in the United States of America

To those I have aspired to emulate:
Ellery Queen, P.D. James, and Alastair MacLean

Let justice descend, you heavens, like dew from above,
like gentle rain let the clouds drop it down.
Isaiah 45:8

Chapter 1

Sunday, November 4
58 hours until polls close

"Well. That's not something you see every day," Maggie said.

The woman's body stretched along the walkway to her door, her feet, still in stylish heels, on the concrete slab and her back along the flagstones. Dead eyes stared up at the gray November sky, and a few colored leaves had fallen onto the neatly buttoned but damp suit coat. A briefcase and an overstuffed tote bag had fallen from her left hand, and her right clutched a knot of keys. No blood dried in the crisp air, no struggle had mussed her perfectly curled hair, nothing about her gave the slightest clue to her demise—save for the black streak on her right hand.

"First time I've ever seen something like this," Riley agreed, gazing not at the woman but at her front door.

Jack, as usual, said nothing.

Maggie Gardiner had already taken her "overall" photos—the yard, the exterior wall of the house, the body—and now turned to what had killed the woman. The front door to the woman's house had a heavy metal screen door with a design of curlicues and latticework, made to fit its surroundings, a brick century home. Its front yard seemed more like a courtyard, ringed by an eight-foot-high brick wall with a matching gate that led to the street, where the victim had parked her car. No driveway, no garage, but only one street from the lake and surrounded by other old-money homes on the edge of Cleveland's city limits. The cute courtyard, with a few wrought-iron bistro tables, mini lights, and even a Beer Meister kegerator under the protection of the elms, gave Maggie and the homicide detectives the ability to work in isolation. The high wall kept the dead woman's situation from both offending the delicate sensibilities and feeding the prurient interests of neighbors, media, and onlookers. A mourning dove sat in the branches above them, cooing a morose sigh to complement the scene.

From the woman's ice-cold body and complete rigor, she had apparently lain there all night, unseen, until staff had arrived to escort her to her first appointment of the day and had found her.

The woman's own home had killed her. Someone had cut the extralong cord to the squat kegerator, then peeled the wires inside the cord away from one another. A black-coated one had been snaked up the side of the metal screen door as far as it would reach, about three-quarters of the height. Its end had been stripped to the bare wire and wound firmly around one of the curlicues—quite visible in the daylight but tough to see in the dark, and Maggie assumed it would have been dark. The clothing told her the woman had come from work or some professional event, and the days had grown short. Tired, approaching her own door in the night, she would not have noticed the black wire.

Maggie noted the motion-sensor floodlight over the door, but it either wasn't functioning or had a light sensor so that it didn't come on during the day, because it didn't light up now.

From this same plug cord, the killer had taken the white-coated wire and connected it to a metal grate with the proportions of an undersized welcome mat. This he placed on the concrete slab in front of the door.

Then all he had to do was plug the cord back into the wall . . . and wait.

Jack Renner, homicide detective with more secrets than most of his suspects, had materialized at her elbow without a sound. It made her start, but not as much as it used to. Jack was tall, dark, decidedly not handsome, and a killer. She knew that and yet told no one, a fact that, even after six months, still astounded her when she woke to it each morning. "I get it," he said aloud. "When she stepped on the grounded plate and then touched the handle, her body completed the circuit."

His partner, Thomas Riley, stared down at the body. "I'd expect more . . . more. Wouldn't she, like, burst into flames?" Maggie raised one eyebrow at him, and his fair skin colored until he protested: "Well, we had a guy on a construction site who got tangled in a live wire, and he wound up practically cut in half."

"She's got the mark on her hand, and she'll probably have a similar scorch on one or both of her feet,"

Maggie said. They couldn't move or examine the body until an investigator from the Medical Examiner's office arrived. "That's fairly typical. Electrocutions can vary quite a bit, depending on how much power and where it goes. Frankly, it seems like an iffy method of murder."

Jack said, "Maybe. Wearing those probably helped." He gestured to the woman's fashionable shoes. "Thin soles, no rubber. Plus it rained last night."

Maggie examined the grate and the concrete slab without touching it, though the fire department had already pulled the plug from the outlet. The surface had sagged over the years, caving until grime accumulated in its shallow depth, providing the perfect resting spot for the grate. "It was already dirty, so she didn't notice the grate against the dark area. He could have even brushed some leaves over to disguise it. But wouldn't it have been, like, humming? How did it not set the house on fire?"

"They're not touching—the screen door and the grate." Riley stepped closer and pointed to the door's sill, two inches above the ground. "Each one alone is static, perfectly safe until—"

"Until she grabs the screen door handle and completes the circuit."

"Exactly. Then she dies, gravity takes over, her body falls back, her hand pulls away. The circuit is broken, and the door goes back to being a mere door. No fire, no sparking, no wildly zinging electric meter. Kind of ingenious, really." He caught her look. "Don't glare. It's, um, definitely different. Iffy, like you said. If that light worked and she noticed the wires. If the leaves blew away so she wondered why there was a metal grate in front of her door. If she had been wearing tennis shoes, or felt some static just before she touched the latch, or if some unlucky UPS guy came to drop off a package—assuming she left the outer gate unlocked during the day, anyone could have wandered in here—or if the outlet had a ground fault interrupter, it might not have worked."

Maggie glanced toward the covered outlet under which the cord lay among the scattered leaves. After nearly being blown up a few weeks earlier, she knew everything she had ever wanted to know about ground fault interrupters. "Frost-free refrigerators don't plug into outlets with GFIs because of the freezing-warming cycles. And aren't they two-twenty?"

"A small one like that, I don't know," Riley said. "Even one-ten could have killed her, what with the wetness, thin shoes, no gloves, and at her age her heart might not be that great any more. She's sixty-two, eight years older than me, and my doc's already giving me a hard time about cholesterol and coronary arteries. So electrocution might have seemed a pretty safe bet, as methods of murder go."

"Please don't sound so admiring," Maggie said without meaning it. By now, she knew Thomas Riley better than that.

He continued as if she hadn't spoken, still thinking the scenario through. "Even if it didn't work, he wasn't out a lot of work or effort. He didn't have to enter the house or bring anything with him except wire strippers and this metal grate, which—correct me if I'm wrong, Miss CSI—doesn't seem to have a spot on it wide enough to get a decent print from."

Maggie looked again at the latticework of metal

strips, none more than perhaps an eighth inch wide. "Probably not, no, especially after the rain."

"Or the plug?"

"Rubber covered and exposed to the elements? Unlikely. I'll swab for contact DNA, but if he wore gloves—"

"And he's an idiot if he didn't. So he doesn't set up a slam dunk but then he doesn't leave us any clues, either. Unless our dead lady has surveillance cameras set up, and I don't see any. Or if the neighbors saw someone dipping into this yard, and they haven't even poked their heads out to see what all the cop cars are for, so I'm not too optimistic."

"The perfect murder?" Maggie wondered.

"There's no such thing," Jack said. And he, of course, would know.

Within a half hour both the ME investigators and the search warrant arrived. It never ceased to amaze Maggie how finding a dead body on the stoop was *not* considered sufficient probable cause to enter a home, but there it was, and in any case she had been too busy with the scene to be in much of a hurry.

The kegerator fridge did not yield any fingerprints, not even with superglue—only a lot of water marks and dirt. Ditto for the outlet and the decorative grill of the screen door, where the black wire had been attached. The white one had been snaked along the edge of the house in the crack between the foundation and the concrete stoop, and accumulated dirt in the crack helped hide the white rubber coating. In terms of fingerprints, the dirt scarcely mattered, since the wires were too narrow for any usable latents, but she collected the length anyway, planning to take a much closer look at it in her lab. She did the same with the metal grate. The blanket of leaves, charming in their reds and browns and golds, made her nervous. The killer could have dropped his glove or his wallet or his business card on his way out and they might miss it in all that debris. But she didn't particularly want to rake the entire yard, either.

Meanwhile the detectives took the keys from the dead woman's hand and confirmed that the fob did, indeed, unlock a newish sedan parked at the curb. The front seats were tidy, but the rear ones held a variety of papers, folders, and brochures, all having slid around willy-nilly until no order could be detected. Three empty paper coffee cups, each rimmed with the same dark red lipstick as on the face of the victim, sat on the floorboard in front of the passenger's seat. The trunk held only a spare tire and an unopened set of jumper cables. Maggie photographed all of this but left it in place until they could decide what might be of significance.

In the grass behind the large oak, she found a black rubber mat with an open weave design—obviously what had been the victim's welcome mat. The mat was larger and thicker than the metal grate, but what with the leaves, the dark, perhaps hurrying through the rain, the victim did not notice the difference. She would have felt it with that last step, but in that instance it became too late, her hand already on the electrified door handle.

On a whim Maggie looked inside the small refrigerator, but it didn't seem to be missing a black wire shelf. It held a pony keg, shiny and secure and—she shook the entire unit—apparently empty. The fridge had probably been unplugged now that the season for outdoor parties had faded, but Maggie wondered why the owner would leave it outside. But then she didn't have a garage and would have needed help to lug the thing inside or down to a basement, or maybe Diane Cragin simply hadn't gotten around to it. Diane Cragin had been very busy and spent a great deal of time out of town, because Diane Cragin was a sitting U.S. senator, R–Ohio.

And that meant, Riley informed her as if Maggie hadn't already figured that out for herself, that this case was going to be a snafu of epic proportions.

"She had enemies?" Maggie asked.

"She's a politician. Would you like enemies listed alphabetically or in order of importance?"

He seemed to have paid more attention to politics than either Jack or Maggie, so he filled them in on what he could as the ME investigator, and Maggie examined the body. Diane Cragin had been the duly elected senator from Ohio for twelve years.

Diane Cragin had been campaigning on the usual issues of bringing jobs back to the rust belt and cleaning up food stamp requirements, didn't hire any tax-free domestic help, didn't sleep with her interns, and hadn't created any major scandals that Riley could remember, but . . .

Maggie looked up as the ME investigator removed the senator's shoes. "But?"

"A Cleveland guy has been running for her seat, Green. He's head of economic development or something like that. It's been a pretty nasty campaign—par for the course these days—and he's accused her of taking kickbacks, promising Ohio one thing and then flying to DC to agitate for the complete opposite, being paid under the table to lobby for the pharmaceuticals with the large hospitals, trading jobs for votes, basically all the same things she accuses him of doing. Politics as usual, in other words."

"You're a cynic," Maggie said.

"Impossible not to be these days."

Riley told her the unhappy man standing outside the courtyard had been Cragin's assigned Secret Service agent for this week. He had dropped her off still breathing the night before and had told anyone who would listen that escorting her only as far as the courtyard had been standard procedure for a senator who put a premium on her privacy and, after two terms in office, was accustomed to getting her own way. She had earned a reputation as an uncooperative client, and it got worse during stressful periods—such as these crazy days before Tuesday's election. So he had left her alive and inside the gate the night before, then saw the body that morning and had to break the gate door to get in.

"Is that it?" Riley asked Maggie.

"That's it." A scorch mark along the bottom of the woman's right foot had burned through her nylons and peeled a small amount of skin, with only a single round burn on the sole of the shoe.

The ME investigator, a young woman with dark skin and dimples, told them, "It doesn't take much, especially with AC power. Hey, bird," she said to the dove in the tree, which had been heaving its heavy sighs nonstop, "knock it off."

Sudden silence, save for the rustle of leaves in the breeze.

"We'll see if she had any medical conditions that made her more vulnerable. Do we have doctor information?"

"Not yet. We haven't been inside or done any notifications," Riley said.

"She's wearing nylons," the investigator said, as if she found this more perplexing than using a screen door as a murder weapon. Nylons and pantyhose had been out of style for years. Women now left their legs bare, cutting industry sales by more than half until nylons were rebranded as lingerie or "sheer tights." Or worn by older women like Diane Cragin, who wished to wear skirts without exposing every age spot, scar, and mole to the public, always so harsh on women's looks once they passed twenty-five or so.

"It's gotten chilly," Maggie pointed out.

The investigator, who had yet to see an age spot mar her perfect skin, shrugged and put Tyvek bags over the late senator's hands, pulling the drawstring tight to keep them from slipping off. The manicured fingernails would be scraped for trace evidence, not that anyone expected to find it—there had clearly *not* been a struggle or physical confrontation. She and Maggie turned the body to one side, but nothing waited underneath it except more dead leaves.

"That's it, then," the investigator said, pulling off her latex gloves with a definite *snap* as the body snatchers moved in to load up the earthly remains of Diane

Cragin. "You have a fun Halloween? I wanted to wear my sexy vampire costume all last Wednesday, but my supervisor said such frivolity wouldn't be in good taste."

Maggie said, "That's a pity. One does hate to see a good sexy vampire costume go to waste. To be honest, I can't remember the last time I dressed for Halloween."

"That's sad," the investigator said, and Maggie agreed that, yes, it was. But her life had changed that year, and perhaps such frivolity was no longer in good taste. Either that or she no longer had the taste for it.

She went to photograph the interior of the house with Jack and Riley.

Uniformed officers, armed with guns and the usual strict instructions not to touch anything (except doorknobs, as needed), had used the dead woman's keys to go inside and "clear" the house. The knob and keyed deadbolt had been securely latched. No one waited there, not family members, pets, or the killer. So the detectives walked behind Maggie as she entered, camera at the ready, hoping that Senator Cragin had left them some clue as to who had wanted her dead.

The bird started up again.

Chapter 2

The house had been built one hundred years before but lovingly preserved, and kept clean if not neat. The wool carpets were barely worn, the heavy windows sparkled, and the hardwood floors gleamed despite minor scars. It smelled of dust and ammonia and stale takeout. The entryway presented them with a staircase, a pristine living or sitting room on the right, and a cluttered office/dining room/reception area on the left. Maggie clicked a few overall shots of the pristine side, then ignored it to turn to the messy office. Cardboard boxes held printed brochures with Diane Cragin's face prominently displayed above the phrase BRINGING JOBS BACK TO OHIO, and Maggie took a moment to study what her victim had looked like when alive. Not really much different than she did when dead, it seemed, though happier, with blond hair and blue eyes and the figure of a middle-aged woman who watched her weight. She formed the perfect, neutral picture of a strong and competent woman. Only her smile kept her from appearing generic: a wide, almost impish grin, as if she knew something that no one else did and had every intention of keeping it that way.

The dining table, which served as a desk or perhaps merely a staging area, also held myriad papers, newspapers, and a list of voting precincts and their captains. Maggie said, "There's a lot here about polls."

Riley poked one with a finger. "'Getting out the likes campaign.' What does that mean?"

"Facebook," she told him.

"Ye gods. Hydrocarbon forecast?"

Jack said, "EPA business."

Riley continued. "Here's 'Green hammer points.' Not green as in environmental, green as in Joe Green. If they're running against each other, that makes him suspect number one, but isn't that too . . . what's the word?"

"Cliché?" Maggie said.

"Easy," Jack suggested.

"Yeah. Besides, I don't think politicians assassinate each other as often as they would like. Hell, if they ever shot anything more than rhetoric at each other, the streets would run red and we'd have all the overtime we could handle."

Just then, one of Maggie's paper bags started ringing. She had put Diane Cragin's purse and briefcase into paper bags and left them in the foyer to get them out of the elements, and now the victim's cell phone rang. No song or cutesy voice, only an insistent *beep beep beep* like a kitchen timer.

It stopped by the time Maggie pulled on latex gloves and retrieved it from the purse, holding it up for the detectives to see. The screen read "Kelly" with a thumbnail of a young woman with chopped black hair.

Automatic screen alerts told them that she had already called twice that morning, at 7:15 and 8:10. It was now coming up on nine a.m. and Kelly had grown impatient, hanging up and then immediately calling a fourth time.

They let this call go to voice mail as well and kept moving through the house. The kitchen had butcher block counters, antique linoleum flooring, and not much food in the fridge among the cans of Red Bull and Mountain Dew. "She likes caffeine," Maggie commented.

Riley peeked at the shelves. "That stuff will kill you even without two-twenty."

A modern laundry room at the back of the house had no clothes in the washer or dryer and a door leading to a sort of alley without a yard or a parking space. The back door had both a chain and a deadbolt, both fastened from the inside. Nearby steps led to a cellar with a dirt floor and a set of folding chairs, covered in dust. Aside from that and a number of cardboard boxes of Christmas decorations, it did not appear to be used for anything. Maggie did not think the killer had found the metal grate in the victim's cellar. Nothing similar to it seemed to be around, nor were there any rectangular-shaped gaps in the dust.

They made their way to the second floor.

"I'm guessing she's not married," Maggie said. No one had mentioned family, and she saw no sign of male clothing in the small bedroom.

"Don't know, actually," Riley said. "She has two kids, grown now. I only know that because according to Green, they're both the big corporate types who walk over the little guys she's supposed to be working for."

Her paperwork might be messy, but the woman took good care of her clothes. Each item either hung in the closet or sat folded in a drawer, with a few pieces resting in a plastic laundry basket. Cosmetics and creams covered half of the bathroom counter, with two empty coffee cups and a box of tissues on the other side. Maggie had the impression that Diane Cragin spent most of her time in Washington; her local possessions seemed sparse and impersonal. Drawers and cabinets held only aspirin, decongestant, and an expired bottle of lisinopril, 10 mg.

"What's that for?" Jack asked, crowding into the tiny bathroom with her. His proximity didn't unsettle her as much as it used to, despite knowing how many criminals he had murdered without benefit of due process.

Perhaps how many, she corrected herself. She probably didn't know about them all. Jack had been a little fuzzy on details, but then, she hadn't pressed. The more she knew, the less she could justify her complicity in her own mind.

Best not to ask. Best to focus on the task at hand. And he had abandoned that habit now . . . or so he said.

She told him, "High blood pressure. A mild dose, and high blood pressure doesn't mean you have a weak heart. I'm not a doctor, but I don't think it would make her any easier to kill—with electricity, I mean."

Riley poked his head into the small bathroom. "Anything interesting?"

"BP meds and aspirin," she said.

"No cocaine? What kind of a senator was she?"

"This whole house feels empty to me. Of course, it's not that big."

"She played that up—not living high on the tax-payer's hogs—but Green says it's because she spent as little time here as possible," Riley said. "I guess they rank our representatives every year for how much time they spend with their own constituents, and she'd always be near the bottom."

"You pay pretty close attention—" Maggie began as she opened a tall, narrow cabinet and promptly forgot what she'd been about to say. Because instead of bath towels and shampoo, she now stared at a tall, narrow safe. "Okay, now we got something a little more interesting."

Both detectives crowded against her to see—not that they could help it; the room had only about ten square feet of floor space, and the open cabinet door blocked the entryway.

The safe might have been custom built to fit the cabinet, as it cleared the six-by-three-foot interior by millimeters. The logo read PATRIOT SAFE COMPANY, and though it had an oversized combination dial and a heavy handle, it seemed much too shiny to have come with the house.

"That *is* interesting," Riley said.

"Nothing strange about having a safe, though," Jack said. "There's no one here most of the time. Anyone could look up her schedule online and know the house would be empty."

His partner said, "But in the bathroom? Why not behind the picture of some ancestor in the living room like it's supposed to be?"

"Did you watch a lot of *Scooby-Doo* when you were a kid?" Maggie asked.

"Why do you think I became a cop? Besides, what's she got to keep in a safe? There's barely any personal property around. I doubt we'll find her mother's pearls on the top shelf."

Jack ignored these asides. "The search warrant covers this, right?"

"Don't touch it!" Maggie said. "Let me process for prints first . . . though I doubt I'll get anything. Why people make safes with a textured finish when that's the one place you're really going to *want* a fingerprint to show—" she grumbled, but the men had already turned away. Raised voices could be heard outside, and Riley crossed the bedroom to look out the window.

"What is it?" Jack asked.

Riley turned to say, "I think it's Kelly."

Kelly Henessey turned out to be a slender woman in her late twenties in carefully conservative slacks; athletic shoes carefully designed to look like dress shoes; and short, swingy hair carefully designed to look as if it had been cut with a pair of garden shears. "I'm Diane's chief of staff. I handle her schedule, delegate the tasks she needs done, do research, fend off lobbyists, and issue press releases. Basically every single thing she does in a day, I either start it or finish it." She paused in her agitated pacing along the flagstones— the detectives weren't ready to let her into the house, even though the killer most likely never went inside and they weren't sure what clues they were even looking for, anyway. But Kelly Henessey didn't seem to care or even notice the dead leaves crunching under her feet. "I'm sorry, that sounds really egotistical. I don't mean that I was, like, the power behind the throne or anything . . . Basically I'm a secretary-slash-gofer, but that's what I'm supposed to be, and it was well worth it to work with Diane. I'm learning everything from her. Learned." She paused long enough to face them, her eyes blank and uncomprehending. "Is she really dead?"

"I'm afraid so," Riley said.

Jack studied the woman, blocking the front door and keeping a close eye on her travels. He didn't want her near where the wires had been, though all the evidence had been removed and Maggie had done all she could with the screen door. They had left Maggie upstairs, working on the safe, but he doubted she would find anything. The entire house had been locked up tight, so if Diane Cragin had been killed for the contents of her safe, and if those contents had since been removed, it had been done by someone who had access to the house, had the combination to the safe, and knew exactly what they were looking for.

Perhaps someone, he thought, like Kelly Henessey. He watched her eyes to see if they would flicker to the outlet, the kegerator, the stoop where the metal plate had lain. Nothing.

"But she was fine last night! Fine," the woman repeated, and began the restless movements again, as if physically circling around to the truth she didn't feel ready to reach. "Did she go to the hospital? Why didn't anyone call me?"

"Did Ms. Cragin have any health issues?" Riley asked. Kelly seemed to assume, as most people would, that the death had been natural, and they saw no reason to enlighten her.

"No! Not that I knew of, anyway, and I made her doctor's appointments. She didn't always eat right, of course—way too much high-fructose corn syrup—and she drank alcohol now and then—and she didn't exercise, per se . . . but seriously she must have logged twenty thousand steps a day. I gave her a Fitbit for her birthday to find out." She shook off this memory and asked, "What was it? Heart attack? Stroke?"

"We're not exactly sure yet. But you say her health was good?"

"Yes, but . . . she *was* in her sixties." Which to a woman Kelly's age must have seemed ready for a rest home. "She was fine last night. A bundle of energy, just like every single day I've known her."

"Tell us about yesterday," Riley said in his avuncular way, notebook already in hand. "How long had Diane been in town?"

The answers came promptly and firmly. "Since Friday night. Day before yesterday."

"And you came with her?"

"Yes, a Delta flight, Dulles to Hopkins."

"Do you live here?"

"No! I mean, not in this house—and not in Cleveland, no. I have a brownstone in DC. When we're here I stay at the Marriott. I'm from Cincinnati, originally," she added, as if that might help her standing among them.

"Can you walk me through Diane's schedule yesterday?"

She didn't hesitate, either in speech or step, continuing to move as she spoke, brushing the leaves aside as if she were angry at them. "Eight a.m. breakfast with the Capital Management unit at city Hall. Nine-thirty visit to RNC—"

"RNC?"

"Republican National Committee HQ. Because the election is Tuesday—and don't ask me what the *hell* we're going to do now!"

This thought so upset her that it took a gentle prod from Riley to get her thoughts back on the timetable.

"We were supposed to visit the river site at ten, but Carlyle cancelled, so we rescheduled for today, even though it's Sunday. We . . . we were supposed to be there at eight this morning, but she didn't show up. The ribbon cutting is at ten! I'm going to have to call—"

"You weren't going to pick her up?" Riley interrupted.

"She likes to drive herself. She's not pretentious that way . . . 'not one of those old-money Republicans,' she always says. Of course, Devin follows her."

Riley's eyebrows swept up, and a severe tone crept into his voice, speaking on behalf of taxpayers everywhere: "Does it really save any money to have the Service guys in a separate car?"

"No, but driving around and sleeping is the only quiet time she gets."

Jack stood, arms crossed, watching her as she spoke. Thoroughly discombobulated but not devastated—and that seemed appropriate. Diane Cragin had been her boss, not her mother, so it didn't seem odd to him that her thoughts already turned toward replacing candidates rather than abject grief. Even if she hadn't quite moved the woman into the past tense.

And the pacing had slowed. Now Kelly stayed on one flagstone, feet planted as if the grass had become moving water and she must stay balanced to avoid a soaking. "Because Carlyle cancelled, we were early for lunch at Lola with the money half of Vepo. In the afternoon, a stop at the public employees' union and a tour of Medical Mart with the Google Analytics reps. Three o'clock meeting with state party accountants. Then she came home to freshen up before the fundraiser."

"What time—"

"It started at five, and she was on time for once. Her speech went well. About nine, I think, she told me she was leaving and to make sure Ken and Andre and Jade had everything they needed."

"Did she have any plans to stop anywhere?"

"I didn't ask, but I doubt it. She didn't say anything, and she looked pretty tired."

"Not surprising. That sounds like a pretty busy day."

She blinked at Riley as if this statement baffled her. "They're all like that."

"Where was this fund-raiser?"

"City Club. It's on Euclid—"

"Yes, I know," Riley assured her. The City Club, established 1912, had been in its current location for 35 years. "Did she have any arguments with anyone in town? Any beefs?"

A hint of a smile, the first one Jack had seen from

her, at the old-fashioned term. "*Beefs*? About a million, but nothing unusual. Everyone is on the same page as Diane—they know she's doing what's right for the state and for Cleveland. Carlyle is a pain, but—"

"Who's Carlyle?"

A half eye-roll. "The EPA inspector for the crib renovation."

"Crib?" Riley asked.

"The water intake facility," Jack said. Riley's eyebrows raised again, apparently surprised that a relatively recent transplant like Jack would know the term. The "crib" took in water for the city's supply from a structure about three miles offshore in Lake Erie. Like the senator's home, it had been there for about one hundred years and carefully maintained, but still some extensive upkeep was due. Jack had read about the reno job in the *Herald* once or twice.

Kelly went on. "He's making a fuss about it, but that's what the EPA does—makes a fuss. Diane wasn't worried, the facts will back us up. Wait—has anyone called her kids?" Already pale, she blanched further. "Will *I* have to do that?"

"We can make notification," Riley soothed, and asked where the family members lived.

"Her daughter's in Texas and her son's in Washington—the state, not the city. She has one grandchild . . . I'm not sure if it's her son's or her daughter's. Hey, she has some sort of a niece or something in town here—she can tell Diane's kids. They'd be, like, cousins, right? So that will work."

"What's the niece's name?"

"Oh, hell, I don't know. And we're going to have

some sort of state funeral! I don't even know how to do that!"

Riley continued with the softened voice. He was good at it, much better than Jack. "I'm sure someone in Washington has experience with situations like this. Did she—"

"The RNC will know what to do, but I'll have to—" Kelly Henessey mused, lost in thought over discreet coffins and invitation lists. Doing her job to the end, Jack thought—admirable but perhaps not helpful right then. If Diane Cragin had any enemies bitter enough to murder, or had gotten mixed up in a deal dirty enough to kill, they would have to overcome Kelly's professional reticence. Political second-in-commands existed to protect their bosses from every sling and arrow, and she would continue to polish Diane's star even in death, out of either a sense of loyalty or a sense of polishing her own résumé at the same time. No one in DC would want to hire someone who couldn't keep a secret. "The governor has to appoint someone for the rest of the term—no problem since he's the same party, but it seems silly for two days . . . he'll only pick his choice for the new candidate anyway—but the election. Oh my God, the election!"

"Miss Henessey—"

A breeze swept through the yard, and the chill seemed to jolt Kelly back to herself. The sky remained gray, and the temperature hovered in the midsixties—not bad for November in Cleveland. "Why are we standing out here? Can we go inside?"

"Not yet. We're still processing." But this time Riley's

tone couldn't smooth over the logic. The young woman became still as she stared at him.

"What do you mean, processing?"

He told her that they needed to establish all the facts about her boss's death, due diligence, giving the care and attention, etcetera, and all the while Jack watched Kelly Henessey as a hawk watches a mouse, looking for any sign that she already knew what had happened.

He saw none.

When Riley finally confessed that Diane Cragin's death had been anything but natural, Kelly reacted by not reacting. He may as well have spoken in Swahili.

"What do you mean, homicide? Someone killed her? On purpose?"

"Extremely on purpose," Jack said.

"How? Why? I mean—who? Did they shoot her?"

"No," Riley said. "We'd like to ask—"

"Was she stabbed?"

"No—"

"Then how can you be sure she was murdered?"

"We're sure," Jack said, and his tone must have convinced, because she accepted it—that her boss was not only gone but willfully gone—and then her eyes changed and focused and became hard.

"Where the hell was Devin?"

"The Secret Service agent?"

"Yes, the Secret Service agent! The guy whose *job* it is to protect Diane?"

Riley told her how the senator had banned the agent from accompanying her inside, that he checked the courtyard and saw it was empty, waited for her to lock the gate behind him, said good night, and left, the same as every other night.

The routine of this procedure must have been true, because Kelly did not argue it, only ran her hands through her hair in apoplexy.

"So he did it, then. That fat fu—um, they did it. I can't believe they actually killed her."

"Who did?" Riley asked.

She burst back into full-on agitated, stalking to and fro across the fallen leaves, hands increasing the lift of her hair, voice moving up a decibel or two with every fresh obscenity, until Jack demanded, *"Who?"*

"The Democrats," she snapped. "Who else?"

Chapter 3

The press had begun to gather outside the tiny walled yard, and Maggie had finished processing the kitchen, so the detectives brought Kelly Henessey inside, where her accusations could not be overheard by neighbors or reporters with notepads and parabolic mikes. Maggie steered her toward the old wooden table and its three chairs and away from the countertops, sink, and cabinets, now dirtied with black fingerprint powder. She had collected several prints from the taps and the glasses in the sink but knew they would most likely match the victim.

Then she lingered, not knowing where to place her focus next and not wanting to tell the detectives what she had found in front of a witness/suspect/closest thing to a family member in the vicinity. Besides, she was curious—about the victim and her untimely death, but also about the political arena.

It took Riley a while to settle the chief of staff down to answering the questions put to her. After she had cursed the entire Democratic party with every foul thing she could think of, Kelly had ached to make phone calls to the entire Republican counterpart to discuss press conferences, next week's quorum call, who would replace Diane in the upcoming election, and where on earth the senator would be buried. Riley nearly had to pull the phone out of her hand to stop her from spreading the news just yet, and at least until the woman's own children could be notified.

That immediately proved difficult. Kelly didn't have their phone numbers and wasn't positive of which cities the son and the daughter lived in. Diane Cragin either had not been very close to her children or had been so close that she chose to safeguard their privacy like the Holy Grail. Maggie guessed it might be the former when Kelly said, "Diane gave me the impression they didn't call her much, had sided with their father in the divorce. And don't ask me where *he* lives—I don't even know his name. They split up ages ago, like twenty or thirty years, and she never talked about it." Kelly didn't know of any other family members at all, not siblings or aunts or nephews. Maybe Diane Cragin lived in a personal vacuum. Maybe she had simply been too busy to stay in touch.

Normally police would turn to the victim's address book—formerly kept in decorative volume and stored in a desk, now kept in digital format on cell phones. But Diane Cragin's phone, once the screen went to sleep, required a passcode, and Maggie knew better than to mess with that. Enter the wrong code and most phones would lock the user out for a period of time. After several it might wipe itself clean altogether, and all those contacts, texts, e-mails, and search histories would be gone for good. Maggie wished she could at least put it into airplane mode to keep it from any external interference, but without a passcode she couldn't get to the settings. Instead she'd called the IT department and a tech had made the fifteen-minute drive to pick the phone up from her. The IT tech hadn't even argued—her first indication of how different the investigation into the murder of a senator within city limits would be from the average drive-by or domestic case. Unfair, but undeniable.

After turning over the phone she photographed the contents of the handbag and the briefcase. They were both stuffed but, like the dining room table, Maggie couldn't guess if any item held a clue to her death. She would spread out the items at the lab, but a cursory look didn't find any threatening letters, illegal drugs, weapons, or large sums of money. If the agendas and reports were clues, they weren't very obvious ones.

Meanwhile, she listened to Kelly as she offered to ask the victim's hairdresser and pointed out that the woman who had been dying Diane's roots for over a decade might have more personal information. "But you've got to let me call somebody. We have *so* much to do."

"I get that," Riley said. "But it's important that we do everything correctly here, right? And that means getting as much information as we can before—"

"I saw the press outside, which means they're probably airing as we speak. Fox News will jump on this with everything they've got, and we have to manage the message."

Jack, not the soul of patience, spoke. "Your boss is dead. That's a little more pertinent than this month's election."

"No, it's *not*! I mean because she *is* dead. The last thing we can do is let them get away with it. They'll spin this around so that she was killed by the rich corporate Illuminati rather than the oh-so-hardworking street thugs that fat asshole caters to."

"I'm going to level with you," Riley said. Maggie assumed that meant he intended to do everything but, and from the skeptical look on her face, so did Kelly. "We're starting from scratch here. Ms. Cragin's world obviously spread pretty wide, and the killer didn't leave us any indication whether his motives were personal, political, monetary, or he just likes killing people. So let's start with the *first* person you would suspect. Even though he might be the *last* person you would—"

"Joe Green," she said, reiterating a statement she'd already made several times in as many minutes. The Democratic candidate for United States senator from Ohio."

"Okay. Why?"

She scrunched her bottom more firmly onto the chair and shook out her fingers as if preparing for a typing test. "He's running for her senate seat, as if he would know the slightest thing about a national office. He's only some stupid chief of, like, the Economic Development office in the city—" She paused, as if realizing that full-time Clevelanders might not appreciate her dismissal of a local position, then cleared her throat and pressed on: "And he hasn't raised half the funds she has. I mean, not even a whole million, only $708,000 to her $3,347,000, which means even the Dems know he hasn't got a chance, because if he did, they'd give him more money."

"You think he'd be desperate enough to murder?"

"I doubt it would be the first time."

"Really," Jack said. "Who else has he killed?"

She backpedaled, but with obvious reluctance. "I don't know offhand. But he's been bribing, extorting, and corrupting his way through Cleveland government for a long time. Take his latest project. He's getting some kid financed to buy up riverfront land and build an 'innovation center,' a building where start-ups can rent a little space along with copiers, printers, and phones and start their own business, because we all know someone who turned their science fair project into the next Starbucks or Apple, right? That's all cute and fine, except he's asking the city to approve a *twelve-million-dollar grant* to pay for this—that's not a twelve-million-dollar tax *loan* or tax credit or even subsidy, it's just a twelve-million-dollar blank check. I don't know how much of that is kicking back to Green, but I've heard estimates as high as sixty percent."

"What has that got to do with Diane?" Riley asked when she paused to take a breath.

"Diane is the whole reason anyone is paying attention to it! Green had been keeping this as far under the radar as he could. Somehow he got the levy passed last year, but since then he's quashed anyone who even mentions it, except when he wants to announce how he's bringing jobs to Cleveland." Her fingers made air quotes around the last four words, derision dripping from her voice. "Then he talks up a storm about how innovation and entrepreneurship are the keys to the future—well, yeah, because no one can make a freakin' livable wage in this economy. But the media, news channels, a newspaper reporter who's been trying to follow the money trail—they were all stonewalled. Diane was trying to help find the truth."

Riley said, "Okay. Anything else?"

"Else? What else do you need?"

"We'll check out his whereabouts. But—"

"That won't help. He's got a cadre of loyalists, his own doctor to keep his happy pills off the books, mechanics to sweep for bugs or plant a few, and I'm sure there's a few professional assassins in the lot. Look, he—I mean, you live here, you must know about this guy. He's chief of Economic Development, which is in the Regional Development division. So he's right in there with Community Development, Building and Housing, City Planning, even the port. As they can tell you in New Jersey, that's where the money is. Utility contracts, building contracts, construction, rezoning—anything you want to accomplish in the city of Cleveland, you have to grease Green's palm. You want specifics?" She gestured with both hands, pointing her right index finger to the left and the left to the right, illustrating the interconnectedness of this circle of favors and funds. "A halfway house system gave him a refrigerator and a trip to Las Vegas to get a partnership arrangement with the Department of Corrections. A paving company that did some work in the park system, the, um, Emerald Necklace place—"

"The Metroparks," Maggie supplied.

"Yeah, that. They also paved Green's driveway and his sister's. The union negotiator for a housing development along the lake gave him limousine service for three years. One guy got a lease for an ice-skating rink at the same time Green got a speedboat that had belonged to the guy's restaurant business. A bank executive had sex with him a few times to get her daughter a teaching position at a downtown charter school. What else would you like to know? I can go on and on."

"One thing," Jack said. "Do you have any proof of any of this?"

"That's not the question you should be asking. You should—"

"Don't tell me what questions I should be asking!" Jack shot back, his voice suddenly thunderous in that way that sucked all the air out of the room and made time slow to a crawl. Even knowing him, knowing as much as she did about him, and even though it wasn't directed at her, it made Maggie's heart flutter to a skitterish beat.

But then, fear pervaded *because* she did know quite a bit about him.

Kelly, of course, didn't have that knowledge. She didn't know that Jack had deceived everyone around him far more thoroughly than any politician could. "Don't try the good cop, bad cop bit on me. It's going to take a hell of a lot more than that act to throw me off."

This almost made Maggie smile, because the two men were not putting on a show. Riley really *was* a pleasant, fairly compassionate officer. And Jack was— well, Jack.

"We don't act," Riley said, calmly but more coolly than usual. "Your boss has been murdered, and we are going to find out who did it. We need facts, not all the rhetoric. Now, do you have evidence to prove any of this?"

Her shoulders slumped about an inch. "If I had

proof, we wouldn't have needed to spend a penny on the campaign."

Riley asked, "Speaking of the election, would killing Diane really make it a slam dunk for Green? Wouldn't another candidate—"

"We'll never get the ads, the name recognition, queued up fast enough. Even if we got someone already known—like the governor . . . that might be cool if he hadn't already said he wasn't interested. Two days? Impossible. All we can do is throw ourselves on the mercy of party loyalists and hope that is enough. And it may not be," she added morosely. "There's an awful lot of Independents these days."

"Didn't anyone else run in the primary?" Riley asked.

"Three, but they're out of money, and the party wasn't interested in any of them, anyway."

"What about the voters? Were they interested?"

Another one of those long, perplexed looks, as if Kelly wondered what color the sky was on Riley's planet, while the color of his skin began to flush with annoyance. Patiently, she explained, "Voters decide on the winner, but they don't decide on who runs in the first place. Parties do. They pick the people they think could win, pay for their ads, and finance everything they need, depending on how much they need it—which depends on the district. If your district is ninety percent red or blue, obviously you don't need to spend a lot of money." She glanced at all three people in the kitchen to assess their tracking abilities, without appearing reassured, and went further. "Someone doesn't wind up in office because they woke up in their bungalow in Podunk, Iowa, and decided to run for office. They get into office because their party needed a candidate and went looking for one, buttered them up, wooed them away from their jobs and homes, agreed to take care of their campaign, and sent them into the ring."

"The other candidates are only there to make it look like a real contest," Jack translated.

"Sort of." Her shoulders slumped from the weight on them. "That's why I have to get back to the HQ, so we can start figuring out who to pick."

"What about you?" Jack asked.

Her jaw dropped a millimeter or two. "*Me*? I'm not a politician. I *work* for politicians."

It didn't seem like such a far-fetched idea to Maggie but was clearly laughable to Kelly. It also seemed to remove any *All About Eve* type motivations from Diane Cragin's chief of staff.

Riley asked, "Let's suppose it isn't Green. Who else did Diane conflict with? Had she been getting any hate mail? People getting in her face at public appearances?"

"Um, everyone, yes, and all the time. That's politics these days. Conflict drives interest, and without interest people don't donate. But other than the usual rhetoric, I can't think of anyone really . . . scary. Except maybe—"

A knock sounded at the door, and Riley went to speak to the scene contamination officer, who wanted to know if the chief of homicide and a few other bigwig looky-loos could be allowed into the yard. The detective went out to give them a guided tour, and Kelly moved over to the stacks of haphazard paper on the dining room table. "As I recall, these are physical letters, these are printouts of the e-mails, and these are ones we flagged for some sort of action, like referring them to someone in their precinct. Do we have any coffee? I'm running a quart low, and I'm going to need it. Can I *please* call DC now?"

"In a minute," Jack said.

"And some of them," she continued as if she hadn't interrupted herself, "get kind of weird." But instead of explaining, she crossed to the sink, hand reaching for a cabinet, before Jack could mutter a *hey*!

A frown of annoyance. "I just want a drink of water."

Jack deferred to Maggie, who said, "Go ahead, I'm done with it. There might be black powder on the cabinet and the faucet, though."

Kelly had the sense to stop before her pricey-looking clothes brushed the dirtied countertop edge. She got a glass from the second cabinet she opened and filled it from the tap. Then she noticed black powder from the faucet handle on her fingers, turned it back on, rinsed, turned off, still had traces of black. She finally solved the conundrum by soaking a paper towel and washing off the handles, then rinsing her fingers and filling the glass before turning the tap off, talking all the while. "I mean, this could be some psycho stalker, right? Someone who thought she was sending him love messages through the press releases and then imagined a rejection as well?"

Jack donned gloves to look through the pile, and Maggie did the same. "Did she have stalkers?"

"A few in the past. Nothing recent. Usually the FBI would pay them a visit and they'd decide to switch their attentions to someone else."

"We'll take a look. Are there any that aren't here? Are some thrown out upon receipt?"

"Nothing is thrown out. You want to make a point to your congressman, send an old-fashioned letter. Not a phone call, not an e-mail. Someone has to actually open a letter, read it, and put it in a file, where it stays."

Maggie read over Jack's shoulder as he quickly skimmed the letters. Nearly every one accused Diane Cragin of being a racist and usually added in another form of bigotry such as homophobia, zenophobia, or ageism. Some insisted that charter schools were destroying the American educational system by letting public schools deteriorate while private concerns used taxpayer-provided subsidies to steal all the best students. Many linked her with big oil and big energy, which explained why solar power and electric cars couldn't get a foothold in the country's business model.

If this represents a sampling of the suspect pool, Maggie thought, *this investigation is off to a rough start.*

Kelly, meanwhile, pulled a bottle of prescription meds from her purse and worked the childproof cap between her palms.

Jack asked, "Who is Randy Cunningham?"

A sigh of the greatly put-upon. "Used to be a representative. California."

"This letter refers to he and the senator collecting bribes."

"Ancient history," she sneered, and then remembered to add, "and not true. At least not on Diane's part."

When she saw this did not satisfy him, she explained in more detail. "This was a really long time ago, like 2005."

"Oh, yes," Jack said with a straight face. "Ancient history."

"Randy Cunningham was on the Defense Appropriations Subcommittee for a while. During that time he sold his house for close to two million dollars to a guy named Mitchell something. This Mitchell something owned a defense contracting firm, specialized in counterterrorism analysis and all that. Mitchell's company begins to get defense and intelligence contracts figuring into the tens of millions."

"Wow," Maggie said.

"About fifty percent of the national budget goes to defense—the discretionary budget, I mean. Of the *entire* budget, fifty percent plus is health costs and Social Security, and defense is actually about seventeen." Her shoulders quivered in a small shrug. "It's still a lot of money to play with."

"How does the senator figure into this story?" Jack asked.

"Mitchell eventually resells Cunningham's house at half the price. Meanwhile, when Cunningham is in DC, he's living rent-free on a yacht that belongs to Mitchell. Eventually this all comes out, some reporters in San Diego get a Pulitzer, and Cunningham went to jail for a couple of years."

"And the senator?"

"Diane was his chief of staff at the time. And . . . she had sold her condo for way more than market value to some woman who worked for a subsidiary of Mitchell's company. But, as I said, never charged."

Jack pointed out, "This e-mail says Diane was a crook then and is still one now."

Kelly remained unimpressed and popped two pills into her mouth, then swallowed the water. "It's not a secret."

"Did anyone consider themselves particularly harmed by Cunningham and the senator?"

"I have no idea. I was in, like, ninth grade at the time."

Now Jack sighed.

"Look at this," Maggie said.

A handwritten message addressed to Senator "Jezebel" Cragin stated that she had clearly been paid off by the company that got the crib renovation contract, since they had a terrible record with water construction projects. The letter ended by pointing out that she proved Andrew Feinstein's maxim that politicians are like prostitutes, only considerably more expensive.

The words weren't particularly ominous, but the handwriting—all capital letters that didn't stick to the lines and became more unstable toward the bottom of the page—indicated a strong emotion. The writer had not signed a name or left a return address on the envelope.

Maggie said, "He says she will be struck by lightning." She and Jack exchanged a glance.

Kelly said, "Yeah, that's the one I thought was weird. They're not opioids."

"What?" Maggie asked.

"These." She held out the bottle long enough for Maggie to read *Sarafem* off the label. "I'm not crazy and I'm not addicted to pain meds, or alcohol, or oxy. I have a medical condition."

"Okay."

"Not everyone in DC is a coke-sniffing addict." The woman stowed the bottle and hung her tote bag off the back of a chair. "They'd be a lot easier to get along with if they were. I'm going to need Diane's stuff—her phone, her organizer, her laptop . . . even though she really didn't do a lot on her laptop. *I* did it all on *my* laptop. For a former lawyer, she wasn't much of a typist."

"All her personal property will eventually be released to her next of kin," Jack said.

Kelly's face contorted with horror. "But her kids—they don't care! They won't even know what all the party stuff is, and we can't wait that long, anyway. And technically, you know, it belongs to the RNC."

Jack sounded implacable. "We can deal with disposition once the investigation is complete."

"But—"

Riley came back inside. "I got rid of the powers that be, but some guy in a suit just showed up." He looked at Kelly Henessey. "He says he's your lawyer."

"I don't have a lawyer," said Kelly Henessey.

Chapter 4

Before Riley could hustle her outside to deal with the not-her-lawyer guy, said guy had managed to dart around the contamination officer and into the small foyer, where he thoughtfully wiped his feet on the mat and paid no attention to his supposed client.

"Who are—" Kelly began.

"My name is Raymond Stanton. I'm the Central Committee Chairman of the Cuyahoga County unit."

Riley protested. "I thought you said—"

"And I double as an attorney for the party. I'm here to take possession of all RNC equipment."

"You're prompt," Riley said.

"Has the house been cleared? I can collect the items now."

"We can't disperse any of the woman's possessions until it's all gone through probate."

"I am here only for RNC equipment. Of course I have no interest in any of Ms. Cragin's personal possessions. Items such as campaign materials, her laptop, her phone, RNC paperwork, were all loaned from the committee and never actually owned by Ms. Cragin."

"Yes, but her next of kin—"

"Have been notified."

"What? You called this woman's children—"

"Of course not. They were personally visited at their workplaces by members of the RNC from their locality. We didn't want them to hear it on the news, where it will probably appear in the next few minutes."

Huh, Maggie thought. Despite attorney Stanton's cold tone, it couldn't have been a worse way for loved ones to hear the news than having a uniformed officer show up on their doorstep.

"Well, that's nice of you," Riley said. "But this is a crime scene, and nothing is going to be removed until we have cleared it."

"But RNC items—"

"Aren't going anywhere until we have completed our investigation."

The attorney scowled but didn't argue. Maggie figured he hadn't truly expected to win that battle. "What can you tell me about Ms. Cragin's death? A lot of people are going to have a lot of questions."

"No doubt. But at present we have no details for release. When we do, I'll be sure to let you know."

Stanton looked as if there were several comments he could make in response to Riley's tone of voice but knew better than to waste his time. "Miss Henessey? First we have to cancel that ribbon cutting and then we have much coordinating to do. You best knew the senator's contacts."

She took a few steps into the kitchen to retrieve her

tote bag, then walked out the door without so much as a good-bye.

As she watched their retreating backs, Maggie couldn't help but ask, "Are you going to let her—"

"Yeah, for now," Riley said. "We've gotten a time line and the basics from her, and we know where they'll be. They're a straightforward lot, I'll say that for them."

Jack said, "That isn't the word I would use."

Maggie said, "There's something I need to show you."

Maggie had examined the senator's bedroom upstairs for signs of disturbance but found no sign that the killer had searched the house. She did note a streak through the dust on top of the antique dresser, pointing straight at a pink heart-shaped porcelain box with flowers spelling MOM on its lid. Black powder now marred the gloss, with a sharp outline where Maggie had lifted a piece of fingerprint tape from across the capital M. "Only some rings inside," she pointed out, lifting the lid so they could see the jumble of inexpensive jewelry nestled against worn velveteen, "but look at the bottom."

She flipped it over, where a piece of paper had been taped to the bottom. *14-138-67* had been written in ink.

"The safe combination?" Jack asked.

"Maybe. Carol does the same thing with her Windows password and her electric stapler."

"Did you try it?"

"Of course not. I was waiting for you two."

"And it's processed?" He meant the safe.

"Yep. Didn't get anything—big surprise with that surface. But not even from the handle, which is smooth steel."

"Like it was wiped?"

"We don't make assumptions like that in real life," she scolded gently. "Sometimes people don't leave prints. They have dry skin, they just washed up, they work with abrasives."

Riley, meanwhile, had already gloved up as if more than pumped for the experiment with the vision of a *Mission: Impossible* type burning fuse motif dancing in his mind. "Let's give it a shot."

It took him three tries, carefully spinning the oversized dial. He finally tried starting left instead of right and snickered with delight when the handle clicked and turned. Maggie and Jack crowded over him to get a glimpse, hoping against hope that the contents of the safe would tell them in an instant who had murdered Diane Cragin.

The contents did not.

But they certainly raised a number of new questions.

At first Maggie saw only a stack of reusable grocery shopping bags, the lightweight mesh kind that she kept hooked over a shelf in her own pantry. They formed a pile of roughly square shapes that could have held more campaign flyers or file folders. Riley pulled up the top edge of the uppermost bag so they could peek in.

Money. Stacks of it.

"Holy shit," Riley said. Maggie's mouth opened. Jack said nothing.

Riley pulled the bag out—getting fingerprints off the mesh would be virtually impossible anyway—and rested it on the floor so he could open it all the way. The bag had been filled to half of its volume with bundles of cash, used and uncrisp bills, held together with rubber bands. Mostly twenties, but Maggie caught sight of tens, hundreds, and even ones. A few of the bundles had been wrapped in what looked like ordinary kitchen plastic wrap or put in plastic sandwich bags. Some fanned out freely from their rubber bands.

"How much is that?" she asked.

"Hard to guess with the different denominations. Did the lady not believe in banks? Is this bribes, kick-backs? Maybe she was embezzling from the party. Or hell, it could be legitimate campaign contributions for all I know," Riley said. "Maybe this is what the lawyer-slash-chairman wanted to pick up, along with the senator's laptop and her chief of staff."

Jack asked, "Whatever it is, it's one big stack of motive."

Maggie said, "But why kill her and then leave it?"

"Because they knew they could get it later?"

"Or they didn't have the combination."

Jack asked Riley, "Are they all filled with money?"

Riley reached for another bag, but Maggie put a hand on his shoulder. "We have to document every single step of this. Impounded cash creates suspicion that never goes away. If I were you, I'd call your supervisor right now and get a few more witnesses here." She snapped a photo of the open safe door and the bag with the money.

"Don't get paranoid," Riley protested, but weakly.

"We work for a police department. You can smoke

pot or beat your wife or bring your dog to work, but there's two things you can't do: You can't talk back to your supervisor, and you can't steal." She took another photo. "I'm just looking out for you, bro."

He pulled out another bag and said, "And yourself. This is all going to have to go to the lab."

"The lab?"

Jack agreed as Riley pulled out a third bag filled with cash. "Prints, DNA, whatever we can get. I don't know about you, but I'm curious to know where this came from."

Morosely, Riley told him: "Us. The taxpayers. That's where it came from."

It's said that money changes everything, Maggie reflected, but that wasn't entirely true in this case. They had left the senator's house shortly after finding the money, but only because there had been nothing more to accomplish there. The killer could have used the senator's keys to enter the house, but if so he—or she—had done so without leaving a smear of mud on the floor or any sign of a search. Maggie had processed every obvious surface, including the inside of the safe—which had no more usable prints than the outside. The place seemed to be more of an office than a home, and from the variety of lipstick shades on the glasses in the dishwasher and two brands of cigarettes in the tray in the yard and different entrees from the same take-out place in the fridge, Maggie assumed that many more staff members besides Kelly had been inside.

Riley got two patrol officers to help move the money and hung on to them so that they would be the ones helping to count it as well. Limiting the personnel involved while documenting their presence would keep everyone's story straight, as well as streamline the paperwork.

The mourning dove had soughed them a chorus as they left, either happy to have the yard to itself again or warning them of some clue they had missed. Maggie hoped it wasn't the latter.

She had called her boss, Denny, to warn him, and Carol had agreed to come in and help for the overtime. The older woman had cleared and cleaned the large examination table in the center of the lab and now considered the large stacks covering the stainless steel surface.

Maggie glanced at her. "I swear this isn't my fault."

"You've been saying that a lot lately."

"Doesn't mean it isn't true."

"She was really *electrocuted*?"

"Yep."

"That's a new one on me."

"My reaction exactly."

They gave each of the two patrol officers and the two detectives a piece of paper and a pen to tally the amounts. Maggie photographed each bag, each bag with the top opened, the contents of each bag after removal, close-ups of each stack, then each stack with a sticky note assigning it a unique number, then each stack next to the tally sheet showing its total. Some of the bundles had a piece of paper tucked under the rubber bands, which noted the amount of money in the stack—so far, those notes had proven scrupulously accurate. Some of the mesh bags had one or two plastic grocery bags inside them, separating the bills further, and these Maggie would label and move directly to the superglue tank, substituting fresh paper bags for the removed plastic ones—thus designing a system on the fly to be able to reconstruct which bills had been in which bags with which accoutrements like notes or trace evidence. And all on the off chance that it might help, in some way, discern who had executed Diane Cragin.

She did not let anyone remove the rubber bands, so they had to count the money while it was still wadded together. There might be trace evidence caught in the bundles, and besides, less handling meant less jostling and disturbing of any fingerprints she might need to process. Secretly she intended to put that idea off for as long as possible. Money, both paper and coin, remained one of the most difficult items to process for latent prints. Coins were small with a textured surface, and bills were porous with complicated and colored backgrounds. They passed through a lot of hands during their lifetime, giving a suspect the foundation to say that they'd handed that dollar bill to a cashier at the GetGo one time, not to the victim. Of course there could be something said for volume—explaining one's prints on one bill would be easy. Explaining them found on 80 percent of the bills in Diane Cragin's safe, much more difficult.

At any rate, not having to unbundle and rebundle the stacks of bills saved everyone time, so she heard no complaints. At least not about that. She did hear mild grumbling about the disposable lab coats, sleeve guards, and latex gloves she made everyone wear to protect any trace evidence that might be mixed in with the cash. This money had been, obviously, collected over a period of time and from more than one person—hence the different styles of sorting, sometimes mixing the denominations, sometimes noting the totals, sometimes binding with rubber bands. Perhaps all this money had a completely legitimate explanation, and even if it didn't, it might not have a single thing to do with the murder. But Maggie wasn't about to take that chance.

Jack and Riley chafed a bit, no doubt anxious to get out and retrace Diane Cragin's last steps, interview all her known associates, and start writing a request for information to her cell service provider. But it made an interesting alternative to arresting drunk drivers and car-hopping kids for the two patrol officers, for they had a marvelous time discussing how finding a safe with this much money in it could outfit one heck of a man cave. One of them leaned toward a maximum amount of sports channels, the other toward an extremely well-stocked bar.

"One hundred ten inch," one said. "4G."

"Two blenders and a margarita machine," said the other.

Riley said, "I want to know *when* this guy—person—set up his little electrocution machine. The assistant said Cragin went home before the fund-raiser and was on time for that. From her place to City Club, the very latest she could have left her place would be four forty-five. The Secret Service agent escorted her home around nine-thirty. That gives our guy close to five hours."

Jack said, "The sun sets at seven-thirty, but he didn't necessarily need the cover of darkness. No one can see into that yard unless they actually stop and look through the outer gate."

Maggie asked if the outer gate would have been locked during the day.

"No," Jack said. "Only at night, according to the Secret Service agent."

Riley said, "Lots of trees and only one streetlight, at the corner, but I'll bet it's pretty dark at night. Much less risky than during the day." He picked up another stack, latex-gloved fingers easily paging through the bills.

"It depends on the neighbors—if they're professionals who are at work all day, then daytime would be better. If they're nosey old-money types who spend all day peering through the blinds, then not so much. What about cameras? Somebody on that street—probably *everybody* on that street—must have home security."

"Negative." One of the patrolmen spoke up. "I helped with the canvas, and I didn't see cameras unless they were really well hidden. One house did, but it's at the very end of the street. Another one had a doorbell camera, but it also had a walled yard like the victim's, so they're not going to see anything beyond their front stoop."

"We'll have to send out another team when people start getting home from work," Riley said.

"Every possible channel, too," the patrolman said to his cohort, returning to their running conversation. "DirecTV."

"No way. You can stream all the subscription ones, get anything you want that way."

"Netflix and stuff? Every time I think, 'That sounds good, I'll have to see that,' they never have it."

"But there's never anything on satellite, either. Why pay that big monthly bill? Much more economical to stream."

The first patrolman nodded at the table. "I got all this money, what do I care about economical?"

"Just 'cause you got the cash, don't mean you gotta waste it."

Maggie bagged up his finished cash in fresh brown paper and removed the plastic bags from another set. The plastic went into the superglue chamber, and the kid began to count. Then he whistled.

"What?" she asked.

"This is all hundreds."

"So's this pile," Jack said.

"I got twenties and tens," the other patrolman grumbled.

"Mine have notes," Riley said. "Scraps of paper. Think a handwriting expert could do anything with this? Might be very interesting if it isn't the victim's." He held up a two-inch square of lavender-colored notepaper on which had been written *3325*.

Maggie said, "I'm not sure what they can do with numbers, though that two looks pretty distinctive. That's the amount?"

"Yep. Guess they didn't bother with a dollar sign. Come to think of it, Miss Diane didn't bother with a ledger or tally or little black book. This much money, you'd think she'd keep track of the running total."

"Maybe it's on her laptop," Maggie said. "Our digital gal says it's got a passcode, but she might be able to crack it."

"Try her birthday," one of the patrolmen suggested. "It's always their birthday."

"They've got equipment to download and copy the whole hard drive," she said.

"A computer system to crack other computer systems," he said. "Sounds disloyal."

"What's this?" Jack asked. He had found another tally note, but this one had something on the other side. It had been torn from what looked like ordinary copy paper, with printed words on the other side: *426–115th Co* and below it *ealth Adminis* and under that *Our Own Directiv*.

"A report? Meeting minutes? Press release?" Maggie suggested.

"Could be anything."

Maggie photographed it and slipped it into an envelope, labeled to correspond with the relevant stack and bag. Then they went back to work. Maggie made coffee. Carol made several "Look! A squirrel!" jokes as if she might pocket one of the stacks while their heads were turned. Conversation between the patrolmen moved on to which fast cars to put in the garage of their newly lavish homes.

The final count: $964,858. And, mercifully, no cents.

Then they all had to trade stacks and recount to make sure the first person had gotten the number right. Any discrepancies meant the stack had to be counted a third time. By the time everything jived, all six people had cricks in their fingers as well as their necks, but it was done and could be sealed and locked and noted and signed for so that Maggie could process all of it at a later date. If any of it went missing, a later count would reveal that.

Long past their lunchtime, the two patrolmen were especially happy to go.

"You'd think counting money would be fun," one said.

"Only when it's yours," said the other.

Chapter 5

Jack and Riley went to find Kelly Henessey at the Republican National Committee office to ask, among other things, if anyone knew the name of Diane Cragin's niece. Jack had even Googled his way to the senator's website while Riley drove, but it did not mention any family members by name, saying only that Diane Cragin was "a mother" and that she "had family in Cleveland."

"Maybe she wants to protect their privacy," Riley suggested.

"That's a charitable view."

"I'm a charitable guy. Full of faith and hope. These days, even chastity," he added, clearly unenthused about this last bit.

"What happened to . . . um . . ."

"Marcia. Wasn't going to work. I got tired of catering to her while she catered to her loser son."

"Oh. I noticed you—" He stopped.

"Noticed I *what*?"

"Looked like you lost a few pounds."

"Oh. Yeah . . . weird, I guess, how that works. When I'm not seeing someone I have the time to eat less restaurant food, get plenty of sleep, work out once in a while. I thought men were supposed to be healthier when they were *in* a relationship. Not that it matters, since I don't have much of a choice."

"That's too bad," Jack said, trying to convey sympathy and loyalty as well as a complete lack of necessity to hear anything more about the situation.

"Not you, though, huh?" Riley said.

This startled Jack away from his Googling. "Oh. Um. Gardiner talked?"

"Have you ever known Rick Gardiner to keep a secret?"

Riley referred to the knowledge that Jack and Maggie were sleeping together—which they weren't, not in any way, shape, or form, but Maggie had decided to tell her ex-husband that in the hopes it would explain the private conferences she and Jack occasionally engaged in. She had also hoped it would prompt Rick to avoid any thought or mention or especially investigation of Jack, and by extension Maggie. This had seemed like a good idea to her, because sleeping together was not illegal, whereas covering up a murder quite definitely was.

She had apparently miscalculated. Embarrassment or distaste had not caused Rick to keep the information to himself—obviously—and he may not have stopped digging into Jack's past.

In the meantime, he would have to smooth this over with Riley. Unwritten rules forbade holding out on your partner, particularly when it involved good gossip. "I should have clued you in."

Riley lucked out with an open meter space on Huron and killed the engine. "No problem," he said, meaning it clearly was.

They climbed out of the unmarked vehicle and walked up the alley between the Halle Building and the Cleveland Athletic Club. Halle's department store had been an elegant institution for 91 years, expanding beyond Cleveland to several other states. It had also become the namesake of Halle Berry. Johnny Weissmuller, Tarzan to fans, had once set a world backstroke record in the Athletic Club's pool. The buildings had more than 200 years of experience between them but did not impart any of that wisdom to Jack, who struggled to find his words. "I was going to tell you, but it's . . . new."

"No, it's not."

They had emerged onto Euclid Avenue but now Jack froze, blinking to adjust from the dimness of the alley and the inexplicable certainty of Riley's pronouncement.

Riley noticed, and explained: "It's hardly a surprise, pal. I saw this coming from the minute you two met."

"What does that mean?"

Jack's partner sounded almost grim. "It means that when you two are together, it's like no one else exists." Riley pulled the glass doors and stepped inside, but returned to the street a second later. "You coming?"

Jack pulled himself out of the stupor into which this observation had thrown him and entered the building in silence.

It wasn't hard to locate the Cuyahoga County division of the Republican Party, since the window wrapping of two large panes facing Euclid advertised its presence. Once past the spacious marble lobby with its bank of brass elevators and soothing fountain, the party rooms were cramped and utilitarian. Old desks, lots of filing cabinets, one large conference table that seemed to be used for storage and stuffing envelopes, and a dry-erase board large enough for a high school classroom were crammed into the wide main area. Jack smelled both dust and sweat, as well as day-old pizza and fresh coffee.

They were told by a short, effusively polite girl in very pink lipstick that both Kelly and Raymond Stanton were on a conference call and would be with them shortly. Jack could see the truth of this, since he could watch both through the glass of a meeting room. They were at a long table surrounded by agitated men with loosened ties and women with harried expressions. Kelly took notes on a legal pad, not bothering to sit. Stanton dictated, and several other people gave their input. Kelly would write a few words, say something, there would be more discussion, and finally she would write some more. No one seemed to be arguing, not too bitterly, but they all seemed very, very stressed.

The polite girl offered them coffee, told them the police were all heroes, and added with a pink-smearing sniff how they reeled in devastation by the loss of Diane, a great American who cared deeply about—but someone called her away to deal with poll results so they never learned what Diane had cared so very deeply about. They were left to cool their heels on a worn leather sofa next to a woman Jack tended to avoid when possible—the intrepid Cleveland *Herald* reporter, Lori Russo.

Not that there was anything unpleasant about Lori Russo, a beautiful blond mother of two, other than being the only member of the news media who hadn't given up on the vigilante case. The series of murders earlier in the year had claimed the lives of some of the city's worst offenders, murdered by the same person.

That person had been Jack.

So he wasn't crazy about Lori Russo's admirable work ethic.

"Detectives!" she greeted them. "Care to make a statement to the press?"

"Sorry," Riley said, sounding genuinely regretful. "Not yet. Too early. What about you? Find out anything you'd like to share?"

"Only that she's dead. That's all I've been able to get out of anyone here so far. They told me they'll have a release in less than a half hour. I gather that's what they're working on, and maybe a further statement on who is going to take her place in the election."

Inside the conference room, Kelly opened an electronic tablet and showed it to Stanton. Its screen made him blanch. "Before her body cools?" Riley asked.

"The election is the day after tomorrow and we're in a heavily Democratic area. I'm surprised they haven't burst into tears of frustration."

Riley sat next to the reporter—and why not, currently down a girlfriend as he happened to be—but she patted the sofa on the other side of her. "Have a seat, Detective Renner. Rick Gardiner tells me you're taking over the vigilante killer investigation."

He said yes, he was, then looked away and hoped she would be more interested in political assassination than months-old unsolved murders.

"He told me that was because you had some sort of history with the case. Followed the guy from Chicago and maybe some of the cities I had researched before that—Atlanta and Phoenix."

"Thank you for your help."

Flattery didn't distract her. "Not that you needed it if you already knew all that. He says you've been working on it for years. *Obsession* is the word he used."

"I'm not the obsessive type," he said, knowing that of all the lies he had told, that one had to be the most egregious.

Riley pointedly left Jack on his own. He couldn't have felt much obligation to run interference for a partner who hadn't even told him he had something going with the hot forensics girl.

Jack watched the conference room door, hoping someone—anyone—would emerge to distract Lori Russo and then tell him something helpful about Diane Cragin.

But Lori pressed: "How's that investigation going? Anything new you can tell me?"

"No."

"Nothing?"

"When I do"—he forced a smile—"you'll be the first to know."

Her eyes widened, and she didn't seem the least reassured. Even Riley looked at him strangely. His reassuring smile must need work, because Lori Russo froze and perceptibly shrank a bit, like Red Riding Hood recognizing wolf teeth under her grandmother's cap.

An uncomfortably apropos analogy.

"What's that?" he asked in desperation, pointing to the large dry-erase board. A list of names ran down one side of a casually drawn grid, followed by a column for district numbers. After that, a column labeled only with a dollar sign listed numbers. These had obviously been sponged off and rewritten until neatness no longer counted. Round dollar amounts only, no cents, ranging from $2,681 to $800,000 plus. Next to the name *Cragin* someone had written *769,422.*

Riley ignored him, but Lori said, "Money. It's how much each member has raised and provided back to the party."

"They keep that on a board?"

"Fund-raising is a huge part of each candidate's job," she told him with slightly mocking sincerity, her equanimity restored. "How can they effect any change in this country without funding to get the right people elected?"

"How indeed?" Jack tried a more relaxed smile, and since it didn't seem to horrify anyone, he continued: "Ohio has two senators and, what, fifteen representatives?"

"Sixteen," Riley said, and blushed when Lori rewarded this apt reply with a smile. "But four are Democrats."

"There's more than thirteen people up there."

Lori said, "Those are the people who, in some way, represent the citizens of Cuyahoga County—from the governor to the state auditor to county councilmen to common pleas court judges. Basically anyone who lists a Republican Party affiliation on their campaign literature."

"The amounts vary quite a bit."

"Well, what a candidate can reasonably do depends on their district's socioeconomic makeup, the percentage of party members in their populations, how long the person's been in office, how many national or local events they have. And some simply don't need a lot of money. When Cuyahoga used to have a coroner instead of a medical examiner system, our coroner never spent a penny to run for the office, because she never had an opponent. But a campaign for governor can run into the millions, easy."

"So you're on the political beat now?" Riley asked her. "I thought you were on crime."

"Everybody's on everything in today's world of journalism. It's the new cruelty."

Riley, the guy currently down a girlfriend, took over the conversation, which suited Jack fine. At least it had gotten Lori Russo away from the vigilante murders. The activity in the conference room had cooled physically but not emotionally. A few members of the group had sat down but appeared to be throwing mental daggers at each other over the chipped Formica. Kelly's expression of desolate worry hadn't changed. Stanton had turned his back to them all and now watched Jack watching him through the glass.

Riley said, "Why do they post it like that? I mean, why would the common pleas judge care how much the state auditor has raised? They're in completely different races. And why is Smith up there? His term isn't going to be up for another four years."

"Ah, you've hit on the heart of it, my friend," she said, glowing with the thrill of a good tale. "That's the dirty little secret that the parties never talk about, because this board isn't for the politicians to keep track of each other. It's to remind the politicians that the party is keeping track of *them*. That isn't the money that they've raised for their own campaigns—it's the portion of the money raised for their campaigns that they have kicked back to the party. And you can bet there's a similar board over at the DNC. I know, because I've seen it."

Jack stared at her in confusion. Riley just stared at her.

Her hands tumbled over each other as she tried to explain. "Have you noticed that political parties pester you for contributions all the time now, not only for a month or two before an election? I remember bawling a kid out for calling me *after* election results had barely been tallied, but I've since stopped arguing. Parties fund-raise all year, every year. So these office holders or candidates or whatever are expected to raise money all the time, election or not, whether they need it or not."

"Why?" Riley asked, but she had already continued.

"Established incumbents, especially ones from districts where the vast majority of the citizens are one party or the other, can raise money the most easily and need it the least. If you're the Republican candidate in a district that's eighty percent Republican, you're going to win—once you get past the primary. You don't need to campaign at all, pretty much. But they spend as much time passing the hat and hosting thousand-dollar-a-plate dinners and calling their friends and supporters as the guy who's a newbie in a swing district. Ask me why."

Jack felt sufficiently intrigued to turn away from the conference room. "Why?"

"Because no one turns down money," Riley guessed.

"Exactly. Because they can and because they want

to." She gestured toward the board. "The more money you give back to the party, the more powerful you become, and the more you're expected to give, and on and on in a circle. It's pay to play to the nth degree."

Riley asked, "What does the party do with it, other than use it for their campaigns?"

"That's the sixty-four-million-dollar question, isn't it, detective?" Lori asked, making Jack's partner blush again. "They use it for paying the rent on this place, I'm sure, and paying their salaries, and buying air time and campaign literature for that newbie in the swing district who needs a boost. They recruit candidates when necessary. They throw big-ticket fund-raisers to drum up even more money. Beyond that, I would really like to know what they do with it. That's a story I've been working on for a while, but if you thought the vigilante killer could make like a ghost, the party accountant could give him a lesson or two."

"Is this legal?" Riley asked.

"Sure. There's nothing wrong with shifting money around when you're all in the same club. If you don't want to do it, don't be a member of the club."

This presented Jack with a new theory about the money in Diane Cragin's safe. Perhaps that had been funds she should have given to the party headquarters and hadn't. Skimming from the top—something that had gotten people killed since money was invented, and probably before that. "What if someone wants to be a member but wants to hang on to their funds at the same time?"

"They can," she said. "There's nothing that says they *have* to give a certain amount back. They can keep every penny they raise if they want to."

"But—"

"But you'd better not need the party's help for anything, ever. If your opponent launches a smear campaign against you and you need some slick TV ads, don't think the party's going to give you the funds. If you're, say, a judge and you want to run for state treasurer, don't think you're going to be the party's candidate for that position. They'll have already picked someone, and you can run as an Independent if you want to, good-bye and good luck. And if you want a seat on the Ways and Means Committee or Armed Services, forget it. You'll be lucky to be a junior on the Joint Committee on Printing. How do you think senators and congressmen *get* assigned to a committee in the first place? The party's steering committee portion those slots out as they see fit. If you get a plum spot on Foreign Affairs, you'll be expected to produce more funds than your colleague with a seat on some low-profile thing like Education Workforce."

"I see," Jack said. "Hence the board."

"The wall of shame."

"Or extortion."

Riley said, "It's like we're back in Stalin's Soviet. The party is everything, controls everything, dictates everything, and if you're not in a good position within the party, you're nobody. Except that instead of one party, we have two."

Jack glanced at his partner, figuring his mind had formed the same theory about the murder. But how to prove it? Someone, somewhere, must have kept a tally of how much Diane Cragin had raised and how much she had returned to the party and how much she *should* have returned to the party—unless Diane kept the only sums and that information rested inside her laptop or her phone. But maybe she had been too busy for that and those accounting duties fell to her girl Friday, the hardworking Kelly Henessey.

Lori said, "But back to the vigilante murders. How's that going? Last time I talked to Rick Gardiner, he had spoken to the Phoenix PD but hadn't gotten anywhere."

Not getting anywhere could be described as Maggie's ex-husband's modus operandi, but that didn't comfort Jack now. Officially the investigation of the murders that Jack had committed had been turned over to Jack— a good thing—but Rick had not given up on ferreting out Jack's connection to them. A bad thing. Maggie had thought that telling him of their fictitious love affair would get Rick to avoid them both, but it had only given him more incentive to deconstruct Jack.

But it sounded as if Rick had at least stopped talking to Lori Russo. Perhaps he had finally figured out that the happily married woman would not be slipping him any benefits in return for a story.

Jack said, "No. Dead end."

"What about the murders in Chicago and Atlanta?"

If he could feed her enough tidbits—fake tidbits, of course—it would keep her from digging on her own. Especially since they currently had a juicy political assassination to keep her busy. "I'm going back and starting from scratch on those. It's difficult in Chicago because they have more murders than they know what to do with."

Lori said, "I wish I could help, but we've been so busy with this election coming up."

He made a sympathetic grunt. At least she hadn't

found the murders in Atlanta and Minneapolis. He needed to keep her away from Rick Gardiner. It would be nice if he could keep everyone away from Rick Gardiner.

"But I may be able to get to Phoenix early next month."

No, no, *no*! "Really?"

"The paper is planning a big spread on the immigration crisis, and my editor wants to send someone to Yuma, visit the border, check out the Minutemen and plans for the wall and what all. I'm hoping to get the assignment—it's practically unheard of for the paper to pay for travel these days—and if I do, I could take an extra day and go to Phoenix. It's only three and a half hours away."

He schooled his voice to sound casual, and thought he almost succeeded. "What will you do there?"

"Line up appointments with the officers who worked the cases I found. I know you said they weren't connected, but it would still make an interesting sidebar to the story. Maybe it's a national phenomenon. Lawlessness picks up in times of cultural stress, and Lord knows we're stressed."

His adopted name couldn't get him in trouble in Phoenix, but he knew of at least three places in the police station itself with his picture displayed. All he needed was for Lori Russo to walk by, glance around, say to her escort *Gee, I know this guy*, and Jack's current world would disintegrate. He'd have to be out of the city with no trail left by the time she landed at Hopkins International. Go to his house long enough to pick up the go-bag and the cash, grab Greta, and head for some part of the country he'd never been to before.

Don't hesitate, don't look back, don't repeat the same mistakes. Don't ever see Maggie Gardiner again.

Maybe the paper's budget would prove too tight. Maybe.

He really needed Lori Russo to *not* visit Phoenix, Arizona.

Diane Cragin's chief of staff rescued him by emerging from the conference room and waving the cops toward her.

"Thanks for the lesson," he said to Lori Russo. Might as well stay on her good side.

"Don't mention it. Just keep me up-to-date on your hunt for the vigilante killer."

"I will," he lied, and walked toward Kelly Henessey.

Chapter 6

She invited them into the conference room, but Riley told her they preferred to conduct individual interviews—meaning her and her alone. She led them to a tiny room with no window, which she said served as her office when she and Diane were in town. Kelly had lost the discombobulation of the morning but also any last bit of patience.

"What are you guys doing here? I mean, I want to find whoever did this to Diane, obviously, but I don't see how I can and I have an awful lot to do and it all needs to be done immediately." She slumped into a swivel chair and didn't seem to notice that the two cops had no choice but to stand. Or maybe she did, but in either case nothing could be done about it, as the space had no room for more chairs. "And on top of everything else, I'm technically out of a job."

None of this made Jack feel sympathetic. "Like it or not, you seem to have been the closest person to Diane Cragin. We have no choice but to start with you. First of all, we need the passcodes to her laptop and phone."

He flipped open his notebook, pen at the ready, all business with no room for bullshit.

She said, "I don't know."

"Really."

"Seriously, I don't know. Why would I? I have my own laptop, I never used Diane's for anything. If she wanted me to have a document or a file or an e-mail, she would forward it."

"She never wrote those passwords down? Had no contingency plan for if she forgot them?"

"A, Diane never forgot anything"—*Yet she wrote down the safe combination*, Jack thought—"and B, she had me. If she wanted an e-mail sent, she would dictate it to me. If she needed to read a bill, I would forward it to her phone and she'd use the audio feature. Frankly, I don't think she was too computer savvy. . . . I doubt she used her laptop for much, and mostly made calls with the phone."

"Imagine that," Riley said.

"But she was also supersensitive about privacy. That's why I don't have a key to her house or a password for her phone. I don't think I'm even on her Christmas card list. She tormented poor Devin, always trying to get rid of him for an hour or two. She regarded both of us as necessary evils instead of vital helps—Hey, wait! I think she may have used one of those online programs for passwords, something called Dashlane? I remember because the annual charge came up on her Visa bill and I asked her about it."

"You opened her Visa bill?"

The woman laughed out loud. "I *paid* her Visa bill. With her online banking. You think Diane would have had time for that?"

"I thought you just said she was a privacy nut."

"About her personal time and personal thoughts, yes. She couldn't care less about her bank balance."

Of course not, Jack thought, since she kept her real bank account in a safe in her bathroom.

Riley said, "Fine. Open this Dashlane and give us the passwords."

She looked a bit sorry for him, as if his advanced age made understanding this sort of thing difficult. "I don't have it—the actual app. It's on her phone. I can't guarantee she even used it, only that she paid for it."

"She only had the one phone?" Jack figured they might as well make sure of that.

"I guess. She could have had a pile of burners for all I know."

Jack knew all about burner phones, ones bought from convenience stores for cash with no identification. He had one at the bottom of his pocket as they spoke, fully charged in case he got a call from his cousin in Phoenix to let him know that Rick Gardiner—or maybe, now, Lori Russo—were at the police department asking about a cop who used to work there. It had not rung in a while, and he hoped it wouldn't.

"What's that?" Riley asked abruptly. He had been staring at a long list of names and titles, blown up to poster-size and hung on the wall. Jack didn't know if he asked the question to throw Kelly off, a standard interrogation technique, or felt curious. Riley got curious about the strangest things. Jack only hoped he never got too curious about Jack.

The list started with the chairman, committee members, general counsel, regional political director, regional political coordinator, down to directors of the Faith

Initiative and the Veteran Outreach and Hispanic Initiatives programs. Plus one that sounded confusing, Chairman of the State Chairmen. "That's the organizational chart of the party. Why?"

"Surrogates and Media Training? What's that about?"

She smiled wearily. "That does sound funny. I assure you it's not some sci-fi androids or something. Surrogates are volunteers who work in their localities to provide expertise and commentary on TV shows, attend speeches or rallies of our candidates and their opponents, ask good questions, and generally coordinate with us to help out in the field."

Sounded like sci-fi androids might be more accurate than she thought. "Plants, in other words," Jack said. "Ringers."

"No—" Kelly argued.

"I was thinking of women having babies for other women," Riley said.

"Not that, either."

He said, "I'd want to be the War Room Director. That sounds cool."

"That's where the core staff of the party can come together so that decisions can be made quickly."

"Is it healthy for a campaign to be thought of as a war?"

Now she laughed aloud, but not in a happy way. "The truth? Nothing about this is healthy. What you're looking at is the people who really run the country. Not Congress, not the president—these people. They set the policy directives, focus the resources, put the most useful candidates in place."

Her candor might have been due to shock, or impatience, or lack of sleep. Or perhaps she had grown weary of the whole charade, because she went on: "It's like this. They don't actually make the decisions—the people in Congress vote for the bills, and the citizens of the country vote for the people in Congress. But they decide what's going to *get* decided, who's going to run, what's going to be law. You can debate for yourself which is the greater power."

"You sound cynical," Riley said.

The woman shrugged, dug a bottle out of her pocket, and shook two pills into her hand, swallowing them without benefit of water. "It is what it is, and this is what it's always been. There are groups with influence and groups with less influence. Say a million years ago you had five people living in a cave and the only word they knew was *ugh*. I'll still bet each one could tell you who was top dog of that cave and who was in the number two slot, all the way down to five. That's not corruption. It's reality."

Jack asked, "What about the combination to the safe?" He and Riley hadn't wanted to mention the safe or the money in it, figuring they would keep that one quiet until someone wanted the funds enough to admit knowledge of them. But they were getting nowhere fast, or even getting anywhere slow in this investigation. They needed to start making things happen.

But Kelly merely blinked at him. "Safe?"

"The one in her house."

Still, only a mild frown. She gestured with her hands, sketching a square in the air. "You mean like an actual safe? A box?"

"Yes."

"Huh. I didn't know she had one."

And Jack had to admit she didn't seem particularly

interested in the idea—meaning either she had been unaware of the stacks of cash, or she knew of cash but didn't know where it had been kept . . . or she was a very, very good actress.

An older man whose tailored shirt did a good job of concealing his paunch poked his head in the door. "Morton's in. He'll be here by this afternoon."

Kelly's face burst into a wide smile, the first genuine one Jack had seen on her. "Fabulous!"

"Taxes look clean, wife has a job. Two kids, though—gotta put them through the wringer. We can't have any surprises."

"Ages?"

"Six and ten."

"No problem. I can do that."

Riley said to the man, "Excuse me. We're in the middle of an interview here. Would you mind not disturbing us?"

The guy glanced at the detective, seemed unable to interpret this non sequitur, and continued speaking to Kelly: "Mark will get you the Facebook buys and the video digital pre-rolls in about twenty."

"Got it," she said, and the man left. Jack watched his partner's face flush to a deeper hue. Not since they'd investigated a firm of financial mavericks had the cops felt so disregarded, and at least the mavericks had been somewhat interested in who had been killed and by whom. Former senator Diane Cragin seemed to have been tossed out with yesterday's newspaper. But, he supposed, they had little choice—the election dictated that work had to be done and done quickly. The staff probably assumed they couldn't help solve the murder anyway . . . especially if no one there had actually committed it.

Kelly was explaining to them that they had found a replacement for the dead senator, an assistant state treasurer who had shown talent for community appearances and could deliver a killer speech. They weren't entirely sure of his stand on charter school vouchers, but he seemed willing to listen. He'd been agitating to run for governor and had jumped at the chance to go straight to a national setting. He would be willing to listen to a lot of things.

Riley said through slightly clenched teeth, "Ten-year-olds need a lot of vetting?"

"Are you kidding? Kids and spouses are land mines. Their exes, jobs, finances, hobbies. Did the wife smoke pot in college? Is the kid flunking math? Getting in fights at school? Cutting? You'd be amazed at how many school-age children are on Prozac. We're starting from scratch with two days to go. They can dig up a lot of dirt in two days."

Riley didn't bother to ask who *they* were. "Well, let's hope the kid doesn't pick his nose on camera. If you can't give us the passcodes to her electronics, then at least give us the account numbers so we can write a search warrant. If you paid the bills, you must have them."

She opened her laptop and gave him this information without comment. "Oh, and someone here remembered the name of Diane's niece. It's Minella, Collette Minella, and they think she lives in Bedford, or maybe Barberton. Also, Diane's will is at her office in DC. I knew that, and my secretary overnighted it to me. Who do I give that to—you guys? Her executor? I used to be a lawyer, you'd think I'd know this stuff."

Riley said that probate was not the job of the detective unit, though they would like to know the executor's name. "But right now we need to talk about the personal side of the senator. As we said, you knew her better than anyone."

"Happy to help, but full disclosure—I've only worked for Diane for a little over seven months. She was demanding but fair, and I've learned more in that seven months than I did in three years with the assistant governor of Oklahoma, but it was still a work relationship. We weren't besties. We spent about sixteen hours a day together, so we didn't go bar-hopping afterward or catch a movie on the weekend. If she had regular sex with anyone I don't know who that might be. If she hated someone—well, besides Joe Green—she didn't tell me. And if she felt terrified to death that one particular person wanted to kill her, she never mentioned it. That EPA guy is always giving her a hard time, but I'd be amazed if he had the guts to kill somebody. Like, astounded. If that's what you were going to ask."

Yes, Jack thought. *That's exactly what we were going to ask.*

Riley hesitated as well, then said, "No critics who were especially vitriolic?"

"These days? That's the only kind there is."

"Diane was polarizing?"

Kelly shook her head, black locks swishing back and forth over her shoulders. "The audience comes pre-polarized. *Conservative* and definitely *liberal* are no longer adjectives, they're titles. *Moderate* is an epithet."

Riley qualified his question. "Any that were particularly credible in some way?"

She appeared to give this some thought, shaking her head no, until a memory came back. "OMG, yes! I mean, not in person, but I know we had a second letter that mentioned being struck by lightning. Hang on, let me find it."

She bustled into the next office, partly visible through the open door, and dug through a box on the floor. Returning with a yellow sheet of legal-sized paper, she almost made it to the door before a young man came by and thrust a schedule under Kelly's nose, pronouncing radio spots as the best he could do. She disagreed. He disagreed with her disagreement. She said she wanted the rush-hour times and he should not take no for an answer.

No sooner had she dismissed him than a middle-aged man who looked as if he should have a cigar clamped between his teeth stepped up and unfurled a poster featuring a gap where a photo of the new senatorial candidate would be placed. Bright red letters above the white space screamed VOTE FOR TRUTH IN POLITICS ON NOVEMBER 6. Beneath it in smaller caps: BECAUSE SOMETIMES YOU FEEL LIKE A CROOK, SOMETIMES YOU DON'T. "What do you think?" he asked anyone in earshot.

"It's not exactly subtle," Riley said.

The man snorted. "Who the hell has time for subtle? In the last few weeks, much less these last few days— we're competing for the least informed, the least engaged, and the least intense voters out there. Subtle ain't gonna cut it."

"Get them up," Kelly ordered.

He rolled up the paper and strode off, muttering "Subtle" under his breath as if it were a filthy word.

Kelly handed the piece of paper to Riley and said, "See, right there, it says she will be struck by lightning. I mean, that's not a new prediction when it comes to politicians, but—lightning? When electricity killed her? That makes sense, doesn't it, in a twisted sort of way?"

"Yes," Riley murmured. Jack read over his shoulder and commented on the greeting ("Jezebel") and the all-caps handwritten font, both similar to the letter they'd found at the victim's house but with one significant difference—a signature. "We'll check this out. But Kelly . . . how did you know she'd been electrocuted?"

With a look more pitying than guilty, she said, "Some friend of a friend of a friend called and told us an hour or two ago. There's no way you were ever going to keep a lid on *that* detail—it's too bizarre."

Riley's molars made a grinding sound. "We were hoping to. It helps to hold back some facts to weed out the false confessions. We expect a boatload of them in this case."

One side of her mouth turned up. "This is politics. We have no secrets here." Then she amended: "Not for long, anyway."

Chapter 7

The writer of the "Jezebel" letters, Harold Boudelet, lived in a nondescript bungalow in Maple Heights, with a sagging roof and a canoe resting on the front porch. Jack pressed the doorbell. Riley went over and nudged the canoe's peeling paint with his toe, as if checking a sleeping dog to be sure it still breathed. Nothing happened as a result of either action. Jack gave up on the cracked button and knocked.

Riley had grumbled through the whole drive that this interview would inevitably be a waste of time. Every politician in the world had to have a stack of hate mail, and Diane Cragin had much more likely been killed over the cash in her safe, but Jack insisted.

Boudelet needed a shave and wore a pair of pajamas pants and a rumpled T-shirt over a pot belly the size and shape of two basketballs, but his eyes were clear as well as clearly suspicious. Their names and badges did not prompt him to invite them in; he held the door with his left hand as if he might have a rifle in his hidden right, stashed. But once they said they wanted to ask him about the letter he'd written to the senator, he grew downright welcoming. His face cleared, the door swung open, and he ushered them into his living room. He even offered to make coffee. They politely declined as Jack scanned the area behind the door. No rifle.

The cops took a seat on the threadbare sofa as Boudelet plopped into a leather armchair across a cluttered coffee table. No sound came from the rest of the structure, which smelled of overcooked beans and rice. Jack could not guess Boudelet's age, race, or cultural background from his mottled, dry skin or the wisps of an unfamiliar accent, but even if he'd been curious he didn't have time to ponder these details, since Boudelet began to speak before Jack even settled onto the faded chintz.

"I wrote the senator a few times, not that it did any good. That woman has no shame, but then most people in my former line of work didn't. It's the only way you can stand yourself. But I wanted to remind her that people like me exist, people who know what was done and where and when. The companies might keep all our names off their memos and their grant applications, but we still exist."

"Okay," Riley said. "Let's keep this simple. What was your former line of work?"

"EHM."

A pause, during which Jack waited for that to make sense. It didn't.

Riley opened his mouth as if to ask for clarification, but he needn't have bothered. "Economic hit man," Boudelet said. "Corporations find a country with natural resources we want. I go in and say, look, let us help you build a power plant and put a bunch of your people to work and lift the economy of the whole country—sounds great, right? You've got no money to pay us for the expertise and the infrastructure, but we'll arrange a loan for you. The rulers are wealthy families who don't care about long-term effects as long as they're making a bundle, and since they *make* the rules, they don't need to worry about a pesky parliament or those damned citizens asking questions. For example—"

"I think we understand," Riley said.

"For example, we went into Indonesia in 1971, purportedly to 'help' them build an electrical grid for the island of Java and, to make it more palatable, save the country from Communism. That was big then. I made up all sorts of logical-sounding economic forecasts on behalf of New England Electrical of how the new grid would pay for itself, elevate the populace from poverty, blah blah blah—so overoptimistic as to be an outright lie. The grid was set up, yes, but didn't generate nearly the projected income, the loan proved crushing, and Indonesia owed out the wazoo. Then the oil companies moved in, and there wasn't much the country could say about it. If any uppity locals argue, like Mossadegh in Iran and Torrijos in Panama, they have mysterious accidents."

"What's this got to do with Diane Cragin?" Jack asked when Boudelet paused for a hacking cough. A dog wandered in, missing half of one ear. His tail wagged to see visitors.

"She was one. An economic hit man for Parsons Corporation, like me. We worked together on my last project, before I finally grew a conscience and got out. Diane, if she ever had a conscience . . ." His graying, shaggy curls quivered above faded green eyes.

"And that project was . . ."

"Site location specialist work. It's the domestic version of IHM work. Instead of raping a country for its natural resources, we do it to our own cities for their tax breaks and subsidies. We convinced the state of Washington to give Boeing the largest corporate tax break in the country's history, with an estimated lifetime value to Boeing of nearly nine billion dollars. *Billion.* The problem isn't Boeing, the problem is the public servants who don't seem able to crunch grade school math."

"Again—"

"I just wanted to remind Diane where she came from."

"You called her a soulless jackal."

"As I had been. Difference is, I admit it. Why does the media spend all day pushing our buttons instead of telling us why, after seventeen years, we're not getting anywhere in the Middle East? Because it's easier to get people hot and bothered about abortion and gun control and flag-burning amendments than it is to impart real information. It's easier to sell Us versus Them than it would be to propose any real solutions or even ask any real questions. Because people on both sides have a full-time job dealing with that issue." He slumped back into the armchair, his spine hitting the leather with an audible thump. "I sold my soul for a job that made me a ton of money and then gave it all away, trying to buy it back."

The dog had wandered out but now returned, carrying a bag of treats in his mouth as gently as if it were a newborn kitten. It presented the bag to Jack with reverence. "Uh-huh," Jack said. "About Diane Cragin—"

"Let me tell you about foreign aid."

"No." Riley said. "Tell us about Diane Cragin."

"I *am*. Because that was the last place I ran into her. As I said, I had found a conscience—so I did the logical thing and started working for a charity, an NGO . . . that's a non-governmental organization—"

"I *know*," Riley said.

"Figuring I could use my mad economic skills for good and not evil, right? What an eye-opener! Unfortunately—okay, people's hearts are in the right places, or at least they start out in the right places, but foreign assistance on a large scale can become one more group of issue people. They've found a cushy job and don't want to give it up."

Jack gave the dog a treat, which it smacked happily and noisily. "Diane—"

"Getting to it. The earthquake in Haiti, 2010. I ran into Diane working with an NGO to install a water filtration system to replace the earthquake-damaged delivery system. The company's name was Vepo. Sounds like a brand of gum, right? They were headquartered in Utah, and she wanted them to get the contract for Port-au-Prince. Did you know we've sent over two billion dollars to Haiti since the quake? Do you know how much of that went to Haitian firms and organizations? Less than two percent. Sixty-five percent went to firms within the DC area. Engineering materials, specs totaling a few hundred million. Not a million dollars, a few *hundred* million. And the kicker? They still haven't finished. Years later this charitable effort is still milking the taxpayers and dehydrating the Haitians."

Jack sealed the treat bag and set it on the end table. The dog's gaze turned reproachful at this grievous disappointment.

"Then Diane comes to Ohio and brings in Vepo to work on the water intake renovation. The facility out in the water has to be inspected and cleaned and installed with newer state-of-the-art equipment for detecting dead zones—"

"We know," Jack said. "So that's why you wrote the letter?"

Boudelet leaned forward, and the dog looked toward him with renewed hope. So did the cops. "The same concepts that I used to convince third world countries that letting Shell build a refinery on their coast would solve all their economic problems can be used to sell Cleveland a water system renovation that it probably doesn't even need. Lots of money comes in, one company gets rich, maybe two or three Clevelanders get jobs they wouldn't otherwise have, and most of the funds get eaten up by consultancy costs or feasibility studies. Diane goes back to DC, and the city has a huge debt to pay off. It's a sad situation that's been repeated over and over again until no one even argues against it anymore. I see a tidal wave coming, but why bother to get off the beach?"

"So Cleveland gets overcharged. Then—"

"It's not just money! While the work is being done in the lake, the water intake is going to be switched to the river. They've built the temporary crib, you've probably seen it, what looks like a little house suspended over the river—"

"Yeah."

"Problem is, the EPA reports say the pipes they're going to use won't work and that there may be toxins in the river—but do you think Diane's going to say, Hey, let's wait before we start sending drinking water to a million and a half people and first make sure it's safe to drink? And Vepo sure as hell isn't going to speak up."

"Because they want to keep their jobs," Jack said.

Boudelet gave a pleased look as if an exceptionally slow student had answered a question correctly. *"Exactly."*

"So why do you think Ms. Cragin was killed? For the sins she committed elsewhere, or the sins she's committed here?"

Boudelet's mouth fell slightly open. The dog's tail stopped wagging.

"What?" he asked. "She's *dead*?"

Chapter 8

With her lab back to its more normal quiet hum, Maggie powered up the stereo microscope and held a mental debate about lunch. Wrap or pita? She had not had a tough-enough day to indulge in a burger. What about a portabella burger? Decadent or no? She examined the plug and wires without finding anything of interest. The kegerator had been the victim's own, so there would be no point in tracing its manufacture. Maggie found no interesting hairs or fibers or adhesives or paint sticking to it. She packaged it carefully; wrapping the ends in their own piece of brown paper on the off chance that they found, somehow, the killer's wire cutters; and then found an analyst who still did toolmark comparisons. Without all that, the wires could not help them.

Carol emerged from the DNA lab, stripped off her gloves, and rubbed the back of her neck.

"You still here?"

"Might as well milk the OT. Mama needs a junket to Atlantic City. Where'd all the money go?"

"Locked up tight."

"You didn't have to do that. I'm not really going to filch it. Not much of it, anyway."

Maggie pulled the metal grate from its brown paper evidence bag and placed it on a clean piece of examination paper. "I know. I have complete faith in you."

"Well, that's fifty percent more than I do. That much cash would turn stronger heads than mine. Is the coffee fresh?"

"Just made it."

"Are you really going to iodine every single bill?"

"I am not." Paper money, printed on paper that was technically cloth with ink that technically never stopped drying, presented one of the most problematic substrates for latent prints. Powders didn't work—the paper was too porous for that—and ninhydrin and other dyes had limited success. Iodine worked the best, though it involved using a rubber hose to blow through a glass tube full of carcinogenic iodine crystals to force fumes onto the bills. Then the brown ridges, if present, wouldn't last but would eventually fade to invisible. Other than *that*, it was cheap, effective, and easy. "I'll do the outside bills on each pack and hope we didn't inadvertently shuffle any when we were counting. We want to know who handled them most recently as bundled packs, not everyone who ever touched them during each bill's lifetime. Of course I say all that to justify why I'm not going to process every single bill."

"I hear you."

"I'll drag my feet for a while. Yes, having half a ton of cash in your safe seems sketchy, but it still may have a legitimate explanation. For all I know, it could be how they normally handle campaign funds. And even if it's stolen or embezzled or extorted, it still may not have anything to do with the murder. The killer never needed to enter the house, but even if we say he did and he killed her over the money, then why leave it there? I plan to let the detectives work a little more before I haul out the iodine."

"Even though Jack wants it processed?" Carol asked, resting one hip against the counter, an implacable force.

Maggie looked at her. Looked away. Busied herself positioning the grate under the lens.

"I promise I'm not going to lay a guilt trip on you for not cluing me in."

"There's nothing to tell." Carol couldn't know how true that was in some ways and how utterly untrue in others. Maggie had a great deal to tell about Jack, none of it romantic. But she never would.

At least she didn't think so.

"Sure," Carol said, and waited.

Maggie cranked the lens up a bit. A stereo microscope functioned as a large magnifying glass, allowing her to look at a solid object in three dimensions, instead of a transmission microscope, which looked at very thin section of something with light transmitted through it. She saw the surface of the grate's tines, rough and pockmarked at the high magnification. Other than the faint coat of rain and outdoor grime, it seemed fairly clean,. "I wonder if the killer scrubbed this. It would make sense, I guess, if he wanted nothing to interfere with the current. Dirt, anything that created a barrier, might work as insulation."

"You know that's not what I want to hear about."

"I do know, but I'm ignoring you."

"You can try, but you won't be able to hold out."

The underside—or topside for all she knew—of the tines had a concavity to them. Maggie popped a sterile cotton swab out of its packaging and ran it along one of them, picking up a black streak. "There's gunk in these crevices . . . looks oily."

Carol snorted. "Seriously? You finally take up with a man—*any* man—after a longer dry spell than a woman your age and appearance should have, and you don't even tell your closest friend? By which I mean Denny, of course."

Maggie tore herself away from the grate long enough to say, "Carol. You know you're my bestest. But you also know I don't kiss and tell."

The DNA analyst sniffed. "I could pretend to be more hurt if I were surprised, but with you? It's par for the course. Your divorce had been in the works for three months before you told me."

Maggie's spine eased by a vertebrae or two. "See what I mean?"

The relaxation died a quick death because Carol pulled up a chair, settling in for a laser-like stare at one side of Maggie's flushing face. "Oh, there's *lots* you can say. What set this off? Where do you see it going? Does he say more than two words at a time when it's just the two of you? What's he like in—"

"Carol!"

The older woman leaned an elbow on the counter. "Sometimes you are not much fun. Okay, fine, we'll come back to this topic at a later date."

"We will *not*."

"For now tell me why you're looking at a piece of somebody's old grill."

Maggie sat up from the oculars. "You think that's what it is?"

"Sure what it looks like."

Maggie considered the object, approximately ten by twelve inches, through renewed eyes. "It would have to be a pretty small unit, wouldn't it? Like maybe a tabletop hibachi?"

"Or a really large one where the grill surfaces come out in sections so you can take them out and clean them more easily. Haven't you ever broiled a steak in your backyard?"

"I live in an apartment."

"When you were a kid?"

"Dad was in charge of barbequing." Maggie had been an adult when her parents died together in a car crash, but her memories of them always seemed to jump back to the elementary grades, herself in a school uniform, she and Alex playing in the creek behind their house, life about as perfect as it could get.

"Then take my word for it. Did this woman have a grill in her yard? Gas or charcoal?"

"Neither." Maggie smeared the swab on a glass slide and placed the slide on a standard transmitted light microscope farther along the counter. It showed her a swirl of oily-looking blacks and browns, dotted with flakes of various colors. "You'd think she would have, along with the beer keg fridge and the tables and chairs. But the killer would hardly have used the grate and then towed the Weber down the street with him."

"So maybe he brought it from home. Hey, you know what?"

Maggie would love to know what, provided it had

nothing to do with Jack Renner and their nonexistent love life. "What?"

"Animals have their own DNA, so even if your guy scrubbed all the caked-on gunk off, maybe I could get the traces that seeped into the crevices. If you could find the steak that the killer grilled on that grill, we'd have a DNA match." She seemed quite enthused by the idea.

"I see. So our killer buys a steak at the grocery store, grills it on this grate, and then uses the grate to electrocute our victim."

"Right."

"Then where is that steak now?"

Carol's enthusiasm faded. "He ate it."

"Yep."

"Damn killer."

"Yep."

"It would have made a great article for the American Academy journal."

"It would have, yes."

The timer in Carol's pocket went off, meaning that some part of the analysis process in the DNA lab had ended and she needed to tend to her samples. "Well, good luck with your barbequing killer. Keep me posted. Not about him, I mean—about the tall, dark detective."

"I will."

Carol, of course, knew better. "You lie."

"I do," Maggie said. "You have no idea how much."

Chapter 9

Having found no more promising leads, Jack and Riley decided to go and at least talk to the purported number one suspect: the senatorial candidate of the Democratic Party, Joe Green.

Their party offices were housed in a red brick building on Superior Avenue, where the cops had to drive around the block twice before a parking space opened up.

Riley pointed across the street as they exited the vehicle. "See that place? Great Korean food."

"Really? What's that like?"

"Korean? Marcia got me hooked on it—just don't try to pronounce the entrée names. You've never had it? You need to expand your horizons, partner."

Jack wondered what his partner would think about some of the things that had appeared on Jack's horizon. "I'm not so sure."

They hadn't called ahead and had no idea if Green, or anyone, would even be there on a Sunday, but with only two days to the election it seemed a safe bet. And having seen the Republican HQ, Jack wanted to get an idea of their similarities and differences. Once a young man let them in and agreed to find candidate Green for them—as he was, indeed, on the premises—Jack concluded that the Democrats were slightly less concerned with security, and slightly less frenetic. But only very slightly, and the fact that their candidate *hadn't* just been murdered had to be taken into consideration.

Lori Russo had been right. A large dry-erase board on one wall posted names and their corresponding totals. The dollar amounts, while not quite as high, were close and within a similar range.

It didn't take long for Joe Green to appear, a rotund guy with his dress shirt untucked, a rapid pattern of speech, and an unflagging smile. He shook their hands with a quick pump and a lightning squeeze that stopped a hair short of bone-breaking. Jack took this as Green letting them know that he could make them wince, could snap a few joints should he choose to. Then Jack caught himself—less than half a day in the presence of politicians and he had already begun to examine every statement for the spin.

"Gentlemen," Green began, his voice rising above the cacophony around them and reverberating off the ceiling tiles. "Officers. What can I do for you? If this is about the rally last night, I assure you that won't happen again."

Riley said, "Um . . . no. We'd like to ask you a few questions about your rival."

He seemed to hesitate ever so slightly. "The late Diane Cragin?"

"Yes. How did you hear of her death?"

"It's on her website. They posted a statement—and

one of our volunteers burst in, all agog with the drama. This girl, Tina." He literally grabbed an anorexic teenager with purple streaks in her hair as she walked by. "You told me about the dead dragon lady. Who told you?"

"My cousin lives on her street," the girl squeaked, both terrified and enthralled by this attention from her idol—that seemed clear from the way she gazed up at the big man. The stiff file folders in her arms nearly slid out before she got a tighter grip. "The snobby one."

"The snobby street?"

"The snobby cousin."

"You're a delight, Tina. Are those for me?"

"Are wh—oh, yes." She handed him the top four folders, which came in a rainbow of shades. "The blue has the schedule for Tuesday, and the pink has the flyers you need to approve."

She made a respectful retreat, backing away instead of turning around, as one might when leaving the presence of a lesser mortal.

"Tina."

She halted, eyebrows raised in hope, as if he might again tell her how delightful he found her. But no such luck; he merely stared in silence and a mood *not* of delight.

"Oh—so sorry!" She burst forward, rearranged the files while still in his hands, and again backed off. "The schedule is on top."

Green had no trouble turning his back on her and strode away. The detectives decided they'd better follow him, and when they caught up, asked for a space to talk in private. Green suggested his office at city hall, but of course they didn't want to wait, so they convened instead in a corner of the large main room, past the haphazard sea of tables and desks and semi-cubicles. Four television sets at various locations each showed a different twenty-four-hour news channel, but at least the sound had been turned down. Green pulled over a desk chair and let the two detectives fend for themselves, establishing the pecking order evidently more important than manners.

Jack commandeered two folding chairs, and they settled as best they could, closing in to hear him over the dissonance of ringing phones and varied conversations.

"We'll have to make this quick," Green said right away, propping one ankle on the opposite knee. "I have a meeting at two, and I need to make a few stops on the way."

"As you know, this is a homicide investigation." Riley said sternly, and Green all but rolled his eyes. "What was your relationship with Diane Cragin?"

"What, seriously?"

"You had met, I assume?"

"I've been instrumental in the advancement of this city for thirty years. If it affects Cleveland, it's my business, so, yes, I've met her. We even saw eye to eye on a few things in the past—the new stadium, the beltway expansion, some tax levies—but you could say that of nearly anyone in this county."

"You're running for her senate seat."

"I've done everything I can for Cleveland from the inside. Now I need to wrench the funds we need from the national market."

"Last week," Riley began, only to be interrupted by an elderly volunteer bearing a clipboard. Without a word she thrust it under Green's nose, who glanced at it, signed the paper clipped to its surface, and handed it back. She gave the cops a baleful stare and trundled off. Riley took an audible breath and tried again. "Last week you said she had been spawned in hell."

Green laughed. "Yeah."

"And that her own children had moved across the country to get away from her after the way she treated their dying father."

"That, too."

"Standard campaign rhetoric?"

"Hell no! This country has had enough of standard rhetoric—more empty words are the last thing we need. What I said was completely true. Her ex-husband, the father of her children, died in hospice without so much as a phone call from her."

And her chief of staff didn't even know he was dead, Jack thought. But then husband and wife may have been separated for decades.

"Her son and her daughter won't take her phone calls. Why do you think there's never a picture of them in her mailings? She can't—couldn't—even remember the names of her grandchildren. I'm not kidding, a reporter asked her that and she said *Amber* instead of *Agnes*. What's your point? That I killed her to win the election? Has that ever actually happened?"

"There's a first time for everything," Riley said. "So purely for fun, and to show the voters that you have nothing to hide, tell us what you did yesterday."

"Sure." He seemed genuinely pleased to do so. "I went to work, because I actually have a real job. I live with my beautiful wife and three great kids in the Bingham. I walked to city hall, got into my office around six-thirty. No one can vouch for that except the security guard, because no one else shows up until nearly eight. Meetings with the parks department over waterfront expansion and with my deputy director about the casino. Lunch with the mayor's secretary to push for extending the Hub, a quick stop at the office here, back to city hall to firm up the budget reorganization proposal, an hour with StartUp Central, and then spent the rest of the afternoon and evening with the studio shooting more commercials. Which reminds me . . ." He snapped his fingers a few times but didn't tell them what it had reminded him of. "That was about it."

"What time did you wrap up with the studio?"

"About nine, I think. My wife knows better than to expect me for dinner these days. I'm lucky she's not one of those clingy types who throws your laundry on the lawn if you don't show up by six. Does that give me a decent alibi, or am I still at the top of your suspect list?"

He never stopped smiling. He also never stopped looking at them, switching his gaze from Riley to Jack and back again. He seemed impervious to the activity around him. Maybe that made him charming, Jack thought, that ability to give someone his full and complete attention. Maybe he really didn't trust cops.

Riley said, "It's not that simple. Investigating means learning as much as possible about the victim."

"In that case"—Green dropped his foot to the floor and leaned forward, as if he'd been hoping for exactly that opportunity—"let me tell you all about Diane Cragin."

Before he could, however, a slim blond man approached, crowing, "Joey!" Green rose, greeted him with a hug, then promptly led him out of earshot. A quick conversation ensued while Jack made a bet with himself that he and Riley figured into it, from the way the blond guy eyed them over Green's bulging shoulder. When it ended, the man left without a backward glance.

Green retook his seat as if the interruption hadn't occurred. "Diane was a smart lady, I'll say that for her. She perfected the art of kickbacks, giving and receiving, for a long, long time. Why the Yardrow brothers got away with overcharging the city of Columbus for streetlights? Diane. How did the cost of a fishing license go up but the state never saw an increase in cash? Diane. A private company builds a retreat in the state park system? Diane. Everybody knows, but nobody can prove. Or if they can prove, they don't want to, because she knew to make cooperation worth everyone's while."

Jack couldn't stifle a sigh. This sounded like more of Kelly's fervent mudslinging. How, he wondered, were he and Riley going to wrap up this case when everyone involved had become practiced in the art of talking for hours without saying a single useful thing?

His partner must have been thinking along the same lines. "What about recently? Very recently."

"Who'd want to kill her, you mean?"

"Yes."

"Other than me?" Booming laugh. "I didn't, by the way. Didn't need to—she was getting me elected all by herself by being the worst legislator we've seen so far this century. Okay—you know the water intake crib is being renovated, right?"

"Yes."

"Diane bent arms until the city hired a company called Vepo—I know, sounds like a cab service, right?"

"Or a brand of gum." Riley shot Jack a somewhat mischievous glance.

"—to do the job. They put the lowest bid—lowest by like two dollars, so hmm, sure sounds like they knew the price they had to beat, right? I worked like hell to get a 'flat fee' clause in there to keep the price from doubling with change orders and supply costs, etcetera, but no matter what I did, Diane's lobbyist dogged every person in the decision-making process until Vepo wound up with the contract. Okay, that happens a lot with city contracts, fine."

Jack must have looked a trifle impatient, because Green held out a hand as if to keep him from leaving. "But what Diane kept under wraps the whole time this temporary crib was being built, until the *Herald* and I spilled the beans, was that Vepo had done similar work in Montana, installing a water purification system for an Indian—Native American—reservation because they had natural gas intrusion in the groundwater after a fracking incident. Don't start me on fracking," he added firmly, as if either of them had tried. "The pipes Vepo used reacted with the residual gas and gummed up the filters so that the water coming out of the so-called purification unit was no better than the water going in, and sometimes worse."

He paused.

"Okay . . ." Riley said.

"One screwup, any company can have. Yes, they cashed their check and cleared out and left a bunch of Indians with no decent water, but hey, we all make mistakes. Problem is, before they were Vepo, they were Trident, a manufacturer of water filters specifically for dam systems. A small town downriver from a dam in Montrose, Virginia, had grown to the point where they needed a municipal water system. Vepo—excuse me, Trident—dug up all the streets and laid down new waste and source piping. The water coming out of the filters wasn't bad, not at all. The state inspected, and it passed every test. But inside the pipes were plastic liners from China—don't ask me the exact chemistry of it, something about the pH of the water reacted with the pipes and created acid. That caused the liners to flake off and left the water exposed to the next layer. But again, Trident cashed their check, moved on, and the citizens of Montrose are still on bottled water and have cancer rates five times the national average. Meanwhile, Trident becomes Vepo Construction and Consulting Inc. and arrives in Cleveland."

"And what are they doing here? Bad filters? Crumbling pipes?" Riley asked.

"Again, don't quote me on the chemistry," Green said, sitting back again, shoulders loose, the picture of relaxed poise—except for those eyes, ever vigilant. He monitored Riley and Jack as if they were coiled snakes, currently docile but potentially lethal. "Sections of Lake Erie can sometimes turn to dead water, meaning no oxygen in it, something to do with warm water on top, cold below. Two buoys out in the lake monitor these zones, can detect the levels and turn off the intakes, sound the alarm. When the city chiefs vetted Vepo about it, they didn't have any idea what we were talking about or have any plan for counteracting the low pH in the dead water. Operations chief wasn't impressed and leaned instead toward a subsidiary of Siemens. Bids come in, the department chiefs discuss it, and bingo, Vepo has the contract."

"You said they were low bid," Jack reminded him.

"Yeah, but that has to be balanced against their qualifications. Instead the whole question went away. Once Diane and her lobbyist went to work, all the city department chiefs developed collective amnesia—and not only about why Vepo got the contract but why there was a contract to get in the first place. Water has always been handled by the Cleveland Water Company under the purview of my esteemed colleague at the head of Public Utilities. They do a fabulous job, as you know by the great stuff that comes out of your tap—if you live in the city. You have to live in the city, right, if you work at the PD?"

"Not since 2006," Riley said, "but yes, I do. So you think Diane Cragin may have been murdered—"

"By the water commissioner. Hah! I'm kidding, though he is apoplectic that the city decided on an outside contractor. But my esteemed colleague in Public Utilities needed the Water Commission to take one for the team, because he's working to get an INFRA grant."

Jack had the strong feeling that Green was purposely getting them lost in the trees so that they'd miss the forest. "That—"

"Is a grant from the Infrastructure for Rebuilding America, discretionary funds that they might hand Cleveland to take care of the unglamorous things like roads and bridges and sewers. If it sounds as if I'm being sarcastic about my colleague in Utilities, I don't mean to. If ever a city could use a lump of money,

Cleveland can, and if he's gotta suck up to the senator to make it happen, then that's what he's gotta do."

"Okay," Riley said. "So Diane wanted an outside contractor—"

"In order to get a kickback from said contractor. She's not going to get a kickback from the Water Company—they're a utility, they don't need her help to get paid to do what they would normally be paid to do. But Utilities wants the grant, and to get the grant they had to demonstrate need, and to demonstrate need they—"

"Described a high-dollar project," Riley finished.

"Politics," Green said. "The art of the possible. All else being equal, this would not be a completely horrible development. Clevelanders' needs get served, which is the most important thing. No one's salary was going to go up at Water even if they did the contract, because to them it would just be another day on the job. This way Utilities will get the grant, pay Vepo, and have money left over to fix potholes on the Shoreway and inspect the Valley View Bridge and improve traffic in the Flats. However, the reason they decided to switch the water intake to the river was purely to inflate the budget, since it will require even more pipe and filters and lead time. Citizens will have to put up with water switches and disruptions for twice as long, but hey, omelets and eggs."

"Won't that solve your dead water problem?" Jack asked.

"No, because where does the dead water go? The lake water flows into the river, where we combine the already dead water with industrial runoff and illegal dumping. Does Flint, Michigan, ring a bell? We'll be another Montrose or another Indian reservation in Montana. Diane will have another drop in her slush fund, and Clevelanders will get . . ."

"A mouthful of dead water?" Riley suggested.

Without the slightest show of exaggeration, Green said, "Poison. Most of this city will be poisoned. The best we can hope for is that most of the deaths will occur quickly, in time for the finance department to put a stop payment on the check."

More political rhetoric? It didn't sound like it to Jack. For one brief, shining moment, he thought he heard the whole truth and nothing but.

"Who was the lobbyist?" he asked.

Green coughed. "What?"

"You said she worked with a lobbyist. Who?"

"Dunno, and it doesn't matter because they're all the same—not as thick on the ground here as they are in DC but still plentiful, and they all follow Diane around like flies after a circus car. Word was she hasn't paid for a meal, a bar tab, or a theater ticket since 1992." He busied himself pulling a small plastic cylinder out of his pocket, shaking out two orange pills, and sliding the bottle back into his pocket. "Excuse me for a short trip to the water cooler."

Two strides took him out of the room on fireplug legs. Jack heard a soft clunk and got up to see what had caused it.

"What do you think?" Riley asked.

"That this isn't getting us anywhere."

On the other side of the table the sound had been caused by the pill bottle. Green had missed his own pocket.

"Agreed. Even if he's willing to kill for a spot in Congress, he's a politician. They can do the *admit*

nothing deny everything make counterallegations thing
in their sleep. If he killed her, he hired some flunky to
do it and made sure we'll never place him within ten
miles of the murder spot."

Jack glanced at the bottle in his hand, then left it on
the chair before retaking his seat. "He's also popping
antidepressants."

"His competition died. He should be celebrating."
Riley stretched, sticking out his legs and reaching his
hands up in a puff of aftershave and coffee breath.
"But you know what the docs say—good stress, bad
stress, the body can't distinguish. So that prompts one
to ask, Is he on happy pills because he's the one who
offed her, or because this assistant state treasurer replacement might be some dynamo who will be even
tougher to beat?"

"Could be neither. I bet everyone here is on antidepressants," Jack said.

"I will not take that bet."

Green returned and dropped into his seat with renewed energy. "So, anything else? I've got a sit-down
with an alderman in twenty minutes. Tell you what, I'll
help you out and cut to the chase. I didn't murder
Diane Cragin. I don't know who did. As for who might
want to . . . should we go alphabetically or in order of
importance?"

"Mr. Green—"

"Order of importance, then. Me. The Water Commissioner. Valley City Enterprises, after she screwed
them over on the zoning regs—that was three years
ago, but who's counting? East Cleveland's planning
division, since she torpedoed their freeway exit grant.
Her niece—"

"What about her niece?" Jack asked.

"Hah! That poor kid—well, hardly a kid. She's a dorky, pale, pudgy thing that looks like crap on camera, but all of a sudden Diane reconnects with hugs and kisses so she could use the niece's home address to fulfill the residency requirement. She'd come to the deep and soul-searching decision that she wanted to be an Ohio senator . . . but that had nothing to do with her failure to get anywhere in Utah, of course. Diane spent a few months trying to work the girl into some kind of asset, push her into a more prestigious job, but lipstick didn't help the pig, and once the residency thing got sorted out, she let the little wallflower slink back to the sidelines."

"Okay," Riley said. "Anything else?"

Green consulted his watch and said there wasn't. He picked up his bottle and the folders and moved toward the door, drawing the detectives along with him. Riley asked for contact information at the studio.

"Are you actually going to verify my alibi?" The idea seemed to surprise him.

"We like to be thorough."

"Huh." The man didn't appear annoyed or even exasperated but did stop and think. Jack could almost see the wheels turning, the slots rotating, the possible scenarios flashing like movie trailers. Being suspected of murder would hardly help his campaign. Cooperating with the police would show him as honest, with nothing to hide. Being suspected by the cops might be a situation voters could identify with, since everyone had been unfairly suspected of something in their lifetime, from chewing gum in class to drug dealing—being hassled by the cops might reinforce his image as a man of the people. An improper arrest would make him a hero, but no need to go that far. "Tina! What's Malik's number?"

The skinny girl had been struggling with a tower of cardboard boxes in the entryway. "It's in the blue folder."

"Tina," he said more quietly. "Tina, Tina."

She took the top box off the stack, staring in horror as it teetered. When it settled and didn't actually fall, she hastily set down the one in her hands and reached for the folders Green carried. With nearly comical deference she took them, shuffled them around so the blue one was on top, and placed them back in his hand, blushing furiously all the while. A repeat of the backing-away exit backed her right into the stack of boxes. They collapsed quietly but heavily, each causing a reverberation through the floor to Jack's feet.

"It's a good thing that girl has tits," Green said to the men, lowering his voice without lowering it enough. Hard to tell since Tina's cheeks were already too inflamed to flush further. "Here. Malik Hybannon. He's on East Twenty-Second."

The detectives thanked him and left. As soon as they cleared the building, Riley asked, "What do you think?"

"He hasn't got my vote. But I'm not sure he killed Diane Cragin."

"Me neither. Shall we move on to the number two suspect?"

"The EPA guy?"

"The EPA guy. But only after lunch." And Riley headed across the street to the Korean place, determined to broaden Jack's horizons whether he liked it or not.

Chapter 10

The Environmental Protection Agency didn't actually have an office in Cleveland. Its Ohio headquarters was in Columbus, with five district offices around the state, the closest being twenty-five miles away in Twinsburg. David Carlyle, the officers discovered when they called him, having gotten his personal number from Kelly Henessey, had been given space in the Cleveland Department of Public Health on the second floor of the Erieview Tower. Remarkably, he said he would be in his office on this particular Sunday. Even more remarkably, he wasn't there alone—an older woman in sweatpants sat at the reception desk. Her eyebrows leapt up to meet her bangs when they introduced themselves. "You guys got here fast."

"We did?" was all Jack could think to say.

"He came screaming out of there only a few seconds ago. Really, how'd you—well, never mind, there he is." She waved an impressive manicure toward a thin young man of medium height, his most prominent feature being straight black hair that fell in a sort of layered cut to brush his shoulders. "David, these are—"

"Thank God you're here," he said with an intense fervor. "Someone just tried to kill me."

"Nice nails," Maggie said to the receptionist about twenty minutes later.

"Thanks."

Curious, Maggie asked, "You work weekends?"

"Oh, hell, no. Just flexing some time. In fact, I'm out of here, so if you need anything you'll have to ask the drama king. You can go right back, sweetie, they're around that corner—oh, there he is."

Jack said, "Thanks for coming."

"No worries." She followed him to a small office with one skinny window from its floor to its ceiling and a collapsible table for a desk. Riley and a dark-haired man about her age and weight waited at the doorway—just as well, since there would hardly be room in that space for all four of them. These were the only observations she had a chance to make before Jack said, "Mr. Carlyle received a letter with a white powder inside. He thinks it may have been an assassination attempt."

She halted. "So it might be anthrax? Plague? That's not what I do, Jack, I do blood spatter and bullet casings. You need the CDC for this."

"That's what I said," the young man told her.

Jack said, "You have the equipment to keep yourself safe, right?"

Riley said, "The powder isn't loose. Take a look, okay?"

"And what is *looking* at a white powder going to tell me?"

"You don't have to touch it."

"Trust me, I *won't*."

Jack said, "We can call the CDC."

Riley hesitated. Maggie figured he didn't want to appear too cavalier regarding her safety, but neither did he want to be casual about the investigation into the death of a sitting U.S. senator. "That'll take forever."

"Then we'll wait."

"I can handle it," Maggie said. "I'll treat it like fentanyl."

She let them all stand around while a disposable lab coat, plastic sleeves, shoe covers, three pairs of gloves, and two different face masks were pulled from her crime scene kit, Mary Poppins–like. She donned it all, knowing that if this powder really was anthrax or bubonic plague or even fentanyl, these measly precautions might not save her. But no matter what, the stuff needed to be contained.

Then she stepped into the office.

The occupant—she assumed it to be the man in the hallway—had not been given much of an office to work with but had tried to organize it as best he could. Milk crates held binders with unfamiliar labels. The table had the normal complement of tools—a coffee mug holding pens and markers, a stapler, and a tape dispenser. Two tall filing cabinets had their contents clarified with sticky notes on the drawers, taped there for added permanence. A framed photo of a dog, breed unknown, with a child of perhaps four, definitely human. The laptop had been plugged in and opened, but the screen remained dark. Papers ringed the empty work area in the center where three envelopes sat. The topmost had been slit open and its missive removed—a sheet of plain white paper. A clear zip-top baggie perhaps two inches square had been taped to the center of the page and did, indeed, contain a white powder. Above the baggie, someone had written in block letters: *TEST THIS.*

Maggie couldn't be completely sure, but she didn't think this was how terrorists did the biological weapon thing.

The she noticed that toward the bottom of the page the writer had added: *And leave Vepo alone.*

"I can't do anything here," she said when she noticed the three men watching her as if they awaited some profound Sherlockian observation, the masks muffling her words. "We'll have to send the powder out. As for the paper and envelope, we've got ninhydrin, DFO, indented writing reagents, but it's all at the lab." The other two envelopes appeared to be junk mail. Using a forceps, she flipped the opened envelope over and noted that it had only his name and no stamp.

"Exactly," the man said, peering from the doorway. "So it didn't come through the mail. Someone got in here and put it on my desk, or at least with the mail for the office. Probably on Friday—I was out all afternoon at a department meeting in Twinsburg."

The sheet of paper appeared to be plain white copy paper with nothing on its reverse side. Maggie noted that whoever folded it obeyed the one-third/one-third/one-third rule of creasing a business letter to be sent in a standard number 10 envelope. She refolded it, slipped it inside a larger brown paper envelope, sealed it, and then slipped that into a paper bag, which she also sealed.

"Is that all you have?" Jack asked, and the young man looked a bit disappointed as well.

"I told you to call the CDC. You think I travel with an isolation unit?" She repeated this process with the envelope, which had even less to show her. Someone had written *DAVID CARLYLE* in block letters, and nothing else.

"Maybe you can get DNA from the person who sealed it," David Carlyle—she presumed—said.

Riley said, "How stupid would you have to be to lick an envelope with anthrax in it?"

Maggie dropped the envelope into its own brown envelope and paper bag. "It may be self-sealing. I can't tell until I can take a closer look. The other two envelopes are regular mail. Have you asked the mail clerk, or whoever takes care of that?"

Carlyle said, "The receptionist you spoke to *is* the mail clerk. And the supply clerk, the lunch orderer, and the pinch typist when you need something at the last minute. She says she didn't notice it but can't be completely certain whether it was in with the stuff she brought from the mail room. I'm not exactly her favorite person."

Jack asked if it could be a joke.

The man paused to give this serious consideration. "I suppose it's possible. I'm, um, not *anyone's* favorite person here. I'm sort of a squatter to begin with, actually out of the Bowling Green office. And last week someone bugged my desk. Well, I *thought* someone bugged my desk."

Behind him, Maggie saw Riley roll his eyes.

"Why Vepo?" Jack asked. "Why mention them specifically?"

"It's a water plant contractor. I guess it's Greek for 'water' or something, the name. They've put in a temporary water crib in the river, and they're going to be doing the renovation on the permanent one—the water intake plant for—"

"We know about the water plant."

Maggie put the collected letter and envelope into yet another bag. She held up the other two envelopes one by one so that David Carlyle could take a look, decide that they were nothing he couldn't live without, and that it was fine if she bagged and collected them as well. Then she removed the first layer of gloves and brushed black fingerprint powder over the clear surface of the desk, observing a great deal of smudges and an oily streak, possibly from a past lunch dish, and nothing else of note. The fake-wood laminate top had been textured to prevent fingerprints from forming to lower its need for regular cleaning, and Maggie damned its efficient soul for doing such a great job of it. She pulled off the second set of gloves.

As she worked, Carlyle explained that he had sent a memo to the state EPA office in Columbus to recommend halting the renovation until such time as Vepo could demonstrate that their equipment would guarantee safe water standards during the upgrade. "The problem is that the outflow pipes they're intending to use have been approved only for desalinization plants, in other words largely a pH neutral environment—"

"Yes, and dead zones in the lake would have a low pH," Jack said.

"Exactly. The liners won't hold up under those conditions, and the outer pipes will start sloughing phthalates. Liver and reproductive system damage—"

Jack didn't seem interested. "And Vepo didn't appreciate your memo?"

"Honestly, I can't tell if they even read it. I can't get a meeting with anyone—*anyone*—there, not the engineer, not the construction manager, not the kid who makes the coffee. As near as I can tell, none of them physically work here in the city, anyway, just fly in and back out again. Everyone in America thinks the EPA has all this power, that we can roll in and shut down a factory without notice, that we can lead a march of frightened citizens clamoring for protection. But the truth is we're a lot like Homeland Security—given a pile of responsibility with very little authority."

Jack said, "You were supposed to meet the senator on Saturday at ten a.m. You cancelled. Why?"

"Yeah . . . my car wouldn't start. I had to put a new solenoid in it. We rescheduled for today, but—"

"You often schedule business meetings on Saturdays and Sundays?"

The young man lifted his shoulders, then dropped them. "The senator was only in town on the weekends— I guess Congress is in session during the week—and I was hoping to convince them to hold off opening the sluices at the temporary crib today. And I had time. My weekends, um, aren't too busy." He sucked in an embarrassed breath and turned to Maggie. "Do you want to see the bug?"

"The—you mean someone *did* bug your office?"

"That's what it looks like. But I haven't had time to check it out." Now that the possible threat had been bagged and tagged, he squeezed past Jack and moved up to her side, next to the table, then sank to the carpet as if his knees had given out, and he tucked himself under the table's surface. She bent down, and he gestured to the side of the file cabinet, hidden from a standing viewpoint by the surface of the table-desk. Maggie dropped to her knees as well.

"See, it's—"

She grabbed his hand before he touched his finger to the object he meant to point out and felt a tiny tremor run though his warm skin. "I don't mean to get grabby, but don't touch it."

He said, "Of course. Sorry."

The "bug" was a rounded disk with perhaps a quarter-inch diameter and a gleaming surface of tiny pockmarks, stuck to the side of the cabinet. Maggie crossed her legs, skooched a bit closer, and took a picture.

Carlyle said, "Honestly it might have been there the whole time that I've been here—about six months. I only noticed it because I spilled coffee and was trying to soak it up with paper towels . . . luckily this carpet is decorated to hide stains like that, but you can still see it right . . . here."

Legs also crossed, he pointed to a brown stain at the edge of a blue poppy.

"Is it attached to anything on the inside of the cabinet?" she asked.

"No. I poked at it—"

She paused in the act of brushing fingerprint powder over the side of the cabinet.

"—sorry, wasn't thinking about prints. I figured it was a magnet or something. But it didn't budge, and then I got distracted by work, and then I decided to leave it there until I could talk to the supervisor in Twinsburg and ask him what to do about it. I couldn't see what anyone would gain from it—you can't even call this an office, it's only a place to write up reports. I don't have meetings here or even an office phone. I submit all my reports via e-mail, so hacking my laptop would be a whole lot more productive than listening in on my cubby. I don't even talk to myself. Much."

Trying to see prints in black powder on a black filing cabinet while stuffed under a table required oblique lighting, so Maggie held her pocket flash at a forty-five-degree angle to the dot. It nearly hit Carlyle in the face. "Sorry."

"Not a problem. Want me to hold that?"

"No, thank you. Do you leave your laptop here at night?" She wondered if she should process that as well—for fingerprints, not evidence of hacking. When it came to electronic evidence, she would use the same technique she had used with the senator's phone—put it in a bag and turn it over to the forensic IT department.

"Uh-uh, it goes everywhere with me. Though I do use the Wi-Fi here . . . don't know how secure that is."

She lifted a few prints from the cabinet's side with tape, labeled them, and then collected the item in question using proper scientific techniques. That is, she wedged a thumbnail between the disk and the filing cabinet until the adhesive gave way, and she dropped it into what used to be called a "coin envelope" by old-time forensic techs. "What if it's not a threat? The letter, I mean. What if someone, in an anonymous, obscure, clumsy way, is telling you that Vepo isn't the problem and that this white powder and wherever it came from is?"

As before, he visibly pondered this. "Most of my work is regarding brownfields—properties contaminated by former occupants like factories or gas stations. Nothing that would produce a white powder."

"How long will it take to figure out what that powder is?"

"Honestly, I don't know. Our toxicology section is there to deal with things like heroin and meth. They rarely see any other kind of poison."

"Don't you have a mass spec?" He meant a mass spectrometer.

"Of course, but the parameters are set to identify illegal drugs, not any possible substance in the world. Scientific instrumentation doesn't work like that—well, you know. There's no such thing as a Batcomputer."

"That's disappointing." He smiled for the first time.

"It is! Actually your agency would probably have better equipment to identify toxins and poisons than we do. There may be a way to give it back to you, if we can determine that it isn't toxic per se."

He looked doubtful as she continued to think out loud.

"If it is indeed someone trying to blow the whistle on a situation, then no crime has been committed and this would not be evidence. But we can cross that bridge when we get to it."

Jack either couldn't hear their under-the-table conversation or felt left out, because he abruptly crouched to eye level. "Let's get back to Senator Cragin. Do you have any proof that she or Vepo planned to knowingly endanger their customers?"

"No," he admitted. "Except that she's done it before. Why are you asking about the senator, anyway? Do you think she sent me the powder?"

"We're trying to determine who had a motive to kill her. And so far—"

"Wait, what?" The small amount of color in the young man's cheeks drained in an instant. "She's dead?"

Maggie found it impressive how long Jack balanced on his feet with his knees in a deep crouch in order to talk with David Carlyle. They hardly needed the privacy and quiet since there didn't seem to be another soul in the entire office complex. Perhaps he thought it helped to have Carlyle hemmed in and immobilized by three employees of the police department, interrogation-wise. But Carlyle only grew more relaxed and enthusiastic as he warmed to his topic. Perhaps he had built a lot of sofa cushion forts as a child.

"I met Senator Cragin a long time ago," he began. "2004. She wasn't a senator then, and I was in DC doing my thesis project on the impact of government funding on environmental solutions. She was on the board of this nonprofit called the America's Clean Water Foundation, which supposedly worked on water efforts across the country. The EPA gave this group grant money for two projects—assessing environmental problems and solutions at meat and dairy farms and helping states, territories, and Indian reservations get into compliance with the Clean Water Act . . . the amended 1972 one."

"Uh-huh," Jack said, and the man hastily continued. She could hear Riley milling around in the doorway, either listening or checking his Facebook page.

"Luckily for us, and, well, the American taxpayer, the Foundation's own accounting firm did a routine audit in 2004 and found kind of a mess. First the Foundation reported spending over half a million—on costs that they didn't record or couldn't prove—more than they actually shelled out. Normally taking in more than you spend is a good thing, except they were supposed to be putting the money to use and instead it's floating around in their coffers for no apparent reason. Then, of these costs, they duplicated or billed a lot more labor hours than had actually been recorded."

Maggie listened. She didn't often deal with white-collar crime, because it didn't usually involve violence. Usually. Of course it involved a great deal of lying, perhaps more than street crimes, lying to co-workers, families, clients, people who believed you were there to help. Exactly what she had been doing since she met Jack Renner.

"Then they awarded contracts—the devil is always in the contracts," he confided to Maggie. "Over twenty-one million dollars to the National Pork Producers Council and one of their wholly owned subsidiaries to conduct on-farm assessments. No bidding, no cost or price analysis, just 'Here you go.' The subsidiary over-billed by more than six million dollars, then gave a side contract to a different company—only fifty thousand, so maybe they figured no one would notice that the chairman of the company was also the vice president of the Foundation's board."

Jack, as always, stayed on target. "What's this got to do with Vepo?"

"Nothing," Carlyle admitted. "Except Diane Cragin was on the Foundation board, and it ruined her chances to become deputy director of the EPA after the nomination committee brought this up."

"So you think the senator had a grudge against the agency?"

"Hah! No, I think she couldn't care less about the agency one way or the other. I think she will ignore environmental concerns to move up the ladder, that's what I think." He leaned closer to Maggie, and Jack behind her, as if imparting a dangerous secret. "So by the next year, she helped Cheney write the Energy Policy Act of 2005. It exempted the fracking industry from complying with the Safe Water Drinking Act, the Clean Water Act, and for good measure the Clean Air Act— the Halliburton loophole, it's called. If you can't repeal the law, then exempt your buddies from it."

"Does that work?" Maggie asked.

"Does it ever! Illinois needed cash, so their state EPA changed the emission requirements to keep the coal plants operating and taxpayers employed. Wisconsin not only handed Foxconn a bank vault's worth of money and a few freeway lanes, it exempted them from permit requirements for everything from construction on lake beds to filling up wetlands. So do I have grave reservations about Senator Cragin handpicking the company that's going to supply drinking water to everyone in Cleveland? Yes, I do. Did."

"And that concerned her?" Jack asked.

"She doesn't want me talking about it, that's for sure."

Maggie asked, even though it really wasn't her job to ask, "What does that mean?"

"I ran into her coming from the Public Works Office. She reminded me—where no one else could overhear, of course—that she still knew a lot of people at EPA and no matter how naive I pretended to be, most people at the agency are realists."

"And that translates to—"

"That there's only so much we can do, in both a legal and political sense, and that we need the cooperation of politicians to do it."

"When did this conversation take place?" Jack asked.

"Last week. Tuesday." If it occurred to David Carlyle that he might be talking himself into the number one suspect slot, he gave no sign.

"Have you discussed this with Joe Green?"

Carlyle's nose wrinkled ever so slightly. "No. I make my reports to my supervisor."

"You're sure? You never spoke with Green?"

His expression turned from disgust to something like despair. "Oh, Mr. Green and I have talked quite a bit about water over the past few months. In fact he's summoned me for a conference at the brownfield in about"—he checked his watch—"twenty minutes. But it won't have anything to do with Senator Cragin, Vepo, or the crib renovation."

"What, then?" Jack asked.

Chapter 11

"What did they say?" Carol asked when Maggie reentered the lab.

"They said to get it the hell away from them."

"That's toxicologists for you. They can't think outside the petri dish." She stood at their tabletop copy machine, making copies of her recent DNA reports before sending them on to the officer, the detective, and the records department. Even though it had been entered in the department-wide computerized reporting system, Carol liked to make sure no one could claim they hadn't been informed.

"It's not their fault. Their job is to test for marijuana and Xanax, not mysterious powders enclosed in threatening letters. Apparently that's the purview of the Ohio Department of Health. Their closest office is in Parma, but they don't have the facilities to test it there and would send it on to the main one in Columbus."

"Road trip?"

"I think so, if Denny approves. We've got to know what this stuff is. Was someone trying to kill him, terrorize him, or send him a sample of some environmental contaminants?"

"Maybe he sent it to himself to get the day off?"

"I doubt that."

"What was the guy like?"

"Kind of cute." Maggie closed the letter with the white powder in a fume hood and pulled off her gloves before catching Carol's curious expression and remembering that she was supposed to be in love, or at least lust, with Jack. "Um . . . if you like . . . he had that sort of soulful look . . ." Damn, this was hard. "Apparently he and the victim had been butting heads over this public contract, and the note mentions that. Of course she's a politician, which means she always has a target painted on her back and her murder may have nothing to do with the EPA and drinking water. But we can't even guess until we know what this stupid powder is. So yeah, I think a four-hour round trip would be worth it if Columbus can give us a clue."

"Not to mention that if it *is* anthrax, I'm with the drug guys. Get it the hell out of here."

"There's that, too."

Jack and Riley stood in the middle of an empty parking lot, with Tower City on one side of them and the Cuyahoga River on the other. A wind that shaded from fall into winter blew in from the lake, brushing an icy touch of moisture on the backs of their necks. The lot was basically used for overflow from the parking garage tucked under huge Tower City, on the other side of Canal Street, and the leftover space received only secondhand maintenance. One end of it petered out into patchy weeds growing around a pile of debris, the shells of two brick walls, and a brand-new construction trailer with a backhoe parked next to it.

Cars zoomed along Canal and Huron and over the interstate bridge. Rush hour had begun to form, and workers from the Sherwin-Williams building next door straggled out to their cars in fits and starts, sparing no more than a glance for the three men standing at the edge of the unused lot. Farther up the river sprawled an electrical substation. When the wind died down, Jack heard faint guitar riffs from the Hard Rock Cafe. A tanker made its slow way past the Cuyahoga's hairpin bends and around the sparkling white building right off the east bank, the new temporary water crib. It looked like an uninteresting two-story office building with painted concrete block walls and a few windows, connected to land by a narrow catwalk. But the catwalk had two sets of locked gates topped with barbed wire, and more bunched around the base of the structure where the water lapped at its foundation.

"So this is a brownfield," Riley was saying, allowing a teensy bit of skepticism to creep into the words.

David Carlyle said, "The term refers to a property that's contaminated enough to be a danger during future development, contaminated enough to ruin the value for future buyers. Developing the land may take longer because of cleanup efforts, and lenders won't loan to a business that's located on property that might have a liability issue down the road."

Jack said, "So you're trying to help out the real estate market?"

"It doesn't improve our environmental infrastructure to have abandoned properties around—and more to the point, leaving contaminated land vacant only exposes that to the community at-large. So if we can direct and help and maybe come up with a grant to clean it up, everyone benefits."

"Okay. So the point is—"

"That this parking lot used to be the Cleveland Asphalt Company. After decades of functioning on this site and then a dismantling, the ground is saturated with petroleum product—hydrocarbons, volatile organic compounds like benzene, toluene, xylene. Heavy metals like arsenic. Also polycyclic aromatic hydrocarbons—"

"We're going to need the SparkNotes," Riley told him. "If you don't mind."

"Oh, sure. No problem." The young man ran a hand through his hair, which only made it messier instead of neater. "Is, um, that lady—Maggie—is she coming?"

Jack said, "Back at the lab. Does this trailer have something to do with your problem with Green?"

"Yes. He and his Economic Development office have gotten behind a wunderkind who blew into town to build a facility for entrepreneurs."

"A what now?" Riley asked, pulling the sides of his blazer closer together. "That wind is getting strong."

"A guy named Connor Scofield is providing the backing. He calls it StartUp Central. It will have more than 50,000 square feet of varying office sizes to provide small start-up companies with space, phones, copy machines, Internet access, everything they need to get a new business off the ground. I think he also plans to have a restaurant or a food court and maybe some retail . . . anyway, that's not really important."

"Then why are we here, exactly?" Jack asked as

nicely as he could, which probably wasn't very, because Carlyle sort of gulped and rushed on.

"The EPA doesn't care what goes inside the building, it's the process of building itself that's the problem. It will disturb all this ground that's been saturated with hydrocarbons and what all, break it up, let it loose, and every time it rains those components will run off right into the river." He waved his hands around, illustrating this movement of contaminants.

Jack made the connection. "Where it's going to be picked up by the temporary water intake that Diane Cragin was arranging."

Carlyle paused, blinking in deep thought because, apparently, this coincidence had not occurred to him. "I suppose so. Either situation is bad by itself. But together, yes, they form a perfect storm."

"These hydrocarbons—" Jack tried to formulate an intelligent-sounding question—unnecessarily, because Carlyle went on to answer even without a prompt.

"The volatile organic compounds, in high concentrations, damage the central nervous system and give people headaches, nausea, and fatigue. They will depress the immune system and decrease the white blood count. Benzene has been associated with anemia and is a carcinogen, causing leukemia especially. The polycyclic aromatic hydrocarbons increase the risk of lung, skin, and bladder cancer, liver and kidney tumors, and is terrible for pregnant women, lowering the birth weight and increasing fetal abnormalities."

"So bad stuff," Riley summarized. "But isn't the rain washing through this ground already?"

"Not much, because of the parking lot itself. The layer of concrete binds up a lot of the bad soil, keeps humans and animals from exposure and keeps it from moving into the groundwater. We call this 'capping in place.' If Mr. Green moves in with his jackhammers, the cap is removed."

"So the EPA is opposing the construction."

"That's been my recommendation. And my supervisor's recommendation." His gaze focused on a spot somewhere behind the cops, and his pale skin turned an even more milky color, emphasizing a slight scar over one eyebrow.

Jack turned. Joe Green exited a car parked next to Jack's. A young man also emerged, as well as two guys who were both older and much larger. Two other cars pulled alongside, and then a van from Channel 15.

Behind them, two large trucks emblazoned WILEY CONSTRUCTION pulled in.

Green had arrived for his meeting. With reinforcements.

"What are you guys doing here?" he asked the detectives as they approached, raising his voice over the cars in the distance and the rise and fall of the wind. He didn't sound unfriendly, only curious.

"Learning about the environmental aspects of brownfields," Jack said.

"I see you brought an entourage," Riley said. Another car arrived with Lori Russo, then another van from Channel 15's rival station. The men from Wiley Construction emerged and began to don fluorescent yellow vests and hard hats, boots clattering on the cracked concrete.

"What are you doing here?" Carlyle spoke to Green

but couldn't take his gaze from the men in the vests and hats.

"Moving Cleveland into the future."

"You can't do that."

"Move Cleveland into—"

"Break ground."

"Not really up to you, is it?"

"Actually, it—"

"And you can explain any objections to the press, here."

Carlyle's voice quavered in time with the hum of the interstate. "I'm not authorized to make public statements. That's not really my job."

"That works out well for both of us, then." Green unabashedly waited for the straggling members of the media to catch up. Lori Russo reached their knot and gave Jack a smile.

The man with Green, a trim blond in a sweatshirt and faded jeans, seemed even younger than David Carlyle but completely at ease. Instead of a cigar he had the white paper stick of a lollipop protruding from his lips, and now he pulled it out to wave around and speak in a puff of watermelon-scented breath: "No worries! We're only here to give everyone an update on StartUp and address your concerns at the same time, before we break ground."

David Carlyle might be a bit hapless, but he knew the arranged leaves and flimsy sticks of a hidden bear trap when he saw them and opted for a strategic retreat. "Fine. I'll be over here."

He turned his back on the group and walked to the trailer, where he took a seat on the two steps suspended under its door.

Green's brow never creased. He turned to the media group and introduced the blond as Connor Scofield. The other two men from his vehicle stayed in the back and were not introduced. They had the look of body-guards, but Jack wondered at the political sense of walking around with personal goons. Perhaps Green had enemies other than Diane Cragin, more potent ones.

Connor Scofield gave the current assembly and all the world at-large a brilliant smile and started off through the weeds at a brisk pace, speaking with the enthusiasm of a kindergarten teacher at the history museum. "Great! Well, all this gunk you see will be cleaned up and leveled out, and this will become a parking garage. It will have walkways to the building, for when that wind whips off the lake."

"Like today," Riley grumbled, hands shoved into the pockets of his worn blazer, even though the temperature hadn't dipped below sixty degrees. But he had stopped holding it around himself as soon as Lori Russo had appeared on the scene.

"Like today. Which'll be super nice in February when its well below freezing."

"You're from Cleveland originally?" Lori Russo asked, pen and notebook out, scribbling as she walked, easily handling the rocky terrain in her rubber-soled shoes.

"Raleigh. But I love it here. I've totally adopted this as my hometown. I want to marry and raise my kids in this city." He waved his arms to sketch a large rectangle in the air. "This will be five floors of office space and other areas. Two of the floors are exclusively for start-ups, and the top two floors will be set aside for corporate innovation offices for larger companies and service providers."

"When does construction begin?" one of the reporters asked.

"Right now. We can all be a witness to history," Green said without a hint of insincerity.

Jack said, "Aren't you waiting on an all clear from the EPA?"

"Why would we be? We haven't received any such ban."

"And the election is in two days," Riley murmured.

"But the mayor's committee hasn't approved the draw yet," Lori Russo pointed out.

"The grant is approved," Green stated. "Approving the construction draw is a minor formality that will be taken care of at Tuesday's meeting, and these guys know it's all good. They're ready to get started."

"They'll never get the building closed in before winter hits," another reporter said.

Scofield said, "The timing is not ideal, but we'll have to push through. If we wait for spring it will put us a year behind all the newest tech releases. Now, the ground floor will stay as flexible space depending on what's going on, cubbies for the smaller start-ups, coffee shop, maybe a restaurant, meeting rooms, an open central area big enough for a modest trade show. Legal and accounting professionals will also have a presence in the building so that the newbies don't just have a coffee machine and a copier but immersion in the support areas that they need."

They had reached the construction trailer, and he paused. "I can show you the blueprints, if you'd like to see them."

The reporters politely agreed. David Carlyle, apparently unsurprised that the crowd had wound up in front of him again, stood up from the steps and moved to the side. He seemed to disconnect one call and dial another, apparently trying to get a supervisor on the line with the authority to stop the men in hard hats. But no one felt like picking up on a Sunday afternoon.

Scofield went inside, then promptly reappeared in the trailer's doorway and unrolled a copious set of oversized blueprints. He couldn't hold them to be readable without one corner or the other rolling up again, but a score of digital cameras made digital shutter sounds.

Jack, meanwhile, stared at the two metal steps hanging off the side of the trailer below the door. They had black metal grate insets, roughly the size and shape of what he had found on Diane Cragin's stoop. None, however, were missing. They also had rounded edges, whereas the grate they'd found did not.

Scofield stowed his blueprints where they had been inside the construction trailer. From a glance through the open doorway, Jack didn't see much else except some crates of hand tools and extension cords.

Lori Russo asked, "What is the estimated benefit to the city? In dollars and cents."

"That's impossible to calculate," Green said. "Obviously some start-ups will fail."

"Probably most of them. That's the nature of the beast," Scofield admitted cheerfully.

"And others will lope along, and yet others will become the next Google or Starbucks. The Economic Development office looks at not only the jobs generated, concrete employment figures for the initial construction, of course, but also the long-term operation."

"Let's take a look at the site," Scofield said, jumping from his perch on the metal steps, and leading them on a hike across the weeds. Carlyle trailed them, dialing yet another number.

"How much?" Jack heard a reporter ask.

"About twenty million. But who's counting?" Scofield tossed this last off with a laugh that Green echoed.

Lori Russo said aloud, "Taxpayers. They'll be counting."

A television guy asked, "Where is the money going to come from?"

Scofield swatted at a fly that buzzed his face, holding on to the last vestige of summer air. "Me. I'm the angel investor here. Me and other venture capitalists. That's what StartUp will focus on, unlike similar forums—not merely giving new people a place to work but luring venture capitalists from other cities and even countries. Put those two entities together, and it will take us into a new game."

"Where is *your* money coming from?" Lori asked. "No offense, but you seem a bit young—"

"Twenty-two," the guy said. "On my next birthday. I know it seems weird when my peers are still on the couch playing video games, but I've been working forty hours a week since I was fourteen. Six years ago I started a website design firm called Grand Slam. Two years ago we were the fastest growing firm in the country, and one year ago I sold it. I'm a hard worker, yeah, but I'm also really lucky that timing has usually been on my side."

"If he wants to be taken for a grown-up, maybe he should take the sucker out of his mouth," Riley said to Jack sotto voce.

Scofield pointed to a partial wall of concrete block, about twelve feet high at the tallest point. "This used to be the main part of the asphalt plant. Watch your step. This would be a hard hat area if there were actually a roof left."

Lori said, "I looked online. I couldn't find a lot of information about Grand Slam, other than it had existed."

"We were the power behind the thrones, not the thrones themselves."

"Or an entry on any list of fastest growing companies."

"We didn't get an *award* for it. That's simply what the numbers said." Jack found it impossible to assess the kid's truthfulness. For one thing, he never stood still, either due to hyperactivity or youthful exuberance or because he knew it was more difficult to assess veracity when the body wasn't still. Police officers had a reason for sitting suspects and witnesses down in a small room with nowhere to go and nothing to distract or explain the motions of their limbs. Humans had gotten very good at schooling their faces to keep up an act, but from the neck down it got harder to do. Feet described most honestly what a person thought or felt. And this kid's seemed to be made of rubber.

They spread out through the empty shell, Riley kicking at loose stones tucked between tufts of weeds, Lori poking at an abandoned bird nest in a recess that must have anchored a large piece of equipment. Graffiti depicted body parts and faces but mostly words in bold and colorful fonts. A metal stairway lay on its back along the floor.

"I love these old places," Scofield said. "You can stand here and breathe in the history."

From what Jack breathed in, this particular old place had become a makeshift men's room, but he said nothing. Instead he wondered how he and Riley were going to explain to the homicide unit chief why they had taken a tour of the Flats instead of figuring out who had brazenly murdered a sitting U.S. senator on her own doorstep. They had followed a breadcrumb trail of evidence, but it had left them lost in a vacant lot.

Now that the group had shuffled during the move, Scofield took the opportunity to shake some more hands, coming round to the young EPA agent as if he had only now noticed his presence. "Don't know if we've been properly introduced, but I'm Connor Scofield. David . . . EPA, right? You were at that one committee hearing, can't remember exactly when that was—"

"Last Thursday."

"Oh, yeah."

"This young man is from the EPA." Green announced to the crowd, giving Carlyle's employment status the grave tone usually reserved for informing a patient of serious health issues. "He wants to tie up the project indefinitely in order to do tests, tests, and more tests, when the Economic Development office has shown that the increased tax base can be used to fix any environmental problems that may develop down the line."

Spots of red appeared on Carlyle's high cheekbones, and he muttered, "I doubt that very much."

Lori Russo said, "I thought you said that was impossible to calculate?"

"The total benefit. The tax base will increase by ten to fourteen percent."

"Did you know," Riley murmured to Jack, "that sixty-eight percent of statistics are made up on the spot?"

A roaring sound started up, and they moved out from behind the wall to find the cause. The construction crew had strung caution tape along the road and at the edge of the Sherwin-Williams plant parking lot, and three of them now warmed up their jackhammers. They obviously planned to start at the far edge, safely away from the reporters' parked cars. A bit close to Jack and Riley's, however.

Green's smile stretched his face. "Beautiful day for progress, am I right?"

"Stop!" David Carlyle screamed.

Chapter 12

"They can't do that! You can't break up this ground!" Carlyle spoke so fast that his words ran together, and he moved toward the construction crew as if he planned to throw himself in their way to save the concrete lot. But after a few steps he realized the futility and whirled on Green. "I *told* you that! The hydrocarbons—"

"You got a cease and desist order? No? Then get the hell out of my way."

"You can't *do* this!" One jackhammer began to bite into the lot, its *rat-a-tat-tat* jarring the air.

Green made a show of patience. "The Cleveland Asphalt Company existed here a hundred years ago—"

"Sixty," Carlyle corrected, shouting over the noise.

"And no one in Cleveland has been poisoned yet."

"But we've been getting our water from the lake. What happens when we get it from the river at the same time you're breaking up this brownfield?" He glanced at the two cops, as if grateful for the bullet point.

The reporter asked Green, "So you're not happy with the EPA reports from this site?"

"They're vague and unhelpful, full of generic but dire predictions. And I'm still wondering how a copy of an incomplete governmental agency report made its way to the desk of a *Herald* reporter."

Lori stated clearly, "It wasn't hard to find. The reviews are posted online, if anyone cares to look."

"If people care to look, they'll see that Cleveland is suffering because its rust belt economy has deteriorated to the point where we can no longer ransom today's survival for tomorrow's ideal."

Carlyle's voice climbed another octave. "How about ransoming today's survival for tomorrow's survival?"

Technically, that did not make his stance more appealing, but it was a good quote, and the reporters wrote it down. A slight scowl crossed Green's face. "I'm the head of the brownfields and special projects team. I have had much more exposure to this issue than the average joe. I know every bit as much about the topic as some EPA head-in-the-clouds, tree-hugging, Kumbaya-singing extremist who intends to let everyone in town lose their jobs to save a nest of a tufted titmouse or whatever."

Through visibly clenched jaws, Carlyle said, "We haven't even calculated the danger to animal life here. We've been too busy adding up the number of human dead."

Recalling what the EPA agent had told them, Jack thought he exaggerated. But hyperbole always begat more hyperbole. The smell of concrete dust began to waft, enveloping them all.

One of the TV reporters stepped closer, pressing a

video camera into Carlyle's personal space. "You don't care for Connor Scofield's big idea?" Pitting the two young men made for a great video clip. Caution versus optimism. Dark versus light. Good versus evil. But which was which?

"It's a fabulous idea," Carlyle said. "The only problem is the dirt where he wants to build. It needs a massive cleanup first, for which their budget and schedule does not allow."

"Then why didn't we all die when they put this parking lot here?" Green jeered.

"Capping it in place with the slab worked because it didn't require disturbing the ground in any significant way. Churning it all up, digging a foundation, will release volatile organic compounds . . . They're a slurry, not a hard rock, so they're much harder to get control of . . . One good rain will flush—"

Public speaking was not his forte.

"Benzene in particular is associated with disorders of the hematopoietic system—"

"Hermaphrodite, you say?" Green looked the EPA agent up and down. "Yeah, I can see that."

The reddened cheekbones became bloody swords, and before Jack could see it coming, the young, mild-mannered EPA agent swung a fist at the city's Director of Economic Development.

Or at least he tried, because Green *had* seen it coming and choreographed the scene in his mind, so Green held up one forearm to block the blow. Judging from the resulting *crack*, audible even over the jackhammers, this took perhaps more effort than he had expected, but it worked.

Unfortunately Carlyle didn't stop there. Among the patchy weeds, in full view of the interstate, the Tower City complex, and most of Cleveland's major media stars, he followed up with a left jab and stepped in closer for an all-out assault.

Jack stopped him—only because if he didn't, Green's two heavies would, and with much less concern for Carlyle's tendons and bones. From behind he took control of each wrist and pulled the kid back. The wiry strength in those arms surprised him, and Jack felt a surge of apprehensive readiness as the EPA agent bucked, then half turned with a stare of pure hate.

Which instantly faded into frustration and embarrassment.

Jack and Riley hustled the young man away. Green watched with great satisfaction, and that irritated Jack more than anything else that had happened that day.

"You played right into his hands, kid," he told Carlyle as they guided him back to his car, taking a wide berth around the workers. "That's why he told you meet him here. That's why he came with reporters in tow."

Carlyle groaned. "I know. I knew it at the time, and I did it anyway. Now it's *really* like no one is going to listen to me. But he can't do this. One good rain and we're all in trouble."

"I'm afraid he's doing it, kid."

They reached his car, which looked as if it needed much more than just a solenoid, and advised him to vacate the premises.

A spark of hope lit his eyes. "I'm not under arrest?"

Riley shook his head. "Nah, get out of here. If Green wants to press charges, we know where to find you."

They watched the young man pull around the trucks and drive away.

"Partner," Riley said. "I don't like being manipulated."

"He's a politician. That's all they're good at."

Riley said, "I'm not so sure Green is the only one doing the manipulating. Maybe our little EPA analyst isn't the total dweeb he seems."

Jack turned his face to the wind. "I'm pretty sure he is."

"Surely if the situation was that dire, someone else at the EPA would be acting to see that Clevelanders aren't poisoned by their tap water. Maybe little David is way out on his own limb here. He could have played Green like a harp, and he could have sent that letter to himself to bolster his persecution claims or simply to get the receptionist to like him again. Or maybe it was sent by someone who likes to send letters."

"Baudelet? But why warn him *off* Vepo?"

"Reverse psychology?"

"That's so reverse it's perverse."

"Partner! You made a joke. Or a poem."

"Something like that." At least, Jack thought, Riley seemed to have forgiven him for not telling his partner about the fictitious romance with Maggie. *One* of them should carry a drop of that human kindness milk, and it certainly wasn't going to be Jack.

They returned to the group in time to hear Lori Russo ask Green, "What did Senator Cragin think about the project?"

Green's head snapped up. "Not her damn business." Then he clarified, saying that it had nothing to do with federal interests.

She gave Jack a conspiratorial glance and said, "That's a good question. In an interview with me she said that you had vastly overestimated how many jobs would be created by StartUp Central."

"It wouldn't be the first time she'd made up her own numbers."

"What does that mean?"

Some of the cameramen had begun to get arty shots of the burly men in hard hats with Scofield in the foreground, and Green clearly wished to join them. But he stopped to face her with his back straight and chin up, gazing directly down into her eyes, the way politicians must learn very quickly to do.

"It means when Diane Cragin ran the Utah development office, she arranged for a tax credit award to Kohl's—the department store?—if they would put a headquarters there. She told the state that the sixty-two million—*million*—dollars in tax credits they were giving up would net three thousand new jobs. I don't know if no one there knew how to divide or what, but they went with it. She campaigned on the virtues of being a job creator and took credit for every one of those three thousand jobs—except only five hundred came into existence. But obviously someone in Utah has brains, because shortly after that she decided to make Ohio her new home."

Russo didn't blink. "There was something else she told me. About Mr. Scofield and a venture in Florida."

The young man had been citing examples of successful StartUps to another reporter, but now he reacted to the sound of his name. "Me? I love it when people talk about me. What'd she say?"

"That you had been the CFO of a company called

VR Labs, to which the city of Fort Myers, Florida, gave an incentive grant of four point seven million dollars two years ago. VR Labs was supposed to open a plant to make nutritional drinks and employ over two hundred people. But it never made either a drop or a dime."

Scofield said, "I did the website for them, that's all. That hardly made me CFO."

The other reporters made notes. Green watched them making notes. Jack watched Green.

"The husband and wife team listed you on their letterhead."

"I never asked them to do that. They were old friends of my parents and thought it would give my résumé a goose, that's all."

His angelic smile didn't stop the reporter, who went on: "Some of the money went to retrofitting an existing building. A lot went to the husband's American Express bill. Some of it went to subcontract the bottling company, a new organization run by a pal of theirs who had no experience in bottling anything and simply subcontracted again to get the specs for the plant. When the construction workers wanted to be paid, they went to the county, who discovered that VR's paperwork contained a fictitious address."

"You can't condemn this kid for his parents' friends," Green said, stepping up to the two of them.

Lori said, "Of course not."

Jack and Riley watched this exchange as if they were at a Cavs game. So did the other reporters, who took more notes and captured more video. The construction workers ignored them all.

She said, "But you can ask what happened to the

rest of the four point seven million. Because instead of creating jobs, many people lost theirs when their companies weren't paid. And now here you are with millions in venture capital."

"What are you saying?" Green asked, his voice low and hard.

"I'm only pointing out the similarities. Someone talked up VR Labs to the county commissioners in Florida until they forgot to check prior financial records, any history of business success, or evidence that anyone involved had ever seen a bottling plant or mixed anything more than a jug of Kool-Aid." She switched her gaze from Scofield to Green. "Something like what you've accomplished getting the chief of Regional Development and the mayor's committee to consider handing Mr. Scofield here a twelve-million-dollar grant."

She didn't add *to a twenty-one-year-old kid whose only verifiable track record involves an out-of-state swindle of epic proportions*, but she didn't have to. Green flushed.

Said kid spoke easily: "Apples and oranges. This situation is entirely different, and besides, I had nothing to with VR Labs except in the most peripheral way."

Green said, "And why would he finagle it out of Florida only to come here and give it to Cleveland?"

Lori said, "Is that what he's going to do? Because he hasn't done it yet. The architect who made those blueprints in your trailer says he was paid through a credit line you got from Bank of America."

Scofield gave her a soft look, as if pitying her advanced age. "Of course I paid him through a credit line. It makes the bookkeeping much more transparent. But why would B of A *give* me a line in the first place? Because of the chunk of money I'm putting into this project."

"But haven't yet."

"Look around you, Mrs. Russo. Why do you think Wiley is here with the backhoe when we haven't even gotten the first draw yet? Because I've committed my personal funds from the sale of Grand Slam. Are you going to take any pictures? Because these guys make a great backdrop."

He stood in front of the looming backhoe, appearing fresh-faced, energetic, the perfect picture of a modern city's future. The other reporters dutifully snapped, videoed, asked a few softball questions, and then hurried back to their offices to Google everything they could find on VR Labs in Fort Myers, Florida.

Lori Russo lingered. So did Jack and Riley.

Green tried for one last pronouncement. "Anyone who doesn't support this project wants Cleveland to keep rusting until we crumble into dust. That was Diane Cragin. She would have been perfectly happy to let such a largely Democrat populace die and disperse and then move a money maker like StartUp to Columbus."

Lori Russo said, "I'm sure you're right."

Green had already opened his mouth to say more, and shut it with an audible *click*.

"But that doesn't make her statements inaccurate," the reporter finished.

Green closed the gap between them in two strides,

aggressively enough that Jack and Riley both snapped to attention and moved closer, smoothly, quietly, on pure autopilot. "Look, chick—"

"Chick?"

"You can sling all the mud you like, but this is a done deal and it's going through. Anyone who interferes with it had better be prepared for a few different kinds of holy hell to rain down on them."

Stupid, Jack thought. Green had to know that threats are like catnip to a reporter.

Or like a red flag to a bull. "What exactly are you trying to say, Director?"

"That I know that your husband is a plant mechanic for Lubrizol and that your kids go to Montessori."

Stupid, Jack thought again, to *ever* bring a woman's kids into it.

Because Lori Russo stepped forward until her nose nearly touched Green's, or would have had she been three inches taller. "Keep talking, Director, because this is all on the record. And I'm sure your supporters would like to know the real you."

But Green was a kind of bull and affected by red flags himself. "And after Montessori I'm sure they'd like to go to a fancy college, the expensive kind. Pity that the job market is so iffy for print media today." He grabbed the back of her neck with one hand, pinching her hair in it. She winced, and he began to say more, but didn't get a chance because Jack had taken that hand and squeezed until he heard the bones creak.

Green let go of Lori Russo, and if he felt any pain it didn't stop him from switching his rage to Jack. "The PD's budget isn't looking so great this year, either."

"Is that the best you've got?" Jack asked.

Riley crowded Green's elbow, his face thunderous. Scofield threw his empty paper stick into the weeds and said, "Uh, guys, come on. . . ."

Green breathed in and almost certainly reminded himself of the upcoming election. "Don't interfere in matters above your pay grade, Detective. It will only be a waste of your time." He gave Lori Russo a warning nod, turned, and walked away, barking *"Connor"* at Scofield as if he were a Labrador. And indeed, he gave the rest an apologetic look and trotted away.

"Are you hurt?" Jack asked Lori Russo.

"No," she said, "but I think I'd like to sit down."

Chapter 13

"It's not going to do anything, no matter how long you stare at it," Denny told her after finding Maggie standing in front of the fume hood, looking down at the letter David Carlyle had received.

"I know. But I don't know how to proceed."

This admission must have made him curious, because he paused to stare at the letter with her.

"There's some indentations in the upper right-hand quadrant. It would be really nice if we could see if there's anything legible there, but—"

"You also need to process for prints. I thought you were on your way to Columbus."

"I thought you were home with the fam."

"Giving a TED talk at Case Western in an hour."

"Oh. Well, I'm going but I wanted to get this started first. Whether it's anthrax or not, we still need to know who sent this note."

"You think it's that important—I mean, assuming it's *not* anthrax?"

"Either way, yeah, I'm a little concerned for this

guy. Someone executes a U.S. senator on her own door-step, and the same day—or maybe the day before—someone drops a letter to the EPA guy who had conflicted with her? Two bizarre events so close together can't be a coincidence. Can they?"

"But if he and the senator were in opposite corners, wouldn't whoever killed her be on the EPA guy's side?"

"Excellent question. I have no idea."

"Or her murder has nothing to do with the EPA issue, and maybe in that case this isn't anthrax and he's safe."

"Maybe that, too. Denny, I thought the financial firm was confusing—but at least they all had the same goal."

"Money."

"In this group, everybody has different goals."

"Plus the kind of nuts who electrocute people and mail anthrax. You know that even if we get the answer, there's no guarantee it will actually make sense."

"You're not making me feel better," she told her boss.

"Sorry."

"But that's why I'm not ready to downplay this letter. We have the indented writing kit with the solutions, but if I soak it with those, I'm probably destroying the ridge detail I'd get by treating it with ninhydrin or DFO. But if I use those first and get the prints, they'll have made the paper wavy enough to alter the indentations."

"Obviously the 'rubbing it with the side of a pencil tip' technique is out."

"Obviously."

"Too bad. It always looks so cool in the movies."

"I tried the ALS but didn't get anywhere. Different wavelengths work great on inks but not so much on plain paper. I—oh, *crap!*"

Her outburst made her boss jump. "What?"

"Iodine!"

"Ah," he said. "Best of both worlds."

She could process the paper by packing iodine crystals into a tube and blowing through it to expel the fumes onto the paper, careful not to inhale the potentially carcinogenic fumes. They would turn the amino acids in any fingerprints to a brown color she could photograph before it faded. Once the prints were saved for posterity, she could use the indented writing solution. "I can't believe it took me so long to figure that out!"

"Well, you're distracted."

She glanced at him as she clipped the letter and its envelope to clasps suspended from the top of the fume hood.

"Or so Carol says. Don't glare, it's no big deal. You know I won't pry. Not much, anyway."

"Glad to hear it."

"But is the tall homicide detective going to be driving you to Columbus? I have a legitimate reason to ask, I swear! I was going to take the city wagon to the TED talk. No big deal, I can donate a few miles on the Dadmobile to the PD."

"I'm sorry, but I'm sure he's not. I mean, a senator just got murdered on her doorstep—the powers that be will expect him to be finding clues and questioning suspects rather than playing chauffeur for his . . . um . . ."

"Girlfriend," Denny supplied. "It's okay, you can say so."

But that's it, she thought. *I can't.* "What's the lecture about?"

"Dadmobile it is. And you don't have to change the subject, I can take a hint. No prying." He pushed himself off the counter and crossed to the doorway into the main lab, where he turned again. "Not even a little."

She pulled out the iodine fuming kit; a plastic box with an old glass tube, open on both ends; and even older rubber plugs and latex hosing. She stuffed in some fiberglass wool, desiccant, iodine crystals, more desiccant—

"Not even the tiniest bit," Denny, still in the room, added, causing her to spill some beads of desiccant onto the counter, swear, and order him from her presence, all of which made them both laugh. "You know you can do the baggie method."

He meant she could simply place the paper in a zip-top plastic bag with the iodine crystals—much easier and should produce the same result. But she had never had much luck with it.

"I'm old-fashioned," she told him.

"Apparently." His voice imbued the word with a double meaning, but when she turned, he really had gone.

Fumes the color of burnt sienna swirled over the piece of white paper, turning it to a light brown color. This faded instantly in most areas but persisted in others, and when she looked more closely she could see the distinct lines of friction ridges. There were several around the edges, where one would usually hold a piece of paper, but also some in the center of the page where the baggie had been attached. A fairly clear one straddled both the paper and the piece of tape, which had held the baggie. The sender had had to press down on the tape to make sure it adhered to the paper.

She repeated the process on the back of the paper and the envelope, then moved both to the photography setup to record them. She gently positioned each print underneath the camera with a scale and a magnetic bar to weight it down to the metal stage underneath. This not only kept the paper from moving with any shift in the air but also kept it flat so that all the ridges would be in focus at the same time. Photographing prints on paper was easy. Prints on, say, the surface of a Pepsi can, not so much.

From the placement she would bet money that they belonged to Carlyle. One would hope that anyone sending anonymous, threatening, and possibly lethal letters would have the sense to wear gloves when they did.

When she had photographed everything of interest and scanned the entire page and envelope, she put the iodine equipment away and got out another old plastic box. This held a supply of small, disposable paint-brushes and a collection of tiny glass vials whose contents came in two varieties—weak indented writing and strong indented writing, depending on how deeply the furrows had been made into her piece of paper. She chose weak.

A natural inhibition to permanently alter evidence made her hesitate. *"Catus amat piscem sed non vult tingere plantas,"* she said aloud, with no idea if she pronounced it correctly. *The cat would love to eat fish but hates to get her feet wet.* She shook the vial, inserted the tiny brush, and painted the upper corner of the paper with dilute ammonium thiosulfate. As far as she knew, it would not react with the iodine, and if it did, that might be a good thing, rendering the fading iodine print into a more permanent color. She might discover a new technique for stabilizing iodine prints. Or she might make the colors run together and the indented writing harder to see.

As it was, the iodine did not interfere and some shapes formed in a darker brown shade against the now light brown paper. Letters appeared: *ne Sat 10.*

Interesting, Maggie thought. But not at all useful— at least not to her. She would have to ask David Carlyle if the notations meant anything to him, because if they did, perhaps the letter had come from some coworker who didn't like him very much. Or one who was not above accepting money from Vepo to work on their behalf. And Jack and Riley would have to ask, since questioning witnesses was not her job.

The envelope yielded no other writing. It did have some prints, which she had photographed.

She put the indented writing kit away, left the paper and envelope in the hood to dry, and prepared for her trip to Columbus. She had one stop to make first.

"I should be used to people yelling at me," Lori Russo said. They had taken refuge where the crumbling brick wall blocked some of the noise of the workers. She perched on the waist-high edge of the fallen metal staircase without regard for her khaki trench coat. "But somehow I never am."

Riley, unusually intense, said, "If he attempts any sort of retribution, you let us know immediately."

Jack thought, not that we'll likely be able to do anything about it. Politicians knew to keep their visible business one inch inside the legal fence, with people to take care of the *in*visible business.

The reporter said, "I can't stand to see this huge pile of taxpayer cash about to be pushed off a cliff and no one seems to care. These tax credits and grants and outright payoffs to bring jobs to town hardly ever work out. I get that since the economy crashed, cities have been grasping for jobs and acting like another Great Depression is right around the corner, even though the unemployment rate is back down to normal. Yes, it's always good to be prepared, but not good to be so desperate that you debit the future just to—well, just to get yourself elected."

"You think StartUp Central is a pipe dream?" Riley asked.

"I think it's a flat-out con, and Senator Cragin was our last chance to stop it. She could have gotten the committee to hold off the money until all questions are answered. The committee is so eager to make their mark that due diligence has been tossed out the window. I don't mean to be ageist, but who hands control of twelve million dollars to a kid with no verifiable track record? Maybe Scofield actually believes he can do what he says he can, but I sure don't. And I'm sure Green knows better."

"You think part of that twelve million is going to come back to Green?"

"I have no doubt. And whatever he gets as a direct kickback is only part of it. A project this size isn't one contract, it's a series of contracts, and Green will have a finger in all of them. The wall panels are coming from a company called Wiley that's owned, on paper, by the father of the guy who hired an ex-assistant of Green's as a salesman. The ex-assistant kicks part of his increased salary back to Green, and lo and behold Wiley gets to sell wall panels to the StartUp project. I know that because his sister told me. The guy who will put in all the wiring owns a company that turned Green's backyard into a resort—and I know *that* because I crashed a party there once—another reason he doesn't like me. He doesn't invite people who can't keep their mouths shut."

Thinking like a cop again, Riley asked, "Can you prove any of this? Or is it simply business as usual?"

"That's the question. The currency of politics has always been jobs. Lincoln traded jobs for votes to get the thirteenth amendment passed. I'm sure several bags of rice changed hands to build the Great Wall. No politician ever had enough money to buy votes indefinitely, but give a man a job, and without spending a penny, he is indebted to you forever. Give a man a *contract* and the same applies, plus he pays *you*."

Jack said, "And becomes a co-conspirator, should things turn sour."

"It's got to catch up with him eventually," Riley said, more hopeful than positive.

Lori said, "But by the time it does, he'll be a senator in DC and this will all be ancient history."

"If he wins."

"That may be a given now that Diane Cragin's dead. Maybe not. It's a numbers game now. It probably won't matter that the new candidate will be someone the voters never heard of until today, or what he's done or hasn't done. All that will matter is that he's Republican. There is no crossing party lines at the voting booth anymore . . . and that's my fault as much as anyone's."

"Your fault?" Riley asked.

"The collective me—the news media. We in print media at least modify it a little bit with actual stories and information about events other than politics, but the twenty-four-hour channels—the talk shows that pretend to be news shows—have discovered the key to job security. Sorry, I'm being obscure." She spoke with her hands, long fingers dancing through the air to sketch her thoughts. "Two things have changed this country. One, the political parties have gerrymandered all the districts so that each has a majority of one party or the other. Once a candidate gets past the primary, they don't need to do much else. If the district is largely Republican and they're a Republican, they're going to get elected. If it's largely Democrat and they're the Democratic candidate, they're going to get elected. It doesn't matter what a candidate does, what they've done, what they're planning to do. Both parties have trained the populace to think *only* in terms of party. Any political advertising or platforms or sound bites you see don't say a word about 'Candidate A believes in charter school vouchers and hopes to get funding for a new dam to generate green power in the valley.' They say, 'Candidate A is the candidate for party A and we can't let any more B representatives get into Congress.' They behave as if that's all the voters need to know, until the voters come to believe that *is* all they need to know. That's certainly all they're *told*—and who has the time to do their own research while they're earning a living and taking the kids to soccer practice and maintaining the house?"

Riley listened, his attention due to either his interest

in politics or his interest in beautiful women. Jack listened, wondering if this could get them any closer to who killed Diane Cragin. Maybe so. If the political world had become so either/or, why wouldn't murdering your opponent be the simplest, easiest, even cheapest way to victory? But according to Lori Russo, changing the candidate wouldn't change the numbers. So had someone killed Diane Cragin for nothing? Or for a different reason altogether?

"The second thing is me, us, the media. I'm not trying to absolve myself, but obviously it's mostly the twenty-four-hour channels, who have discovered the same thing: the economic beauty of a built-in customer base. They can chat away for hours and hours, not about what has actually happened but about what *might* have happened and what they *think* might happen and their *opinion* of what happened or what they think *should* happen. Why? Because it's easy and it's cheap. You don't have to do any investigation or any real news-gathering. All you have to do is pick one party or the other and you have the same defined, built-in customer base that the parties do. Of course your goal is ratings, not votes, but either way its job security. So for their own reasons, the media in this country have jumped on the bandwagon with both feet." She tucked a lock of yellow hair behind one ear, then gave them a sheepish look. "And that, gentlemen, is what's wrong with this country. According to Lori Russo."

Perhaps Riley's thoughts had been more on target than his partner suspected, because he said, "So who do you think killed Diane Cragin?"

"I'd love it to be Joey Green," she admitted. "But I have nothing to back that up. All I can do is bust his chops over StartUp Central. If he did kill the senator and my pestering distracts him, maybe he'll screw up and reveal something to you two. *And* it will distract him from my real story."

"What's that?" Riley asked.

"Sorry. I can't comment on an open investigation," she said with a devilish grin. "I'm trying *not* to turn into another Roberta Baskin."

"What does that mean?"

"Roberta Baskin did a great expose on Nike sweat shops in Vietnam, got a lot of attention, but CBS pulled the story when Nike sponsored the Japan Olympics— aired on CBS. I don't want to give Green any heads-up. Influence can travel by a number of different avenues. Suffice it to say that StartUp Central and all the money swirling in its orbit is only the tip of a very large iceberg."

Then she stood up and brushed off the back of her coat, holding it out and twisting to see if the fallen staircase had stained the back of it. Jack looked too, but not at her coat.

The metal staircase had had metal steps, with risers made of rectangular metal grates, two to each step. Apparently they had simply rested inside the step's frame and then slipped out when the structure collapsed. Several rested on the ground. They looked quite similar to the object found on Diane Cragin's doorstep. He leaned past her and picked one up.

Riley stared. Then he said, "I'll get a bag."

"What?" Lori Russo asked. "What is that?"

"Long story."

For a reporter, she knew when not to press. Or when

to change direction. "Hey, guess what? My editor approved the New Mexico travel. I'm going to Phoenix."

If I have any acting skills, Jack thought, *now is the time to use them*. But it seemed impossible to make his face calm when his stomach had clenched into one iron knot. "Great. When do you leave?"

"This weekend. Is there anything you can think of that I should ask when I talk to the Phoenix PD? Any lingo that would make them take me seriously?"

He pretended to think about this as they emerged from the ruins. The wind cut through his blazer, and the sun had begun to sink toward the West Side Market on the other side of the river. He still carried the grate, and in the distance Riley rooted around in the trunk of their car. Jack wanted to cut the conversation off, but if she kept talking until Riley returned, she might get his partner's attention. So far Riley had been okay with considering the vigilante murders to be unsolvable ancient history. Should he drag his feet and get her onto another topic before his partner returned? Or cut his losses and tell her they had to get this grate to Maggie for comparison as quickly as possible?

Managing people proved so much easier when he planned to kill them in the same sitting. Then he could say anything he wanted.

"No. You know all about the murders here—ask if they had anything similar. Especially similar to the caliber of the gun and the locations of the bodies." At least these last two would broaden the number of murders under consideration instead of narrow it, and with luck she'd get someone with little patience or time or inclination to help. Someone who might send her on her way without encouragement, or worse, a tour of the facility.

His safest bet was if she didn't go at all.

She picked her way through the weeds and thanked him.

Riley approached and held out a paper grocery bag, into which Jack dropped the metal grate.

"Are you guys going to tell me what that thing is?" the reporter asked.

In unison, they told her, "No."

Chapter 14

Maggie stepped in through the rear door of the Medical Examiner's office and signed in under the casual glance of the deskman, such a familiar face that she might as well work there. Without greeting or preamble, the deskman told her in which autopsy suite her case could be found. He didn't have to ask which one. Only a very high-profile victim such as a sitting U.S. senator would be autopsied after hours on a Sunday.

A large black man stood next to the table, absently washing off the body of the dead senator. "Don't matter who you get to be in this world," he announced to no one in particular. "You still wind up cold and naked on a piece of steel."

"Hi, Maggie," the pathologist said. "What're you here for?"

"Fingerprints. I doubt fingernail scrapings would give us anything. She may never have set eyes on the guy who killed her, much less got in a fight with him."

The pathologist joined the diener in shaking his

head over the corpse. "Electrocution. That's a new one on me. As a murder, I mean. We get a utility worker caught in a wire at least once or twice each year. A month ago I had some guy drilling for a phone pole— big thing, like a backhoe only with a drill where the bucket would be—the guy put his hand on the drill top to guide it to the right spot at the exact time the tip of the—" He made a jagged gesture with his hand, sketching an inverted V.

"The drill arm tower," the diener supplied, hauling the wet body of Diane Cragin to one side in order to flop her over onto her stomach.

"Yeah, that. It touched the power lines overhead. Five hundred volts, which isn't even that much for a power line, and poof, guy was dead. And looked like her—little scorch on the hand, little scorch on the foot. Otherwise, nothing."

"This was plugged into a household outlet. An outdoor one, but two-twenty."

"That would be plenty. Electrical current starts to hurt at ten milliamps. By twenty or so she'd be in paralysis."

"She couldn't let go of the knob," Maggie said, staying out of the way of the diener's hose.

The doctor picked up the woman's right hand. The fingers had loosened as rigor passed, and he examined the scorch mark. "The bones in the path of the current get warm. We'll probably see some burns of the finger muscles and ligaments when we open it up. At forty it would be hard to breathe; at ninety, ventricular fibrillation throws her into cardiac arrest. By one hundred, she's dead."

"And this was over two hundred."

"Volts," the diener said, his voice a low, easy rumble.

Maggie and the pathologist looked at him, but he finished with the hose and put it to one side, returning with a shiny, deceptively small metal scalpel. With it he sliced a Y-shaped incision in Diane Cragin's chest.

"That's right, I wasn't thinking." Maggie said. "So how many volts would it take, if one hundred milliamps kills you?"

"That can depend on the wattage."

Maggie and the pathologist waited as the diener peeled back the thin layer of skin, fat, and muscles covering the rib cage. He picked up a pair of long-handled pruning shears and began to snap through the ribs, one by one. "The body can take a lot of volts. It's the current that kills you—the amps."

The pathologist said, "I'm pretty sure you're speaking in tongues."

"That's what happens when your dad's an electrician."

Maggie said, a trifle uncertainly, "Right. If it were plumbing, then volts is the water pressure and amperage is how fast the water is moving. So how many amps would she get from a two-twenty line?"

Snap. "That depends."

"On what?"

"On the ohms." He snapped a few more ribs, but after an amused glance he took pity on them. "Ohms is the resistance to flow, like the size of the pipe in the analogy. Big pipe, less resistance. This poor lady, thin shoes, wet skin, resistance goes down. Plenty of volts, nothing to slow down the amps. Zap."

Snap.

Maggie still couldn't quite picture the relationship, and she repeated her question about the amps.

"Two-twenty? About twenty. One-ten is usually about ten to fifteen."

"That's what I don't get—he said twenty would create paralysis, but it doesn't get fatal until over ninety. So why is she dead? Weak heart?"

"Because the amps and the voltage multiplied make the *power*—or watts. The force with which the water comes out of the pipe."

"*Oh*. So it's more than just numbers."

Snap. "Exactly. Of course that's AC—alternating current. AC causes tetany in the muscles."

"Contractions," the pathologist translated for Maggie, though she had figured that out.

The diener said, "That's why she couldn't let go of the knob. If it was DC, it would have knocked her on her ass in one huge convulsion. Still probably kill her, though. Because DC is direct current, and that—"

"No, no," the pathologist said. "Stop now. My head's starting to hurt."

The diener appeared indifferent to this topic and snapped another rib, freeing the cage structure over the front of the torso. When he removed it, Maggie could see Diane Cragin's lungs and liver and the other things packed tightly inside her body, dark and glistening red.

The pathologist broke his own moratorium, asking, "But why didn't it trip a breaker?"

The diener said, "Because frostless refrigerators cycle on and off and would trip the breaker every time it cycled on. That's why two-twenty lines don't have them."

"Huh," the pathologist said. "So it zaps her, her muscles freeze up, and it keeps zapping her. The heart seizes up and goes all arrhythmic."

"How long would that take?" Maggie asked.

"Pretty quick."

Maggie looked at the dead woman, mouth agape, hair wet, missing a chest wall. "I'll bet it wasn't fast enough."

Then she asked if it would be all right if she could roll the woman's fingers and palms and get out of there.

"You're not staying for the whole post?"

"Sorry. I have a long drive ahead of me."

He didn't ask where or why. "Well, I'll let you know if I find anything unusual—other than petechial hemorrhages in the internal organs, the ones in the path of the current. Elevated creatine kinase. Macroscopic hemorrhages in the ventricle. Pulmonary edema. Like that."

"Sure," Maggie said. "Like that."

She thanked them and left.

Chapter 15

"How was Columbus?" Denny asked her the following morning.

"I got there in time for rush hour."

"There's no rush hour on Sunday," he said.

"Tell that to Columbus."

She drank the coffee she had made in the hopes it would revive her. She had gotten to bed very late after waiting at the Columbus ODH for the analysis. "The good news is, it's not anthrax."

"That *is* good news. What is it, then?"

"Baby powder."

"Damn babies."

She laughed. "They signed it right back out to me— no sense cluttering up their evidence room—and I brought it back to fingerprint the baggie. I don't expect much after all the folding and manipulation and the fact that it probably had a layer of powder on it before the person even taped it to the note."

"Is it still a case now, if all that's happened is someone played a nasty joke on the EPA guy, which doesn't necessarily have anything to do with the dead senator."

"True. But it's still threatening a public official, right? A federal employee? Is that a crime?"

"It probably ain't good."

Carol came into the lab, lunch bag, tote bag and a Windbreaker dangling from her arms. She told Maggie that she had a visitor.

"A what?" The crime lab did not receive unexpected visitors. Buried in the Justice Center above the floors of police departments, they didn't have a waiting room or a receptionist and the AUTHORIZED PERSONNEL ONLY sign on the door did not hang there merely for show. The door was locked, and visitors had to sign in and could not remain without lab personnel present. They weren't set up for the casual drop-in.

"I found her loitering outside the door, a pudgy little thing brimming with determination. And she asked for you. Don't ask me why, because I don't know," the older woman added hastily as Maggie opened her mouth to do just that, "but she seemed harmless enough, so I told her you'd be right out."

"How'd you know I was here?" Usually they arrived at work at about the same time.

"Where else would you be?"

Maggie chose not to ponder how this could be a rather sad commentary on her personal life and went to the nook inside the lab door to find her visitor exactly as Carol had described. A woman of about thirty, dark hair, medium brown eyes, a nose with an unfortunate upturn, and an outfit made of a great deal of spandex. Lumpy curls spilled over her shoulders. She gave Maggie an apprehensive smile. "Are you Specialist Gardiner?"

"Yes. And you are?"

"Collette Minella. I'm Diane Cragin's niece." She panted slightly, as if she had taken the stairs instead of the elevator.

"Oh . . . yes. I'm . . . I'm sorry for your loss." Maggie had been around plenty of grieving family members during her career but didn't usually need to interact with them. She certainly didn't have them show up at her lab. "What are—how can I help you?"

"Is this your signature on this form?"

Collette held out one of their standard chain-of-custody forms. It listed the items that Maggie had removed from yesterday's crime scene, including the victim's cell phone, laptop, a prescription bottle of blood pressure meds, and "money from safe, unknown amount." As per standard operating procedures, Maggie had signed and dated this form and left one of the carbons inside the home, to give the family a list of what had been removed. "Yes, it is."

"Okay, great. How do I get these things back?"

"We're not finished processing them yet."

"What does that mean?" she asked with worry in her tone. Her gaze darted past Maggie's shoulder, scanning the lab as if the items might be in plain sight.

"We're examining them for information that may be related to your aunt's death. Have you spoken to the detectives?"

The woman blinked. "No. Who are they?" When Maggie gave her their names, she said, "Well, more power to them, but that's not really my concern. Apparently I'm the executor of the estate, so I have the right to all her belongings."

"Um, okay . . . but I can't release anything until we have finished processing—"

"And how long will that be?"

"—and the detectives sign off on the case. It's really up to them." Maggie had no qualms about passing the buck in matters like this. He who has the authority can also bloody well have the responsibility . . . and the handling of grieving family members.

Collette Minella's breathing grew even harsher. "Let me be frank. I don't really care who killed her. I mean, I can't do anything about the fact that she's dead. I can do something about my own future. So I just want her stuff back."

"I get that, but I can't affect it," Maggie said, equally as firm. "But let me find the detectives for you. They will be able to answer some of your questions—and I'm sure they have a few for you."

They convened in one of the homicide unit's smaller interrogation rooms, four people fitting into a space meant for two. Maggie remained to find out if Collette Minella might have any idea what her aunt's phone and laptop passwords might be, because so far the forensic IT people had been stymied. She also wanted to hear for herself any explanation for the cash in the safe, still hoping for a reason *not* to spend months pro-cessing the whole kit and caboodle for fingerprints.

The detectives sat next to each other, across the

small table from the victim's niece. Maggie sat at the end of the table, a third corner to the triangle—or an impartial observer? As usual she and Jack said nothing to each other and he barely acknowledged her presence. Riley, on the other hand, kept glancing over at her with a considering look, and she didn't want to know what he might have been considering. It would have been funny, this charade of romance, except that she didn't seem to find much amusing these days.

"You can have her phone, I don't care. Anything that will help with the investigation," Collette said as an opener. "I only want the money and any jewelry taken."

Maggie assured her that they had not removed any jewelry.

Riley went through the basics—where Collette lived (Barberton), what she did for a living (hotel clerk), when she last saw her aunt (a good seven years ago), and, for fun, where had she been the day of the murder (work, grocery, library, and home to watch *Game of Thrones*). Maggie watched her with a purposely sympathetic expression, hoping to put her at ease by having a fellow female in the room, both because she felt a minor duty as said female and because she hoped that Collette Minella could tell them something—*anything*—that would give the investigation a focus. The victim had been dead for twenty-four hours and, as far as Maggie knew, they weren't a single step closer to finding out why. The life of a politician covered too large an area.

Collette Minella, for her part, didn't seem to expect or need sympathy. She spoke easily, twisting her hair with a foot jiggling at the end of a crossed leg, a sign of relaxation. But she also professed to zero ideas on who might kill her aunt. She couldn't even remember the last time they had communicated in any way. "I think I sent her a Christmas card, three, four years ago. Then I stopped sending them."

"To her?" Riley asked

"To anyone. Nobody sends them back anymore—too much effort. You would think everyone would have gone to e-cards, but they don't do that either. Kind of sad."

"So you and your aunt weren't close."

A short bark of laughter. "Was anyone? Her own kids won't speak to her."

"Why not?"

"I don't know. They don't speak to me, either!" She seemed to find this genuinely funny, but then added more soberly, "No reason they should be in touch with me, really. I think I only met them once, at someone's wedding long before my parents died. And Aunt Diane sure as hell wouldn't tell me what her deal was."

Riley again asked why not. Next to Maggie, Jack shifted in his chair, giving off the faintest odor of aftershave and impatience.

"If she had any weaknesses—and I suspect she didn't—the last thing she'd do is ever let me in on them. Let me summarize. Aside from that long-ago wedding, I've never encountered the whole family. Mom didn't talk about them much, but I always kinda thought that was because they lived in another state and we didn't see them regularly. It wasn't as if she *disliked* her or her cousins or anything. So about thirteen years ago, I guess it was, I get a call out of the blue from Aunt Diane saying she's going to be in town and would like to have lunch. She couldn't make my mother's funeral, but she wants to have lunch. Okay, fine—look at me, I never miss a lunch—"

She paused as if giving the men a chance to assure her that she shouldn't worry about weight. It didn't seem to surprise her when no one did and she continued: "—especially if someone else is paying for it. She told me she wanted to use my address temporarily to establish residency in Ohio to run for senator. If she won, of course, she would get her own place. I had an extra bedroom in my condo and nothing else to do, so I said sure. I didn't really mind—it was interesting, watching all those type-As come and go and gab to each other about market share and 'message.'" Her fingers made air quotes around the last word. "I didn't even mind that they took over my living room for crunch projects, though mostly they worked out of their offices downtown. And mostly they paid no attention to me."

Again, she stated this without rancor. No one had paid attention to her since her mother, Maggie guessed. Now her closest living relative dies, and instead of planning a memorial service, she visited the police department to "get her stuff back." Life hadn't made her bitter, but it had made her realistic.

"Neither did Aunt Diane, unless they wanted to make some sort of statement about family ties. Then she'd parade me in front of the cameras—not to say anything, of course, just to stand and smile lovingly, after her assistants spent an hour making me presentable."

"Presentable?" Riley questioned.

"Not as much of an embarrassment, in other words.

She would have liked Malibu Barbie with hipster glasses and a job at the prosecutor's office or something, and instead had a Cabbage Patch Kid with no college who made minimum wage. I got it. I wouldn't mind being Malibu Barbie myself," she said with a touch of wistfulness. "I didn't mind. I liked the way they styled my hair, actually—I've never been able to get it exactly like that since. Of course they hated everything in my closet, but did dear Aunt Diane ever buy me anything new? Or give me a penny for the months of free rent or restock my fridge after her workers pulled an all-nighter? Not a chance. Anyway, point is then she won the election."

Collette stopped there. It seemed the rest should be obvious. But it wasn't to Riley, who prompted her to go on.

"That was the end of my usefulness. She packed up her ball and bat and flyers and got her own place. I don't think I've seen her since. No, she sent the team over to pretty me up for a few fund-raisers when she ran for reelection. If I obeyed strict instructions to never say anything negative about Aunt Diane, our family, my own life, etcetera, etcetera, I could sit next to a well-dressed man and eat a free dinner."

It seemed to Maggie that Collette enjoyed this opportunity to finally express her true thoughts about her famous aunt, and she couldn't blame her one bit.

Riley asked gently, as if he were empathizing instead of probing a potential suspect for motives, "You were okay with that?"

The woman gave a guileless shrug. "Sure. It didn't cost me anything, and I had nothing better to do. At the time. And she *was* family."

Jack spoke. "You must have meant something to her. She made you her executor."

"I doubt it. I'm local, and she probably didn't trust anyone she worked with—who would, you know? They *are* politicians. Though maybe she thought a piece of her estate would pay me back. Whatever."

"She did have children . . ." Riley began.

"She's divided the estate equally between them and me, one-third each, so maybe they weren't that estranged. Maybe she made me executor instead of burdening her own offspring with the job because they're successful. All I know is that I'd like to do a decent job of something, for once." The self-deprecating humor faded into a thousand layers of regret, but only briefly. She must have learned long ago that it did no good to dwell on what wasn't. Or maybe she knew better than to let the detectives investigating her aunt's murder think that there had been bad blood. "That's why I'm here. I need to get this house on the market—getting a decent price is still a little rough in these parts, I'm sure I don't need to tell you—and gather all her possessions. So I need the stuff you took back. I mean, I need the stuff you took, back."

"Miss Minella—"

"It's no problem. I understand why you needed to, like, investigate and all. But the property now belongs to me, so . . ." She let the word trail off, waiting for their response. The relaxed pose of legs crossed now shifted to the more tense, feet on the floor, ready for fight-or-flight stance. She leaned forward.

"The items we took might give us clues to why your aunt was murdered—"

"But they now belong to me."

Her and her two cousins, Maggie thought, but why quibble?

"No argument there," Riley said in a jovial tone. "Who they belong to is up to the probate court, not us. But how long we examine them for evidence, is."

The woman's body language continued to shade from relaxed and outgoing to aggressively needy. Her hands snaked out, palms up in a conciliatory way to convince them that she was being as reasonable as a stand-up citizen could. "I understand about the cell phone and the laptop. But I need you to return the money so I can get the estate settled. I mean, money is just money, right?"

"It's part of the investigation." Riley spoke quite easily himself, since he had no intention whatsoever of parting with the evidence before its time. "Speaking of the cell phone and laptop, would you happen to know Ms. Cragin's passcodes?"

A sneer slipped out, and Collette clamped one hand to her mouth. "Are you kidding? I didn't even know her middle name until I saw it in the paper this morning."

"Well, that's okay. But we will need you to sign a consent to search her phone and laptop. It's a very simple form."

Her skeptical expression seemed to say that Riley's smooth tone didn't fool her one bit, but at the same time the contents of her aunt's electronics held no interest, because she said, "Sure. But about the rest—I didn't want to mention it, but Aunt Diane wanted me to have that money. She told me so last week."

"Really? I thought you said you never spoke."

"No, we did—now and then."

Riley lost the smooth act and smiled, a much less honest and friendly smile than Maggie usually saw on him. He wasn't above enjoying the sight of a fish squirming on the end of his line. "You know, we haven't counted it yet—how much is there?"

"I'm not sure of the exact amount."

"Ballpark."

"My parents taught me not to talk about money. . . ." At their disbelieving looks she hastened, "But it was quite a lot. A large amount." Her lips flattened until they nearly disappeared before she said this, which indicated to Maggie that Collette Minella was lying. Not about wanting the money—she clearly wanted the money—but about knowing about the money or having any idea how much there was of it. She had simply read the evidence sheet Maggie had left on the kitchen table and had seen "money found in safe."

She'll be a happy girl when she learned the total, Maggie thought. Unless the Republican Party could find a way to lay claim to it, Collette Minella had just hit the lottery.

Jack had been rocking his chair in the time-honored tradition of bored students and now let the two front legs fall back to earth with a thud that the sound-deadening panels in the room couldn't completely disguise. "Miss Minella, do you have any idea who might have wanted to murder your aunt?"

She didn't care for the change in subject. "Everyone who ever met her, probably."

"Really?"

Collette Minella gave up on the plan to walk away with a large pile, or even small pile, of cash that morning. That the world remained as disappointing as usual did not come as any surprise, and relieving herself of the stress of trying to pretend otherwise prompted her legs back to their relaxed, crossed position. She gave them a small smile. "I mean, she's a politician, right?"

Chapter 16

"That was a bunch o'nothing," Riley complained. "I bet our victim's neighbors know more about her than her niece."

Maggie thought aloud, "She did live with her for a while, so she probably knows how she took her coffee and other personal habits. But I doubt that's going to help us find who killed her."

"She's an excellent suspect, motive-wise—kinda bitter, needs money. But I can't see her hooking up her own version of an electric chair."

"It wouldn't take a lot of technical knowledge," Maggie said, but without any real conviction. "And it wouldn't require access to the house, to which I'll bet she doesn't have a key."

Riley said, "Until probate gave her one along with the will. I'll bet my tickets to the game next week that she never knew dear Aunt Diane even *had* a safe until she did a walk-through and saw its door hanging open. She certainly has no clue how much money was in it."

"So why murder for it?"

"Anything on that grate?" Jack asked her.

She figured he meant the one he and Riley had found at the old asphalt company. "It's not the same. Slightly smaller but with thicker tines. And I ran the residue from each through the infrared spectrometer. Your grate has minerals and synthetic compounds, and the one used in the murder definitely has organic fats on it."

"So someone did grill their steaks on our murder weapon."

Riley said, "I'm not going to make any inappropriate analogies to grilling a politician."

Maggie thanked him. "In the meantime, I really wish the niece had those passcodes."

"Your guys haven't cracked the electronics yet?"

"The laptop, yes. They should get the data dump to you later in the day. But with phones it's not like it used to be—by which I mean four years ago. There *is* no unlocking an iPhone without the passcode. And as law enforcement has learned in the past, Apple won't give it up even for higher-profile crimes than this one."

"Your guys can't guess?"

"You put in the wrong code three times and it locks you out for a while. When that while is up and you still make a mistake, the while gets longer. After a certain point it wipes the phone entirely—and we'll never get that information back." She paused in front of the elevator, preparing to go back to the forensics unit.

Riley said, "I thought they always said deleted doesn't mean deleted."

"Sometimes. Sometimes not. Android tends to delete in bundles, so stuff may still be there. The iPhone deletes more piecemeal, so it's usually gone when it's gone."

"I see," said Riley, who clearly didn't.

"I did give them the bill that you got from Kelly, and they'd hoped to at least access her iTunes account."

"Seriously? You think her taste in music will tell us something?"

"Well, iTunes backs up your phone every so often, and sometimes we can retrieve some information. Don't ask me what or how—tech is *so* not my area. In the meantime, they sent the phone to Cellebrite. For a couple thousand dollars they can unlock it for us and send it back, then our guys could download it. For once the prosecutor's office isn't quibbling over the price, so IT is trying to talk the higher-ups into releasing enough funds to have Cellebrite do the whole data dump. That way we'd even have what she had deleted."

"You mean they're not? The higher-ups even have to think about it?" Riley protested.

"It's a lot of money. The two thousand is just to unlock it."

"So we have to wait around for the higher-ups to cough up the funds, or until it comes back for our guys to work on it and hope she didn't delete anything important?"

"Maybe not," Jack said.

The other two looked at him. Behind her, the elevator doors opened.

"We're surrounded by politicians, who are supposed to wield power and influence. . . . Maybe we could make that work for us."

Riley latched on to the gist. "If her party wants to know who killed her—"

"Especially if it turns out to be the other party, right before the election."

"—they should be willing to pull all the strings we need."

"Unless it *was* her party who killed her," Jack pointed out.

"Speaking of which." Maggie nodded toward two people now walking up the hallway toward them. Kelly Henessey and Raymond Stanton strode with determination, gazes fixed on the detectives. "I don't want to abandon you gentlemen. However . . . yeah, you're on your own."

But the elevator, tired of waiting, had left without her.

"Gentlemen," Stanton opened, "we're here to retrieve Senator Cragin's property." He ignored Maggie, either out of chauvinism or snobbery toward someone without a rank, or because he knew enough about police procedure to know this decision wouldn't be up to her.

Yet she still had to stumble through another explanation of why they hadn't gotten anywhere with the victim's electronic devices, and why simply having the account numbers they had provided had not helped. Neither he nor Kelly seemed to be listening, and shortly they got to the real reason for their visit.

"The money in Senator Cragin's safe," Stanton declared, "are funds of the Republican Party and need to be returned to same."

"Really. You always keep a great deal of cash around?"

The circles under Kelly's eyes had darkened and swelled, while her skin's flush illustrated an unhealthy level of diastolic blood pressure. "Many campaign donations are in cash. Diane had the support of working-class people. They donate whatever they can to help her help their state."

Collette Minella must have already stretched Jack's patience, because he said, "She's dead, Ms. Henessey. You can lose the rhetoric. How much money did the party have stored in a safe in a private home instead of at party headquarters, by the way?"

"I don't have the exact amount."

"Ballpark," Riley barked, for the second time that morning.

Stanton said, "What, is this like someone leaving an earring in the ladies' room? Describe it and we'll give it back to you? The funds belong to the party. Don't make us get a 6343 order to force you to release it. The police have gotten enough bad publicity in recent years."

"Go ahead. I would love to see you explain that much cash in writing. I would also love to know how you knew it was there without entering a sealed crime scene that was only released an hour ago. Either Collette Minella went to you first, or you had another key to the house."

"No key," Stanton said, "and it *was* released."

"Collette? What's she got to do with—" Kelly began, but Riley held up a hand.

"Stop. Any further discussion needs to take place in a proper setting. We need a room and a few forms signed, and then we'd love to trade whys and wherefores with you."

The attorney and the chief of staff goggled in perfect unison.

"What," Kelly said, "like we're *suspects*?"

Stanton said, "You're going to read us our rights like we're common criminals? I think not."

"Then we're done here. Go file your motion, because our prosecutor's office will also file a request for a grand jury."

The chairman immediately saw the public relations disaster of party officials being hauled before a grand jury. "Okay. Fine. The money certainly isn't important compared to finding out who killed Diane."

Really? Maggie thought. That's not what it just sounded like.

"We will be happy to cooperate with the investigation in any way. We will call you later today to set up an interview. In the meantime, we'll retrieve the phone and laptop."

"Uh, yeah. That's not going to happen, either."

Thus followed another round of Stanton and Kelly insisting that the electronics were party equipment and belonged to the party, and Riley pointing out that they were used as personal possessions and therefore went to the next of kin, aka her executor, who had just signed a consent to search, and Jack explaining that whom the items actually belonged to was not nearly as relevant as the fact that they had been found on a murdered person and as such there was no possible way they would be leaving police custody anytime soon.

Then he brought up the abilities of the external company and that speed required funds. Would the victim's party care to subsidize the investigation?

No, Stanton said. It wouldn't do for a political party to interfere in a government agency's functioning.

"Seriously?" Jack said. "Isn't that exactly what you've been trying to do for the past ten minutes?"

"Insulting us will not do you any good, Detective. In any way."

That might have sounded ominous, Maggie thought, applied against anyone less already ominous than Jack Renner. She said, "What about the account? The phone account?"

The other four stared at her.

She explained, "We can't get into the phone itself, but the provider—you said it was Verizon?—will allow online access to the account. That will at least give us the numbers she called, received, and texted, even though it won't provide the actual texts or photos or voice mails."

"I tried—" Kelly began.

Stanton cut her off. "Even if we have that information, we can't release it. There may be confidential items of national importance on those devices."

"There may also be clues that point to her killer," Riley said, secure in a foundation as solid as Gibraltar.

"If we have to get a court order—"

"Again, counselor, whatever. We're not releasing anything until we've completed our investigation, and I must say I'm mystified at your lack of concern. After all, it was your candidate who got offed."

Stanton glared for all he was worth, but then turned and walked away, snapping out a cell phone to make a call. Kelly waited until he was out of earshot, then confided, "I'm sorry, by the way . . . that I can't give you the phone records. I couldn't get into Dashlane, either; if Diane ever set up a password, I can't guess it. Me and Diane, we weren't pals, but I appreciated the chance to work for her, and she always treated me fairly. I don't want to do anything to protect the guy who killed her, so if the phone calls could help—"

Riley said, "If you know—"

"I don't! Diane would never let anyone else have access to her stuff. But I wish I could at least access the call history from the online account."

"How about now? Give it to us now," Jack said.

Kelly only needed a push, Maggie thought, to do the right thing. She seemed to be walking a tightrope of decision over a chasm of conflict. The fluorescent lights of the hallway cast a death-mask pallor over her face. She met Jack's gaze, reluctantly, briefly. "I can't. I gave the info to Stanton and it's up to him . . . and it was her private account, so I'd probably be violating some privacy law—"

"You woul—" Jack began.

"—and I'd never work again," she said more firmly. "Not for either party. The one thing no one in Washington wants is someone who can't keep a secret."

Riley said, "I thought you said there were no secrets in politics, between social media, infighting, and twenty-four-hour news."

She gave them both a smile that made Maggie feel extraordinarily naive. "Only the 'who's sleeping with whose boyfriend' kind of stuff. The secrets that *really* count—they stay buried."

Stanton had finished his phone call, and Kelly turned to join him. They walked away without another word.

Riley watched them go. "Everybody wants the money. Finding whoever killed their dear friend and colleague follows a distant second."

Maggie said, "I think Kelly wants to know, but only if she can use it in the campaign."

"They had no idea that money was there," Jack said, "or they would have asked about the safe before her body cooled. Ditto the niece. The esteemed senator from Ohio kept that money a secret from everyone."

Maggie thought aloud: "Including the killer, or he would have waited around until she got shocked and died, and then taken the keys out of her purse, gone into the house, and taken the money. Except he didn't have the combination."

"Or he knew that the money would come back to him eventually," Riley said.

"But it's going to the niece."

Jack said, "Or he didn't care about getting the money back, only that she took it in the first place?"

Maggie said, "And knew that if he killed her, it would come to light?"

Riley ran a hand through his hair, which didn't help its shape. "Or the money has nothing to do with anything, and she was killed because someone didn't like how she voted on the charter school issue. Either way, that much cash is like the smell of popcorn. Anyone who catches a whiff is going to want it."

Jack said, with a rare spark of humor, "Even if it means filing the 6343 you just dared them to draft. By the way, what *is* a 6343?"

"Hell if I know."

They both turned to Maggie.

"Don't look at me. I don't have the U.S. Code committed to memory."

Riley said, "We need to figure out where this cash

came from. It's too big a motive to disregard, and anyone who knows isn't likely to tell."

She punched the elevator button once more. "Fine. I'll process the money."

The detectives turned away, but she gave Jack's elbow a gentle grab. His bicep tensed under her fingers and his expression became apprehensive, as if afraid she might say something, well, *personal*.

She did not. "We've had that phone for twenty-four hours and this is the first they've mentioned it, right?"

"Yes."

Riley paused and listened.

"Why are they now so concerned about what might be on her phone?"

"They've had time to think about it," Riley suggested.

Maggie said, "We asked Kelly yesterday to pull the account information."

Jack made the connection. "And today they're worried about the phone. She saw a phone number in the call history that made them nervous."

"That would be my guess."

"Great," Riley said, "so now the people closest to the victim are lying to us."

"Everybody lies," Maggie said before she realized it, and this time it did feel personal.

Chapter 17

Maggie did not make it back to the questioned funds, however, as Denny caught her inside the lab doors. "Grab your go-bag. We've got a homicide. Josh is at a traffic death and Amy's working a missing person, so it's just you and me."

"Go-bag? Seriously?"

"I thought it sounded all special-ops-like. Like"—he waved his arms—"ninjas."

"Someone has a ninja costume left over from Halloween, doesn't someone?"

"Well, duh."

Not at all upset at having to put off processing the money, she asked, "What is it, and where are we ninja crime scene techs going?"

"Dead woman, found shot by her car next to the lake. Not far."

Twenty minutes later, most of which had been used up getting the police department issued vehicle out of the parking garage, she discovered the accuracy of that description. There was a car, a dead woman, a bunch of patchy grass, and the lake. And that was it.

They had arrived by driving down an old road at the end of Burke Lakefront Airport and through a chain-link fence, past a maintenance building of sorts. The gate had been opened for them. A marina sat to their right and empty land to the left, perhaps a natural buffer zone in case a runway proved too short for a particular plane. The road they used could hardly be called a road, more of an access path that hadn't been paved since the last millennium.

Maggie and her boss joined two patrol officers standing between the body and their own car. A Ford sedan had been parked half on and half off the road-way, its passenger door hanging open. The woman's body stretched in front of it, body in the grass, head on the asphalt. Her purse and its contents lay scattered across the road next to the driver's door.

"You beat the detectives," one of the officers said.

"Do I get a bonus?" she asked. "Who's coming out?"

"Gardiner and Dembrowski."

Her ex-husband. The day just kept getting better and better. "Who found her?" Obviously they weren't in a well-traveled area.

"Some maintenance guy goofing off. He said he was conducting a routine check, but I saw a fishing pole in his cart. Pure chance he found her—she might have stayed there for weeks."

The lake tried to distract her, the sound of the waves, the smell of the water. The overcast sky turned its surface to silver. The breeze hadn't warmed up from the night before.

"Does she work here? At the airport?"

"They're not missing anyone."

Denny said. "Is that gate we went through normally closed? I would think even a small airport would have pretty good security these days."

"Dunno, boss," the officer said. "They had it open to let us in."

Maggie photographed, and Denny sketched. Rick and his partner, Will, arrived, Will as sunny and friendly as usual, Rick scowling. Usually Maggie and her ex got along fine now that the divorce had faded into the past, but since she had told him she and Jack were sleeping together, all pretense of amiability had been tossed in the circular file.

"Hi, Will," she greeted them. "Rick."

"Maggie," he said, so deadpan she almost smirked, but didn't dare. Jack had convinced—or apparently convinced—her ex-husband that Jack had been moving around the country investigating the vigilante murders instead of committing them, but it did not feel like a permanent solution. Vengeful ex-husbands could be unpredictable. Best not to poke the bear.

Denny began to gather measurements to go with his sketch, not easy in such an open area. He managed to find a small structure about the size of a bus shelter off the road and used that as a fixed point, getting a distance to the vehicle and the body. This required use of their extra-long three-hundred-foot tape measure, with one of the unlucky patrol officers standing in the weeds to hold the "dumb end."

Maggie took a picture of the victim's purse, a large leather tote that lay on its side. Lipstick, pocket calendar, wallet—which had been opened, and a dollar bill left protruding—two pens, and a set of chopsticks from China Jade rested beside it.

She moved on to the body; facedown, the woman's blond hair obscured her features. She wore those supercomfortable type of Mary Jane shoes with rubber soles, a blouse, and snug jeans so dark and new they appeared to be dress slacks at first glance.

The blouse, a pale pink, had two large blood-encrusted holes, one in the right shoulder and another lower and to the left. For such wounds the staining seemed minimal; either she had died very quickly or the fluid had obeyed gravity and exited out the bottom—probably both. The palm of her left hand, down at her side, was clean, meaning she hadn't even had a chance to clasp it to her chest before collapsing. A large pool had gathered beneath her, telling Maggie to expect at least one corresponding hole in the woman's front. She would be a blood-soaked mess when they turned her over.

The detectives had remained back with the purse. Will Dembrowski had donned gloves and now picked up the victim's wallet. "Cash is gone, but the cards are all here."

"Robbery?" Rick said aloud.

"Out here? A parking garage downtown, I'd say yeah, but what would this chick even be doing out here? She sure doesn't do airport maintenance dressed like that."

"Meeting a pilot? Maybe she's a stewardess. Is there any airport ID in there?"

Maggie took some close-ups of the bullet holes. They appeared to be exit wounds, with the threads forced away from the torn flesh, but she couldn't be positive.

Will dug into the small leather wallet. "No . . . bunch

of pictures of kids and some guy who looks like an Italian model . . . her DL . . ."

"What's the name?"

Will peered at the plastic card and read, "Laurine Russo."

"Holy shit!" Rick exploded, so loudly that both Maggie and his partner started and stared. "I know her! She's a reporter."

Maggie looked down at the woman as if she might confirm this, which of course she did not.

Rick approached and examined the body. "Let's turn her over."

"Not until the ME gets here. You know that."

"She's been dogging me for months."

"Who was she a reporter for?" Maggie asked him.

"The *Herald*."

Will had joined them. "Oh, *that* one. Holy crap, was this an assassination? She getting too close to a story or something?"

"That only happens in the movies," Rick said. "And real hit men don't take the few bucks out of your wallet when they whack you. I bet she was meeting somebody here, either for a story or for a quickie before work, and ran into some homeless dude instead. Lone woman, middle of nowhere, no witnesses, easy cash. Yeah—she was into me, calling, showing up at the unit. Really persistent."

Preening over the woman's corpse . . . but class had never been Rick's strong point. Maggie ignored him and took a picture of the back of the woman's head, the clean, blond hair shifting slightly in the lake breeze.

Rick straightened, put his hands in his pockets, and circled her and the body in slow steps.

"What story did she call you about?" Maggie asked, to make conversation. It might behoove her, and especially Jack, to stay on his good side.

"The vigilante murders."

"What?"

She didn't hide her shock, couldn't, and stared up at him, mouth open, fear that she didn't even understand yet coursing through her. Then she dropped her face to her camera, made herself fiddle with the buttons on the back, changing settings that didn't need to be changed, anything to avoid eye contact and buy herself time to recover. She let curtains of hair fall forward to cover her flaming cheeks. "Really?"

Rick, of course, hadn't missed her reaction and swaggered a little more. "Oh yeah, she was all hot and heavy for that story. Thought it might be related to murders in other cities."

Don't look at him. Don't look at him. But she couldn't fiddle with camera buttons forever.

She should say something noncommittal like "Oh," but didn't trust herself to speak. Did Rick have something on Jack? Had he found out more about Jack's trail, things he hadn't yet told the higher-ups?

Her ex-husband said, "I'm surprised she didn't call you about it, try to get a quote or something. Since you got up close and personal with the killer."

She managed a "Huh."

"She was probably going to, but I wanted to keep you out of it."

"Thanks." Letting him take credit for something he didn't do regarding something that didn't happen . . . if it made him happy.

Maggie forced herself to take a breath, then got busy taking a photo of Lori Russo's face without dipping her camera or her own hair in the large pool of blood, which had spread about a foot past the borders of the body. She set the camera on the asphalt, aimed, and clicked, then examined the result via the screen on the back. Then she set it back down with a slight change to the orientation and tried again, as if this were a monumentally important part of crime scene processing instead of a way to avoid eye contact with Rick, or Will, or even Denny, still out of earshot.

Rick had nothing on Jack he hadn't had before, she told herself. If he did, he would have acted on it already. Rick had all the patience and self-discipline of the average toddler.

"Of course, your boyfriend has that case now. So maybe she's been dogging him about it . . . calling, stopping in . . ." Rick went on, coming to a stop in front of the car. Then, as if that stroll had been taxing, plopped his bottom down on the hood of Lori Russo's Ford.

"Get off that!" Maggie cried instantly, startling both cops. "Fingerprints!"

So much for staying on his good side. "The *car*? Why on earth—"

She girded her emotional loins. "I'm sorry for shouting. But—the passenger door is open. The killer might have walked around the car to get the purse, or been in the car with her and had someone else pick him up."

"And then put his hands all over the hood?"

She kept her voice level and returned to photographing Lori Russo's face. "I don't know, but we have to try."

Will had been making notes and interrupted, perhaps to keep the investigation on track or to give Maggie some breathing room. He'd always been diplomatic that way. "We'll have to talk to her editor, see if anyone at the paper knows what she's been working on. Her husband, too. Maybe it was something risky."

The Medical Examiner's investigator arrived, one of the newer girls—young, trim, bounding with life. Her chest and legs would go a long way toward distracting Rick. He pointedly engaged her in extra conversation as if this would annoy Maggie. Instead it gave her time to examine her own roiling thoughts.

No way would Jack kill Lori Russo. He would not kill an innocent woman just doing her job. He would not.

Her hands shook.

"Maggie?" Denny appeared at her shoulder, having finished his measurements. "You okay?"

"Getting cold. I should have brought my jacket."

He nodded; somehow she had pulled that off. "Yeah, that wind off the water feels good at first, but then it gets through the layers." He helped the investigator spread a clean sheet alongside the body so they had a place to flip her onto.

The victim had been a reporter, and the vigilante murders were months old. Surely more recent stories could have put her in danger, especially if she'd been as persistent as Rick said.

"How long do you think she's been dead?" she asked.

The investigator examined the woman's back, poked her skin for signs of lividity, and felt for any warmth. "Not sure. I need the arms." They turned the body over, revealing the full horror of a bloody death.

Blood soaked the clothing, the entire blouse, and the pants down to the knees. At first Maggie couldn't see any bullet holes, but then the investigator pointed them out—two small tears near the center, entrances smaller than the exit holes in her back. They were nearly invisible in the now dark red cloth and without any tearing or fouling. Not close shots, then.

Lori Russo's eyes were open. Still-gummy blood coated her entire face, masking what must have been an attractive one, and thick clots stuck here and there. Her right arm had been twisted beneath her.

"She's holding a notepad," Maggie said—a small spiral-bound pad, clutched between fingers and thumb. Maybe the reporter had written a clue for them, but it might take some work to be able to read the blood-soaked pages. She worked it out of the hand.

What if it mentioned Jack? What if she had been meeting Jack?

Maggie held it out for the investigator to see, her heart pounding so hard the blood crashed in her ears. Nothing she could do about it. There was nothing she could do.

But the girl merely glanced at the sodden, illegible pages and snorted. "Good luck with that."

"She was working," Will said, "not meeting somebody for fun and recreation. She was chasing a story."

Rick said, "The guy called her up and said he had a hot tip."

"But they had to meet in secret. No witnesses."

"Made her easier to kill than a Craigslist hooker."

Maggie noticed a pen had also fallen beneath the body and that the notebook rested in the right hand. Perhaps the reporter was left-handed, or had not begun to take notes. Still greeting her interviewee, perhaps, putting them at ease, warming up to asking questions. So even if it *had* been Jack—

Stop.

The ME investigator, meanwhile, examined the face, the teeth, pulled up the eyelids to check the whites and insides of the lids for petechiae. "Doesn't seem to be any damage, even landing face-first on the street. I figure she didn't get in a fist fight before getting shot, but we'd already guessed that." She moved down to the chest, lifting the blouse to expose a sturdy black bra and two bullet holes, one above, one below its left cup.

I'm sorry, Maggie silently communicated to the dead woman, *that we're pulling your shirt up in view of the whole world. I'm sure that's something you didn't do while alive, save for a Mardi Gras kind of situation, when it was your choice. I'm sorry for the tiny road stones now embedded in your cheek. I'm sorry that everyone around you is behaving as if this is completely routine, because for us it is. I'm sorry that your feelings and modesty are not a consideration for us. But we really are trying to find out who killed you.*

The investigator wiped some of the blood away and poked the skin, checking the lividity. When her fingerprint turned white and stayed white, they knew it had become fixed, that the blood inside the veins had clotted and would not flow back in once pushed out. Then she pulled on the arm, trying to unbend the crooked elbow.

"I'd say about six hours." She meant time of death. "She's pretty stiff in the joints but not the abdomen. It would set in a little more slowly because it's cool out here, unless she's got some medical condition that affects rigor."

Maggie said, "So early this morning. Before any of us were at work."

Any of us, she thought.

Chapter 18

Carol stood in the doorway, her gaze swiveling around the lab. The plastic bags, having been superglued the day before, were in the fume hood, drying after their dye stain bath. Some bundles had been placed on pieces of clean examination paper, their rubber bands removed and a sticky note with a number placed so that each grouping could be distinguished in the photos—which Maggie clicked at every stage of the dismantling. "Let's have lunch. In Paris."

"I wish."

"I think you're going a bit overboard on documentation, kiddo."

Maggie looked around at the meticulous placement, the warm-from-frequent-use camera, her single-spaced bench notes now spreading into a second page. "There's nearly a million dollars in this room. In cash."

"Yeah," Carol said. "That used to be a lot of money. But okay, I see why you're dotting all the *i*'s and checking off the *t*'s. We still don't know why the lady had all this stuffed into her closet?"

"No clue. Everybody wants it, but no one wants to explain how it got there."

She had texted Jack before leaving the scene: Call me when you can.

He hadn't responded. She had gone to the homicide unit upon returning to the building, but Jack and Riley were out. With every breath, her body screamed at her to go back, find him, track him down, and tell him Lori Russo is dead and what does he think about that? He may need to know. He may need some warning before and if Rick got in his face. And she wanted to see his reaction, didn't she?

Why?

She didn't really believe he did it. Could do it. Would have done it.

So she forced herself to work instead. Slowly, methodically, giving it her full attention . . . or at least as much attention as she could spare.

She realized Carol was speaking. "Payoffs. Bribes. Kickbacks. That's how it got there. What else is she going to do with it? Put it in a bank and wait for the IRS to notice it doesn't jibe with the 1040? Because don't they have to release their tax records? Members of Congress?"

"Nope. Some do, but they don't have to."

"How many is 'some'?"

"Like, eight percent. Come look at this." She directed the other woman to the oculars of the stereomicroscope. Its lens hovered over a twenty-dollar bill. Money, up close, had a lot to look at between the pressed fibers of the paper and the complicated patterns of the ink. But she had found some light-colored dots that didn't add to the artwork.

"What are those?"

"I have no idea. I thought it was just dust or some kind of lint, but when I prodded one it was so hard that it zinged off onto the counter somewhere and was lost."

"Let's not tell Denny that. Losing evidence tends to be frowned upon in this establishment. Do you think it's significant?"

"I didn't. Until I found it again in those bundles." Maggie waved at three more dissected stack of bills on a different piece of examination paper. Then she pointed to three others already repackaged. "But not those."

"Huh. Still, something that tiny—could be cross-contamination. You guys were counting all this on the same table."

"Possible. And if it's only in these two stacks, you're probably right. We'll see if it turns up in any more."

Carol twisted the dial to move the lens, trying to get the focus even sharper. "And you have no idea what it is?"

"It's hard, and round. So it's not dust, dirt, a paint flake, a skin cell . . . the surface is smooth, so it's probably not some kind of mineral like asbestos or plaster dust. I tried putting it under transmitted light, but it's not quite *that* small—I see a tiny opaque sphere. I'm thinking it's some kind of spore."

The task chair skittered away as Carol jumped back from the counter. "You mean it really *is* anthrax?"

"No! I'm sure the Ohio Department of Health knows what they're talking about. And the powder was with David's note, not the money. Different case. Besides, I Googled—anthrax spores are more football shaped, not spherical."

Carol wheeled the task chair back but refrained from sitting in it again. "Oh, well. If you *Googled*."

"And if it *were* anthrax, we'd be dead by now."

Carol continued to stand, the better to watch her with a baleful stare.

"Think of them as seeds, if that helps."

Carol admitted it did, a little.

"And that's not all I Googled. This is one of the tally sheet pieces of paper that was in bundle number 25A." She gestured toward a scrap of plain white paper, torn from a larger sheet of printing which left only *426– 115th Co* and below it *ealth Adminis* and under that, *Our Own Directiv*. "I searched all of it at once, and came up with Senate bill number 426, the Grow Our Own Directive: Physician Assistant Employment and Education Act of 2017."

"What the heck is *that*?"

"A bill for a pilot program at the VA to train veterans as physician assistants."

"Sounds good. But why is a piece of that bill turning up in this senator's loot?"

"Excellent question. For which I do not yet have an answer."

"*Yet*. I admire your confidence, kid. Any other trace evidence?"

"Spots of blood in three different bundles."

"The plot thickens."

"They're pretty tiny—think paper cuts rather than a scene of slaughter. I pulled them out, but there's no sense having you run the DNA just yet." *Don't look at your phone*, Maggie told herself. It would have vibrated if he called or texted. "Some dog hairs, some cat hairs, one human hair, blond with a gray root, probably our victim's, another one that's dark brown."

Carol opened her mouth.

"No root."

Carol shut it again. Useless for nuclear DNA analysis.

"A number from the same dog, I think, with consistent color and length. A bichon frise."

"I hate those little yappy dogs."

"But if you're allergic to dogs, that's the dog to get. Then there's some vegetation."

Carol raised her eyebrows.

"That's my term for 'something tiny that came from a plant'—pieces of leaves, one or two that might be stems or thicker parts of leaves, I don't know. It's not pot. I also found a bunch of fibers, nothing too consistent. Four tufts of fibers that look like the rats-nest type of pressed synthetic bundles, that we see in Tyvek suits and reusable grocery bags."

"Wasn't some of this found in reusable—"

Don't look at your phone. "Yes, but it doesn't match any of them. My tufts are all brown, and the bags from the safe come in blue, a different shade of blue, green, purple, and gray."

"I'll bet they're from the person who gave her the money—they had it in a brown grocery bag and dumped it into her blue one. Sort of like trick-or-treat . . . you're bribing someone, you'd have to do it on the sly. Then she takes it home and counts it."

"Hence the scraps of paper with the amounts on them—but those are inconsistent, too. Some have them and some don't. I'm no handwriting expert, but the shapes of the numbers look very different." She pointed to one set where a white rectangle sat next to the cash with *3700* written in a spidery scrawl. The paper had three precut edges, and one torn one with light blue lines running from side to side, apparently from an index card. The next bundle had *2500* neatly printed in pencil on a triangle of pink paper with two precut edges and one torn. "Different combinations of denominations—"

"Say that five times fast."

"—different orders of the denominations. There's no rhyme or reason to it. Either she was completely disorganized about her bookkeeping, or these bundles all came from different sources, some of whom included tally sheets and others didn't."

"They probably did. That's how kickbacks work. You have your hand in everything. A zoning regulation is suspended, a new school opens, one county gets their roads repaved, and you get a little off the top of each one."

"Our tax dollars *not* at work. I'll fingerprint the scraps of paper—that's easy and it's more directly related to the money being given to the victim, rather than a print on a bill that floated through the economy and then ended up with to the victim." *Don't look at your phone.* But I think this may be much more productive." She held up an evidence bag and let Carol peek inside. "It's four fresh stacks. Crisp bills with a bank band around them. The patrol officer who counted these commented on them at the time, but we were so overwhelmed that we didn't think much of it. These had to come directly from a bank."

"And *haven't* been randomly floating through the economy before winding up in the victim's safe. So—fresh prints?"

"I'm thinking more that the serial numbers can tell us which bank they came from and whom the bank gave them to."

"Is that possible?"

"I have no idea."

Denny poked his head into the room. "Maggie. You have a visitor."

Her heart went into jackhammer mode. "Jack?"

"No. Nobody I know."

She stifled a groan. *"Again?"*

Chapter 19

David Carlyle waited in the entranceway to the lab, by the small table with the sign-in sheet and the forms for the officers to fill out to have their items of evidence tested. His naturally somber face brightened as she approached.

"Hello," Maggie greeted, uncertainly.

"Hi, uh . . . I thought you'd want my fingerprints. To compare to any you got on the letter that somebody sent me . . . you know, like to rule mine out?"

They didn't usually obtain elimination prints, but it certainly couldn't hurt. If all the prints she'd obtained matched Carlyle, then there would be no point in asking any potential suspects for their exemplars, something that tended to put a damper on community relations anyway. "Ah, yes. Of course. Don't bother to sign in—we'll have to go to the booking room."

He accompanied her through the white hallways, down the elevator, and across the atrium with enthusiasm that flagged only a little when they reached the grimier jail area. But the LiveScan machine sat near the front of the facility, a wheeled, squarish contraption that reached Maggie's waist. With a monitor perched on top, it looked more like a portable EKG machine than police equipment. Maggie opened the program and typed in Carlyle's information, name, birth date, ethnicity, then labeled the prints as *Elimination* so that they would not get sent to the criminal database and searched against all outstanding crime scene latents. This protected Carlyle's civil rights, though she did not feel entirely sure he warranted this category. In her heart of hearts, the jury remained out on David Carlyle. He might be a victim. He might have something to do with the senator's death. He might be playing a game all his own for reasons she could not yet guess.

She wanted to ask about the indented writing: *ne Sat 10.* His own jotting of an upcoming meeting, unaware that this had left an impression on the threatening note, supposedly sent to him by a stranger? It didn't appear on the envelope, so he couldn't have made the impression himself before opening the letter. Or someone else's jotting of an appointment for the *following* Saturday, the tenth, with *-ne* belonging to a name other than Diane. She found it doubtful that he would refer to the antagonistic senator by her first name, anyway. She would have to tell Jack about this latest clue. And Riley, too, of course.

But now it was time to roll. Literally.

She started with his right hand. His fingers were cold, and she held them briefly between her two palms to warm them up and make the skin more pliable.

He asked if she had, indeed, found any prints on the letter, envelope, or baggie—which most people would have asked first, as it might spare themselves the tedium of having their prints rolled. She told him yes, but she did not say anything about the notation she had found in the indented writing. As much as she would like to, the cops would need to handle that, just as they had been the ones to give him the happy news that he had *not* been exposed to anthrax.

The first images to collect were "plane" impressions, meaning first the thumb and then all four fingers together were placed straight down on the glass platen. After that she needed to roll each digit by itself from side to side, preferably all the way from one edge of the fingernail to the other. This required some dexterity, and she ordered him to relax his hand. Relaxing any part of his anatomy did not come easily to him, and his index finger remained stiff, smearing the image. The program rejected it, and so she wiped the platen and tried again after again rubbing his hand with both of hers.

"That's nice," he said.

She looked at him, and he audibly gulped.

"I mean, it's . . . you know . . . like a hand massage or something . . . sorry. I'm really not the complete dweeb I must have appeared to be yesterday. I'm just tense."

"You're in a jail. It makes most people tense."

He laughed, which echoed off the bare concrete walls. She continued to manipulate his fingers. A patrol officer came in with a swaggering, swearing youth in baggy pants and handcuffs, and Carlyle's fingers stiffened again in the wake of the kid's attitude and miasma—Ralph Lauren's Polo and sweat.

Maggie moved on to the left hand, rubbing again.

"How do you do this? Work around, like, criminals?"

She smiled at him, which only made his fingers difficult to work with again. She explained, "A, they're in handcuffs. B, there's an armed police officer right there. And C, I'm an unarmed forensic tech. I'm not a physical threat, and if I give them a nonjudgmental, pleasant look, I'm not a threat to their self-esteem, either—which, make no mistake, is the more significant concern in their lives. So I'm never in any real danger. Unless of course one grabs a cop's gun and decides to take everyone in the room hostage—then, yes, but that's never happened." *Yet*, she thought.

He chuckled along with her. "I'm a little sensitive to guns. One of my first assignments was the Elk River spill in West Virginia."

"What happened there?" she asked. Chatting made his fingers relax.

"This place called Freedom Industries, which made coal-mining chemicals, sprung a leak and released seventy-five hundred gallons of methylcyclohexanemethanol into the river, spoiling the water source for about three hundred thousand people. I was collecting samples of drinking water from the houses and one old guy ran me off his porch with a shotgun."

Maggie made an appropriately shocked-sounding noise.

"He and his son and daughter all worked at the plant and didn't want the place to go under. I get it, I guess. They could live on bottled water for a while, but they couldn't live without an income."

"That's a harsh choice."

"The irritating thing is that the EPA hadn't found the plant in violation for years, just let it go—hardly the job-killing thugs we're supposed to be. But then when something bad happens, we're incompetent and maybe corrupt. We can't win for losing."

"Try working for a police department. We're either overzealous bullies or don't care."

"I can see that! What you are depends on what they want. I talked to the guy a couple weeks later at a town meeting. There were few choices for employment in the area, and he and his kids had pensions to think of, too. So I get that Vepo could create a lot of jobs that this area really needs. I get that StartUp Central could take this city into the future. But if I let that influence me, then bad things can happen, like a tank next to a river springs a leak and suddenly three hundred thousand people are drinking poisoned water. Or no matter *what* I do, the next time it rains, hydrocarbons are going to wash into the new water intake and a chunk of the city will develop leukemia or cancer of the bladder."

Maggie studied him. All of a sudden she really hoped he hadn't killed Diane Cragin.

"Is that it?"

She had finished the last finger. She also realized that she hadn't thought about Jack and Lori Russo in a whole three minutes, and that she still held Carlyle's hand. "Oh! Yes. All set. I will get the card printed out and then delete you from the system so you can't be searched again in the future."

"That's okay, I don't care. I've got nothing to hide."

"It's standard protocol. Let me walk you out."

She guided him back to the atrium in the center of the building. He took a breath as if steeling himself, and then thrust out his hand. "I know it wasn't the best circumstances, but it was really nice to meet you."

"You too. You never know, we may run into each other again during another investigation."

"I hope so," he said. "I really do."

She continued on to the elevator bank back to the lab. She did not turn to see if he would still be standing there, watching her go. But when she returned to her piles of money and its various trace evidence, Carol said, "I see what you mean."

"About the serial numbers?"

"About your EPA boy. He *is* kind of cute."

"Mmm." Maggie returned to her microscope.

"But don't tell your new boyfriend I said so. He scares me." The DNA analyst returned to her micro-tubes, her feet tapping lightly against the linoleum.

"Sometimes," Maggie muttered to herself, "me too."

Chapter 20

Just as she thought she would start screaming in a long keening wail, he called her back. "What's up?"

"Where are you?" she asked.

"At my desk."

"Don't move."

Three minutes later she found him right where he said he'd be, clicking morosely through screen after screen with an external hard drive plugged into his computer. An overcast sky had turned the air of the normally bright homicide unit to a dull gray, and most of the desks were empty, the detectives out at lunch or working on their cases in the field. One flipped through a yearbook in the corner, most likely searching for a suspect, and another wrote a report, two fingers pecking at his keyboard.

Jack glanced up, saw her face. "What is it?"

Without pausing her forward momentum, she pulled a spare chair along with her and sat down in it, her gaze never wavering from his. She kept her voice low. "Did you know a reporter named Laurine Russo?"

A line appeared between his eyebrows, either at the question or her use of the past tense. "Yeah. *Herald* writer."

"She's dead."

No reaction at first, then: *"Shit!"* loud enough to make one of the other cops slam the yearbook and the second pause, fingers as rigid as wooden stakes.

Okay, Maggie thought. He didn't do it.

Jack's acting ability lay in *not* showing emotions. *Showing* them was not something he could do convincingly, even, it seemed, when they were genuine.

At least they *seemed* genuine.

She shouldn't second-guess her own mind into oblivion. That way lay madness.

He found words, with uncharacteristic speed. "What? How? Where? When?"

She told him everything she could. This was not telling tales out of school—the detective unit was indeed a unit, and anything one member knew could be shared with another.

He didn't question, an insidious little voice in her head pointed out, that she'd been murdered. You just said dead. It could have been a car accident or natural causes . . . *except I wouldn't have come over here to tell him in person that the woman had suffered a coronary over her morning coffee, now, would I?*

"Rick and Will are at the autopsy now," she finished. "They didn't ask me to go—not much for me to do there. With the clothing intact, the notebook in her hand—obviously no assault, so no sense taping for hairs or fibers or collecting fingernail scrapings. And Rick probably didn't want me around, and Will didn't want to listen to Rick being obnoxious because I was around. Not to mention cause of death was pretty damn obvious."

She was talking only to be talking, as if that made things normal, as if this were purely a dispassionate, professional exchange of information. And why wasn't it? she wondered. What had gone on between him and this Lori Russo?

Jack didn't appear to be listening, anyway. He even jumped up and paced around his desk for a lap or two, the movement as uncharacteristic as the rapid speech. "You don't have her phone?"

Why? Who would show up in her call history? "It's the only thing missing, aside from cash from her wallet. We *assumed* cash from her wallet, unless she made a habit of walking around with only a dollar bill sticking out of it."

"Trying to make it look like a robbery gone bad," he said, apparently to himself.

"As if she'd be out for a walk in such an isolated location for no reason at all. Someone had left the gate open for her—the grounds manager said it's always locked, accessible only by keycard, and every employee's card had been accounted for. One of them got paid off to open it up, Will figured, and now that it ended in murder, they're too afraid to fess up."

Jack sat again. "We have to find that person. And check her e-mail, her phone—that's probably how he arranged the meet. If we're lucky."

"You mean Rick and Will can check. It's not your case."

She heard his teeth grinding against themselves.

"You think this is connected to Diane Cragin?"

He stopped grinding. "I don't know. Russo could

have been poking under half a dozen different rocks . . . that's what she did. Damn! She's got two kids."

He looked stricken. Maggie leaned closer, wanting to reach out but not knowing what to reach for, feeling a qualified relief that Jack had not . . . killed the woman. She forced her brain to finish the thought. He had not killed Lori Russo. Right?

Jack said, "She hinted at a bigger story about Green. I hope her husband or her editor has all her notes. She would have left notes."

She let him muse for a bit, then asked, "What's that? What you were working on?"

He glanced at the monitor and the external hard drive plugged into the small box that now represented his desktop computer. "Contents of the senator's laptop."

"Anything?"

"No. I mean, a silo full of e-mails and bills and reports and drafts, but anything that might tell us why she was killed? Who knows?"

"Nothing in the e-mails?"

"No threats—apparently all the nuts have to write to the main party e-mail and couldn't get her personal one—no sex, no talk of transferring funds or secret meetings. If she had a hidden agenda, she knew better than to put it in writing." He rubbed his face, and Maggie wondered if he'd been up all night combing through the crime scene photos or witness statements. "What do you have?"

"I have something on the money," she said, though he didn't seem particularly interested. "The sequential bills came from the Federal Reserve—our Federal Reserve, the one that's two blocks away."

"So a payoff here in Cleveland, not DC."

"It was part of a withdrawal that went across the street, literally, to Fifth Third, three weeks ago."

"And from there?"

"No idea. But that's not all. Elsewhere in our bundle o'bills—" She explained about the piece of paper regarding Senate bill 426.

"Physician assistants?"

"I did some more Googling. One does wonder how crimes were ever solved without it. Senator Cragin had nothing to do with Senate bill 426. Didn't work on it, it didn't go through her committee, she's not linked with any of the sponsors."

"Is it a bribe for her vote?"

"It's possible, of course, but I doubt it since the bill is still in committee. It's not even close to being voted on yet."

"Does it have anything to do with Cleveland in particular? This bill?"

"No. It's national."

"So it's nothing Lori Russo would have been working on."

His mind still lingered on Lori Russo. And it would, Maggie knew, until they found who had killed the wife, mother, and dedicated reporter.

Jack was saying, "So where did it come from?"

"I'm thinking there could be a million routes. I'll bet members of Congress get a copy of everything they have to vote on and some industrious intern cut up discarded paper to use as a notepad. Or she was in someone else's office and needed something to write on. I did find two prints on it, but neither is hers."

"Have you found her prints on anything so far?"

"Yes. Some of the other scraps, and all of the bags. The plastic bags—of course I can't do anything with the mesh ones. Also on that *Mom* tchotchke with the safe combination taped to the bottom."

"Okay. So she isn't being posthumously framed by someone. She definitely had her hands on that money."

"Yep. For the sake of argument, let's rule out industrious interns to explain the scrap of paper. Maybe she didn't have a connection to Senate bill 426, but whoever gave her the money did."

"Possible," Jack conceded.

"I don't see how that helps much. But maybe this will." She slapped another set of printouts on his desk, creating a breeze that ruffled a surveillance video screen shot from last week's robbery and a napkin from Pei Wei. "The IT guys got into her phone account through the laptop. The automatic feature filled in the passwords for them. It's only the call history—no texts, photos, or websites, simply calls in and out, but at least it's something."

Jack's hands went to the pile like a drowning man after a life preserver. He flipped pages, flipped back.

Maggie added, "They did the same thing with her Fitbit account, but that didn't help much. She didn't have the GPS turned on, and besides the shock that killed her killed it, too. It last sent an update to the site via her phone around nine p.m. Nothing after that, which is consistent with what we already know."

Jack muttered, "Reverse order. Calls pretty steady, back and forth, all day. Several after five, not answered."

"She would have been at the fund-raiser—probably had the sound turned off or just ignored them."

"This was the last outgoing—nine-twenty p.m."

"Kelly said she left the fund-raiser at about nine."

"She spoke to someone for three minutes." He stared at the number, then went to pick up the phone on his desk. "Might as well—"

Maggie put her hand over his, gently pinning the receiver in its cradle. "Wait. Search the number first."

Right then Riley returned, carrying a Styrofoam cup of coffee and a small paper bag. "Am I interrupting something?" he asked, his tone not as light as he had probably intended.

This time Maggie remembered that she and Jack were supposed to be dating and managed to *not* look confused. Jack caught his partner up on Lori Russo's death. Riley reacted with the same amount of shock, and Maggie found herself the teensiest bit jealous of Lori Russo. Every man in the department seemed to not only know her but knew her with a healthy amount of feeling.

Jack, meanwhile, then explained about Diane Cragin's phone information. He typed in the last phone number dialed. "Bruce Haywood."

"Fabulous," Riley said, spreading cream cheese over half of a sliced bagel. Grief for a murdered reporter had not ruined his appetite—or perhaps it had, as his movements were rote and absent. "Who's that?"

Maggie peered over Jack's shoulder. "A lobbyist at Garfield and Corning. East Fourteenth, Hanna Building. Fancy website that doesn't say much—how they're great guys, their clients are great guys, and here's our e-mail address."

"They're lobbyists. They let the money do the talking," Riley said. He took a bite, and a dollop of cream cheese landed on the napkins piled below.

"A senator talking to a lobbyist is hardly suspicious," Jack said.

"Not suspicious at all," Maggie said.

"We should go talk to him," Riley said, chewing. "Not call. Show up on his doorstep."

"Definitely," Jack agreed. "Just for the hell of it. Though the killer didn't need to call her—the wires were set up at her own home. She had to go back there eventually."

Riley warmed to an idea. "Maybe he was *at* the fund-raiser, saw her leave about nine, and wanted to be on the phone with her when she bought it to establish an alibi."

Jack said, "And then never called to tell us, hey, I was on the phone with her when she died?"

Maggie asked, "Then how did he install the wires if he was at the fund-raiser?"

Riley said, "Yeah, never mind. I guess we'll have to let him tell us where he was and why she called him. It will be some routine matter and nothing to do with the murder, and we'll be right back where we started."

"Or he will say that she was upset about a fight she'd just had with someone."

Riley grunted his lack of confidence in her cheery scenario. "Who else did she call?"

"No one after the fund-raiser began. She received two." Jack searched the numbers; they belonged to the League of Women Voters and someone named Nancy in DC. The calls she had answered before the fund-raiser came from the Black Women's Political Action Committee, David Carlyle, Channel 15, and someone named Marge Winston, also in DC. Senator Cragin had also *made* two calls shortly before the fund-raiser, both to the same number. When Jack typed it in, nothing came up.

"Burner," Maggie said.

"Interesting," Riley said. "Why is our senator calling a burner phone? Drug deal?"

"The toxicology came back clean," Maggie said. "They had rushed it, of course, but all the standard illegal substances came up clean."

Jack said, "Money, then. That's the other thing you discuss over untraceable phones."

"Or sex," Riley said.

"This case, I'm guessing money."

"You think people stop having sex after sixty?" Riley demanded, an uncomfortably sharp edge to his tone.

"I hope not," Jack answered, with an utter absence of inflection.

There seemed to be a subtext to which Maggie wasn't privy, but then when it came to men and sex, it seemed like she understood very little—at least according to Rick—other than it seemed to be their number one, all-time raison d'être.

At any rate, the chief of the homicide unit entered the room, distracting them all. Immaculately dressed and slightly hesitant, as if he had never been in the room before and wasn't sure he should be. He crossed over to them.

"Renner. Riley." He glanced at Maggie but said nothing. She figured he didn't want to admit that he did not know who she was or what she was doing there, yet unconcerned since she wore a PD uniform of sorts.

"I've been told that the Republican Party—some guy named Stanton—is going to be sending over a sub-poena for the senator's phone and any downloads or printouts of same. They don't seem to care about the laptop."

"That's because there was nothing on it." Riley swallowed. "They want the phone—"

"They want it and everything about it. Basically we are not to read, examine, copy, or access any informa-tion found in same, on the grounds of national secu-rity."

Jack snorted. "Seriously? They're pulling out 'na-tional security'? What's in her call history, the nuclear launch codes?"

"It's Washington. They can claim that about every-thing," Riley said. "What it means is, they don't want us to know where that money came from or where it was going."

Jack said, "The niece signed a consent to search."

"Not valid," the chief said. "It doesn't belong to her. The party paid for it and provided it to the senator. Technically it's their property."

"But it's her personal information," Jack argued.

The chief commiserated but said getting a search warrant would be much faster than trying to figure out who had the authority to consent to a search and who didn't.

"We tried that. The judge denied the warrant based on jurisdiction."

"He was afraid the murder case would go to the feds," Riley explained, "and didn't want to 'dilute' the evidence."

Jack laid one large hand over the stack of printouts from the laptop download. "Besides, it's too late, boss. I've already got—"

The chief held strong opinions on the better part of valor and all that, because he practically shouted. "Don't tell me! I don't want to know. Just box it up until they decide on a special investigation team or whatever."

Riley said, "Right now we can't even do that, since the phone is at Cellebrite. Are they sending them the same court order?"

"I don't know. Maybe they trust Cellebrite not to talk about their clients. Us, not so much. Either way, it's their problem."

"The feds should have taken over the whole thing from the beginning. It would certainly have been all right with me."

"Me too," the chief said. "But apparently they want to leave us on the hook for it—"

Jack said, "But without any of the evidence to work with."

"It's not ideal, but we're in a pretty tight corner here. The pressure is unimaginable. I've already been asked to be on all the local channels and most of the national ones. Fox wants to do a half-hour segment."

Riley coughed. "Well, you'll, um . . . make us proud I'm sure. . . ."

"No, the mayor and the governor both advised me to stay out of the spotlight." He spoke with deep unhappiness, the spotlight always his number one goal. "And I've heard from other sources, too. The middle of a political fight is not where we want to be. These guys have been making people disappear for decades, and the badge isn't going to protect me. It won't protect you, either," he added to his two detectives, in a voice so somber that Maggie would have found it amusing if not in such deadly earnest. The chief could not be said to hold high esteem among his staff, but he wasn't a total idiot. If he had been so thoroughly cowed by these unseen forces, there must be something to be genuinely feared.

"So . . . what are you saying, Chief?" Jack asked.

"That we do our jobs without going out on any limbs. We comply with the government's requests, document everything, give them what they want, and if we don't get anywhere because of their limitations they can give the whole investigation to the FBI with my blessing. And you"—he pointed at Maggie—"don't say a word about this conversation."

"Absolutely," she assured him.

The man left. Riley popped in the last bit of his bagel and mumbled, "Where does that leave us?"

Jack said, "About to go interview Bruce Haywood."

"But—you heard the guy!"

"He said to turn over the phone downloads when we get them from Cellebrite. He didn't say anything about the phone account sheets. Relax. Haywood's a lobby-ist. If he's got national security secrets, then this country is in trouble."

"You think it's not?" Riley swallowed his last bit of bagel. "But, okay, let's go interview the skeevy, slimy lobbyist."

Maggie said, "I'm picturing a cadaverous guy in a trench coat with sunglasses, or an overweight white guy with gray hair and a cigar clamped between his teeth."

Riley crumpled a napkin and used it to sweep crumbs

off his desk. "Watch it, missy. You're describing me, except for the cigar, and that's only because they won't let me smoke in here."

Maggie told them she would call if she got any further with the trace evidence on the money, then headed for the door. Jack folded the senator's phone account sheets and put them in his pocket. Riley gazed from one of them to the other, then gave Jack a slight frown.

"What?" Jack asked.

Riley raised an eyebrow, and as Maggie reached the hall she heard him say, "You two are like no couple I've ever known."

Got that right, she thought.

But at least, she added to herself, I can be sure Jack didn't murder Lori Russo.

She pushed the elevator button. Pretty sure.

The car arrived. Relatively sure.

But by the time she returned to the forensics lab, she no longer felt sure of anything at all.

Chapter 21

Bruce Haywood, Jack immediately saw, didn't resemble either of Maggie's imaginings. Inside his small but perfectly appointed office, everything about the trim, fortyish, medium-height, brown-haired, clean-shaven man in a crisp shirt suggested professionalism without tipping into intimidating superiority. Old enough to have experience and be taken seriously but not old enough to be old-school and inflexible. Tall enough to reflect a client's status, without challenging their alpha position. Casual and hardworking enough to take off the jacket, but with a pressed and expertly knotted tie to indicate complete mastery over his surroundings.

He's a psychological masterpiece, Jack thought, *and he hasn't even opened his mouth yet.*

"How can I help you, Detectives?" Haywood said, the wording completely in line with his image so far. There to put every resource possible toward solving your problem.

"Tell us about your relationship with Diane Cragin."

"The senator?" he asked, as if there could be another

Diane Cragin that homicide detectives might be asking about. "Terrible about her death. Such a lovely woman. I had met with her on behalf of my client, Vepo Construction and Consulting."

"The crib renovation."

"Yes."

Jack reached forward and took a mint out of a crystal candy dish on the corner of the man's desktop. That, a phone, a wooden cup shaped like a mushroom and holding exactly two pens, a framed photo, and a cell phone were the only other items on it. Complete mastery . . . prospective clients must find it reassuring, along with the chameleon-like ability to adapt from one rough-hewn contractor or a gaggle of charitable ladies to a green first-year representative to a bluenose, golf-playing cabinet member. What surprised Jack, however, was how sincere the guy seemed—as if truly concerned about the woman's death and more than eager to tell them something that might help. He answered the next questions with vigor. Yes, he had spoken with the senator on the night before last. He didn't recall what time but would have it in his phone—here, she had called him at 9:20 p.m., and they had spoken for about three minutes, about the negative press Vepo had been getting locally.

"I told her I'd send over some rebuttals and talking points that she could use the next time they asked. She said fine. That was about it."

"Wait—*you* were going to send *her* talking points? Like, you're writing her speeches?"

"No, of course not. I give—gave—her information to help clarify the situation. And only about Vepo. They're the only client I currently have with the senator. Had.

For instance, some reporters have asked about Vepo's track record, so I got with Vepo and they explained their resume in some detail. They had built a water purification plant on a Native American reservation in Montana—I can't remember the exact name, I confess it was two tribal names I'd never heard before, Salish and something else—anyway, now the water is better than ever and as a bonus, employment has risen seven percent. I relayed that information to Diane, and she used it in the next media interview."

Riley said, "So Vepo tells you everything is hunky-dory, but we heard the filters gummed up from natural gas intrusion—"

"Oh, no, we do a little more due diligence than that! I sent an associate from our Helena office to check out the rez, the local media, do a few man-on-the-street talks. She reported directly back to me. Yes, they are still having water issues in the area, but that's due to the local fracking. Vepo can't be blamed for that. Can I get you two anything? Coffee? Tea? Water?"

Jack's partner operated on the premise that a good cop should always accept any offer of hospitality, as it put the interviewee at ease and established rapport. Jack had suffered more day-old coffee, stale doughnuts, and brick-hard cookies than he cared to think about, but this time Riley must have figured this guy didn't need help to relax—Haywood already seemed as relaxed as possible for a man to get while still wearing a tie. Or maybe the breakup with the girlfriend had thrown him off more than Jack realized. At any rate, Riley said, "No, thank you. Is that a standard part of being a lobbyist? If you don't mind my asking."

"Don't mind at all! I know most people think lobbyists walk around bribing legislators to put in a casino next to the middle school and that sort of thing, passing wads of cash in smoke-filled rooms."

Jack pictured Bruce Haywood in a trench coat clenching a cigar, and smiled. Then he remembered the piles of cash in Diane Cragin's safe, and stopped.

"Lobbyists simply facilitate the communication between different groups—corporations, trade unions, cities and counties, charities—and their elected representatives. I risk sounding like my grandmother when I say this, but the world has become so complicated these days. You can't have a group of farmers send one of their own to the state capital or to Washington to tell their senator that they need a few subsidies and a new dam, because the dam will alter land use in a nearby suburb and might cause flooding, fertilizers the farmers use will hit these new pockets of groundwater, yet the dam forms a bridge so that the school buses can take a more direct route, and subsidies are a very questionable system now that most farms are corporate owned. So you see—issues are complicated. The farmers, the utilities, the kids' parents don't have time for in-depth study and analysis of the issues. For that, they hire me."

"To write the representative's talking points."

He chuckled, and fiddled with a pen—the first sign of possible evasion Jack had seen. Evasion or perhaps boredom. "We'll write more than points. We'll write the whole bill."

Riley's eyes popped.

"That's pretty common these days. If I can take a second to blow my own company's horn, this is one of Garfield and Corning's strengths, the technologically complicated issue, the stuff that representatives simply do not have time to become subject matter experts in. Excuse my syntax."

"And Senator Cragin didn't have time?"

"None of them do. They're only in Washington for three full days a week and then it's back to their districts to listen to people there and campaign for the next election—and there's *always* a next election. That's why they all live on four or five hours of sleep, never see their kids, and have really understanding—or uncaring—spouses."

"I see," Riley said with a hint of disapproval in his voice. "What talking point did she need help with that night?"

"As precisely as I can recall, she expressed concern about the upcoming EPA report and his assessment of the water quality in the river."

"Ah. You've spoken with David Carlyle?"

"Not directly, but I've seen all his reports. He's worried about the pipe sleeving and an influx of hydrocarbons—"

"From the asphalt company?" Jack asked.

"Yes. I told her that filters have been used quite successfully in the Niger Delta, where a recent Harvard initiative found their health symptoms largely alleviated, and that I would send her the citations."

Riley asked, "Did she say anything else?"

"No."

"Did she mention the fund-raiser she'd just left? Were you *at* the fund-raiser she'd just left?"

"No, and no. I'd been at my son's baseball game and then met a client for a quick drink."

Nice public places, Jack thought. Easy to verify, if

we suspected him of murder . . . which so far they didn't. Good thing, because from all appearances, if Bruce Haywood decided to kill someone he might apply the same mastery and control of his job to getting away with it. Jack reached for another mint and turned the framed photo so that he could see it. Screwing with people's desks could be the most direct route to screwing with their brains, and he needed to throw Bruce Haywood off his very good game.

The photo wasn't of a wife or a kid or even a dog. It showed the man himself holding up a small pot of plants—mushrooms—adorned with a blue First Place ribbon.

Jack asked, "They actually have mushroom shows?"

"No! Well—they might, I don't really know. My wife gave me that ribbon as a joke. I do grow them, though. Only ones to eat—nothing hallucinogenic."

"They sell those, you know," Riley told him. "At the grocery store."

"The ones I like are pricey. It's a hobby," he added a bit defensively, as if the detectives had given him an odd look.

Which they had—Jack could feel it on his face. Mushrooms. Why not grow some lichen while you were at it? "Did Ms. Cragin express concern about anything else? Any other projects, or . . . people?"

"No. As I said, it was a very short conversation."

"What was her mood?"

He blinked, apparently not expecting this question. "Typical Diane. Pleasant but brisk. To the point."

Riley asked, "Did she seem worried about the EPA report?"

"Not worried—more like annoyed. Remember the Vepo deal is already done. The city could, of course, cancel the major work on the permanent crib, but it would take a major problem to get them to reverse a decision."

"Major like a fatal health issue?" Riley asked.

Jack said, "Let me get this straight—Vepo is your client, right? Not the senator."

"Yes, Vepo, but the senator was very much on board with the project and wanted it to go forward."

"But she didn't pay you."

"No. Vepo pays me. But providing information to interested parties is a large part of my job, so I didn't mind her calling me for advice."

"Did she express any concern about any individuals? David Carlyle? Joey Green?"

Haywood got to the point himself. "Was she scared of someone? Not that I know of, and she certainly didn't sound fearful when I spoke with her. As I said, typical Diane, upbeat, gung ho."

Jack unwrapped another mint, trying to think of a question that might actually get them someplace. He leaned forward to toss the wrapper in the can next to the desk, noting that the can fit right in with the rest of the office—understated and neat. So neat that it had nothing in it save Jack's two wads of cellophane and one other item.

"Do you also represent StartUp Central?" he asked Haywood.

Mild surprise. "Yes. Why?"

"You know Joey Green?"

"Yes, we've met several times."

"Even though he's on the opposite side as Diane Cragin."

"Yes, of course. Party makes no difference to me— kind of like a law grad will work for either the prosecutor or the public defender. It only matters who wants to hire them. I work for Vepo and StartUp Central, not Cragin and Green."

"What happens if two different clients have incompatible goals?"

His head tilted ever so slightly. "But they don't. They're totally separate projects."

Riley said, "But the EPA believes that one aggravates the other. If only one occurred at a time, not such a problem, but if both projects go forward, our drinking water has a huge problem."

"We believe both issues can be dealt with," Haywood said, "so that the city will be both safe *and* profitable for all its citizens."

"If not, then one of your clients has to lose."

"I certainly don't want that," Haywood said.

Jack and Riley were in the car before Riley asked, "What made you think StartUp was a client?"

"A lollipop stick in the garbage can. Unless a client brought their kid to a meeting with them—"

"To that office? They wouldn't dare."

"And he seemed familiar with Joey Green, didn't have to place the name."

"Everyone in Cleveland is familiar with him. You can't get through a commercial break without seeing one of his campaign spots. Watching TV in real time is impossible. I have to DVR all my shows, and even then my finger is wearing out from hitting fast-forward." Riley sat in the driver's seat but didn't start the car, instead staring at the huge chandelier suspended over Euclid Avenue in front of the theaters. "What did you think of him?"

"I think he works very, very hard on appearing likable as well as straightforward."

"It worked. I sorta liked him. At least compared to anyone else we've met so far in this little drama. You know what the problem here is, partner?"

Jack said, "There's only one? I can think of a lot more than that."

"Usually when we have a murder, the killer is lying about everything relevant to the murder. Other people might be lying about shtupping their secretary or owning a gun, but aside from those kinds of things they generally tell the truth."

"Yeah?"

"In this case it feels like *everybody* is lying about *everything*. Kelly and Stanton are lying about that money belonging to the party, and if and when they figure out where it *did* come from, they sure as hell ain't going to tell us. Green is lying about StartUp Central being a sound economic decision. The little niece is lying about not resenting the hell out of her dear aunt and knowing that said aunt had a pile of cash in her safe. Scofield is beefing up his résumé and pretending to be the next Zuckerberg. The EPA kid—I don't know what he's lying about . . . I can't shake the feeling he sent that fake anthrax to himself. What are we going to do with these people?"

"Arrest them all?" Jack suggested.

"Then put them in a room and let them decide what's going to get built, whose taxes are going up, and who's going to take the blame." He turned the key.

"I think that's what they do, anyway," Jack said.

Chapter 22

The homicide unit meeting took place in the same dingy conference room/storage area where Maggie had first met Jack Renner only six months before. It hadn't changed much, still had boxes of copy paper in the corner and shrink-wrapped bundles of victim's rights brochures piled at one end of the long table. Patty Wildwood still sat at the other end, the practicing head of the homicide unit if not the nominal one, because, of course, the official chief spent his time posing for pictures and hanging out with movers and shakers rather than trying to run murder investigations, something for which he had little experience and no talent. Through unspoken agreement it had been decided that cases actually got cleared when Patty organized things.

She opened with: "Is the Russo murder connected to this election somehow? To the senator's death?"

"Don't know," Jack said.

"According to her husband, absolutely," Will said. "Not Cragin's death, but he is completely positive that one of Green's guys killed his wife."

"Joe Green?" Patty asked, surprised.

"You're sure it wasn't the husband?" Riley asked, only because it usually was.

Rick Gardiner said, "Don't think so. The guy is totally devastated."

"Shattered," Will agreed.

They both sounded uncharacteristically somber, which gave Maggie pause. She had come because Patty wanted to hear what forensics she had found at each scene. Rick hadn't warmed up any since that morning, but he kept the obnoxious burner on low. Getting that close to abject grief could throw a detective off their stride for the rest of the day—part of their job she had never envied.

"Guy looks like an Italian model," Rick went on. "Never stopped crying the whole time we were there. Will would get him calmed down, he'd stare into space for a minute, then he'd say, 'What on earth am I going to tell our children?' and start up again."

"Sad," Patty said, with real sympathy. She had children of her own and could be fierce about any crime that involved juveniles. "Why does he think Green killed her? Where's *that* coming from?"

"Because she was working on a story about him."

"A series, he called it," Will clarified. "She's been researching him for months, gathering witnesses, records, printouts. And she kept it all at home because she got nervous about leaving it at work after she found out one copy editor and a maintenance mechanic owed their jobs to Green. Hubby said five percent of all the workers in this county owe their jobs to Green, at least according to his wife."

Patty asked, "Did she have actual proof of something serious? More than, like, he accepted Cavs tickets from a utility chief or something like that?"

"Way serious," Rick said.

Will sorted through a large file box that he had brought with him. "She kept her research in their little home office, and he gave us every bit of it. He seemed to resent the *Herald*, thought his wife worked too hard for what they paid her, didn't give her enough kudos, whatever. The longer we sat there, the more stuff he pulled out. I've never had a more cooperative family member. Maybe he wanted to procrastinate picking up his kids at school to tell them their mother is dead."

That set had returned to Jack's jawline, Maggie noticed.

Rick looked directly at him and said, "She called you a couple times, didn't she? About the vigilante killings? Hot chick, right?"

Jack said nothing, and Rick gave a little start that made her think Will had kicked him under the table.

Patty wasn't unaware of the Rick/Maggie/Jack triangle. But she didn't care, either—Maggie had been accurate about the frequency of pairings and breakups inside the average police department. "What did he give you?"

"All this stuff," Will said as he continued to page through the stack. "He said we should take it and put the bastard in jail. Then he started bawling again."

Maggie glanced at Jack again. Picturing the scene with Lori Russo's husband didn't set well with him, she thought, pondering that compassion that males could surprise you with just as you had begun to think they weren't capable of any at all. She put her hand on the top corner of his chair back. Not his shoulder, not his neck. He didn't seem to notice, but it made her feel better.

He felt bad about her death.

But not because he had caused it. Though, if anything could cause a crisis of conscience in Jack Renner, killing an innocent, caring, hardworking wife and mother would do it.

Stop, she told herself.

Will found the paper he needed. "This is a summary she had written up. 2013, Cleveland Halfway House LLC was going to lose its funding from the county. Green said they and some other concerned parties should meet for dinner, which they did, and after four hours of steak and lobster, the nine-hundred-dollar bill got dropped in the Halfway House people's lap. It paid off, though, because Green arranged a meeting of county leaders, and *boom!* the funding was renewed and with a new contract for a work-release program. The owners of other halfway houses kept their mouths shut because they saw which way the wind blew. Halfway House kept paying, too—their consulting bill for one of Green's right-hand men doubled. Supposedly it was for extra work, but after Green and his close pals went on a gambling junket to Las Vegas, one of them called to say thank you for the trip. She's got signed statements for two people regarding that."

He went on: "Last year the city decides to ramp up its development program and starts handing loans out like candy. One went to a holding company that housed Environmental Products, insulated wall panels. Green got someone named Gabor a job there as a salesman. Green drove city business to Environmental, and Gabor kicked back a percentage of his salary."

"And Gabor got tired of it?" Riley asked.

"No. It was more than he'd made working for the city, so he was okay with that. And since Environmental never paid back the loan, they had plenty of cash. Instead, since they also owned a construction company, they renovated Green's backyard into a resort."

"Or at least as much of a resort as you can manage in a place where it snows six months of the year," Rick grumbled to himself.

"She told us that story," Riley said.

Will continued. "On the inside of his house, a company called Four Up installed a new video and stereo system throughout. Four Up was granted a loan from the city for eight hundred thousand dollars, which went into bankruptcy without anyone noticing or sending to collections. It goes on and on. She's got stacks of this stuff—statements from people who witnessed bribes to get a guy a job at the sheriff's office, to approving a housing development built by a guy who provided Green with limousine service and use of a condo, to getting some other guy a lease for an ice-skating rink in Lakewood, to bribery of city and county employees so they'd lose the paperwork if and when people came around asking about this contract or that loan. Chief," he said, then stopped, "I mean, Patty, it's going to look bad for the department and the city when this comes out."

She frowned. "Meaning?"

"I ain't saying," he told her. "I'm just saying. You might want to give the chief and the muckety-mucks the heads-up before it breaks."

She nodded solemnly. "Good plan. But it's not going to break from us—political corruption is not our job. Homicide is. The muckety-mucks can decide what to do with this stuff."

"Unless this stuff is why Lori Russo was murdered," Jack said. It sounded as if his teeth might be clenched.

"Unless it is," Patty agreed. "But if we like Green for it, we're going to have to have actual proof of homicide, not corruption."

Rick said, "The husband also gave us her call history. They have a joint account, and he could access it online. The chick's incoming calls went unanswered after seven-thirty this morning. At six-thirty she received a call that lasted less than a minute. We did a computer search, but nothing came up."

"Who wants to bet that was our killer with a burner?" No one took her up. "We need more than a grieving husband and a reporter's notes. We need to find the connections. Autopsy?"

"Exactly what it looked like," Rick said. "Two in the front, went out the back."

Maggie said, "Her notebook."

The other people in the room looked at her.

"It was pretty gummy with blood, but I separated the pages as well as I could to get them to dry. Infrared light wipes out the blood, so I could see the writing. This was on the uppermost sheet."

She passed a piece of paper to Will, who sat closer to her, on which she had written *Nov 5 7 am* and below that *774EWZ*.

She watched Jack's face from under lowered lashes, her entire body poised to gauge the tension in his muscles, his arteries, his cells. But if he recognized the numbers and letters he gave absolutely no sign. Maggie breathed out.

Patty said, "License plate. Who does it come back to?"

"I don't have access to OHLEG," Maggie reminded her. The Ohio Law Enforcement Gateway database could be used only by sworn LEOs, not civilians.

Patty turned to Rick and Will but didn't have to tell them to get on it ASAP. "With luck, the reporter wrote down the plate of the guy who rolled up and shot her. Anything else?"

No one spoke.

Jack sat back, pinching Maggie's fingers, but she extracted them before any real damage occurred. She saw his jaw loosen, and his gaze followed the license number with something like encouragement, as if comforted by the existence of a solid clue to Laurine Russo's killer, and in turn she felt a bit comforted herself.

Because it seemed to be further evidence that Jack had nothing to do with her death? Or because at exactly the same time she'd been suspecting him of the woman's murder, Maggie had been searching for some way to console him?

Why the hell would she want to do that? He was a professional, cops saw people get killed all the time, and her relationship to him was pure business.

And of *course* he had not killed the reporter. She needed to get a grip.

Yet she leaned closer to him to say, as the room emptied, "There's something else you need to know."

Chapter 23

"When did it get here?" he asked as soon as they entered the lab.

"About an hour ago. Amy got the mail but then she got sidetracked by a traffic death, so it sat on her desk until I noticed it." She handed Jack a white Tyvek envelope with the return address of the analysts who had examined Diane Cragin's cell phone.

Riley said, "That puts us in a nice little moral dilemma. We're supposed to put our fingers in our ears, hum a tune, and send this right over to the people who probably killed her in the first place."

"Maggie already opened it," Jack said.

"I had to make sure which case it related to! The number isn't on the shipping label."

"I'm not criticizing. I'm just saying they won't know that we looked at it."

"There's no point," Riley said. "If we get a lead from it, eventually we'd have to explain in court how we got a lead from it."

"Very true," Jack said, then turned to Maggie. "Do

you have a room I could use? And maybe a pair of latex gloves?"

Riley goggled at him. "You're going to read it anyway?"

"As you pointed out, we're not getting anywhere with this investigation. Diane Cragin kept this phone locked up tight for a reason. It might help us to know why."

"Fine." Sigh. "Let's take a look. I'll be damned if I let a bunch of politicians hide all the clues and then hand us the blame for not solving this case."

"No. There's no point both of us possibly sinking our careers."

"Don't be ridiculous." Riley looked to Maggie for support, but she could offer none. She understood Jack's thinking all too well. He had nothing to lose. He was the man who didn't exist, nothing but a fake name and a temporary address. He didn't have to worry about protecting a pension he never intended to collect. If the feds came knocking, he could disappear to another city and start his extracurricular justice project again without her disapproving eye. Come to think of it, why hadn't he done that already? What was keeping him here?

"The report has everything." She spoke only to keep Riley from watching her while clearly wondering why she didn't seem concerned about her supposed boyfriend losing his job and risking federal prison at the same time. "Call history, texts, photos, websites she surfed. But the numbers called won't do you any good if you immediately give yourself away by dialing them back. The texts, you might fake your way around them for a while, but as Riley said, unless you can come up with another way you would have settled on a suspect, you'd only sabotage your own case. The evidence would be thrown out."

"It's worth a try," Jack said. "Or someone is going to get away with electrocuting a woman on her own doorstep. Besides, we have a signed consent to search. We have not yet received any subpoena to *not* search."

"Splitting hairs," Riley said.

"Or strict adherence to the rules," Jack argued, not too persuasively.

Silence fell, during which Maggie heard Carol humming in the DNA lab. Denny, luckily, had gone to court. A worrywart under the best of circumstances, this situation would give him heart palpitations.

"Make that two pairs of gloves, please," Riley said.

She put them in her chemical processing room, both balancing awkwardly on the waist-high, wheeled task chairs with the hard rubber seats.

"Stinks in here," Riley observed. Errant wafts of ninhydrin and dye stains lingered.

"It won't kill you," Maggie said, holding out a box of latex gloves. "I think."

"I feel silly looking like a cat burglar," Riley said, pulling one on.

"I don't," Maggie said, which made both men look at her.

"You can't be here for this—" Riley began to protest.

"Of course I can. *I* didn't get any court order to cease and desist. My job is only to turn the report over to you, which I have done."

Jack gave a tiny smirk.

They developed a system. Jack read the texts, lingering over any that sounded significant. Riley cross-referenced the numbers against the detectives' case notes to determine if the call came from the phone of an already-identified player, such as Kelly. If any were not familiar, Maggie did a reverse search via the Internet.

"A text two days ago." Jack read: "'Does he have it?'"

"Who's that to?" Riley asked.

"That's the problem. It just says 'Skinny.' But the number is here," Jack said, and read it off so Maggie could search. She did, and came up empty. Then she pulled the gloves back off, since she wasn't touching the phone report anyway, and poured herself a cup of coffee. If she planned to defy the powers that be in order to catch a killer, she would need caffeine.

"We'd already noted it in her call history as a burner," Riley declared after perusing the sheets he held. "So whoever Skinny is, Cragin called him a bunch of times as well as texted. He sounds like her drug connection, but our senator didn't partake, and we didn't find any other illegal objects among her belongings. So it had to be payoffs, toting up that stash in her safe."

Jack said, "Which we can't connect to the texts or calls because we can't establish when any of that money showed up. It could have been there for years, for all we know."

"Clever, in a way, to throw it all in a pile. It can't be linked to any pattern or other event."

"Maybe . . ." Maggie mused, and then continued when both men looked at her. "That bunch of fresh bills that went from the Fed to Fifth Third three weeks ago. If the bank can tell us who they gave it to, that might make some sort of time line."

"Will they do that?" Riley asked.

"Not without a subpoena—I asked. From the Fed to the bank is one thing, but from the bank to a customer, that gets into the bank-client privilege."

"Is that even a thing?"

"Enough of one that, according to the Fed, it will be faster to get a subpoena than to spend a few days arguing about it."

Riley grumbled but pulled off his gloves and said he'd get the warrant started. He trundled out of the lab, and Maggie took over his half of the Cellebrite report. There were so many categories of information—photos, websites visited, downloads. Phones did so much more than make calls.

"Here's another," Jack said. "From someone she named Tubby, shortly after one from a Blondie. I'm sensing a lack of imagination from our senator, as well as a touch of mean-spiritedness."

"Wow."

"What?"

"You made a joke."

He ignored her until she finished searching the number, without results. "She tells Tubby to meet her at four. I assume that's a time, unless it's the name of a restaurant or a place on East Fourth that they're both familiar with. Then she says 'We can work.' We can work out? We can work *this* out? We can work together? This woman's worse than teenagers. At least they use the *same* unintelligible shorthand. Tubby, by the way, responds 'Ok.' Big help." Jack continued through the report. "Here's one from Mole: 'Gave note.' And she wrote back, 'pmt in mail.' No question mark. Sounds like a payment she was *making* instead of *getting*."

Maggie perked up and set her coffee cup on the counter with a soft *clink*. "When was that?"

"Day before yesterday. Why?"

"She paid someone to give someone a note."

Jack got it. "David Carlyle. So Mole is her spy at the EPA."

"Or at the Ohio Department of Health. Probably the guy who had to give up his supply closet to give Carlyle an office." She searched the number, which gave no results. "Does *everyone* have a burner phone?"

Jack coughed. "She sent one to Skinny that says 'turkey wheat.' No reply. What does that mean?"

"Stock tip?" At his look she explained, "Turkey is the world's largest flour exporter. I read that somewhere."

He considered this. "She's got a lot of cash, has to invest it somewhere. Why not in Turkish-grown wheat?"

"They don't grow it. They just mill it."

He gave up on that line of inquiry. "Another one from Tubby. 'Don't mention su at fr.' She writes back, 'okay water contract Tue mtg.' He writes, 'K.' Wait, another new player—Wawa. Wawa writes, '$ on way.' She writes, '$50K?' Wawa sends a Y. Here's the number." He read it off, and Maggie typed at her keyboard.

"Nothing."

"This isn't helping. She kept everything sufficiently vague, and now that she's dead, these contacts can make up any story they like to explain their texts. Plausible deniability, the politician's stock in trade." He pulled his phone out of his pocket.

"What are you doing?"

"Calling Tubby," he said.

"No, wait—"

But he had already dialed and held the phone to his ear. He said nothing, listened, and his eyes widened just a flicker before he hung up.

Maggie said, "Your number will come up on the caller ID of whoever you call. They'll know you're from the police department."

"Um . . . not that phone."

She paused, coffee cup halfway to her lips, gazing at him with both surprise and a touch of betrayal.

"Like you said, everybody's got one."

She set the cup down. "And everybody lies. I can't scoff at the politicians when I—"

"And even if the PD did come up on the phone screen, I don't think it would bother Tubby."

"Why? Who is he?"

"Joe Green."

This surprised her out of her self-recriminations. "So the two mortal enemies had made a separate peace."

"Or a mutually beneficial arrangement."

"Su is StartUp? Don't throw StartUp Central under the bus when you're talking to—fr? Fund-raiser? Financial Revenue Committee? Mr. French?"

"In return, he doesn't bring up Vepo's history with water filtration."

"It's hard to tell which of these two people had the worst environmental record."

"Does it matter? Let's try Wawa." He dialed the number, listened, and told Maggie that someone named Clinton invited him to leave a message. "Now, Skinny."

She searched, got nothing. "Maybe that's Kelly. 'Turkey wheat' could mean exactly what it sounds like—turkey on whole wheat. It's a lunch order."

"She uses a burner phone to order lunch? If it is Kelly, she's not answering."

"A phone is a phone. And Kelly seemed to do everything short of scrubbing her toilets so it makes sense."

"What about Blondie?" That, too, was unlisted in cyberspace, so he dialed its digits.

Maggie searched it. "That doesn't come up, either."

"Blondie doesn't answer. Maybe she's with Skinny-slash-Kelly."

Maggie got up and glanced over Jack's shoulder at the texts. They had already established that outgoing activity had ceased after 9:30 Saturday night when, presumably, Diane Cragin had returned to her home to be electrocuted by her own doorknob. Before that, there had been the call to the lobbyist at 9:20 and a photo uploaded to Facebook at 8:30, Maggie now discovered in the section of photograph information. The report even gave a thumbnail of the photo—a group of people in a large room, obviously the fund-raiser event. Jack leaned close to her long enough to point at a group of print next to the thumbnail. "What's that?"

"Metadata. It will give information about photo, time, even location if you have location services turned on in Settings. Let's look at the cell tower information." She tapped keys on her laptop, then said, "This text to Green at four p.m. went through the cell tower on Breakwater Avenue. That's in Lakewood, nowhere near her house. Her house is practically right next to the East Seventy-Seventh tower."

"Opposite side of town," Jack said.

She cautioned, "That doesn't necessarily mean anything. If the closest tower gets busy, it will bounce signals to other towers. Although I would think it would bounce it to the downtown ones first . . . but this really isn't my field."

"It sounds as if they agreed to meet at four o'clock. Can either phone tell us where?"

Maggie went back to the Cellebrite report. "Maybe. Now that we're looking at the time *before* the fundraiser when we had assumed she was home . . . the last photo she took . . . here. At 4:16 p.m. she took a photo."

Jack leaned over her sheets. "A mushroom? She took a picture of a mushroom?"

"I guess so," Maggie said.

"Who did she send it to? That lobbyist guy is into mushrooms."

Maggie said, "She sent it to Blondie."

"Weird."

"But the metadata along with the photo gives the location, in latitude and longitude. She must have had location services turned on."

"How are we supposed to figure out by latitude and—"

She had already typed it in. "Wendy Park. It's a spot in Wendy Park, on Whiskey Island. That explains the Breakwater cell tower." She tapped some more keys. "It looks like, if you go nearly to the end of Whiskey Island Drive and cut back into the trees, away from the river . . . you could park there and be fairly hidden."

"Especially in early November. Nobody on the volleyball courts then."

"You play volleyball?" She tried to picture that, and couldn't.

"Not since grade school. She's meeting Joe Green on Whiskey Island. At 4:10, he's not there yet. Even if they kept it short, how does she get back home on the east side and then to a fund-raiser downtown? Kelly was sure she had arrived right on time at five, apparently unusual for her. And where is the Secret Service guy all this time?"

"It was Saturday," Maggie pointed out. "No rush hour. But why were they meeting at all? They were deadly enemies, both running for the same Senate seat. Isn't it unethical for them to meet privately . . . like, you know, prosecutors and defense . . . well, they meet all the time, but like prosecutors and judges without defense—"

Jack said, "The only thing I am sure about is that 'unethical' wouldn't bother either of these two characters. Were they agreeing to rig the election—but in whose favor? Was one paying the other to forfeit? But that wouldn't help, since if one stepped down, the party would put in their Plan B, like they're doing with the assistant state treasurer."

"She couldn't have done it," Maggie announced. She had been tapping away as they talked.

"Who couldn't have—"

"According to Maps, even if he arrived at 4:11 she couldn't have gotten from Whiskey Island on the west side, driven to her home on the east side, and driven back to the fund-raiser to arrive by five o'clock. Not without driving ninety miles an hour on inner-city streets."

"Which we assume somebody would have noticed," Jack said. "Preferably one of our patrol officers."

"So maybe she went straight to the fund-raiser."

Jack gripped her arm, finding the words. "This changes everything. We had assumed the killer set up the wires to electrocute her during the fund-raiser, between five and nine p.m. But if she hadn't gone home all day, then they could have been installed any time after eight a.m. Cragin had a breakfast meeting, and then she and Kelly were going nonstop until a meeting with David Carlyle at three-thirty. Again, she must have gone straight from there to be on Whiskey Island at four."

"But why don't Kelly and the Secret Service guy know that?"

"Good question. Whatever their story is, the window for our killer just got a whole lot wider. It also puts Green back in the running, TV studio or no TV studio. He could have stopped over to Diane's at any point during the day."

Maggie said, "He doesn't even have a Secret Service guy to ditch or bribe or whatever."

"Very true," he said absently.

"What's up?" Denny asked from the doorway.

Maggie's heart leapt, spiking with guilt even though she had nothing to feel—oh, wait, she did. She had a great deal to feel guilty for but tried to force that knowledge from her face. It should have gotten easier after six months. "Um . . . nothing."

Jack stayed still and didn't speak.

Denny studied their sheepish looks, said that was all right then, and turned away with a slightly disappointed expression that made Maggie think he would be searching for a way to send a gentle reminder that canoodling would have to be done on her own time.

Jack began to gather up the papers.

"What are you going to do?"

"I'm going to deliver this report to the RNC," he said, "like the good little boy I am."

"Okay," Maggie said uncertainly. "Good luck." She thought of adding *Happy hunting,* but that would pass a little too close to the bone in Jack's case. And in hers.

At least she had forgotten about Lori Russo for ten whole minutes. To keep it that way she thought about mushrooms, and not only because she had skipped lunch.

Chapter 24

Jack and Riley found Kelly Henessey and most of the RNC staff a mere block away, at the convention center. A mini debate forum had been set up in the global atrium, the noise of a thousand conversations echoing off the shiny floor, the soaring metal rafters, and the wall of windows until it grew into a deafening wave. Hong Kong streets were less crowded, Jack estimated. In the thirty seconds he'd been there, he saw two people stumble on the deceptively asymmetrical steps, too intent on their discussion to watch where they trod.

A low stage had been set up opposite the window wall, with nothing on it save three microphones on stands, arranged haphazardly. Kelly Henessey's shock of black hair flickered from a spot next to the platform, surrounded by people but speaking on the phone. Jack could see the former assistant state treasurer bobbing in her orbit, with no fewer than seven people hovering around him in turn, like ants around a discarded piece of watermelon. One read to him from a sheaf of papers, the other held out a clipboard for him to sign, a third adjusted his tie, and the other four milled around with worried looks on their faces. The object of this activity appeared docile, or perhaps simply exhausted, dazed with the tsunami that had hit his life.

Ten feet behind them stood Secret Service Agent Devin, his weary gaze darting restlessly around the cavernous space with a look of despair. That must be the worst job in the world, Jack thought. It must be like trying to protect one ant in an anthill, one bee in a hive . . . impossible, in other words. On top of that, the huge windows against the dark night created a mirror, doubling the visual crowd to a dizzying number.

Jack tugged on Riley's arm and nodded in Kelly's direction. Riley clutched the Cellebrite report to his chest as they pushed through the crowd, a Trojan horse to give them safe passage.

"Kelly," Jack shouted as they neared.

She glanced at the cops and at first didn't see anything there to interest her, turning back to her phone call. "Get the club to provide rides to the polling station. Elderly, disabled, anyone who has a hard time getting out. *Yes*, that's your job! You're the precinct captain." She disconnected and rubbed one eye, turning to face them. Jack wondered if she had slept at all since the senator's death. "Did you find out who killed Diane? Please tell me it was that guy."

She hitched a thumb over her shoulder to indicate the other end of the stage, where Joe Green and his own entourage conducted their own last-minute confabs.

"No, but—"

"Then tell me who the hell thought a debate the

night before the election was a good idea?" she demanded, sweeping everyone around her with a single gesture.

"You did," said a young man with beer stains on his tie and a cell phone to his ear.

"That was when we had Diane."

The former assistant state treasurer seemed to be hyperventilating, spreading his fingers over his chest to help himself stop. "It will be all right. I'll be okay."

"Of course you will," Kelly said, with not the slightest shred of sincerity. "You have the employment stats, right—hey, does he have the employment stats?" She spoke again to everyone around her.

"Kelly—" Jack said.

"Wyatt's got them." The young man, still on the cell phone, waved wildly toward the rear corner.

"Who the hell's *Wyatt*?"

"The 3-D volunteer coordinator."

"For how long? And you're letting him hand talking points to our candidate—"

"I vetted him."

"How well?"

"As well as you would! You think you're the only one who knows what you're doing around here? Yes, I'm still here," he added into the phone. The fact that they had been shouting did not seem to bother him or, indeed, anyone around them, perhaps because everyone was shouting and because Kelly needed to shout, her voice weak and hoarse, her lips dry and beginning to crack. The less-than-trusted Wyatt pushed through the throng and handed Kelly a piece of paper; he started to explain some of the figures, but she waved him away.

"Kelly," Jack began again, "we need to ask you some questions."

"Not now."

"Yes, now. This is a murder investigation."

"This is an *election*! Where's your wife?" she asked the candidate. "Are those kids ready? They're going to sit still while the cameras are on, right?"

"They'll be fine," the man huffed. "Naomi will keep them under control."

"*Kelly*," Jack said. The space, though vast, contained a great deal of body heat with too many people packed too tightly for too long. He wondered what effect a collective lack of oxygen could have on a mob. "We have the report on Diane's phone records. And we have some questions about her last day."

Kelly guided the candidate up the steps to test the height of the microphone. "No fiddling with it on camera. Don't *touch* it on camera." To Jack, she said, "Fine, give it to me and I'll give it to Stanton. What about her last day? Weird . . . to think of it that way."

"We'd like to know what her meeting with Green was about."

"What meeting?"

"The private one they had in Lakewood before the fund-raiser."

"What are you talking about? I was with her all day, until she went home to change. We never met Green." A light dawned in her eyes. "Was he waiting at her house to kill her? Is that what you mean?"

Jack repeated the information about the meeting but didn't get too far before Kelly interrupted by shouting and waving to get the Secret Service agent's attention.

Jack watched as Devin wearily spoke into a small shoulder mic and moved toward them. He didn't work alone, of course; Jack had spotted three other men and one woman in the vicinity dressed in matching black suits that must be overwarm under the circumstances. Contrary to popular media, however, they did not wear sunglasses at the indoor venue.

Kelly, meanwhile, had grabbed another woman to tell her: "Get up there and remind him that the moderator is going to be Hayley from Channel 15, pretty little thing but she's going to have her producer Mac on her earbud screaming at her to go for the jugular, so no matter what comes out of her mouth he can't yell back, got it? Because all anyone's going to see is him beating up on sweet little Hayley, not that bastard Mac."

The woman nodded so hard it seemed her head might fall off, and dashed up the steps.

"He doesn't look capable of yelling at an invading Mongol horde," Riley commented, eyeing the pale, clearly overwhelmed man.

This did not reassure Kelly, if that had been his intention. Instead she said, "He doesn't?" and gazed up at the stage in horror until Devin arrived to distract her from her client's shortcomings.

Kelly asked him where Diane had been at four p.m. on Saturday afternoon.

"Closeted with you," he said.

She scowled, and said that wasn't right.

He clarified: "In a meeting with the state party accountants. At headquarters."

"No! That ended at three-thirty!"

A few people closest to them noticed the commotion and openly listened. Kelly turned her back on one and gave another the evil eye. It had no effect. They kept listening.

Devin raised his voice to match hers. "No, she was holed up in that little room at the back you guys use, gave me strict instructions to guard the door as if it were the Unknown Soldier's tomb and not let anyone even knock, until four-thirty, quarter to five. I don't know where you went, but she came out and said they were done, and I drove behind her to the fund-raiser at the City Club."

"No, no, *no!*"

The Secret Service agent had evidently had enough of preelection nerves. "Yes, yes, yes. We arrived at the RNC at 3:10, and I followed her to the fund-raiser at"—he checked something on his phone—"4:45 p.m. Why? What's the deal?"

Kelly stopped yelling at him and grew pensive. "She told me she was leaving. Sent me home for some dinner and a change of clothes."

"Did she change her clothes?" Riley demanded. "Was she in a different outfit at the fund-raiser?"

Understanding dawned in her eyes. "No . . . but she did that, picked one dress that would go through the day. . . . Devin, you mean that small meeting room in the back, next to the stairwell?"

He nodded, then listened to his earbud and looked around.

"So on the day of her death, in between your meeting at the RNC and the fund-raiser that evening, she ditched Devin," Jack said, trying to hurry this interview up before the show started because Kelly would grab that excuse to ignore them, "then drove herself to Lakewood and met with Green. Why?"

Kelly managed to appear confident of her words. "That's not true. That didn't happen."

"How do you know? Obviously you weren't there."

The pressing crowd forced them closer, but that was all right. Kelly seemed to be sweating in more ways than one. The young man who hired Wyatt moved past them with a half-full water bottle, which she snatched out of his hands without even looking at him, then drank from it as he rolled his eyes. She tried to hand it back, but he told her to keep it; she either didn't notice or didn't care about his sarcastic tone. Instead she told him she had Diane's phone report; who could they spare to take it to Stanton?

"Wyatt—"

"Not Wyatt," she literally screamed. Then she flagged down the earnest young woman the cops had met on their first visit to her headquarters. Meanwhile the young man with the frayed temper rolled his eyes again and guided their candidate toward the stage. Kelly handed the bottle to Jack as if that might be his entire purpose in life, took the Cellebrite report from Riley, and gave the girl sufficiently dire instructions until the girl hustled away, heavy envelope clutched to her chest as if it were her only child in a room full of pedophiles. Then Kelly pulled a plastic vial out of her pocket, shook out some pills, couldn't cap the vial without spilling the pills in her hand and handed the pill vial to Jack, took back the water bottle, and drained it.

All of this activity, he knew, had been designed to give her time to think up a story, so he broke in. "Why is it such a problem to admit that your boss met with Joe Green?"

"You mean the bastard who just dug up all the hazardous waste?"

"Isn't reaching across the aisle, conferring, compromising, what they're *supposed* to be doing?"

She tried to give him the empty water bottle back, and he refused to take it. She handed it off to a random volunteer, who made the mistake of passing too close to them. Then she took her pill bottle back, thoughtfully recapped it, stowed it in a pocket, and told them, "I don't know what you're talking about. I have no knowledge of such a meeting and don't believe it ever took place."

She and the two cops were, for a brief second, completely still in the midst of chaos and noise. Kelly had located the party line and stepped back behind its velvet rope. They couldn't blast her out even with an overpriced battleship and a hellacious straw poll.

"We may have a code pink," Devin announced, and moved toward the front doors.

"Take care of it," Kelly screamed after him, then waved wildly for two other volunteers to follow him. "And tell me again whose idea it was to do a debate the night before the election!"

"What's a code pink?" Riley asked.

"Someone who wants to cause a disturbance, shout insults, heckle the speaker. Enemy plant."

"Why pink?" Jack asked. But Kelly had already gone, disappeared into the crowd toward a knot of RNC volunteers gathered at the back of the stage.

"Well," Riley said. "That was a bunch o'nothin'."

"Maybe, maybe not." Jack nodded toward the other side of the stage, where Joe Green glad-handed up a storm, and suggested they venture into the enemy camp.

"Will we need a password?" Riley asked.

"No, but we might need a letter of safe conduct."

"For us or him? We can't pin Russo on him, not yet. You know that, right?"

"Yeah." Jack glanced at his partner, perplexed.

"Good," Riley said as they threaded their way through the frenetic assembly. "We'll get him for it. Play it cool."

I am not the actor I think I am, Jack realized, because in truth all he wanted to do was put his hands around Green's throat and squeeze. Riley had only to look at him to know that.

But Jack could wait.

The camera-ready moderator had also taken the stage, standing at the rear. The candidates would have to answer her questions without looking at her, but apparently that was preferable to standing with her back to the audience. All three people onstage knew that to be seen was the only purpose of the proceeding.

At first glance Green's exuberance seemed the opposite of Kelly's stress. He greeted the cops with a manic joy, clearly thriving in the arena of public competition and confident of his ability to come out on top. Only on closer inspection did Jack see the broken blood vessels in the eyes, the razor stubble on the chin, the webs of dehydration in the corners of his mouth. A large man with large pores stood at his elbow, obviously muscle, obviously on border guard duty, and not caring who knew it.

"Officers!" he crowed. "How nice of you to attend!"

"Why did you meet with Diane Cragin in Lakewood on the day she died?" Jack demanded.

Green had been lying to people since before Kelly

Henessey was born and was consequently much, much better at it. "I didn't."

"We're ready to start," a young black man said to him—or shouted, rather, given the noise level. "Don't flirt with Hayley like last time, okay? You know Laila said—"

"Yeah, yeah. No problem. I'll be a very good little boy."

"Did Taylor ask you about the balloons? We've got the bands lined up for election night, but what about the balloons?"

"What about them?"

"She needs to know what colors you want."

"Red, white, and blue, dumb-ass. What the hell else would we get?"

"I know, I know! But Taylor thought we might want to be different."

"About the colors of the flag? No. We don't."

"Way too much Red Bull flowing through the veins around here," Riley observed to Jack, then shouted to Green: "What was the deal between you two? You know she told Kelly all about it. We just want to get your side."

Green waved off the young man and the debate about balloon colors, his smile never dimming, making it abundantly clear that Joe Green didn't give a single, solitary crap what the cops thought or what they knew. Within twenty-four hours he expected to become a United States Senator, and nothing they could prove or accuse him of could affect that, not at this late stage. "Kelly would never part with even a fraction of Diane's sins. It would tar her with the same brush. But by all means, keep asking. Always happy to help a fellow public servant."

"Ready?" the young man asked.

"Completely." Green spared a glance at his muscle. "Carl? You good?"

"Never better." The man's gaze never ceased scanning the room.

Green studied his opponent from the shelter of the crowd, perhaps noting the well-cut suit, the precisely clipped hair. Then he took off his own jacket and handed it to Jack, interlaced the fingers of both hands until the knuckles cracked, and charged up the steps to land on the temporary platform until its surface reverberated under the heavy feet, clearly the "regular working stiff" alternative to the prissy, well-to-do enemy candidate. Jack thought he should have kept the jacket to cover the dampened armpits and sweat-wrinkled creases at the waist, but perhaps he was wrong, because the crowd erupted in applause. The moderator waited for it to die down enough that she didn't have to screech to announce the beginning of "this brief mini-debate."

Thus ended the interview of suspect Joseph Green.

The muscle moved to the side of the stage, but Jack grabbed his elbow. "Carl? Carl Nero?"

The behemoth barely paused. He threw off Jack's hand like a fly at a picnic and took up a position at the foot of the steps, in a position to block anyone who tried to storm the dais via the risers and that much closer if anyone leapt from the floor.

"Who's that?" Riley asked.

"Someone whose print turned up in Cragin's stack of cash."

"Once again, we're getting nowhere at a steady pace."

"At least you haven't been turned into a bloody butler," Jack said.

Sudden movements toward the rear of the dais caught Jack's attention. Two men in suits—either Secret Service or private, he couldn't tell, each with an arm clasped firmly on either side of Harold Baudelet. They moved his solid form toward the door without pause, though he didn't seem to be struggling overmuch. As they passed by, Baudelet gazed at Jack and Riley and his mouth moved, but if he spoke to them, Jack couldn't hear it over the crowd.

Jack handed Green's jacket to the young man who had been speaking to Green and they reached the exit behind Baudelet and the guards, before the moderator finished her opening platitudes. They never heard the searing questions of vital public interest posed to these potential representatives.

"So Green talked to Kelly," Riley said to Jack, musing on this as they plunged into the open air.

"Not surprising. Kelly was her first line of defense."

"You guys!" Baudelet called to them across the flagstones. "Tell these goons I'm not nuts."

"Not so far as we know," Jack hedged as the cops caught up, and flashed his badge. The guards promptly lost interest, happy to dump the guy with them and get back inside with the action. Baudelet swore he'd leave the premises, and after snapping his picture with a cell phone, they chose to take him at his word.

He stood on the paved walkway with Jack and Riley, straightened his sweatshirt, and told them he had merely wanted to ask the new candidate if he would continue

Diane's deal with Vepo. "A reasonable question, don't you think?"

On impulse, Jack asked, "What did Diane Cragin say when you confronted her about Vepo? You must have gone to see her. You wouldn't have sent a piece of paper and thought that would do the job."

"Of course not! But her staff kept her cordoned off like the crown jewels. I never got near her."

"What about Mr. Green?"

"Him? *Pfft*. He's small town. Corrupt enough to put me and my former employer to shame, but he'll never have the reach to do any real damage."

"Okay. Well, good night, Mr. Baudelet." Riley took a step in the other direction.

But Baudelet seemed reluctant to part. "No, I never saw Diane. Only that girl of hers."

Riley and Jack both stopped. "Girl?"

"The one with the chopped hair. Her chief of staff, I think. Told her all about my adventures with Diane and how much better life got for the Haitians and the tax-payers of Washington."

"Really," Jack said. "And she listened?"

"Attentively. Yeah, that was almost weird, come to think of it. Hey, there's my compatriots—gotta go." He trotted over to a motley crew of sign-holders approaching the glass doors with an air of determination that would have made Edmund Hillary look like a dilettante.

In the sudden quiet, Jack realized how crisp and cold and utterly clear the outside air seemed. He drew a deep, grateful breath of it, in, out, then noticed Riley doing the same. They both laughed.

Then they began to make their way back to the police department, insanely happy to be out in the cold, dark space of the evening.

"I am never, ever running for office," Riley promised aloud.

"Or working for the Secret Service. Little Devin is going to have some explaining to do."

"It sounds like this wasn't the first time. Kelly told us right away that the senator liked to slip away. I thought it was to collect her payoffs without witnesses, but after that chaos in there I can't really blame her if she freaked out and did a runaway bride sort of thing now and then."

"But they're not about to admit it now. Even after death."

Riley came to a halt in the middle of the sidewalk along St. Clair. "I get it."

"What? Who killed Diane Cragin?"

"No. Why the secrecy." He waved toward the convention center with only a streetlight illuminating his arm. "It doesn't matter if Cragin took bribes—she's dead and buried, case closed. It doesn't matter if she gave her own Secret Service detail the slip—again, old news. But what they absolutely cannot have is a member of their party consorting with the enemy. That breaks down the whole us/them structure they've funneled us all into. We're Oceania and Eurasia in Orwell's *1984*, thirty-plus years later."

"Better dead than red," Jack mused. "They'd rather have her bribery revealed—though they're not admitting that, either—than even speaking to someone of the other party."

"Wow. That's—" Riley gave up on words entirely.

"It is, partner. It is."

Chapter 25

Jack and Riley arrived at the Regional Development budget session at city hall in time to rescue Kelly Henessey from Joe Green in the hallway outside the meeting room.

The slender young woman—for the first time Jack realized how well she fit her boss's nickname for her, if indeed that was the case—had both her arms up to protect her face. Green had not struck her, but his fists were balled, his face blood-red, and his hair stuck out as if he'd touched the same wire Diane Cragin had. His voice echoed off the marble walls.

The other few people in the hallway looked, saw, and pretended not to notice so long as Kelly remained physically untouched. His was hardly the first meltdown ever seen in those hallowed halls. The building dated to 1916, a Beaux Arts expression of how far city government had come from its first meeting in a log cabin.

Connor Scofield stood to one side, expressing a desire to intervene with ineffectual flaps of his hands.

"I don't give a shit what you think! That was the—" Green caught sight of the cops, broke off, and stepped backward.

"Something wrong?" Riley asked, as if the elevator button had stopped working or they'd run out of coffee. His tone did little to calm Green, who snarled that this was none of Riley's business.

Then he stalked off to the traditional location to have a time-out, regroup, or rethink one's strategy— the men's room.

Jack asked Kelly if she were all right, and she said yes, fine. But she didn't look fine. Her eyes were bloodshot at a bad-horror-movie level, and her hands trembled. Blush and eye shadow had sunk into her pores hours, or perhaps days, before.

"Sorry, dude," Connor said to her. "But this is really important."

"You think I don't know *important*?" she snapped.

He shut up, unwrapped a lollipop, and put it in his mouth. At Jack's look he spoke around the ball of hard candy: "I'm trying to stop smoking, and the patch thing doesn't quite cut it. Actually it just makes me pee a lot." With this he slunk toward the men's room, passing David Carlyle coming out. If either noticed the other, they gave no sign.

Carlyle saw the cops and hesitated. Jack thought he might, for no discernable reason, run. Or perhaps the sight of them simply brought back memories of possible anthrax, because he wound up standing in the middle of the hallway floor at a spot equidistant from the men's room, the cops, and the meeting room, an electron simultaneously repelled by all unattracted charges.

Perhaps a bit ironically he stood in front of the painting called *The Spirit of '76*—not the original version of the painting but a copy painted by the same artist, Archibald Willard. Carlyle resembled the nervous drummer boy much more than the bloody but unbowed fife player.

"What are you doing here?" Jack asked Kelly.

"Diane had planned to present a position statement on StartUp's funding. We need to see her work through."

This woman talks in sound bites, Jack thought. Perhaps that had become an unconscious habit, and perhaps a great deal of work and discipline went into it.

Green emerged. His color hadn't improved much. He pulled a pill vial out of his pocket, shook two pills into his hand, and stalked five paces to the water fountain to swallow them. His orbit bounced off David Carlyle and forced the young man to move closer to the cops until the gravitational pull broke entirely and he greeted them, addressing Kelly as "Miss Henessey." Maybe he felt safer in their clique than Green's.

"Why are you here?" Jack asked him.

"I have the latest test results to explain why they have to stop excavation until DC can issue a protection order. Breaking up the parking lot was bad enough, but if they start hollowing out below ground level—"

"Think it will work?" Kelly asked.

His shoulders sagged. "Probably not."

Green returned, glaring for all he was worth at them, Kelly, Carlyle, the door, and a light above the door that had one small red and one small green light. The red one glowed.

He asked just what the hell the cops wanted.

"We're investigating a homicide," Riley told him. "I'd hate to have to investigate two."

"We're having a difference of opinion," Kelly said. She sucked in air, but the effort cost her. The embarrassed flush in her cheeks faded as if the oxygen molecules had absorbed it. "I'm afraid our new candidate isn't endorsing StartUp Central either, and doesn't believe the federal matching funds are going to materialize. It's going to be one of the cornerstones of his campaign."

"Of course it is," Green fumed. He walked around in a circle to, Jack guessed, get himself under control.

Connor Scofield now exited the men's room in time to hear this last exchange. "This guy hasn't even met me and he decides to make my project a campaign issue? How is that responsible governing?"

Kelly said, "Because it isn't personal, Connor. It's dollars and cents and what's best not only for Cleveland but for everyone in Ohio."

Green said, "As if you'd give a—" He turned and grasped the handle of the door to the meeting room.

To Jack's surprise, Kelly put her hand on Green's arm. "Wait. They're not ready." She pointed to the light above them, still red.

"They'll be damn close enough," he said, but waited. "Your fat-cat party doesn't care if the working people of Cleveland can't make a living."

"Fat cats? I'm not the one who renovated my backyard with free labor."

"You leave my family out of this!"

Riley calmly interjected, "Your new guy's out of time to have much of a campaign, isn't he?"

Kelly gave a slight smile with cracked lips. "Until the polls close, there's always time. That's why I'm here on friggin' *election day* to see this through."

Riley's soothing tone usually worked, but this time it had no effect on Green, whose face remained an alarming shade of red. "Going against your late boss's wishes! Diane had begun to see things my way on StartUp. She saw the benefits of encouraging jobs to come to this area. What the hell is the matter with the rest of you?"

Kelly fidgeted, hyperactivity bleeding through. "I can't verify that, and taking a stand against bankrolling a boy who's got nothing to show for his plan except a lot of talk is exactly what we want to do. We've been working to lessen government waste—"

"Waste? You think it's not obvious how Vepo bought her off to shoehorn them in, to pave the way for the graft and overruns and change fees that that project is going to cost us?"

Jack realized he no longer believed a single word any of them said. It was all posturing. He saw the same thing among attorneys who behaved in court as if opposing counsel spent his time clubbing puppies but then laughed with them in the hallway and maybe went out for a beer. The three in front of him could turn those personalities on and off like a toggle, until he had no idea which might be the real one. He wondered if they knew themselves. Or cared.

Connor said, "I know I'm young, but I'm not a *boy*."

"As you stand there with a sucker in your mouth!"

Kelly snapped. "Look, the appropriate place to discuss this is in front of the committee. We also need to make sure they're aware of the EPA report."

Everyone glanced at Carlyle, who clearly wished the floor would open up and swallow him.

"You betcha," Green said. "And you can be sure I'll be calling for a meeting to revisit the Vepo contract, and personally handing the committee a copy of *that* report."

"Our political process at work," she puffed, as if short of breath. Either her boss's death had hit her harder than she expected or the reengineered campaign had demanded more energy than coffee and protein bars could provide. Jack wondered if she had slept at all in the past thirty-six hours.

David Carlyle said, "Is Mrs. Russo here? She was going to attend this."

"That's all the hell I need, that bitch showing up," Green said.

The reporter's death had not been released yet, not even in her own paper, in cooperation with the police. Jack supposed Gardiner and his partner wanted to use the time to let the killer think the body hadn't been found and maybe slip up, which seemed nonsensical to him because whoever had opened the gate surely would have reported back to whoever hired him. More likely they hadn't gotten around to preparing a press release. Maggie's ex was a nonstarter, and Will would never set the world on fire, either. Jack didn't have high hopes for the investigation.

Meanwhile his number one suspect in that murder, Green, looked up at the light over their heads—which was still red—and charged the door anyway. Through the narrowing crack Jack saw committee members standing, chatting, and gathering up papers, so Green's haste probably wouldn't draw any censure. Connor Scofield looked at Kelly, defiantly slurped on his candy, and followed Green.

"So where *is* your new candidate?" Riley asked Kelly.

"A potluck on the east side. Who the hell decided to have this hearing on the second Tuesday in November ought to be first fired and then boiled in lava."

The doors opened from inside, and men and women in suit coats and dress shirts began filing out, chatting. Jack held the door open for them, which seemed as good a method for getting out of the way as any, and allowed him to keep an eye on Green at the same time. "Because there's no cameras here?"

She didn't take offense. "Exactly, Detective. You're catching on."

"You didn't tell us you had met Harold Baudelet."

"I didn't? Must have slipped my mind. But that's why I gave you his letter. I knew he was nuts."

"Yet you didn't know about that money in her safe, did you?"

Her hands went to her stomach, as if feeling it for lumps. "It's party funds. Diane often collected her own contributions—"

"Almost a million dollars' worth? I don't think so. If you had been part of that deal, you would know the amount right down to the penny and have records of every person it came from."

"I'm glad you have such faith in my competence, Detective. That's actually the nicest thing anyone's said to me all week."

"So if she kept you out of it, where did that money come from?"

"You just said I didn't know."

"I'll bet you can make a damn good guess. That's why, once you learned of the money, you and Stanton had to get those phone records. They would lead us straight to Cragin's 'contributors' and the scandal would sink this election for your party."

"*Jack*," his partner said.

He and Kelly both turned, Carlyle still lurking in the hallway behind them. The cavernous meeting room had mostly emptied, leaving rows of vacant chairs, except for three men at one end of the conference table, a young woman setting out fresh notepads, and Joe Green, who staggered, hand to his chest. Then he fell onto the beige-colored carpet. The woman screamed. Jack pushed past Kelly Henessey and into the room.

Green had not lost the flush to his skin, but now the redness took on an ashen hue. His palms were pressed to his sternum, but before Jack could even reach him, their grip had loosened until one hand slid off to his side. The other stayed at his throat, where his windpipe gasped for air, filling the room with the sound of desperate, wet panting.

Connor Scofield knelt next to him, one hand on his shoulder.

Jack wasn't sure what to do. He had been trained in CPR and use of an automatic external defibrillator, but those were techniques for someone who had already suffered a heart attack. He didn't know what to do for someone in the midst of one.

Except for one thing. "Get 911," he told Riley.

Kelly stood behind his partner, watching with huge, slightly hopeless eyes.

Jack pulled at Green's tie. The man might be choking—but on what? He hadn't been eating anything, and there were no snacks or pastries in the room. He tried to turn Green on his side anyway—clearing the airway seemed like a good idea. The large body didn't move easily.

And then, as Jack tried to snake one hand under his shoulders, he died.

Without the wet, gravelly gasps, the room became silent.

"Oh *no*," Kelly whispered.

Chapter 26

"Thanks for coming," Jack said to her.

"I didn't have a lot of choice. If I stop responding to scenes, the city stops sending me a check." Maggie gazed around the room. Riley spoke to a few men in suits off to the side. A woman sat next to some paperwork, texting away. Connor Scofield and Kelly Henessey had been placed in opposite corners. He sat with his head in his hands, and she spoke on her phone, an excited chatter bursting from her now and then despite the pale, horrified look. A man had died in front of her, Maggie thought, and knew from personal experience that even when it was someone you loathed, the experience still shocked the system. But Kelly must also realize that the campaign field had been leveled once more. They had a last-minute substitute, but now the Democrats had no one at all. And hers had a two-day head start.

"Don't know," Maggie heard her say into the phone. "But he's been lining his satin pockets for decades.

You've got the spots for the ribbon cutting lined up? *What?*"

David Carlyle, Jack told her with a suspicious amount of relish, had been present but disappeared the second Joe Green hit the floor. He'd been outside in the hallway and hadn't entered the room, so technically wasn't a witness or they would have sent a cop to run him down.

Curious office workers milled in the hallway, peeking through the doors every time they were opened. The patrol officer who arrived for contamination control didn't bother with yellow tape, since the area couldn't get more controlled—one door, three small windows, and technically this wasn't a crime, anyway.

"It looked like a heart attack?" Maggie asked Jack.

"Clutched his heart, couldn't breathe, had been extremely agitated immediately before onset."

Maggie snapped a few photos of the room in general before moving on to the body. "If I had to pick my most likely candidate for a heart attack—no pun intended—it would be him."

Jack crouched to peer at the victim's hands. "But in these circumstances I'm not about to take anything for granted."

Maggie crouched as well and studied Green's still form without touching it. Physical examination would have to wait for the Medical Examiner's staff to arrive, but she could look. She started at the feet. His shoes appeared to be real leather and, she assumed as she knew nothing about men's shoes, expensive, but they were worn and scuffed. The belt had obviously been a favorite, stretched and scratched with a simple, beat-up buckle. Unlike Diane Cragin's heels with pointy toes, Green dressed for comfort. But of course men have that option, Maggie thought, not that she was bitter or anything. She knew no more about men's pants than men's shoes, but these seemed to be made of a light-weight, wrinkle-resistant fabric that hung beautifully—a sophisticated item designed to look ordinary, right in line with his ordinary-guy persona but still affording him all the comfort he desired.

"Something on his knee?" Jack asked her.

"No, no . . . checking out this fabric. Nice stuff." She moved on to the belt without looking up, hoping Jack wouldn't be giving her a *Let's focus on the job and shop later* gaze.

Behind him, a committee member with a voice that carried told Riley, "I can't believe it. He always had so much life in him."

The shirt, a conservative light blue in some well-wearing blend like the pants, had been ringed with a red tie. The breast pocket had an unidentifiable stain from a recent meal and a piece of paper tucked inside it, which Maggie did not touch. Yet. The quality of the jacket matched that of the pants, a lightweight material with shiny silk lining. She gently prodded the pockets. Nothing in the left, a hard roundish item in the right.

"Probably his pills." Jack told her that he had swallowed some just before the attack.

"I was at his house for a party over the weekend," the guy now told Riley. "He's got a really nice place."

"Who's going to tell his wife?" the committee member next to him piped up. "Someone has to get to her before some idiot or the media call her. And the kids—who's going to—"

"We've sent a Victim's Advocate to the home," Riley said.

"But this whole building is a sieve! No one ever keeps their mouth shut around here."

Green's hands, Maggie noted, were surprisingly unblemished. The skin appeared soft, but the nails had been bitten as far as comfort allowed. He wore a gold ring with a diamond the size of a green pea on his right and a diamond-crusted band on his left. He had a small cut in his left palm and two ink stains on his right index finger.

The first guy said, "She's such a dynamo. Always put up with him no matter what rumors flew."

"More than rumors," the third one corrected. "If you were hot and wanted a job, you had to fu—um, sleep with Joey. What? Everybody knew it."

"Yeah, yeah. Joey liked the ladies. But she stuck by him."

"Well, duh. The kind of life they led? She's going to skulk off and raise three kids on alimony?"

"He worked tirelessly for Cleveland," the second man said, trying to get the conversation back on track. Unfortunately he spoke with all the sincerity of a homemade TV ad.

Green's tie had been loosened, and a few red lines appeared on his neck, most likely from his own fingers as he struggled to breathe. Flecks of foam rested in his mouth.

"It was a barbeque, this past weekend?" she heard Riley asking one of the men.

"Hell, yeah. I'm not talking burgers and dogs—two-inch T-bones and lobster."

The second man put in, "I'm sure that's not what they need to know about right now—"

"And like I said, he had the backyard redone."

A third man said, "Easy to do when everybody owes you favors. That's how he got a roof on his house and a junket to Las Vegas, complete with hookers. Because the guy who got the halfway house contract gave it to him, that's how. What? It's common knowledge."

"A fish pond, jacuzzi, all this garden stuff, like—"

"Flowers?"

"Yeah, bushes and whatever. You should see the new grill he got. As long as the table and uses three propane tanks. Never seen anything like it."

Maggie and Jack glanced at each other over the still form of Joe Green.

Riley, she knew, had caught it too. "New grill?"

"Somebody he knows—Joey knew everybody, remember—had it brought in special from the factory."

"Really," Riley said. "What did he do with the old one?"

The three men, Maggie saw out of the corner of her eye, stared.

"Um, why? Are you in the market for a used propane grill?"

Apparently Jack's partner decided the most direct route was best. "It sounds weird, but I have a reason for asking. What happened to the old grill?"

But the men couldn't help. The third protested to everyone within earshot, "Don't ask me. I've never been wined and dined by Joey Green in my life. How he spends his bribe money, I got no clue."

"Geez, Mick, the guy's dead. Like, lying right there dead."

"Which changes nothing. Except now I don't have

to worry about having my budget appropriated or a landfill going in next to my house because I insisted on open bids."

Riley said, "Okay. What about today?"

None of them had even spoken to the victim before he choked and fell, so they could not add any details to what the cops already knew. In the sudden quiet of the room, Maggie heard Connor Scofield in the back saying, "But will we get the money?" Then he turned down the volume but not the urgency. She saw him cup his hand over his phone, hunching over until his face disappeared under a curtain of hair.

The ME investigator arrived, agreed that it appeared to be a heart attack, but of course they would have to wait for the autopsy results to be sure. The committee member who had waxed poetic over Green's backyard reno asked if that would be necessary, as it would surely distress his wife. The ME investigator pointed out that an unexplained death in a public place would absolutely require an autopsy, even if, as the man emphasized, the attack had been an obvious result of never passing up a piece of red meat or a shot of whiskey in his entire life.

The investigator also pulled out the piece of paper from Green's breast pocket, which turned out to be a parking receipt for a lot several blocks away, stamped that morning.

"Probably going to turn it in to be comped. He never missed a chance to skim a penny."

"Geez, Mick—"

"Yeah, yeah, I know. The guy's dead."

The ME investigator pulled the bottle out of the

jacket pocket. As they expected, a prescription medication made out to the victim. "Nardil."

"What's that?" Maggie asked.

"Phenelzine. It's an antidepressant."

"What the hell did he have to be depressed about?" the third man said, and Riley ushered them and the lady with the files out of the room.

The ME investigator opened the bottle and glanced inside. Then he frowned and poured fifteen or twenty buff-colored pills out into the palm of one hand. "This ain't right."

"What isn't?" Maggie asked.

"This isn't Nardil. Nardils are orange."

Riley returned. His knees gave a creak as he joined them on the floor as if they were football players in a huddle, trying to keep their signals hidden from those not on the team—that is, Connor and Kelly. "That's an old trick—use a real prescription bottle but fill it with something stronger. What are they, then?"

"Dunno." The investigator pulled out his cell phone and fired up a drug identification app, searching by color, shape, and imprint. "That's weird . . . these are fluoxetine. Another antidepressant. Brand name Sarafem."

"What?" Maggie asked in surprise. The three men looked at her.

"Sarafem. Why, are you on it?" the investigator asked.

"No. But I know someone who is."

Riley took Connor Scofield off to find out what interactions, if any, he had had with the victim that day.

Maggie and the ME investigator reached a compromise on the pills, deciding that she would take the bottle to fingerprint it—presuming any prints remained after being shoved in and out of Green's pocket and then the investigator twisting off the cap—and he would take the pills to compare them to what might be found in the dead man's stomach. She poured the pills into a zip-top baggie and dropped the plastic bottle into a paper bag.

Now Jack and Maggie sat with Kelly Henessey in the emptied meeting room. The body snatchers had carted Joey Green off to his second-to-last public appearance, but that faint, stale smell of death lingered in the air.

"What do you mean, where are my pills?" she asked Jack. "How do you know I even take pills?"

"You told us," Maggie said. Jack had wanted her to remain for exactly this reason, in case Kelly tried to end the conversation with a blanket denial.

"They're perfectly legit. I'm not some kind of druggie."

Jack said, "I understand that. What I don't understand is why your pills are in Joe Green's pill bottle."

"Because they're not my pills. Look, mine are right here." She pulled a bottle from her purse and handed it over. "What have any pills got to do with a guy having a heart attack, anyway?"

"What are these for?" Jack asked.

"You can't ask me that. That's medical information—I don't think you're allowed to ask me that." But when Jack simply glanced over at where Green's dead body had been, Kelly said she had a stomach problem.

"I often throw up a lot of what I eat. It's . . . complicated. The doctor thinks these help."

Bulimia, Maggie thought.

"They couldn't kill anyone unless they, like, took the whole bottle, and I'm not even sure that would do it. That's why the doc chose them. She said they were . . . safe."

Jack dumped the contents out onto one of the notepads left for the meeting. About nine buff-colored pills fell out. "You filled this a week ago, sixty pills. At two a day, you're kind of short."

Kelly frowned and rubbed one eye, her only reaction. "That's not right, I had more than that. . . . I think I did. . . . I mean, seriously—my boss is murdered, giving us two days to turn a complete unknown into a viable candidate, and there's—so okay, I've probably been taking more than I should. My doctor can shake her finger at me, but it's not illegal."

"Actually—"

"Okay, technically it is. But it's only endangering myself and has nothing to do with why that guy just died! Why would my pills even kill him? He's on antidepressants, and *these* are antidepressants . . . technically—why would they kill him?"

"I don't know."

"And how on earth would I get my pills into his bottle? It's not like we were friends. I—" She stopped, sat back, and wrapped her arms around herself, each hand under the opposite pit.

"You what?"

It seemed to Maggie that Kelly had remembered something, debated telling them, and finally decided against it. The young woman ran her hands through her hair, for the third time since sitting down. Then she reached over and scooped her pills back into the bottle. "Look, Green having a heart attack is hardly a big surprise, and you have no probable cause to be asking me all these questions. I haven't practiced in a while, but I *am* a licensed attorney, so you can take me into custody right now, or I'm leaving."

She stood up, turned, and left.

"Jack—"

"She's right. We can't prove the pills in his bottle are hers. Right now we don't even know that they caused his death. Maybe he wanted a prescription with a little more kick."

"You said he took some outside in the hallway before coming in here, right?"

"Yes."

"But the ME guy's drug ID app had a picture of Nardil—they're orange, like distinctly orange. How could he shake out pills that were the wrong color and not notice? Unless he literally didn't look at them, as if the action was so automatic that he could do it by feel."

"He never looked at them—too busy glaring at us the whole time." Jack had his arms crossed, one elbow balanced on the other hand, the free hand elevated, and abruptly snapped those fingers. "Got it. He was color-blind."

"What?"

He told her about Green being so hard on the secretary who didn't keep color-coded folders in order and not being able to distinguish between the red and green lights over the door in the hallway.

"That would make sense. But how could the killer—

if there *is* a killer—count on that to slip him the wrong pills? Who would even know that?"

"Probably everyone. The secretary certainly knew it, and the rest of the staff at party headquarters. I bet Connor Scofield does, since he didn't bat an eye at the doorway light thing."

She considered this. "He and Green's coworkers might also have access to his pill bottle, unless he keeps it in his pocket every minute. But that lets Kelly out. Her hanging around his party HQ would be like a Hatfield sneaking into the McCoy's cabin."

"Maybe she sent in some plumbers."

"Oh, hah," Maggie said crossly. "Why does it seem there's almost nothing we can rule out here, other than unicorns and space aliens, and I'm not even sure about the aliens? There's something Kelly wants to tell us . . . something she's hiding, something between her and Green. It's hard to tell—she's so stressed out by the campaign that it throws off her affect and body language."

Jack didn't seem interested in Kelly Henessey's body language. "*If* Green was somehow murdered, is it related to Diane Cragin's murder?"

"Very different methods. One is so obviously a murder, and in the other case we may never be able to prove it wasn't some kind of accidental overdose. And why? Who would want them *both* dead? Aside from, maybe, the assistant state treasurer."

"Hmm."

"That was a joke."

"Or David Carlyle," Jack said.

"To kill—no pun intended—both the Vepo deal and StartUp Central?"

"Yes."

"Seriously? Can you picture David Carlyle murdering two people?"

"You like him." It sounded like an accusation.

"I do. Why wouldn't I?"

A crease appeared between his eyebrows, as if puzzling out a difficult math problem. "But—what if—"

"What if *what*, Jack?"

He leaned forward though no one remained to overhear them. "You're supposed to be dating me. I mean, that's what you told people to get Rick off our backs. If you start going around with David Carlyle . . ."

She couldn't help but smile for the first time since Lori Russo's murder. "Are you jealous, Jack?"

The crease deepened. "This cover story was your idea. At some point you're going to start dating someone else, so then—"

"No worries. We'll invent an imaginary breakup to end our imaginary relationship."

The line smoothed out. "Oh. Will that work?"

"Of course it will work! This is a police department. We have more get-togethers, breakups, and still more get-togethers than the average soap opera."

"This isn't funny, Maggie."

"It's a *little* funny. Look, there's something else. I didn't want to tell you when other people were around."

Now he rubbed an eye, just as Kelly Henessey had been doing. "What?"

"I finished processing all the scraps of paper and the plastic bags that were with the money. Got a bunch of prints, but most were Diane's. Of the seven that weren't, four are still unidentified. Of the other three, one is a guy named Carl Nero, got some minor assault charges, served a few years, lives in Bay Village. Another belongs to a Sharon Novak, a middle-aged woman who had one past DUI, charges dismissed. Thing is, I got the print off a Save-A-Lot bag, and she works at the Save-A-Lot on Olde York, so I figure that's a wash. The third belongs to Connor Scofield."

Chapter 27

"Scofield?" Riley said, steering the car up Cedar Avenue, crunching over leaves the blustering wind had scattered. "How . . . how does that even make sense? What was the print on?"

"A scrap of paper with the bundle's dollar amount scribbled on it, tucked under the rubber band."

"How does money from the kid get to Diane's safe? Was he paying her off to let the StartUp thing go forward?"

"If so, he wasn't getting his money's worth. She battled it up to the end."

"Unless Green was telling the truth when he said Diane was coming around to his way of thinking. The cell phones tell us they had a secret meeting, and the secret meeting tells us they had some kind of deal. The draw approval was supposed to happen today— really too late to affect the election. They could playact until then. I don't think it's a coincidence that Green moved up the start date on the construction to before the election once she died. Or maybe it was Scofield who was paying her off and not getting satisfaction. Maybe that's why he killed her."

"You think he did? Green is the one who recently threw out a backyard grill—our possible murder weapon."

Riley braked at a red light. "True, but I'm sure Connor was invited to the barbeque. And Green will get a kickback or a percentage from StartUp. Little Connor gets the whole shebang—or loses whatever money he's already put in. If it fails, Green isn't out a penny." Riley warmed to his theory. "He's the little boy genius. He's probably got the mechanical know-how to set up the electrified door. He'd notice whether there are cameras on that street and where they are—that generation is mentally tuned to any sort of electronics. He didn't have access to her house, so he had to use the exterior arrangement, and that's why he left the money behind."

"Fabulous," Jack said. "How do we prove it?"

"Well, we have his print—why were his prints in the database in the first place?"

"He got caught smoking some pot in Cincinnati."

"He serve time?"

"No, small amount, nonresident, first offense. They dismissed. I don't know why he happened to be in Cincinnati, but how he touched a piece of paper that wound up in Diane Cragin's safe? That, I've got a theory about."

Riley parked the car in the garage at the county Medical Examiner's office. "I'm all ears."

"He and Vepo both use the same lobbyist."

"Our friend Bruce."

"Exactly. What if, just maybe, Connor is passing

money to Bruce to give to Green, while Vepo is passing money to Bruce to give to Cragin."

"And Bruce mixes it up."

"Who cares which bills they get as long as it's the
right amount?"

Riley got out and slammed the door. "Aside from
proving graft, hardly a massive surprise in this day and
age, that would mean there's no connection between
Scofield and Cragin. The wads of cash were merely
bribes that passed in the night."

Their voices echoed off the low concrete ceiling,
and Jack could hear birds chirping among the brown-
ing leaves outside. "And they don't tie him to her murder—not directly, anyway. He still has a motive, but
he's not the only one."

"Who else you got in mind?"

"Let's assume the worst—that Vepo was paying
Cragin to endorse their contract knowing it would
probably poison a few thousand people. That was a
hell of a lot of money in that safe."

Riley pointed out, "On the other hand, it might not
all have come from them. It could have been years of
kickbacks and payoffs. Why didn't she get an offshore
account or something, to keep it safer? Yes, those
banking records might be found, but on the other hand,
what if your house burns down? Your retirement plan
just went up in smoke, and insurance don't cover
cash."

"Life is risk," Jack said. "Point is, Vepo has given
Cragin a bunch of money to buy her endorsement. If
she was making a deal with Green to go back on it—"

"Why would she do that?"

"No idea. However, now she's dead."

"And Vepo may be screwed out of the big contract."

"Yes. Maybe. Maybe not—Kelly and Stanton could take up right where Cragin left off, especially if they know or figured out where that money came from."

Riley pulled open the doors of the Medical Examiner's office, the darkening skies reflected in their glass. "If they don't, I'm going to be concerned about little Miss Henessey's life expectancy. As you said, that was a hell of a lot of money."

The pathologist doing the autopsy on Joe Green turned out to be a very short, trim woman with a slight Eastern European accent. It made her sound like a Bond villain, an image completely at odds with her cherubic, grandmotherly face.

It did, however, fit her working persona. She announced all Joe Green's physical failings to the world at large without mincing words. The man had been overweight, with black-flecked lungs that spoke of too many cigars and an enlarged liver with nodules and fibrous tissue that spoke of too many drinks. He had hardened arteries from too much cholesterol and an enlarged heart from too severe high blood pressure.

He had nothing in his stomach, meaning he'd had either a very early breakfast or none at all. She bet the latter from the smell of alcohol in the contents. The lack of food also made the half-dissolved tablets that they'd watched him swallow easier to find.

"We think someone might have slipped him those. On purpose," Riley told her as she stood at the counter flaying the stomach to examine its inside walls. It now resembled a burst balloon, only larger, smellier, and much more unattractive. She had dropped the two pills into a petri dish to the side.

"You mean like poisoning? That might explain the postnecrotic cirrhosis—dead liver cells."

He explained about Green's prescription bottle for Nardil instead containing Sarafem. The doctor listened as she sliced through the spleen, dropping a sliver into the quart of formalin, resting nearby for exactly that purpose. Then she gave him a reproachful look. "That's not what I meant by poisoning, Detective. What you're describing would be a drug interaction."

"Okay . . . would it be enough of one to kill him?"

"Fluoxetine and phenelzine? They could create a central serotonin syndrome. The former is an SSRI, a serotonin reuptake inhibitor. Those increase the serotonin levels in the blood. The latter is a monoamine oxidase inhibitor—"

"Yes, but—"

She met this interruption with the disregard it deserved. "—and the interaction of the two will produce mental status changes, agitation, and tachycardia."

Jack said, "He definitely got agitated."

Riley said, "But he was always agitated, so it's hard to tell. Tachycardia is when your heart beats really fast, right?"

"Yes."

"How fast will kill you?"

Another one of those looks. "That depends on the person involved, their age, and their health. An infant's heart beats much faster than adults, with the gap lessening as they grow until their late teens. Medications can change the point where a racing heart turns into tachycardia. Whether or not the person will lapse into sudden cardiac death can't be fully predicted."

Jack worked through all those words to the end. "So taking the two meds together might have killed him."

"Years of an unhealthy lifestyle certainly didn't help."

"How much would it take?"

She eyed the petri dish. "More than two half-pills."

Riley looked at Jack, perhaps to avoid the sight of the doctor cutting the man's brain open as if slicing an eggplant. "We don't know how long he might have been taking the wrong pills. Would it take a while for the mixed-drugs situation to build up to a fatal amount? Days? Weeks?"

This time the pathologist added a patient sigh to the look. "That's impossible to determine, Detective. Interactions vary. Absorption rates vary. Individual reactions vary."

Jack said, "We know one thing. Someone wanted him dead."

Bruce Haywood looked up without alarm as his secretary showed Jack and Riley into the office. "Gentlemen! What can I do for you?"

They both sat without being asked, and quickly, Jack could see, the balance of confidence shifted. Haywood's eyes narrowed a millimeter, and he straightened the papers he'd been signing and put them to one side. Unlike their last visit, the cops now clearly had an agenda, and Haywood had more than enough brains to know it would have an item or two he didn't like.

"For starters," Jack said, "you can tell us why you gave Diane Cragin a whole pile of cash."

He had to hand it to the lobbyist—not so much as the quiver of a single eyelash.

He said, "That sounds a lot like bribery."

"Yes," Riley said. "It does."

"Why do you ask?"

Riley seemed to have lost his patience with double-talk; perhaps he'd been hanging around Jack for too long. "Because it's our job to ask why a lobbyist is plying a sitting U.S. senator with money. Why would we *not* ask?"

Haywood held up a hand and tried a smile. "Detectives. I assure you that I have no idea what you're talking about, and I very much doubt that anything in Ms. Cragin's possession could be traced to me. Other than information regarding Vepo water construction, which is what I was hired to give her."

Jack let a silence ensue, enough to give the guy some hope that they had bluffed and all he had to do was hold out and they'd give up and go away. Then he said, "You're familiar with Senate bill 426?"

Haywood's lack of reaction formed a reaction in itself. "The Physician Assistant Employment Act. Yes . . . why?"

"The Veteran's Administration is a client of yours? They're listed on your website."

"Some departments of it are, yes. Surely you're not suggesting that the VA—"

"No, not at all. Only that you used their extra paperwork to jot notes on."

A slight narrowing of the eyes. Not anger, but confusion. Jack kept it coming. "Also, you're acquainted, I'm sure, with *pleurotus columbinus*?"

That produced a response, but nothing as pedestrian

as a jaw drop or a flushed face. Bruce Haywood merely went still. From his hair to his fingers he turned to stone, a rabbit seeing a wolf at the edge of the tree line. "Yes."

"The blue oyster mushroom. It's what you're growing in your picture here, right?" Jack turned the desk photo to its side. This was a bit of a gamble. Maggie had shown him pictures, but he couldn't tell if the mushrooms in the photo were exactly the same or some variety. Edible fungi all looked alike to him.

But Haywood slowly nodded.

Riley picked up the narrative. "In the not inconsiderable cash we found at Ms. Cragin's place, several piles had tiny flecks sprinkled among the bills. Those flecks turned out to be spores. Mushroom spores. Blue oyster mushroom spores . . . which sounds like a rock band spin-off but isn't."

Jack pulled out his phone and dialed a number.

Haywood allowed himself a breath, no doubt reminding himself that mushrooms were abundant on this earth and that, as Maggie had warned Jack, the pleurotus genus contained the most commonly grown mushrooms in the world. And indeed, his next words were: "Everybody eats mushrooms, Detective."

"I don't," Jack told him.

Now the lobbyist smiled, solid footing restored. "You should, they're very healthy."

His phone rang. He glanced at it, then at Jack.

"Yep," the cop said. "The senator not only had your office phone but your personal cell. She had a nickname for you, by the way."

Haywood couldn't help but look interested.

"Blondie."

"I've been called worse."

"No doubt. She sent you a photo of a mushroom on the day she died, didn't she? Knew about your hobby."

"Yes. So what? Adding spores in Diane's house to my hobby hardly equals evidence. One mushroom is very like another."

"Not really," Riley said. "Did you know plants have their own DNA?"

The smile evanesced.

Riley pulled a piece of paper from his jacket pocket. "Our forensic scientist collected all those spores in the cash. And this is a search warrant for this office *and* your home so that we can collect any and all mushrooms found there for analysis and comparison. And also—let me look at this again—'evidence of bribery, money laundering, public corruption or extortion.' Personally I'm dying to peek in your files. I'm betting we'll open that can and find enough worms to aerate acres of your mushroom farm."

Now the lobbyist paled, turning an instant shade of snow white. Jack could guess how his wheels turned— Diane Cragin was dead, no need to protect that client, and since she was dead he could come up with any far-fetched story of how the money got wherever it did. But if they exposed his current clients, he would be ruined. Most likely jailed *and* ruined, but Jack figured "ruined" weighed more heavily.

The man tried to rally. "That's one heck of a job, to get a search warrant based on a few mushroom seeds. Mind if I look at that?"

"By all means. Take your time, make copies," Riley said magnanimously, handing over the warrant. They waited as Haywood read. Jack wanted him to absorb every word, to know they had not exaggerated one whit. Haywood wasn't stupid. They had to convince him their threats were anything but idle if they hoped to turn him around.

But he tried one more time. "If you really had that much faith in your mushroom spores, you'd have a warrant for my arrest."

"As a matter of fact—" Riley pulled a second set of papers out of his pocket. "We do."

Haywood swallowed hard. He read the warrant. At one point his eyes bulged. "Murder! What's this about murder? Bribery is not—and who is Laurine Russo?"

"Relax," Riley said. "We don't think you actually pulled the trigger." He didn't add that Carl Nero's print had been found on a bag with Diane Cragin's cash. He didn't explain that Carl Nero, formerly of Joe Green's buddy's company Environmental Products, now worked as a bodyguard for Green. He didn't explain that the last thing Lori Russo wrote in her reporter's notebook had turned out to be the license plate of Carl Nero's car. He had probably used his connection to Environmental to lure her to the spot, promising her some dirt on Joe Green. If he had been more observant—or less squeamish—and removed her notebook from her dead hand, they might never have made the connection. But now the links tumbled straight and true from Cragin to Haywood to Green to Nero to Russo. Which left the lobbyist implicated in not only bribery but murder.

But they weren't obligated to disclose those details yet, and let Haywood stew.

He set the pages down on his desk and said, "I'm going to call my lawyer."

"I think you'd better," Jack told him.

Chapter 28

Haywood closeted himself in an empty conference room with his lawyer for only twenty minutes before proposing a deal. In the meantime, Jack and Riley guarded his office door by drinking coffee in his lobby while, across town, a patrol officer watched over the man's home to be sure a worried wife or child didn't emerge to destroy the prized mushroom crop. A prosecutor arrived to review and approve their side of any deal, a paunchy older man with a face like a granite cliff.

"What do you think he'll propose?" Riley asked his partner, refilling his cup under the sad, worried eyes of a very pretty receptionist.

"He'll tell us as little as he can get away with, as long as we don't rifle his filing cabinets," Jack guessed. "We might have done better if we'd hauled him into the station and gotten it over with. This soft approach gives him time to think."

"It's a gamble. But he's pretty smart, so thinking might

do us good. He'll balance what he gives up against what he still gets to keep and do the math. Throw him in jail and he might clam up from the shock."

"It's where he should be."

"Somebody's always greasing palms. It's the way of the world."

"Doesn't make it okay."

Riley sipped. "You're kind of a Boy Scout, you know that?"

"Me? You're the one who lets every person of interest cry on your shoulder."

"That's all a technique, pahdnuh. Or should I make like our boy genius and call you *dude*?"

"I'd rather you didn't." Jack nodded toward the prosecutor. "I hope he's got the authority to keep from giving Haywood a free pass and doesn't just roll over."

"He doesn't look like the rolling-over type. In fact, he looks like you—in another ten years."

Jack studied the man's craggy face. "Hell. I hope not."

Haywood and his lawyer, a near twin to him in terms of looks and attitude of competence, emerged. Haywood's composure had slipped a bit, and he now appeared distinctly worried. But Jack thought that could be an act as well, to convince them of his sincerity, that he would now tell them the whole truth and nothing but. Jack didn't believe anyone they had met in the past couple of days had told the truth or had made any statement even close to that end of the spectrum.

They sat around a round table in Haywood's office. Jack didn't want him anywhere near his laptop or phone and even had paranoid visions of the file cabinets being rigged to incinerate their contents at the touch of a button.

The two attorneys made no pretense to a friendly confab. Haywood's opened with: "We're going to make you a deal. Mr. Haywood will blow the whistle on a situation that could lead to the deaths of thousands of people, and in return he gets full immunity from all prosecution, criminal and civil."

"No," the prosecutor said, and they went on from there.

It took twenty minutes, but they finally established that Haywood would tell the police everything he could about Diane Cragin and this potential threat, but he could not be prosecuted as a co-conspirator to the threat and, what seemed most important to him, all other client information must remain confidential.

The prosecutor pointed out that they had a warrant for *everything*. In return, the other attorney said that Mr. Haywood's cooperation would make the detectives' success possible, as opposed to blindly wading through enough paperwork and computer records to keep them busy until the next decade.

While they worked it out, Riley sipped coffee and Jack watched Haywood, pondering the nature of white-collar crime. Maggie didn't care for the direction of his moral compass in trimming back the violent criminals, but backyard deals with the Vepos of the world created much more destruction than Jack ever could. Just ask the citizens of Virginia, or Haiti, or the taxpayers of Utah and Washington.

I should shift my focus, he thought.

At last the prosecutor agreed to the deal, stressing

that should Haywood hold back on anything—*any-thing*—relating to Diane Cragin, Connor Scofield, or Joe Green, the deal would be off and teams of cops would invade his office and his home.

"Wait—" Haywood said. "I thought this was about Diane."

"We found more than your mushroom seeds in Ms. Cragin's cash," Riley said. "Tell us how Connor Scofield is connected."

"He's not."

Riley moved his head from side to side in regret. "We're not getting off to a good start here, Mr. Haywood."

"No, really—Connor is a client of mine, but regarding a separate project."

"Then why are his fingerprints on Ms. Cragin's money?" Technically it was on the piece of paper *with* the money, but that would take too long to explain.

Haywood seemed genuinely perplexed. "I don't know."

His lawyer said, "Because this Scofield had his own deals going with Ms. Cragin, which have nothing to do with my client."

Riley said, "No. Nope. They were battling each other, not BFFs at all."

The lawyer seemed pretty sharp, but with Haywood's firm's money, Jack wouldn't have expected anything less. "Then Scofield was paying her off. That still has nothing to do with us."

Riley said, "So a wad of cash at Ms. Cragin's had *both* Scofield's fingerprint and Bruce's mushroom seeds? I don't think so."

Haywood swung his face from one side to the other.

"They didn't have anything to do with each other as far as I know."

"Wait, wait," the prosecutor interrupted. "Can we get back to the death of thousands of people?"

Haywood cleared his throat. "Vepo. And the crib renovation project."

Jack exchanged a glance with his partner, remembering the EPA guy's dire warnings.

Haywood said, "I'm no scientist, so don't quote me on this, but basically we're looking at a Flint situation. In order to switch water intake to the river, they have to unshutter a pumping station that hasn't been used in years—right under the Hope Memorial Bridge, between the steel plant and a carbon-processing place. That will get it from the river to the Garrett Morgan treatment plant."

"Carbon?" Riley said.

"Coal, basically. All those influences make the pH of the soil more corrosive to pipes that have been in the ground for sixty years. That is not such a problem, *if* the proper corrosion control treatment is used to keep the rust layers in the pipes from flaking off when the water passes through them. That was the mistake they made in Flint, not using the corrosion inhibitors."

The prosecutor looked slightly ill. "Rust layers?"

"Rust is a fact of life. It won't kill you, unless the corrosion control doesn't work so that the rust releases into the water flow, the rust being full of lead. At the same time this water leaches the iron out of the old pipes. The iron reacts with the chlorine in the water. The same chlorine is supposed to take care of any bacteria, so now the chlorine isn't doing its job, the bacteria count goes up, and we get outbreaks of Legionnaires' disease in addition to lead poisoning."

"And this would kill thousands of people?" the prosecutor asked.

"The Legionnaires', no. It killed only about ninety in Michigan."

"*Only*?" Riley exploded.

"I meant, something like this doesn't leave bodies littering the street. Most of the victims are invisible, because they haven't been born yet. With too much lead in the water, the fetal death rate will go from a normal six percent rate to sixty percent."

Riley said, "Shit."

"Then there's all the kids with underdeveloped brains and abilities from it. That's hard to quantify."

"But you said all this would go away with a corrosion control treatment. Why not just use the treatment?"

"Money. It's very expensive stuff. In Flint they simply forgot it, but I know for a fact that Vepo knew about possible corrosion and decided against doing anything about it. They already had to come in with a competitive price—at least on paper, I'm sure they planned to increase the costs later and blame it on change fees or supply price increases—and in addition to what they were paying Diane, it wasn't enough profit for them."

Riley shook his head. "I thought the problem was the hydrocarbons washing out of the brownfield under StartUp Central."

"StartUp is a completely separate project."

The cop blinked at the lobbyist. "But they both affect water quality in the river."

"Oh. Yes. I suppose so."

"And you were willing to let all this happen and say nothing," Jack said, "until we showed up with a warrant."

A short silence fell. Haywood looked at his hands. Finally he said, "I'm a lobbyist. That's my job, and like it or not this is how things are done—always have, always will. How do you think Omar got the contract to build the pyramid instead of Karim? Because he slipped a few shekels to the pharaoh's project manager. And it will never change, because the people who pass the bills regulating lobbyists are the ones who profit the most from them. Most of them consider Congress only a stepping stone into the lobbyist world—better hours, better pay, less ridicule on social media. Industry, government, and lobbying firms operate with revolving doors, people moving from one to the other that quickly."

"Did you?"

Haywood's head bobbed up and down. "I used to be an accountant at a drug company. Want to know what industry employs the most lobbyists?"

"Defense?" Riley asked.

"No—good guess, because they're one of the most powerful lobbies. If a lawmaker even hints that spending ten billion per design like the Airbus Atlas *might* not be the best use of funds, they're attacked as 'soft on terrorism.' There is no worse death knell for a politician than being 'soft on terrorism.'" Twice his fingers made air quotes around the phrase. "The defense industry is merely more visible with their trail of waste, like the Airbus, like spending over nineteen billion dollars on a futuristic tank model before the project finally shut down, like the Zumwalt-class three-billion-dollar destroyers. But no, the biggest group, the most lobbyists, the most money spent by an industry is pharmaceuticals. Insurance runs far behind them, about two-thirds their amount. Then you get into the manufacturers and the utilities, oil, etcetera."

"So you went through that revolving door," Jack said, to get the guy back on track.

"You betcha. You can look at me like I'm scum, I get it, but I'm how things get done."

"Why go through you at all? Why didn't Vepo just give Cragin the money themselves and save your cut of it?"

"Because it isn't about money." The lobbyist corrected himself: "It isn't *always* about money. Dealing with most of my clients, money never changes hands at all. With Diane, yes, I did not show good judgment."

Ya think? popped into Jack's head, but he kept it to himself. Keep the guy talking.

"It's about persuading people with information and assistance. As I said, I help them write the legislation, check the facts, provide them with what they need to convince their fellow Congressmen or the ones on their subcommittee or the General Accounting Office. Lawmakers want to get things passed or industries hired because accomplishing a goal looks good for them, or the industry is big in their home state or because it's a project they truly believe in. Outright bribery is much more rare than you might believe."

Jack said, "And yet Ms. Cragin had a pile of cash in her home."

"Um, yeah."

"Where did that come from?"

Haywood spoke with reluctance. "Vepo, of course." He told them the company had delivered cash to him and he had passed it on to Diane Cragin. "Technically it was not a bribe. It was campaign contributions."

"Is that what they're calling it nowadays?" Jack murmured.

"Then why wouldn't they take it to the RNC headquarters like all her other loyal supporters?" Riley asked.

"They wanted to remain anonymous, since they're a company bidding for a contract for city work. If they gave her a large sum—it looks bad."

Riley snapped, "It looks bad because it *is* bad. *Because* they're bidding for a city contract is exactly why they *shouldn't* be making 'anonymous' campaign contributions."

Jack doubted they would come up with a way to prevent unfair lobbying practices in the next twenty minutes, so they needed to get back to murder. "All the cash you gave Diane Cragin came from Vepo? *All* of it?"

"Yes."

"How much?"

Haywood blinked. "Money?"

"Yes, money."

"I—I don't recall offhand. I didn't keep a record of it."

"Why not?" Riley asked, and then remembered that they spoke of an illegal procedure punishable by law. "Oh."

"It went from Vepo to Diane, more than once, and I don't remember the amount of each. I played middleman, to answer your earlier question, only as a matter of convenience. The Vepo reps met with her in Washington."

"Yet they sent the money here?"

"She didn't want to deal with this in Washington. Too many ears everywhere."

"Unlike here in the boonies with us rubes," Riley groused. "Ballpark the figure for us."

Haywood didn't like it, to judge from his face, but he finally said, "I would guess about five hundred thousand."

"Total."

"In three payments, yes."

"Hmm," Riley said.

They had figured Cragin's stash had been accumulating for a while, so this did not surprise Jack. What did surprise him was how half a million dollars no longer sounded like a lot after talk of billions and trillions. That was how they got away with it—no one could easily wrap their head around that kind of money. One million seconds equaled less than two weeks, whereas a billion seconds reached nearly thirty-two years.

If more people realized that, Jack thought, they might vote differently.

He said, "So Vepo sent Diane cash. Did Scofield?"

Again that hint of perplexity. "No."

Jack didn't see why Haywood would lie on this point—Cragin was dead, and Scofield didn't seem like a sufficiently lucrative client to warrant climbing out on a limb. "And yet his print turns up on her money. What that tells us is that Scofield funneled money through you as well, and you got your bundles of cash mixed up. One hundred-dollar bill is as good as the next. Who was Scofield paying off?"

"Other than Joe Green?" Riley added.

Haywood hesitated, glanced at his lawyer, glanced at the arrest warrant and the plea bargain on the table in front of him, and then said, "Yes. Joey. Not a bribe but campaign contributions. He thought Joey was a pal, appreciated his belief in the StartUp Central project, and wanted to help him win. But he wanted it to be anonymous as well."

"Then why didn't he send it to DNP headquarters? Let me guess—because, since he'd been angling for public funds, it would look bad."

Haywood nodded, unhappy at the corner he'd been put in. He'd had to choose between a client and himself—an obvious choice to him, but one that would have consequences in the future, even if it kept him out of jail. And Jack figured Haywood wouldn't serve a day—as he'd said, the ones breaking the rules were the ones writing them. "But why not slip him the bulging envelope on his own? Why involve you at all?"

A hint of ego slipped into his voice. "Because Green wouldn't give him the time of day. He took one look at Connor and saw some dreamy kid who would squawk the minute a compliance officer glanced in his direction. Green wouldn't listen to one word about StartUp Central until Connor hired me."

Chapter 29

After Haywood signed his official statement, Jack and Riley headed back to the banks of the Cuyahoga. They parked in the Sherwin-Williams area, now that the abandoned parking lot had been reduced to rubble. The backhoe had gotten to work, as well. A gaping hole appeared in the dirt, the construction trailer perched on its edge.

Riley slammed the car door. "Still don't get why we aren't putting that guy in jail. I'm the one who did it, or rather didn't do it, and I still don't get it."

"You're telling me? We did it because we made a deal. And because prosecuting people for something that hasn't happened yet is always tricky."

"The bribery happened," Riley grumbled.

"That's why he asked for immunity. Besides, that's white-collar. We're homicide."

They stomped over the patchy weeds to reach the trailer. Connor Scofield had told them on the phone he would be there and that they were more than welcome to stop by. He didn't ask why they wanted to visit him,

Jack noticed, but he had to be a pretty smart kid to have gotten where he had by twenty-one. Either that or he really was as sunny and guileless as he appeared.

Jack doubted that.

The wind off the lake had strengthened and chilled—no kidding around now, winter was coming and fall had packed its bags. Yet at the same time thunder rumbled softly in the distance, a quiet warning of what was to come. Farther up the river they saw the new, temporary crib that so concerned David Carlyle. Its windows were brightly lit, and Jack saw two people working on the catwalk railings.

They knocked before entering but didn't wait for an answer.

Connor Scofield stood on his worktable, positioning wires above one of the trailer's few tiny windows. He used a cordless drill to attach a tiny webcam to the ceiling, where it could keep watch over the contents of the trailer. The air inside equaled the cool dampness of the air outside, with an added whiff of locker room tang. "Hey, dudes. Hang on, with you in a sec. Have a seat."

"How did you get here?" Riley asked. "The parking lot is empty."

"Uber. Nobody owns *cars* anymore." He jumped to the ground, his light weight barely causing a quake in the trailer. "What's up? Other than poor Joey being dead and all."

"How much did you give him?" Jack asked. He towered over the kid, at least a head taller, and knew that he filled up most of the available walkway in the trailer. But he didn't see the slightest hint of intimidation in Connor Scofield's face. He seemed as relaxed

as ever. Either the kid had perfected odorless marijuana, or he believed he had nothing to fear.

It would be Jack's job to convince him he had a
great deal to fear.

"How much of what?"

"Money."

"For what? I kicked in some for the television commercials. I felt that was fair since StartUp *is* my baby."

"To get him to write the grant into the Community
Development budget. Let's not call it a bribe. Let's call
it 'information and resources.'"

"Let's not call it nothing, brah. I didn't bribe anybody."

Riley's face expressed his deep disappointment.
"We're not getting off to a good start here, Mr. Scofield."

This pronouncement didn't have the sobering effect
that it had on Bruce Haywood. The young man simply
told him to call him Connor and that he had no need to
bribe anybody. "StartUp Central is *so* clearly what this
city needs. Why would I waste one penny of my hard-
earned dollars, and those of my investors, to buy votes
when anyone who couldn't see it on their own would
have to be a complete idiot?" He gave Jack a little
smile as if that settled the matter, turned to the flimsy
drafting table, and picked up a roll of blueprints.

"We have witnesses and fingerprints that say differently," Jack told him.

"Really? What witnesses?"

"You tell us."

"Oh, no, no, no." He rolled out the blueprints, weigh-
ing the four corners down with a stapler, a can with pens
and pencils, a dirty coffee cup, and a hacky sack ball.

"I wasn't born quite yesterday, Detective—isn't that what old people say? You tell me all about it."

Jack felt his teeth grinding. He hadn't moved from his spot in the aisle, and Scofield had to reach around him to spread the blueprints. His arm brushed Jack's torso, even, but the kid gave this no more notice than if Jack had been a coatrack. "We found your fingerprint with a bundle of money. Care to tell us how it got there?"

Didn't bat an eye. "I'll be happy to, but I need more data. What money, where?"

"A stack of crisp bills from Fifth Third bank to a customer, an LLC called RV Labs—so similar to the VR Labs you were only so peripherally involved with. You're listed as CEO."

"You couldn't think of a new name? We weren't sure they'd tell us," Riley complained mildly, "thought they might have sent all their employees home early to vote today. But apparently banks aren't into that so much."

Scofield said, "Speaking of names, don't you think Fifth Third is a stupid one? What does that even *mean*?"

Jack said, "It means you gave it to Bruce Haywood to give to Joey Green. You didn't even take the paper bands off first."

Scofield rested one hand on the table while his face made a show of deep contemplation. "I'm sure I didn't. Sorry."

Riley said, "The funny thing is that it went from Green to Diane Cragin. Can you tell us about that?"

Scofield said nothing, didn't move so much as an eyelash for several seconds, and Jack knew that this information came as a shock. But shock that Green had gone behind his back, or shock that the cops knew about it? "You're not making any sense. Why would Joey give money to that witch?"

"That confused us, too."

At least he had stopped fiddling with the blueprints. "Well, when you figure it out let me know, brah."

Riley had had enough, his fair skin developing a dangerous flush. "Call me *brah* once more and I'll punt your skinny ass into the Cuyahoga."

Scofield smiled. He had to figure—correctly—that he had won if they were resorting to name-calling and threats. "Ah, but that would be police brutality, and"— he waved at the camera he had just installed—"ready to live forever in the digital world."

"We have Bruce Haywood's testimony," Jack said.

"Well good for you. I still have no idea what you're talking about."

"He says you paid him to get Green to listen to you. He says you gave him twenty thousand to get Green on board."

"He can say what he likes, can't he? That doesn't make it true. Joey needed a project to bring jobs to the area, cement his legacy, and boost him into Congress. I didn't have to pay him. He'd have paid me, except I didn't need the money."

He didn't frown, had no tension in his face except for a barely perceptible narrowing of the eyes and a few beads of sweat glistening at his hairline. Scofield didn't mind being accused of a crime. But he minded very much being accused of a lack of impressiveness.

He went on. "So let me get this straight. My finger-print is on a bill that Bruce used to bribe Diane with?"

"Yep," Riley said.

"And that's a big deal? I probably handed Bruce some cash to pay him back for coffee or something. We've met a number of times over the past few months. Not a big deal, br—Detectives." He began to peel back the first layer of the blueprints, changed his mind, turned, rested his hips against the table that might or might not support them, and crossed his arms.

"We're not talking a dollar bill or even five," Riley said.

Jack said, "But that's okay. You don't want to tell us your side, fine. There will be plenty of time for that after your arraignment." He moved to the door, opened it, and stepped out. In his periphery he saw Riley hesitate, uncertain, but then follow.

Scofield spoke from the doorway, not quite as perfectly confident as a moment before but certainly not rattled. "What does that mean? You're going to, like, arrest me or something?"

Jack straightened his blazer, feeling the wind worm its way through the lining, and spared the kid one last glance. "Have a nice day, Mr. Scofield."

Riley grumbled nonstop for four blocks. "Arrogant little brat. He thinks he can stick his fingers in his ears and Mommy will make the mean men go away?"

"He thinks people who confess the minute the cops show up are lame," Jack said, with a grudging admiration. They paused in front of the public library and waited for pedestrians to cross from the old Arcade. "He's thinking, so what if we found a print on some beat-up twenty— he can find a way to explain that. Then it's his word against Haywood's. He's the bright young star and Haywood's a slimeball lobbyist."

"You're not making me feel better, partner. Or should I say *brah*? What does that even mean, anyway?"

"It means bro, brother, came from either Hawaii or Haiti. They can battle it out for ownership, and we'll have to let the prosecutors battle Scofield in court. The kid's not going to roll over for us. And he doesn't even know—or might not know—that Green and Cragin were having secret confabs. Money may have gone from Scofield to Green to Cragin without involving Haywood, and that's why Haywood doesn't know about it."

"But does that make sense? Green bribing Cragin—to what? Give up her Senate seat? Sounds like all the money in the world wouldn't make her agree to that."

"Unless she felt ready to retire and fade away with her nest egg, though it wouldn't be that easy. Even if she wanted to throw the fight, her party sure as hell wouldn't. We don't really know what was in her mind. She didn't have friends or confidantes. Only a public shell for the rest of the world to see."

"The way I figure it," Riley said, "the fingerprints on the money are explained because it all funneled through Haywood. Vepo gives Haywood money for Cragin. Scofield gives Haywood money for Green. He mixes it together because money is money—as long as everyone gets what they were supposed to, who cares if the actual bills stay in their own little pipeline."

Jack said that made sense. "But we don't have to tell Scofield that. Let him think Green was double-crossing him."

"Though if money *did* move from Green to Cragin, it could have been for her to do a one-eighty on StartUp as soon as the election was over," Riley added, but without much conviction.

"He didn't act like a man who didn't intend to win. If anyone still living can tell us, it'll be Kelly," Jack said.

But at Euclid and East Ninth, as a blink of lightning lit the sky, his phone rang. He answered with, "Has your ex found anything? On Russo?"

"Um, no." Maggie's voice told him.

Figures.

"But David Carlyle is in my lab."

That guy again. "Why?"

"He's afraid Connor Scofield is going to try to kill him."

Chapter 30

"I know this sounds crazy," Carlyle said.

The lab's entire reception area consisted of a chest-high table with a ledger, a bowl of mints, a pen on a string, and a placard reading ALL VISITORS WHO GO PAST THIS POINT MUST SIGN IN, which Maggie had printed herself. But the lab also lacked a conference room, so Maggie gathered chairs around her desk and set aside the small stack of manila folders holding her current fingerprint identifications. Jack hadn't wanted to bother trooping everyone over to an interrogation room in the homicide unit, and hence Maggie sat in on the interviewing of a witness/suspect/victim, depending on what David Carlyle turned out to be. The man in question, meanwhile, kept looking at her with soulful eyes as if she could help him explain the situation.

Which she couldn't. All she knew was what she had told the detectives.

"Never mind what it sounds like," Jack told him, not gently. "What are you talking about?"

"Okay, so. Connor Scofield called me—"

"When?"

"About twenty minutes ago."

Maggie noticed Jack share a glance with his partner. Apparently this meant something to them.

"And he said he'd like to go over my report to get a better idea of it, that Green had been handling getting the committee's approval to release the funds, but now that he's dead he—Connor—would have to handle it by himself."

"So?"

"And he needs to understand every aspect of the report. Since before he'd left that part of it up to Green."

Jack made no attempt to hide his impatience. "*And*?"

Maggie put her hand on his thigh. She didn't pinch, but let it rest there for half a second before removing it. She felt his rectus femoris give a little spasm while Riley's mouth twitched and Carlyle blanched.

"So when do we get to the part where he's trying to kill you?" Jack asked, but less harshly.

Carlyle swallowed.

"He said that it was very important to tell the committee that he is ready to break ground. He said that twice. I said what I always said, that my job is to assess the environmental concerns, not advocate for one decision or the other, that I'm neutral. I truly am neutral," he added to them, placing one hand on his chest. "I don't care whether StartUp Central gets built. That's no skin off my nose. I care only about releasing hydrocarbons into the water."

Again she saw a glance between the two detectives. When they had time she would demand to be brought up to speed.

"The killing part," Jack reminded him.

"So he asked me to meet him at the trailer, and said, 'Just you and me.' He said that *three* times. 'Just you and me can hash this out. I'm sure we can come to an arrangement.'"

"And that makes you think he's luring you to your death?" Jack asked. This time Maggie nearly pinched, but Carlyle spoke with more conviction.

"No. Not until he emphasized how important it is that this project begins on time, meaning next week, and all of a sudden I'm remembering that people are dying under bizarre circumstances, and that Connor Scofield is a little bizarre too, you know what I mean? His voice got kind of strange—as if that lovable stoner persona fell away, leaving who he really is. You know what I mean?"

Maggie expected Jack to blow this off, but instead he stilled. "Yes. I think I do."

Riley asked, "When does he want to meet?"

Carlyle checked his watch. "In an hour. I told him yes because, truthfully, he absolutely insisted and I was afraid to say no . . . maybe not *afraid*, I was at the other end of a phone call, but I figured if I said no he'd appear when I didn't expect him. This way, I'm . . ."

"Forewarned," Maggie supplied.

"Yes! Exactly."

"Where?" Jack asked.

"At his construction trailer. It's very much out in the open, I know, but on the other hand it will be dark by then and the few streetlights are a hundred feet away. It gets *really* dark out there at night. I know because we had to do this one study regarding the northern long-eared bat and—"

Jack said, "Would you be willing to wear a wire to your meeting with Connor Scofield?"

Whatever Carlyle had been expecting them to do for him, this had not been it. His eyes widened instantly, and his mouth formed the word *wire*. "You mean, like, try to get him to say something incriminating? Or kill me while it's being recorded?"

"No," Maggie said.

"Yes," Jack said. "I mean no, we're not going to let him attack you. And I don't think he intends to." Riley nodded assent to back this up, but Maggie did not feel convinced. "He will most likely offer you money or some other incentive to skew the EPA report so he can get his building built. We can do something about it if we get attempted bribery on tape."

The knot in Carlyle's throat bobbed. He paused for thought. A good deal of thought.

Then he turned to Maggie. "Will you come with us? I don't mean to see Connor, I mean in the van or wherever they will be—"

"No," Jack said.

"Yes," Maggie said.

"There's really no reason you have to be there to hold his hand," Jack groused.

"You certainly aren't going to," she pointed out, and slipped the video camera battery out of its charging port.

"No, and you know why? Because he's a grown man."

"Then you should have interviewed him in the

homicide unit and not in my lab. You thought less official surroundings would put him at ease."

"No, I didn't want to waste ten minutes walking
back to the homicide unit on David Carlyle's persecution fantasies."

She dropped a large duffel bag with the camera and
its equipment into his arms. "And now he's going to
make your case for you. So, you're welcome."

"Or we'll find out that Connor Scofield is exactly
what he appears to be, and the EPA savior of the environment is delusional."

He turned to walk out of the lab's supply closet, but
she put a hand on his arm. "Do you think that? Seriously?"

He admitted he did not.

She persisted. "Do you think Scofield could be dangerous?"

"Anyone can be dangerous when they have what
they think is a good reason. Don't raise your eyebrow
at me—I'm not talking about myself. Maybe Scofield
never did anything worse than a youthful DUI. Maybe
not. But right now this seems like the only way to find
out."

"Do you think David is in danger?"

"Maggie. We wouldn't let him do this if we thought
it would put him at risk."

She felt her eyebrow twitch again. "Really?"

"We'll be right there with the audio receiver, a safe
word, and lots of guns."

This did not reassure her as to his honest assessment
of the situation. She ushered him out of the forensic
supply closet and closed the door behind her.

Jack said, "Even if they get into a scuffle, Scofield is skinny enough that Carlyle should be able to take him. Despite being the size of an anorexic girl, who, by the way, seems to think you're the new BFF."

Now her mouth twitched. "That's just catty. People will think you're jealous."

"I'm not—" He lowered his voice as she waved good-bye to Denny. "But we're going to look like fools if Scofield doesn't pull out anything more than his boyish charm."

She flipped her hair over one shoulder, then adjusted the strap of the SLR camera hanging there. Men and their egos. "Is that all you're worried about? No concern for the guy you're using as bait?"

"Nothing will happen to him, don't worry." They entered the elevator, the doors closing them off from the rest of the world. "You like him."

"Of course I like him, Jack. He's a nice guy."

Even though they were alone, Jack cocked his head toward her and spoke quietly. "He's right about people dying in bizarre ways. But Scofield isn't the only sorta-bizarre person in this drama. Green and Cragin were both planning to disrupt the environment in potentially disastrous ways. Both of their projects going forward at the same time equals disaster squared. What if he's taking his job a little too seriously?"

She felt herself frown. "You think he's stepping in to protect the environment the way you step in to—"

The elevator doors opened. Weary workers wanted to leave for the day and waited with less than patient faces for Jack and Maggie to vacate the space.

Once freed, Jack said, "I'm not jealous, Maggie, I'm concerned. David Carlyle was well known to and deeply unhappy with the two people who are now dead. He seems to have a slight fixation on you. I'm just saying, don't turn your back on him."

"Fine."

"I mean it."

"I get it! I do," she added more calmly. "Anything is possible. With luck we'll find out tonight who's the more dangerous, David or Connor."

Or you, she thought but didn't say.

It didn't help her roiling thoughts that thirty seconds later they found David Carlyle with his shirt off. A stone-faced Riley handed him pieces of duct tape with which to attach wires to his smooth chest.

Riley said, "This is the best we can get from the Vice supply on such short notice, and they couldn't spare anyone to help us set it up. It's easy, the guy kept telling me. I don't even know if I have it on him right."

"Does this have a camera?" Carlyle asked, poking at the teardrop-shaped lump taped to his left pectoral.

Riley said, "Nope. Audio only. The fancy surveillance equipment is requested days in advance; last-minute actions get whatever's left on the shelf."

Jack picked up the receiver. "Say something," he commanded.

"The quick brown fox jumped over the lazy dog," Carlyle said, sounding extremely uncertain about both the fox and the dog.

Jack held the receiver closer to his face, watching the colored lines on its small screen. "Nothing. Is the unit on?"

Carlyle held a small black plastic box, about the size of a pack of cigarettes. "It's awfully lightweight."

"Batteries," Maggie said, and Jack and Riley went

off to find a couple AAs. Meanwhile Carlyle stared at a stain in the carpeting and Maggie tried to look anywhere in the room besides his half-naked self.

Finally he said, "You must think I'm the world's biggest dweeb."

"No, of course I don't."

"I *feel* like the world's biggest dweeb."

She had to laugh at this. "I think you've been thrust into a chaotic situation and you're trying to do the right thing."

"Thanks, but—maybe I overreacted to Connor Scofield's call. He's probably just feeling desperate because his champion died and he's got contractors ready to come in."

"Desperate people can be dangerous."

"He's going to be even more desperate than he realizes. All the chemical tests came back with even worse results than before. There's no way he can break ground there, not without a complete removal program in place. The problem in Ohio is that we don't really have a dry season. Even if he did it in the middle of summer, it could rain and wash all those disturbed petrochemicals right into the river."

"Then he'll have to do the complete removal. You're not saying he *can't* build, only that he can't under the current plan."

"They made it clear that complete removal is not an option. Green said 'the numbers don't work.' Meaning it cut into their profit too much."

"Then they can build somewhere else. It's not like there *isn't* a supply of vacant land in Cleveland."

"Not downtown."

"The city isn't going to drink poisoned water. That can't happen. Once it's explained to the committee—"

"You can't be naive," he interrupted, eyes darker than ever. "You have to understand that there's only so much the EPA and the Department of Health and other watchdogs can do. Companies have the money to make massive contributions to the political campaigns of the people who appoint other people to state energy commissions and public service committees. They make the decisions about who can build what and where in their state. Which companies can drill, which can frack, which restrictions to put on solar or green energy to keep them out of the competition. The people on those commissions and committees know they can slide right into a lucrative job as a lobbyist for those same companies, so let's make friends. If the government doesn't want to throw out the rules entirely, they waive them for select clients, like Foxconn in Wisconsin. In California they're still battling the chromium that Erin Brockovich uncovered because under Obama we somehow kept postponing our reports because we were listening to scientists who work for the power company. As soon as Trump was elected, the head of Murray Energy sent him a wish list of regulation rollbacks—not only pulling out of the Paris accords but reconsidering rules meant to protect miners from coal dust. He didn't get everything, but he got quite a bit. We—my own agency—let Dynegy in Illinois delay and delay installing scrubbers to clean the air their plants belch out. So yes," he finished, sounding every bit as discouraged as he looked, "sometimes I feel like I'm waging a quiet little unseen war against invisible forces, which occasionally include the very agency I work for."

Maybe I do as well, and on the wrong side. Maggie put her hand on his shoulder.

Jack and Riley returned. Both faces darkened when they caught sight of the tableau.

Maggie backed up to give Riley room to tape the now-powered-up unit to the small of Carlyle's back.

"This is going to hurt when you pull it off, kid," he warned.

"Better that than have it sliding around so that he notices it," Carlyle said, gulping at the thought.

Maggie took a look, then gently pointed out that the unit showed through the thin white dress shirt he wore. "Do you have a T-shirt you could wear underneath this, or a jacket to put over it?"

"I have a Windbreaker in my car."

"That will work," Riley said, and held up the receiver again. "Say something."

"The quick brown fox—"

"Loud and clear," Jack said. "And recording. Let's go."

Maggie squeezed Carlyle's hand on the way out the door.

Chapter 31

The cops and Maggie arrived at the scene first, tucking the unmarked van into the parking lot at the Sherwin-Williams building. Workers filed out for the day, opening a space for them. The detectives couldn't get a surveillance van, filled with electronic equipment and amplifiers and parabolic mics; the back of this van had nothing but empty space and one ratty jumpseat, which Maggie used, holding the belt buckle together with her hand because it didn't seem to want to catch. Not ideal, but the best they could cobble together in an hour. She set the forensic unit's video camera on its tripod, aiming it between the front seats and out the windshield. The footage would probably prove useless, pixelated grainy shapes moving around in a shifting background, but it might as least verify who was where as long as the daylight held out. Police work was rarely ideal. They could only do what they could do.

They waited for David Carlyle to arrive. No car sat in the abandoned lot, but a light burned in the construction trailer, and of course Connor Scofield was too cool to own anything so archaic as a motor vehicle. Riley fidgeted in his seat. She thought he sniffed the resolution to the case in the air, and it made him as eager as a fox catching the faint scent of pheasant. The skin of the professionally pleasant detective fell away, revealing teeth and sinew.

Maggie had been trying to organize the whole situation in her mind during the ten-minute drive, and now said, "What has changed?"

Both cops expressed perplexity at this question, and she hastened to explain.

"Vepo has been paying Diane to facilitate the water contract—first the temporary crib, and then the permanent crib renovation. Now she's dead and an entirely new candidate thrust into her place who may have never heard of Vepo. He certainly doesn't owe them anything."

"But the party does," Riley said.

"No, the money went to Diane and Diane kept it. The party doesn't owe Vepo anything, either."

Jack said, "Not necessarily. Stanton might know all about the money, and they kept it at Diane's house because it's more secure than a campaign headquarters where dozens of people come and go around the clock. But he or Kelly or both of them can't admit to bribery."

"We have to give that money back to someone eventually. If we can't prove its provenance, it goes to Collette, right?"

"Lucky Collette."

"So they're stuck. We have the money and Vepo is out the cash, with perhaps nothing to show for it."

Riley observed, "That's the problem with crime.

When you get screwed, you can't call the cops. Kelly is the key. We have to get her to crack."

"Which we can't do because we're stuck here," Jack grumbled, sounding as if he were ready to race through the trees himself.

Maggie went on, "Then there's Connor. You said Haywood says he gave a lot of money to Green to get StartUp approved. With Green dead, Connor is out that cash and his influence."

"Hence this desperate meeting with the EPA kid," Riley said.

"Whoever killed them, assuming it was the same person, doesn't seem to have accomplished much except getting both projects tanked."

"And who's the only one with that motive?" Jack turned around to look at Maggie. "David Carlyle, that's who."

Riley had a visible *OMG!* moment. "What if he's setting us up? What if, instead of Scofield intending to do him harm, *he's* actually going to kill Scofield and claim self-defense? He's got the perfect situation—a couple of cops sitting here waiting for exactly that to happen. He'll be out of our sight. We only have audio, not video. He could go in there, say a bunch of stuff, and slaughter the kid, and we'd only have his word for exactly how it went down."

Jack watched Maggie. "You don't believe that."

"It's possible. But if I had to guess who's more likely to be a killer, my money is still on Connor Scofield."

A silence ensued. Then Maggie said, "Can we at least tell David that I identified a fingerprint on his not-anthrax letter?"

"You did? Why didn't you tell *us*?" Riley demanded.

"Haven't had a chance. Besides, it's no one connected to the senator or Joe Green. It belongs to a Helen Sibley. No record. She came up because the state included employment records in the search due to, you know, threatening a federal employee thing. She works for the Department of Public Health."

"Oh, hell," Jack said, "it's the receptionist."

"I guess she really wanted her supply closet back," Riley said.

Maggie said, "Huh. So *Saturday* and the number *10* could refer to an appointment for herself or a message she took for someone else there. But was she the 'Mole' the senator paid off?"

Riley said, "Good question. We'll be having a chat with Ms. Sibley. Rattle her until she bites those perfect nails."

Carlyle's car drove by, slowed. He pulled off the street onto the grass, parking illegally, but traffic stayed light in the area.

"Showtime," Jack said.

Maggie started up the video camera so they could at least establish to a future jury that Carlyle had arrived at the lot and entered the construction trailer. She clicked the microphone off. No one wanted a future jury listening to their banter, sneezing, or off-color jokes.

Through the viewfinder she could see his small figure turn to examine the surroundings. She could see his dismay at the disturbed ground even at two hundred feet in the growing twilight. As if to further illustrate the point, he became backlit by a flash of lightning.

"He's wondering where we are," Riley said.

"He's being obvious," Jack complained.

"It's an empty part of downtown after dark," Maggie pointed out. "Being aware of his surroundings is normal behavior. Plus he can't hear us, and this van isn't labeled. He simply has to trust that we're here and we're listening, poor kid."

They watched him finally slam his car door and pick his way across the disturbed ground to the construction trailer, moving with determination. He had indeed put on a dark, lightweight jacket. Through the audio equipment Maggie heard the rustle of his shirt and the whine of the wind heading up the river from the lake. He said nothing, didn't ask if they were there or express hope that they could hear him, and Maggie figured she knew why. He didn't want to sound like a dweeb.

When he arrived at the trailer's door, she zoomed the camera lens to include only the trailer.

They heard a muffled sound, and then saw Carlyle open the door and disappear inside. Maggie closed her eyes and said a silent prayer for David Carlyle. And for Cleveland, should David Carlyle fail.

"Hey there, brah," they heard Scofield say, as clearly as if he were in the room. "Thanks for coming by."

Riley said, "At least the sound works good."

After that no one spoke. They only listened.

Scofield: "As you know—well, you were there—Joey's dead, so I've got to get the committee's approval for the construction draw all by my lonesome. Without Joey's promises, those crews aren't going to keep working without money."

A pause. Then Carlyle: "Uh-huh."

Scofield: "So I need you to have my back on this. This is so important for the people in this city, man. Jobs have been in the toilet here forever and time, like, technology and innovation have passed this dump by, know what I mean?"

Carlyle: "Cleveland's hardly a dump. But—"

Scofield: "I mean, what's more important, a few ticks on your waterborne solids meter or providing a future for the young people in this city before they move to Austin or Atlanta looking for a future?"

Carlyle: "If they consume a bunch of hydrocarbons via their water system, they're not going to have much of a future anywhere."

Scofield: "Is that just a bit alarmist, dude?"

Carlyle: "I don't get paid to be an alarmist. I get paid to gather samples and have them tested, and that's what I did. The results are the results, and the results in this case are alarming all by themselves."

You go, brah, Maggie thought.

They heard a slight brush as Carlyle shifted his weight.

Carlyle: "The volatile organic compounds are pervasive. There's no cleaning or treatment that we could do to the soil that wouldn't wash right into the river. If we were talking about a lot not so close to a water source, there would be a number of options, but obviously that is not the situation here. And it has to be fixed immediately. Now that you've broken up the concrete it's going to start washing out tonight. We can only hope it's going to be a light rain."

Scofield: "Exactly, dude. It's already done, so you can stop whining about taking up the concrete—"

Carlyle: "Your only choice if you want to build on

this lot is a complete removal of the land at least ten feet down. Even that's not ideal—"

Scofield: "And how much would that cost me?"

Carlyle: "I couldn't say. I mean that depends on who you hire, whether you could get the state EPA to kick in funds—"

Scofield's voice, even digitally transmitted over a distance, sounded much less easygoing than it had only a few seconds before: "Ballpark it."

Carlyle: "I've seen other operations do similar work, and yes, this is not an ideal location with having to get the loads back up that hill. But I'd guess one to two million."

Scofield: "Impossible, in other words."

Carlyle: "Why? The city's giving you twelve."

Scofield: "So you think I'll have plenty, huh? Do you have any idea how much this kind of thing takes? To pay off your contractors, your inspectors, your investors?"

Carlyle: "No, I don't. But I couldn't do anything about it even if I did."

Scofield now took on a different tone: "See, that's the thing. You can. You write the report, right? You send in the samples. What if you sent ones that were taken from the edge of the site? Or maybe slightly over the edge?"

Carlyle: "Skew the results?"

Scofield: "Exactly."

Carlyle: "Why? I mean, why would I do that? No offense, but . . . I admire what you're trying to do here, but that doesn't mean I can let people be put at risk to benefit other people. They may need jobs but they also need health."

Scofield: "Why not both? We'll compromise, do one of the cheaper cleanup options—"

Carlyle: "Won't work."

Scofield: "Will you *listen*? We'll clean it up so that it's good enough, maybe not ideal but won't kill anyone."

Carlyle: "It's too late for that. The rain is about to wash right out into that brand-new crib out there, where the water will go straight to the pumping stations, which aren't equipped to deal with a high influx of hydrocarbons."

Scofield: "Senator Cragin's baby. She's dead, and that bitch is still getting in my way."

Carlyle: "Even if, best-case scenario, it never rains, your *not ideal* means nausea, birth defects, or cancer instead of outright death, and a tripling of the miscarriage rate."

Scofield: "Dude, stop with the Chicken Little stuff. All those hydrocarbons have been leaching out into the river every time it's rained for years and years, so what's the difference if it all happens at once and gets it done?"

Carlyle: "It's barely leaching now, and the difference between a trickle and a tidal wave is obvious."

Scofield: "Fine. Try this: You will send in clean samples because I'll pay you to. How's that work?"

A pause. Riley muttered, "That was easy."

Carlyle: "You mean like a bribe?"

Scofield should have been a little more concerned about self-incrimination, but he must have felt safe. "Yeah, dude, like a bribe. Let me guess, you live in a crappy studio and haven't gotten laid in a year or more, right?"

Carlyle: "Uh—"

Scofield: "You know why? Because girls can smell *no future* as easily as they can smell *success*. Aren't you sick of everyone treating you like dog shit? Stand up and do something for yourself, man!"

Carlyle: "Like poison a city?"

Maggie felt as proud as a coach at the end of a winning game, but integrity didn't impress Scofield: "Come off it! Our world is full of poisons every day— but how many people actually die? Twenty thousand."

Carlyle: "What?"

Scofield: "I can get you twenty thousand. Maybe thirty. How does that sound?"

Silence.

Maggie wondered if Carlyle was actually thinking about it, or if he was wondering what to do next because the mission had been accomplished. She said, "That's it, right? You've got him on bribery. Shouldn't we go in now?"

"Let's see what else he says," Jack told her. She didn't like it but didn't argue, because Carlyle had begun speaking again.

Carlyle: "Do you have it here?"

That seemed an odd question. Regretting his decision to call the cops? Keeping up the patter like a wired-up Scheherazade? Or just curious?

Scofield: "No, of course not. I have to get the draw from the city first—which got interrupted by Joey keeling over, remember?"

Carlyle: "By which point my report would already be on record and I couldn't change it without incriminating myself. You could screw me over and there'd be nothing I could do."

Scofield: "Hey, you gotta put out to get back, know what I mean? But I've never broken a deal, man."

Carlyle: "It doesn't matter. I can't do it."

Scofield: "Twenty thousand, dude. Think what a difference that could make in your life. Enough to make it a whole lot sweeter but not enough to attract attention from anybody. That's the perfect balance. Joey taught me that."

Carlyle: "Can't do it."

Scofield's voice grew less friendly: "You gotta think this through."

Carlyle: "I've thought. Thank you very much for the offer, but my report will be factual."

A rustling sound, as if one of them had begun to move.

Scofield: "You're making a bad mistake here, pal."

Carlyle: "We're not pals. And you're in front of the door."

Riley muttered, "What does he think, we're going to have a sniper take him out?"

Maggie said, "He's letting us know he's trapped. Shouldn't we go in now? He's in trouble."

"He's got a code word if he thinks he needs it," Jack told her.

"What is it?"

"Peachy."

Scofield was saying: "You need to step off that pedestal, brah. You're not Captain America, okay? Nobody's going to pin a medal on you for saving the day."

Carlyle: "Get out of the way."

Scofield's voice plunged to a low, hard sound as cold as steel, so clear and close to the mic that it raised the hairs on the back of Maggie's neck. "I said, you aren't thinking. That bitch senator is dead. Joey is dead. You really want to mess with me, too?"

Another silence. Maggie wrapped her fingers around the handle of the van's rear door.

Carlyle: "Did you kill them?"

Scofield: "You think it's coincidence that they both bought it in the same week?"

Carlyle: "But—but Green was on your side. He got the committee to consider—"

Scofield: "Because I paid him to! That's how the world works, you idiot. But he went behind my back and made his own deal with the bitch. You think I was gonna let that slide?"

Carlyle seemed to give up on staying tough and cool. His voice developed a tremor he could not control: "Get out of my way."

Then they heard rustling, thumps, grunts of exertion, and more thumps, along with Carlyle's frantic shouts of "Peaches! Peaches!"

Maggie turned the door handle. Then she was out of the van, and running.

Chapter 32

For a large man Jack could run fast, even over the broken concrete. Maggie went down once and took a sharp edge to the shin but still lagged behind him by only three long strides as he flung open the trailer door. At that point she had the sense to stop and let the men with the guns take down Connor Scofield. They couldn't all fit through the narrow opening, anyway.

But past them she saw Connor Scofield on top of Carlyle, punching, and blood on Carlyle's face. That propelled her up the steps on Riley's heels. The two detectives peeled Scofield up as if he were a rag doll, and Jack pinned his arms behind him. The young man kicked out once but missed Riley and recovered enough sense to not try it again. Neither detective had bothered to pull out his weapon.

Maggie went to Carlyle, who had already sat up and put a hand to his bleeding nose. "Are you okay?"

He didn't answer, only looked at his now-bloody hands. As the detectives dragged the less than cooperative Scofield outside, Carlyle pulled his legs out of their path as if the young man were a live snake.

Maggie squeezed past them to snatch a roll of paper towels off the table. She yanked off a wad and put it to Carlyle's nose. "Does it hurt a lot?"

"No," his muffled voice said, but not convincingly.

After a few minutes of trying to staunch the flow, she helped him to his feet, feeling the trembling muscles underneath his shirt. Jack poked his head through the door. "You all right?" He looked at Maggie, though the question must have been meant for Carlyle.

The man in question nodded, reddening paper towels bunched against his face. "Peachy."

At the station Maggie stayed with her unofficial charge, and Jack and Riley sat down with Connor Scofield. The boy genius had been cuffed to the table in the small interrogation room, and no amount of appealing to his "brahs" could convince them to bring him a coffee. Jack figured they had caught a glimpse of the real Connor Scofield over the tinny wireless connection from the trailer to the van. Now he had to bring that Connor back.

"Tell us how you killed Diane Cragin," he began.

The face underneath the shaggy blond hair had a few darkening bruises, and they hadn't come from the cops. David Carlyle had fought back. Neither that nor the handcuffs had shaken the kid's confidence, however. He had refused a lawyer and promised to tell all, speaking earnestly as if to show they were all on the same side, to schmooze them into seeing things his way.

Jack, of course, didn't buy it for a minute.

"Dude, I didn't kill *anyone*! I only told the EPA loser that to scare him into changing his report for me."

"After attempted bribery didn't work," Jack pointed out.

"I'd never have done that, either. I was desperate, dude. StartUp Central is, like, crumbling before my eyes before it even broke ground, and this city needs it so bad! I couldn't let some guy who counts blue jays for a living ruin it."

"Or a senator."

"I didn't do a thing to that lady. I don't even know how she died." He sniffled, but not from emotion. His eyes were drought-dry.

"Let me explain something, Connor," Riley said. "May I call you Connor?"

"Of course, brah. I got no use for formality." He sat back, letting his shoulders relax. After all, he excelled at this kind of pleasant chat.

What he didn't know was, so did Riley. "We have you on attempted bribery, aggravated assault, and murder, all recorded and witnessed by police officers and an EPA agent. That means your only chance—your *only* chance—is to hope that the judge will look kindly on your youth and spirit of cooperation."

The kid couldn't help a bit of an eye-narrow at the mention of his age. "I admit that I lost it and went off on the nerd. But I was never going to actually pay him any money to cover up anything—"

"Yet that's exactly what you proposed."

"I was talking out my ass! Like I said, I was desperate. But if no money changed hands, there's no crime, right?"

"Wrong. Just because your mark turned you down doesn't make it less of a bribery attempt. Tell us how you killed her."

"I didn't! Like I told you, I only said that to scare the guy. And it worked." He paused for a smirk. "You should have seen his face. Eyes got all big. I really thought he'd cave."

"But he didn't."

"Amazing," Scofield admitted, giving credit where it may be due.

"That's the problem with thinking that you're smarter than everybody else," Riley told him. "You tend to under-estimate your opponent. And now we're left with this: You are the only one with a motive to kill the senator."

"Oh, come on! She's a politician. *Everyone* has a motive to kill them. If you ask me, Joey did it. Hate to speak ill of the dead and all, but he had way more motive than me. With her out of the way, the election would be a cakewalk. He said that to me, right after he told me she was dead. A cakewalk. Whatever the hell a cakewalk is, anyway."

"A half hour ago you told David Carlyle that she had been working *with* Joey Green. Against you. Sounds like you had motive to kill both of them."

Scofield slumped a millimeter or two, not so chatty on this aspect.

Jack asked, "What made you think Green and Cragin had joined forces?"

"Because the other bitch told me so."

"Who?"

"Her flunky. Kelly Henessey."

* * *

Maggie found herself in front of the bare-chested David Carlyle for the second time that evening. She had gotten a fresh stack of paper towels, but that turned out to be overkill; the bleeding slowed and then stopped, except for the last oozes of red liquid, now faint smears against the white towels rather than the bright red spots they had been. She had enough from the trailer that they had made the trip back to the station without getting any blood on her clothes, or any more on his. She couldn't be sure about the police van but did not intend to fret; surely that van had seen much more blood spilled than this in its day.

"How does your nose feel?" she asked Carlyle.

"A little sore," he admitted. "But it'll be okay. It always bleeds like this, ever since I was a kid."

She pulled the duct tape off his back to release the wires, using the same technique as with painter's tape—peeling at an acute angle with a steady pace. But no technique could make it painless, and his muscles rippled under the skin. Behind him, where she could sound more objective, she said, "That was brave, you know."

He made a comment that sounded like "*Meh.*"

"It was. This isn't your job and you're not trained for it. You weren't obligated to do a single thing to bring Connor Scofield down, but you went alone into a situation that could have turned violent—and did."

He flexed shoulders and twisted his torso a bit, apparently to stretch the now-freed flesh. The duct tape had left angry red lines. "But I wasn't alone. You were there."

She came around the front of him. "I'm glad that was a comfort."

"And this isn't my first fight, believe it or not. I got into a couple when I was little because, you know, that's what boys do." This had a boastful tone until he added, "My propensity to bleed actually helped. I'd start gushing, and the other kids would get so freaked out, they'd leave me alone."

She smiled for what felt like the first time that evening. But when she saw the nearly adoring cast to his face, she thought better of it.

"Are you okay? Your leg is bleeding."

The broken concrete had not only bruised her shin but cut through both her pants and her flesh. "Oh, hell. Yeah, it will be fine, but I'd better go wash it out. I'll leave the recorder here for the detectives to give back to Vice. After that I'll have to get back to the lab. I have more—" She began to say *money* but then remembered he probably didn't know about that. "Stuff to process."

"Thanks for your help. And . . . thanks for being there."

"You're welcome." She wadded up the used duct tape.

"I really appreciate it."

"No problem."

"It would be great—"

"Are the detectives in here?" asked a new voice.

Maggie turned. Collette Minella stood in the doorway to the homicide unit.

She said, "The ones named Renner and Riley. Are they here?"

"They're conducting an interview right now. Do you need them for something?"

"Just an update as to my aunt's property." She entered the unit. Unlike Maggie she seemed perfectly comfortable to stare at the bare-chested David Carlyle, and asked him, "What happened to you?"

"I—I went undercover. Sort of."

"You a cop?"

"No."

She grinned. "Good. Neither am I."

Maggie introduced them, explaining that Collette was Diane Cragin's niece.

Carlyle told her, "I knew your aunt. I work at the EPA . . . but we didn't see, um, eye to eye."

"That happened a lot with my aunt."

"She pretty much couldn't stand me," he admitted.

"Then we have a lot in common."

Maggie sidled out the door. Glancing back, she saw David Carlyle smile at Collette Minella, a hopeful, tentative look, and Maggie breathed a sigh of something very much like relief.

Chapter 33

"What about Kelly Henessey?" Jack asked Connor Scofield.

"She called me. She had called me once before about setting up some kind of public debate over the project, but that scheduling fell through. . . . Anyway, she had my number, so last week she called and was super hot about Joey talking to Diane. She said they were going behind our backs and making a secret deal."

"Deal to do what?"

"I don't know! She was so mad, she wasn't making a lot of sense. She told me to watch Joey and see what happened about the crib renovation project, because he was going to switch sides and support Vepo for the reno. Then he'd stab me in the back and pull out on StartUp."

"Why?"

"Hedging bets. If she won, she'd support StartUp, and if he won, he'd support Vepo. Or maybe because Diane was paying him to, kicking him in on what she could get from Vepo. Kelly wasn't sure if money actually changed hands or if it were some sort of handshake deal. Or if Joey was going to cut her in on what he skimmed off the amount that the city should have given me for StartUp. Here's the thing: If the city releases the money but then the project gets cancelled for whatever reason, a lot of those funds don't get put back. You can come up with expenses to eat up some of it, like surveys and soil grading and architect plans, stuff that's nonrefundable. Not a lot, relatively . . . like five or seven percent. A fraction. Doesn't sound like much, right? Until you do the math. Seven percent of twelve million is . . . um . . ."

"Eighty-four thousand dollars," Jack supplied.

"Yeah. If they could push it up to ten, and they probably could because Joey could pad a bill like a true artist, one hundred twenty thousand—the cost of doing business, right? The city doesn't care. They have well over eleven million dollars back that they're *not* going to have to pay out. They move on to the next idea and forget about it."

"But why? Why would Green bail on his own project?"

"For the *money*. Joey was like a crack whore around money. Wave a few bills in front of his nose and his eyes glazed over. He'd do anything for it. Weird, really." Scofield settled back, taking time to puzzle this out.

"And Kelly was sure of this?"

"One hundred percent. She said the EPA would kill at least one of the projects because both together would hurt the water much worse than only one of them. StartUp might cause runoff into the river, but if the crib didn't relocate to the river, it wasn't that important. If

the crib relocated to the river but StartUp wasn't causing the runoff, then it wouldn't be so bad. She figured
that they figured that one project had a much better
chance of getting past the regulations than both of
them together."

"But what about the election? Wouldn't bailing on
the project guarantee a loss for Green? He'd built it up
as Cleveland's salvation," Riley asked, brushing dirt
off his left leg. Apparently he hadn't made it over the
minefield of the former parking lot without a tumble,
either.

Scofield's shaggy locks fell over his face, releasing
a scent of sweat and body spray with a hint of pot. "He
wouldn't bail until the city gave us access to the funds,
and that wouldn't happen until after the election and
he'd be on his way to Washington, shaking the dust of
Cleveburg off his toes."

"Hell of a risk. And he'd still have to face reelection
at some point."

Another shake. "Joey was very much a live-in-the-
moment kind of guy. At least that's how I would work
it. Look, supposing he got money from Cragin, he's
got that money. He gets folding money from me at the
same time. Say StartUp gets cancelled, he's got the ex-
pense money. If there is environmental damage from
Vepo, it doesn't reflect on him, plus he can use it
against Cragin in the next election on the off chance he
doesn't win this one. Pretty much win-win from his
point of view, the piece of shit."

"Did you ask him?"

"Uh-uh. Never mentioned it."

"Why *not*?" Riley demanded.

"A, I didn't believe her. I figured she was sowing

dissent to shake him up before the election. B, let's say I *do* believe her, then I want to watch Joey and see what he does, get some confirmation before I act."

"And did you?"

"No. He seemed to be right on board with StartUp every minute of every day. He set up that press conference to make the EPA guy look like an idiot. He coached me what to say in front of the committee meeting. I figured Kelly Henessey didn't know what the hell she was talking about. *Or* Joey planned to double-cross Cragin instead of me. That would be like him."

"If you had found reason to suspect Green," Jack pointed out, "that gave you a good reason to want him dead."

Scofield didn't flinch at the accusation. "Okay, make up your mind—did I kill the senator or did I kill Joey? Besides, nobody killed Joey—dude had a heart attack. If you ever saw him eat, you wouldn't find that surprising."

Jack said, "Kelly Henessey said Diane had a secret deal with Green to kill StartUp and usher in Vepo's reno contract."

"Yep."

"Why would she tell you? Isn't that exactly what they wanted? Vepo in and StartUp out?"

"Yes!" Scofield exploded in a billow of exasperation. "That's why I didn't believe her. That's what they had all wanted, so why wouldn't she just keep her mouth shut and let Joey screw me? What was in it for *her*?"

"And she said—?"

"She hung up on me. After telling me to figure out a

way to stop Joey. Like *anybody* could stop Joey."

"What made Kelly so sure of this?" Riley asked.

"She found some text messages on Diane's phone, that's what she said."

"Cragin's phone was password protected."

"She saw them one day when Diane set it down for a minute. That's what she said. I didn't ask what they said or anything, I was too busy trying to pin her down to what that all had to do with *me*. I told you, the bitch was babbling."

A short silence ensued. Jack tried to make sense of this. Scofield lied as easy as he breathed, but Jack had the feeling Green's betrayal might be true . . . mostly because Scofield seemed less than enthusiastic about it. Admitting that not everyone might have been taken with his sparkling personality didn't come naturally to him.

Jack would have to speak to Kelly Henessey. "What day was this?"

In response Scofield asked for his cell phone. Jack handed it to him and watched over his shoulder as he scrolled through an inordinately long call history. "There. Last Thursday."

Jack plucked the phone back. He had no doubt that Connor Scofield knew tech in a way the two cops could never hope to comprehend, but even he couldn't remotely wipe a phone using only mental powers.

"I'm going to get that back, right?" Scofield said.

"Eventually. Have you spoken to her since?"

"Nope. Not until that day Joey died, in the hallway. You were there."

"Yes," Jack said. "I was."

Chapter 34

70 minutes until polls close

"What's happening?" Maggie asked from the back seat.

"Hell if I know," Jack said.

"Let's try this—why am I here?" They headed back to the banks of the Cuyahoga, where Kelly Henessey would be coordinating the ribbon-cutting ceremony for the temporary crib, and Jack and Riley hoped to get some answers from her. Detective work, not forensic work, so she needed her role clarified. Not that there was anywhere else she'd rather be, because after the events of the past few days she wanted some friggin' answers herself.

Riley said, "We're going to need to take her cell phone. We need you to disable it or whatever you do and drop it in one of those spy bags."

"A Faraday bag. It blocks signals so it can't be remotely wiped, and it doesn't require any special technique to use—drop it in and close the top. You have a warrant to take it, right?"

She watched from the back seat as the two detectives glanced at each other.

"Gentlemen?"

Silence.

"She's not going to just give it to you."

"She might," Jack said. "If we tell her it could help make a case against Cragin's killer."

"Unless *she's* Cragin's killer."

"Yeah, that. We'd also like a DNA sample and fingerprints before she heads back to DC. She said she didn't know anything about the money in Cragin's safe, but Scofield says that she talked about payoffs. I'm betting some of those unidentified prints on the money will be hers."

Maggie didn't complain. She'd never been to the main crib, the orange circle of concrete with a white house sitting atop it, three miles offshore in the lake, and was curious to see what one looked like on the inside. Until they arrived and she realized they were walking into a political party's last publicity effort on an election night. All of a sudden there were dozens of places she'd rather be, blissfully quiet places.

She could hear the noise from the grass before they even reached the catwalk with its shiny new paint. Its sixty-foot span held at least as many people, scattered here and there, speaking excitedly to one another or into phones. Three patrol officers working security, at three separate points, stopped them to ask for ID, but of course let the detectives pass without argument.

This new crib's base had been left unpainted, with

the housing still white. Double steel doors had been propped open, and they plunged into the brilliantly lit interior.

Maggie's first impression was one of slight disappointment.

The upper platform formed a wide path around a center hollow with a waist-high railing. A metal cabinet in a corner stood open with a red, white, and blue ribbon strung between the doors. Other than that, the place seemed empty of the machinery or technology she had been expecting. It was not, however, empty of people.

Teen raves were less crowded than the ring of concrete. People milled everywhere. Two television reporters were trying to get the people around them to clear enough space so that their cameramen could get a shot that didn't show their pores. Maggie saw the lawyer, Stanton, looking smug, and the impromptu candidate looking bewildered—but smiling, smiling, smiling. A woman she assumed to be his wife kept a hand on his shoulder, exhausted but somehow more relaxed than the candidate himself. Two small children played hide-and-seek among the throng, their shrieks barely audible above the din. At least they were having a good time. Everyone else, despite the forced gaiety, seemed as panicked as passengers after the *Titanic* hit the iceberg.

Room had still been found for a television set in the corner, tuned to the election results as precincts reported and predicted and updated. Three campaign workers slavishly monitored the screen and shouted breaking news to coworkers, reaching earsplitting decibels to be heard over the cacophony of other shouts. Even the chill November air through the open doorways couldn't keep up with the body heat. Phones rang ceaselessly in an endless variety of music and tones.

Jack spotted Kelly near the railing and tugged on Maggie's hand. They squeezed through the crowd.

The woman looked worse than Maggie had seen her yet, as if she hadn't slept, eaten, showered, or paused in days. Her eyes were red-rimmed and her hair lank as she poked at a tablet and shouted at two people with campaign buttons who appeared nearly as exhausted as she did. They had to thread single-file through a phalanx of college students to reach her, and when they did she glanced at Maggie and the cops as if she had never seen them before and didn't find them significant now.

The inner room held slightly fewer people than the outer, but still at least one person for every two-foot-square space. Jack walked up to Kelly and asked if there was somewhere they could have a private word. Her look in response said that Jack had clearly lost his mind. "Of course not. The polls close in an hour. Mack! Make sure the news vans don't leave the Public Square rally. Give them some good soundbites to make sure they stay!"

"It's important," Jack said. "I don't think you want to have this conversation in public."

Her face contorted to reflect the absurdity of this. "What do you freakin' *want*? I don't have time for this! Talk to Stanton. That's what we pay him for."

"We need to talk to you."

"About *what*?"

"About why you killed Diane Cragin."

"Are you completely insane?" Kelly snapped. "I didn't kill Diane! Why on earth would I kill Diane?"

"Because you wanted the Vepo contract to fail. It was too late for this temporary crib, but the permanent one could still be salvaged," Jack said.

At this her face, her entire body, went still. Only for a split-second, but in the reigning chaos the change stood out like flashing neon. Then she spoke so quietly that Maggie couldn't hear her in the din but saw her lips form the words *What are you talking about.*

Jack said, "We've spoken to Connor Scofield. You sure you don't want to have this conversation in private now?"

Kelly glanced around as if searching for an escape, but then said, "Yeah, follow me."

They threaded after her through the sea of overly warm, overly excited people to a door in the back under a bright red Exit sign. It opened into a stairwell, a blank, dingy gray hole with concrete steps and dim lighting. Kelly wound a cautious way down it until they landed on the lower level of the crib structure, blissfully unoccupied but nearly as noisy since the crowd was only one floor up through an open hole. On top of that, below them the river churned in its pen and instantly grabbed Maggie's attention. By leaning over the railing she could see the huge portal to the north where the water entered, and across from it the closed sluice gate. The water lapped at the walls as if frustrated, forced to wait until the gate opened to continue its journey to the Garrett Morgan water treatment plant—named after the African American inventor of the automatic traffic light and many other useful items. Some of the water's drops made it all the way up the side, and spots on the landing shone with wetness. A gap in the railing to her left allowed access to a rung ladder that descended into the waves.

Kelly stood at the railing as well, but not to admire the technology. "Now what?"

Riley said, "Scofield told us how you tried to sabotage your own candidate."

"Never. I would never do that."

"You would if you thought she had made a separate peace with the enemy."

Kelly couldn't have looked more confused if he had been speaking Swahili, so he clarified: "You told him Diane Cragin was in cahoots with Joey Green, to screw StartUp Central and push the Vepo renovation."

Her face cleared, then turned to a more calculating cast. "He told you that?"

Riley nodded.

"The little shit. Please tell me you had to put him in thumbscrews and beat it out of him."

"That's not how we roll."

"The little *shit*. My fault." She threw up her hands and paced in a small circle around the damp concrete slab. "My fault. I should never have trusted a stupid kid."

"So you did tip him off that Cragin and Green were meeting?"

She came to a halt. "Yes. So what? So I tipped someone off to chicanery in public office."

"Congratulations. But *we're* the guys you're supposed to tip off."

"You wouldn't have recognized the lies. It's not illegal for two elected officials to talk to each other. Scofield had a vested interest in putting a stop to it."

Someone above them screamed with laughter, the shriek echoing around their concrete chamber.

Riley asked, "What could he do that you couldn't?"

"Control the money. The city grant would have gone to him, not Joey. He could turn Joey's head with that, offer him a lot more than he'd get from Vepo."

Jack said, "Start from the beginning. You're working for Diane and you don't like what Diane is doing. Did you discuss it with her?"

"You just said it—I worked for her. I existed to pick up her dry cleaning and write her speeches and book her TV ads. The last thing you can do in my position is argue with your boss. The last thing you can do"—she rested her back against the uppermost rail—"is develop a conscience."

"And you did?"

She stared at the floor. "Politics. The art of the possible. What is doable, what is practical, what is profitable. Forget what is ideal, or even good." She rubbed one eye. "We'd been working on the Vepo thing for five months. I had to read all their reports, prepare all Diane's talking points. Then I got the EPA kid's feedback. I told myself that he was overly cautious, that he only wanted to justify his job . . . then I found out more about Vepo's track record. Then StartUp came along, and even I could figure out that if they kicked up all the toxins in the soil while Vepo's system would already be compromised . . . disaster. Pure disaster."

"And the senator—"

"I tried that! I gave her all those facts. She didn't lis-

ten. I tried to couch it in political terms—that her career would blow up if she had Vepo do the renovation
and then they killed a bunch of people. She didn't believe it. I said, *They're going to kill a bunch of people*,
period. She didn't care. It was just so . . . much . . .
money. Frankly . . . she wouldn't admit it, but I think
she planned to retire for good at the end of the next
term. She had stocks and accounts and of course the retirement plan up the wazoo, but the tax-free cash . . .
she needed to pad that nest egg for all she was worth."

"So you sabotaged your own boss?"

Kelly looked as if he'd slapped her. "No! I wanted
to *stop* her."

"Again, we're the guys you're supposed to tip off.
Why not call us, or at least alert the media? Or the Senate ethics committee or whatever. No, you waited until
she was dead and then steered us toward Harold
Baudelet, let him tell us about the whole Vepo mess."

Again, that look as if he were truly a mental defi-
cient. "Because this is my job. Turn in my boss? Expose her? Yeah, that looks great on a résumé."

She turned and paced the circular railing, shaking
her hands away from her body as if she could shake off
her disgust at his cluelessness. Maggie didn't move,
and neither did the cops. Kelly had to be drawn out at
her own pace.

Directly opposite them, Kelly spoke over the water.
"Remember how I told you everyone in the world is
just trying to keep their job? That's all I was doing. No
matter what happened with Diane, I have a lot more
years to go. I have to think about that every single day.
I have to make good things happen for my person and
not bad things." She gazed at Maggie, perhaps think-

ing she'd be more likely to understand—what? The tightrope women had to walk to stay employed? The sacrifices one makes for their profession?

That one could wind up telling lies without ever having planned to do so.

Yes, Maggie thought. *I understand.*

"I've done a lot of things in this job. I helped a guy keep his mistress under wraps for three years. I wrote talking points against gay marriage for a gay guy."

Above them someone used some kind of loudspeaker to announce that the new candidate would be cutting the ribbon to open the gates and start the process of getting Cleveland cleaner water.

Maggie said, "I know how these things get out of control—"

But Kelly steamrolled on. "I designed press releases to make it seem that a new tax law *wouldn't* lower the tax on the rich and raise it on the poor. But I'll be damned if I'm going to kill people."

"But," Jack pointed out, "you killed Diane."

"Will you get off it? I did not kill Diane. I didn't kill anyone! Why do you keep saying that?"

Riley pressed, "So you wanted to stop the Vepo contract. What did you do next?"

"I called Scofield and told him that Green planned to stab him in the back."

"How did you know Cragin and Green were meeting?"

"She told me! I had to reschedule a few things to make it happen. Why not? Diane got what she wanted—so why would I care? Other than poisoning half the city, all would be great for our side."

"What was in it for Green?" Jack stayed where he

was, Riley behind him, as Kelly moved slowly along the railing. No one wanted to duplicate the claustrophobic effect of the upper room.

"I don't know. Nothing about him seemed to make a lot of sense. I thought he wanted to set her up, get proof of her making deals, and the election would be in the bag. Maybe she even promised to step aside—but of course she didn't. Whatever deal they had, she went back on. That's why he killed her."

"Green killed her?"

Talking usually calmed people down, Maggie knew, but not in this case. Kelly grew more agitated with every word, pacing, reversing direction with sharp turns and starting at every sharp noise from above. "Yes! What I've been telling you from the start! He called that morning, raging. I could hear his voice coming from her phone, calling her every filthy name he could think of."

"Why?"

"I don't know. She hung up on him. We were leaving the breakfast with Capital Management. But I think she called him back from her car, because I saw her on the phone as we drove over here."

"What did she say about it?"

"Nothing."

"Did you ask?"

"Diane made it clear from day one—I worked *for* her, not *with* her. If there was something she wanted me to know, she'd tell me. Otherwise if she didn't tell, I didn't ask. I did point out that I was her first line of defense, so if something might blow up on us I needed to be prepared, right? She said, 'What's he going to do? Tell his party he made a deal with the enemy? No,

StartUp has to go, or Vepo will end in disaster. That little wiener dog at the EPA has convinced me.'"

"But they met later in the day," Riley said. "So maybe they worked something out."

"I doubt it. I can't say I knew Diane that well, but I ran her life for seven months. Whatever she promised him, she had no intention of delivering. I'm sure she was trying to string him along until after the election."

The noise upstairs had dimmed a bit after the first announcement but had already bounced back to deafening.

She paused long enough to rub both eyes with one tightly clenched fist. "I don't know how he figured out that she planned to screw him, but he did. He knew she wouldn't be home—especially if they met, as you said. Did you know his father was an electrician? He's always talking about his working-man roots. He killed my *boss*. Just to win an election!"

"So you used your meds to return the favor?" Jack asked.

"He deserved to be struck by lightning! At least Diane was a transplant. He planned to screw his own friends and neighbors, people he lived with!"

Kelly glanced up the center hole; Maggie didn't know if the girl wished she was up there with them or dreaded having to rejoin the action. But she also stared at the cops as if she wanted to push past them and escape. A peal of thunder seemed to shake the building, loud enough to be heard over the water and the crowd.

"So what did you do, Kelly?" Jack prompted, guiding her, almost gently, back to her story. "About Vepo?"

She had been completing the circle of the center hole, which would bring her to Maggie first and then the cops. She poked the single chain across the railing's gap and set it swinging. The woman's face seemed to tremble on the edge of tears, razor-sharp cheekbones jutting from pale skin. "Nothing. Scofield had been my last hope. I couldn't see a way to stop them . . . the crib project would go on. And I would let it. And now the heavens are going to open up at the same time these gates do and poison us all." She gave a loud sniff and moved her right arm, but instead of wiping it across her face as Maggie expected, she reached under her light sweater and pulled a Glock 40 from the back of her waistband.

Maggie stopped breathing.

From the corner of her eye she saw Jack reach for her arm, no doubt to pull her back and away from Kelly, but the woman swung the gun at the two men and said, "Don't move!"

If she shot at them, she'd have to shoot through Maggie to do it.

No one moved.

But Kelly didn't seem interested in pointing it at anyone; she used it more to gesture with, waving it in exasperated agitation. "Just leave me alone! I just want . . . give me five minutes . . ." She rested her hip against the rail, facing all three of them, the gun at her side but with her finger clearly on the trigger. And Glocks, Maggie knew, had no safeties. If she pulled that small crescent of metal, it would fire.

"Kelly—" she began.

"Don't! Just don't! There's nothing you can say."

"I know." Maggie kept her voice as gentle as she could and still be heard above the loudspeaker as the speaker announced handing a pair of scissors to the new

senator from Ohio. The crowd met this optimistic pre-
monition with cheers, utterly unaware of the drama
playing out beneath their feet.

Kelly didn't want to kill anyone, Maggie knew. She
had simply been forced into a corner, literally and fig-
uratively, both by them and by her own actions. "You're
exhausted. You've been through a wringer in the past
few days and—"

"Stop!" She pointed the gun at all three of them, but
mostly the two cops, swinging her arm from one to the
other. She had to know Maggie would be unarmed.
"Back up. Go away."

"Maggie," Jack said, his voice a low warning. No
doubt he meant to remind her that she had no training
in hostage negotiation and was not wearing a bullet-
proof vest. She knew all that damn well, but she was
there and she was closest to the woman. She had to do
something, or that sweaty, nervous finger would twitch
and the shot would deafen whomever it didn't kill.

Then Kelly swung the gun up and used the tip of the
barrel to scratch her own temple, letting it rest there.

"Maggie, step back," Riley burst out, sounding nearly
as desperate as Jack did. She could feel them behind her,
coiled to move, with only uncertainty keeping a tenu-
ous leash.

Maggie said, "Kelly, listen to me. You're not thinking straight."

"What else is new?" The gun moved back toward
the cops, catching Maggie's position in its sweep.

"You're suffering from the effects of exhaustion.
You're dehydrated. You probably have a headache and
feel dizzy at times. You haven't eaten because you

don't have any appetite and that makes you feel even weaker, like your muscles—"

"It's an election," the woman said. "They're all like this."

Maggie didn't know what else to do but keep talking. "Kelly, no one's been poisoned yet."

"That gate's about to open," Kelly pointed out.

"But it hasn't rained."

Another rumble of thunder ruined this defense, and Kelly snorted.

Maggie kept trying. "The brownfield won't leach everything right away. There's still time. You can get the city to take the reno project away from Vepo and save all those people." She chose to gloss over a possible prosecution for the murder of Joe Green.

"And be the hero?" Kelly asked.

Maggie didn't fall into that trap. Kelly didn't want to be a hero; she just didn't want to be a demon. "You can make it right."

"You can help us bring Vepo down," Jack put in.

The barrel turned up again. The end of it pressed against the skin next to Kelly's right eye. "But I'm the one who propped them up to begin with."

Maggie couldn't help holding out her hands, as if she could guide the gun away. "Kelly, don't do this."

"Maggie," Jack again warned, his voice as tight as she'd ever heard it. But what could she do?

"Three . . . two . . . one," the man with the loud-speaker announced.

"Your body is worn out, but that's a temporary problem."

Machinery started up and the gates began to open.

The water rocked like an excited stallion and a dull roar grew, but on the floor above, a woman screamed—and not with laughter this time. "She's got a gun!"

Maggie made herself ignore all of it, never breaking Kelly's gaze. "You'll feel much better with proper fluids and rest, and then you can fix it. You can fix all of it."

"Turn in all my bosses?" A crooked smile. "I told you how good that looks on a résumé."

Then she pulled the trigger.

Jack saw the trigger finger clench and without thinking pulled Maggie back so roughly he heard a ripping sound from the fabric of her shirt. *Get the gun get the gun get the gun*—but that didn't prove possible. The shot to her right temple pushed Kelly to the left, over the loose chain across the gap. Her body tumbled silently into the roaring waves and disappeared immediately. She took the gun with her.

He had one foot on the edge in a purely instinctive movement before rationality made him take a second look—Kelly Henessey had left half of her brain matter on the damp concrete floor. Drowning would not be the cause of death.

Then he turned to Maggie.

She had screamed—to his ears, her voice ringing above the shot, the water and the screams of the now-aware crowd upstairs—but seemed to have no breath left, tiny bits of red dotting her pale face.

"Are you all right?" he asked.

She stared at him the way a toddler stares at something new and possibly not pleasant, with a pensive, tiny frown . . . not afraid but deeply concerned.

And that scared him, because there had never been anything remotely childlike about Maggie.

He moved toward her and pulled her into his arms. His chest marred the red dots on her skin, but at least it blocked the view of the splotches of tissue representing all that was left of Kelly Henessey.

Outside, the heavens opened, and the deluge began.

Chapter 35

That look had largely disappeared by the following week, though touches lingered around her eyes. Jack noticed it when he stopped by the lab to collect a fingerprint report on the baggie of Nardil that they had found in Kelly Henessey's purse. The assumption made was that she must have dumped the pills in it when she substituted her own Sarafem into Green's prescription bottle.

Riley had prompted Jack to go and collect the report, inventing some errand he had to take care of; he probably believed Maggie may still be in a fragile sort of state and could use a shoulder. A generous soul, Riley. He may not have a girlfriend of his own but wanted to help Jack maintain his relationship with one.

A sudden concern struck Jack. Should his history ever come to light, the fallout might burn up Riley the most. How could a homicide detective face coming to work every day if it became known that he'd been the partner of a serial killer and never knew it? Riley would never live it down.

If for no other reason, Jack had to make sure that did not happen. He owed the man that much. He had walked this tightrope before, but somehow practice did not make it easier.

He shoved his mind back to the task at hand and asked if any prints had been recovered from the baggie.

"Nah. Plastic bags are a pain to get prints from—they're too flexible and get wadded up and stuffed in things, then covered with powder or lint. Our superglue and dye stains can only do so much. But her changing out his pills—seems an iffy way to kill somebody."

"That's what the doc said."

"Maybe she may have only wanted to make him sick enough to knock him out of the race. Frankly, after spending all week listening to politicians, I'm surprised that sort of sabotage doesn't happen all the time."

"That's why the White House has tasters."

"Green should have invested in some. How did she know he was color-blind, though?"

Jack remembered the unfortunate secretary and her colored folders. "It wasn't a big secret. Certainly his whole staff knew and made allowances for it."

"But how did Kelly make the switch, her pills for his?"

"Who knows how—or when? They ran into each other several times, public debates, private payoffs. It would have been tough to prove, if we'd had to go to court."

"I don't know."

He studied her. "What do you mean?"

"The pockets," Maggie said, coffee cup halfway to her lips. "When he died I heard her say something to someone about Green 'lining his satin pockets.' If that's a common expression, I've never heard it. But when I examined the body, that expensive jacket that was made not to look expensive was silk-lined, kind of shiny. How would she know that if she hadn't handled the bottle?"

"Huh," Jack said.

"As you said, they had run into each other on occasion so it could have been something she'd noticed before. But . . ."

Or, Jack thought, she overheard them discussing his clothes at the scene, but he said, "The doctor thought it would have taken several doses to cause a fatal heart attack. Less than that could cause agitation and a racing pulse . . . the symptoms make me wonder if she took some herself."

"I was about to say that she'd hardly take a combination she'd poisoned someone else with. And she didn't put them in her pill bottle—more sense than that— hence the baggie. But she needed any boost she could get to make it through election night in the shape she was in. And if the suicidal bent had been bubbling to the surface for a while, who's to say what she might have done?"

"I had not pegged her as suicidal. I figured all that manic hyperactivity as par for the course for political types."

"She told us her doctor prescribed—maybe *specifically* prescribed—something she couldn't overdose on. Maybe the doctor saw something we didn't, maybe it's standard, I don't know. Clearly she had been getting close to the edge for a long time, to judge from the dry skin, the weakness, scleral petechiae."

Jack said, "The stress of the election, plus having to do everything without knowing if she'd still have a job after Tuesday."

"And of course failing to stop Vepo, that weighed on her conscience. Probably a lot of things weighed on her conscience."

He should ask what weighed on hers, address the elephant in the room. But he didn't want to. He didn't want to know how much of a danger Maggie Gardiner might be to him.

So he sat in the lightweight wheeled chair kept by her desk for visitors, watching her face. "Other people in the party—friends—said she had seemed depressed and worried for months."

"She was exhausted, both physically and mentally, and the antidepressants may have aggravated it instead of helping. This would have prompted her to suicidal thoughts, as well as anger, isolation, hopelessness, and paranoia—she may easily have believed that killing Green was the only way to save the city, or the only way to get justice for him killing Cragin. Above all, she was tired of lying to keep her job."

He couldn't dodge this. "We're not the same, Maggie. Us and them."

She met his gaze. "How do you figure that?"

"Because there are lies and then there are lies. Theirs hurt people for personal profit. You—we— saved future victims at great personal risk. It's *not* the same."

"You believe that?" He heard hope in her voice.

"And so do you. Or we wouldn't be sitting here."

She considered this, and him, for some time. Then the sounds of Denny bustling around the mass spec in the other room jolted the silence, and the conversation moved back to safe ground. She said, "Kelly also had the stress of waiting to see if Green might expose her, or blackmail her or whatever. She no longer had the safety net of Diane's influence."

"You think that might be why she killed him, maybe more than getting revenge for her boss?"

"Huh. Hadn't thought of that, but I guess it could be. No one ever does anything for only one reason."

"Is that one of Locard's principles?"

"No," Maggie said, "that's one of my principles. At least the city is reexamining the Vepo contract. Is the party cooperating?"

"Stanton's trying to find a way to distance all of them from the fact that they were running a candidate who planned to poison a good chunk of the city, but aside from that, they're more than willing to throw Vepo to the wolves. The party improves their environmental record, and it will keep them too busy to ask for their money back. Your little friend David is front and center."

"You still don't like him?"

"On the contrary. Now that he's no longer a suspect in two murders, I'll graciously step aside and set you free to see him. Even if he's a little dorky and can't remember the right code word when he needs to."

"No, thanks. He's a very nice guy, but I think his head has been turned by Collette Minella. Who may soon be a very wealthy woman thanks to all that cash that no one is able to claim without admitting to a number of felonies."

The city had turned the brand-new crib off again, closing the sluice gates, until the water in the river could be analyzed to everyone's satisfaction. The jury remained out on what to do with the StartUp lot, since the environmental damage had already been done. The future of the business depended upon how much financial support Connor Scofield could get once his bribe activity came to light. Not a lot, Jack would guess, which was too bad in a lot of ways. Minus the financial shenanigans and the brownfield it nearly sat upon, StartUp Central remained a great idea.

Maggie said, "Anyway, here's your report. Let me get the baggie, and I can sign that back over to you, too."

"And nothing on it, you said?"

"Some pieces-parts along the top edge," she said, using her own terminology for small wisps of fingerprints, "but nothing I could work with."

Jack nodded as she walked away. That did not surprise him. He had been careful to hold it by its very edges when he dropped it into Kelly Henessey's purse.

Chapter 36

His only target, at the beginning, had been Diane Cragin. Jack had stumbled on Lori Russo's article about the crib renovation and at first had been merely grateful that Russo had turned her attention to something besides the vigilante murders. Her concerns about the water system prompted him, on an idle afternoon, to do a bit of research on Vepo, Diane Cragin, and their proximity to mass poisonings elsewhere in the country. The experiences in Flint, Michigan, also popped onto his radar. Jack also seemed to be the only person in the city reading David Carlyle's EPA reports, which were posted online as public record. All of this, especially Diane Cragin's track record of complete disregard for other human beings and her position of great authority over what happened to those human beings, convinced him that she needed to die.

Or, at least, get knocked out of commission, because he honestly hadn't known whether the electricity would kill her.

He had been observing her in-district schedule for

weeks and did a number of drive-bys of her home. Thanks to a politician's penchant for being seen—except where it wouldn't be prudent to be seen—most of her appearances were announced online. Her Facebook account provided minute-by-minute updates. He had never observed anyone else at her home, even when he entered her yard on two separate occasions; she had few visitors, no houseguests, no parties. The Secret Service detail never entered the yard. Thus he felt fairly safe that he could accomplish his goal without running two-twenty current through some unsuspecting innocent.

Hooking up the wires may have been his riskiest move to date. But she lived on a very quiet street with copious foliage and even in broad daylight—lunch hour, to be exact—he had been completely hidden from view. Dressed in a pair of unlabeled coveralls, he had been in and out in under two minutes. The grill had come not from Joe Green's now-discarded Weber but from some contraption one of Jack's neighbors had thrown out on garbage day two weeks before. Of course he couldn't be sure when Cragin would arrive at her home, but it didn't matter. That it rained beforehand proved lucky for him—but not for her, as her wet shoes sealed her doom.

That would have been the end of it, even if she survived. The murder attempt would give authorities a reason to look into her friends and enemies, such as Vepo. The bribes Jack assumed she had received would come to light.

He had been aware of Green and the environmental danger of StartUp Central through David Carlyle's *other* reports, but that situation did not seem as dire, especially if the river crib was shut down. And, with the arrogance of age, he never thought the city would hand twelve million dollars to a very young man.

He had made slips: showing familiarity with the crib project from the beginning, recognizing the EPA reports on the senator's dining room table, pushing Riley to interview Baudelet.

But then Joey Green had killed Lori Russo.

Jack had no doubt of this. Green's bodyguard's car had been at the scene. Also rumors and even a long-ago failed prosecution had tied Green to unexpected deaths before, and he had withstood his share of scrutiny over the years. But he had never had so much riding on the moment as he had in those few days—a percentage of the twelve million *and* a senatorship. Lori Russo had to go. Green destroyed a good person and devastated a loving family simply for a new job and some money.

As soon as Maggie told him the news, Jack knew what he had to do. Green had to *die*.

But Jack needed to be careful. Maggie took trust-but-verify to heart and would still be watching for any unexpected deaths occurring in Jack's vicinity. The chaos of the debate provided perfect cover to dump the pills from Kelly's bottle into his pocket, then switch them with the ones in Green's bottle, left in the jacket he thoughtfully handed to Jack. Someone in the crowd could have seen him. One of Green's staff might have noticed the color change. Green might have survived the heart attack. Success might not be guaranteed, yet the plan also left little risk to himself. He'd have gladly taken any risk to remove Green from the planet.

But in the end Green's unhealthy lifestyle had cooperated just like Cragin's shoes.

Almost as if the universe approved and wanted to help. Because there are lies, and then there are lies.

It would have been nice to have it written off as an unsurprising heart attack, but he knew the odds were very slim. At some point the ME's office would notice the incorrect prescription. He hadn't counted on that happening right at the scene, but no matter. He would risk losing his freedom to take Green out.

He had *not* intended to frame Kelly Henessey and certainly didn't plan to drive her to suicide. Casting a bit of suspicion wouldn't hurt, maybe even prompt her to clean up her act and stop covering up mass disasters for professional liars. He didn't think the Sarafem could be positively linked to her prescription or that anyone could prove she'd had the opportunity to make the switch. Without that she couldn't be convicted. But with her suicide possibly seen as an admission of guilt, all police investigations could be closed. Green killed Cragin and, via his bodyguard, Lori Russo. Kelly killed Green.

She had even helped by not denying it when they asked her at the water plant. He couldn't help but see that as sad. He really hadn't meant for her to die.

Though, on the other hand, she had been willing to let thousands of people suffer in order to safeguard her job, so he would not be shedding a lot of tears for Kelly Henessey. He did regret that she chose to die right in front of Maggie.

Because Maggie, he realized as she returned and handed him an evidence envelope with a swish of her lab coat and an upward curve of her mouth, was what he had truly risked losing.

She would never forgive him if she knew what he had done.

He would not make that mistake again.

Acknowledgments

As always, I have such a list of people to thank that I know I will miss too many. Thank you to my fabulous agent, Vicky Bijur, and all in her office; my equally fabulous editor Michaela Hamilton and the great team at Kensington; Richard Alan Moore and Tom Avitabile, who provided much insight into political workings; my sisters, who are always available to provide editorial comment and moral support; and my husband Russ, who explained how to kill someone with electricity.

This book required a great deal of research, as constant and frenetic as the topic itself. I found countless articles, documentary videos and news items to give me real-life examples. Cleveland's *Plain Dealer* provided thorough coverage of the Cuyahoga County corruption trials which gave me the inspiration for Joey Green. Some of the books I studied were: Linda Killian's *The Swing Vote: The Untapped Power of Independents,* Susan Delacourt's *Shopping for Votes: How Politicians Choose Us and We Choose Them*, Trey Radel's *Democrazy: A True Story of Weird Politics, Money, Madness, and Finger Food,* and John Perkins' *Confessions of an Economic Hit Man.*

Don't miss the next enthralling thriller in the Gardiner
and Renner series by Lisa Black

EVERY KIND OF WICKED

Coming soon from Kensington Publishing Corp.

Keep reading to enjoy a sample excerpt . . .

Chapter 1

"Well, that's less than helpful," Maggie said of the snow.

The white flakes drifted lazily downward, landing on the frozen grass, the bare limbs of the large trees, the bloodstains sprinkled across the worn stones and the very stiff body of a young man who had not dressed well for the weather. Yet exposure hadn't killed him— he had been dead long before his body froze.

From the deep red stain blossoming from the center of his chest, Maggie Gardiner assumed a gunshot—or shots—had been the likely cause of death. Something had penetrated his internal systems to leak his life-blood out across his white shirt and over the stones beneath him, which marked, coincidentally, a grave. But Maggie didn't say so; declaring cause of death was a pathologist's job and she worked as a forensic specialist. Her job would be to find the evidence around said death in order to help her colleagues at the police department determine who had walked away from this boy's last encounter.

Which would be more difficult to do with each passing moment as the snow slowly covered up the body, the blood, and all her evidence.

She had arrived at the scene immediately before the assigned detectives, and now felt them standing on either side of her, Jack Renner to her right and Thomas Riley to her left. Renner, tall, only a bit dark and not so handsome, and his partner, distinctly shorter but lighter in both coloring and personality. And her, an inch shorter than Riley and nearly half his body weight, pale with deep brown hair falling past her shoulders, no gun, no badge, a civilian employee in a department of sworn officers. A uniformed patrol officer hovered somewhere among the graves as well. They made a somber and all too familiar tableau. A frigid breeze lifted her hair, chilled her neck, and moved on.

"A dead guy in a cemetery," Riley said. "That's—what's the word?"

"Weird?" Maggie suggested.

"I was going to say redundant." He took a step closer to the body and she spread out both arms like a railroad crossing, stopping both detectives. It wouldn't hold them for long, she knew.

She crouched, looking not at the body but the ground around it, finally poking the ground with a latex-gloved finger.

"Shoe prints?" Jack asked.

She answered with disappointment. The canopy of trees in the cemetery kept the grass sparse, and if the man had been killed during a thaw there might be nice prints in the Ohio clay-mud. But the ground had been frozen much too solid for the killer's feet to create prints. At least she didn't have to pour casts, always a chore in any kind of weather, but especially in snow where the reaction as the cast hardened created warmth and melted the print. A forensic Catch-22.

The cops took this as an all-clear and moved closer to the body. So did she. The patrolman stayed where he was. He had already strung yellow crime scene tape across the now-opened gates at either end of the cemetery and the high stone walls protected the rest. Crowd control at an inner-city cemetery on a snowy weekday didn't present much of a problem. Outside those walls, office buildings towered over the scene, only half a mile from the Public Square. Cars hummed along the surrounding streets, calm now that the morning rush hour had ended. She could work in relative, if chilly, peace.

Maggie observed their young victim. He lay facing the sky, eyes unable to shut against the precipitation. He wore jeans, a T-shirt, and a satin jacket that would have been at home inside a disco circa 1985, with thin padding unlikely to be much protection against Cleveland weather in mid-December. Maggie put his age at about twenty-five. He had brown hair, brown eyes, and a deeper hue to his skin even with the pallor of death over it, possibly mixed-race. His hair was cut short, no apparent piercings or tattoos that she could see.

"Any ID?" Riley asked. "Wallet? Phone?"

She patted his pockets—empty—and they couldn't turn him over to examine any rear pockets until the Medical Examiner's investigator arrived.

But under the open jacket he wore a white badge pinned to his shirt. It had rounded edges and red letters which said only "Evan." A streak of red dots crossed right over the *v* and continued along the shirt. Maggie noted some round stains on his chest and abdomen, and an irregular blotch over his collarbone.

Riley said, "So somebody shot him—"

"I'm not so sure. See those drops? Round spots imply blood fell on him when he was already laid out. I don't know why a gun would be that bloody when it wasn't close enough to leave a jagged hole or the powdery soot of fouling. Unlikely that enough tissue would get on the barrel to drip off later."

Jack had followed her reasoning. "So you think it's a stab wound?"

"That is my guess, but I can't be positive either way. Autopsy will tell. But a stab wound would make more sense, if the killer stood here for a second while blood dripped off the weapon and caused those spots. They didn't come from the victim's hands—they're clean."

"So the killer waited," Jack said. "Making sure he was dead."

He ought to know, Maggie thought.

She said, "No injury to our victim's hands. Either he can't throw much of a punch, or he was swinging a weapon himself and the killer took it away with him, or this was a blitz attack. He didn't even have time to put a hand up and feel his own wounds."

Jack looked around. "So the guy walked out of here with a bloody weapon."

"Or not," Riley said. "We'll have to check those cans at the exits."

The patrolman had been checking his social media but listening as well, because he immediately put the phone away. "Me?"

"Lift the lid off, but don't touch anything inside."
As the young man walked off, Riley said, "If it's not
there we'll have to search the whole grounds. Lucky
for us it's not a big cemetery."

Maggie continued her usual crime scene examination. She took close-up photos of the victim's hands,
without moving them. His right lay palm up, his left
palm down. As she had noted, no torn nails, no bruis-
ing, no bloodstains. They seemed in fairly good shape,
the skin smooth—whatever the guy did for a living probably didn't involve heavy manual labor. They were
bare, something she never understood since she pulled
her gloves out of the closet as soon as the temperature
dipped below sixty, and wished she could get them out
of her pocket now—even two layers of her thin latex
gloves didn't begin to insulate against the chill.

Riley said, as if thinking out loud, "We should check
the entire cemetery anyway. This guy was probably
walking home from work or from the bar, and somebody saw a target. There could be homeless camping
in here—handy stone walls to hide behind, nice and
dark at night, not a place that cops or pedestrians would
be scoping out on a regular basis."

Maggie said, "In winter? I'd think they'd want to be
near a steam grate, or up against the window of an oc-
cupied building. I can't imagine anything colder than a
cemetery in winter."

"Yeah, the only people around have zero body
warmth." Riley chuckled at his own joke. "But break
into one of those little mausoleums and you could probably start a small fire without anyone noticing. Or maybe
your standard mugger saw this guy taking a nice, isolated shortcut . . . it would have had to be before this

place closed, though, or our victim couldn't have gotten in. Unless they both jumped the fence."

Maggie took in the victim's pants and shoes, free of scrapes. But then the cemetery had the high stone wall only on its two long sides. The east and west walls consisted of a shorter iron fence. The young man looked agile enough, especially if he found something to climb on first to allow him to clear the spiky finial at the top of each picket.

Jack walked around the large headstone behind where the victim lay and alerted her to the slim wallet lying up against the back of the stone, protruding from the gathering snow. After Maggie photographed it in place, Jack gloved up and opened it. Riley, knees creaking, crouched to scatter the snow with one hand to look for any other clues that might be steadily disappearing from view.

The wallet stayed slim because it contained almost nothing. "No DL, no credit cards, and certainly no money," Jack grumbled, checking all its compartments. Something fell as he did so, and Maggie caught it before it hit the ground. A dark green plastic key card, the magnetic strip clearly visible.

"Credit card?" Jack asked.

She turned it over, showing him that it was blank on both sides. No numbers, no name, only the ghost image, in lighter green, of a scowling face wearing a horned hat.

"A Viking?" Jack asked.

"Cleveland State," Maggie said.

"Their football team?"

"Basketball. They don't have a football team."

"Are you sure? About the school?"

She didn't take offense at the query. He knew her well enough to know she wasn't exactly the biggest sports fan in the world. If that were the only thing he knew about her, things would be so much less complicated.

"I went there. Green is their color, too. This must be some sort of student ID card."

Riley straightened up and looked around at the whitening landscape. "I don't see anything else. I'd feel a lot better if we could have a sudden, miraculous thaw right about now. Who knows what else is out here?"

Jack dug a few scraps of paper with unlabeled phone numbers and the business card for two area tech stores out of the wallet, then dropped the whole bundle into a paper bag Maggie held out. They would have to follow up those leads later, unless they were lucky and the guy had an ID card in his back pocket.

Maggie could see a mugger taking the cash and credit cards but, assuming the guy had one, why the driver's license? "Maybe the mugger resembles the dead boy enough to keep the DL in case he needed it to use the credit card, or cards?"

Jack said, "Risky. We could check surveillance videos wherever the cards have been used in the past, say, twelve hours . . . of course that's *if* we knew the guy's name."

"Maybe that's why he took the driver's license."

Riley said, "Your average mugger isn't that smart. Trust me on that."

She did. "So our killer is either really smart or really dumb."

"Or this guy didn't carry any identification," Jack said.

Maggie shivered. She couldn't stop thinking about her last visit to the Erie Street Cemetery. She had first entered Jack Renner's orbit that day, eight months and a lifetime ago. The gravesites had been dampened with spring grass and the body of a young girl. Trafficked, abused, murdered, and disposed of.

Jack hadn't killed the girl, of course. But a day later he killed the man who'd killed her. Maggie had discovered that and done nothing about it. Then Maggie had made her own violent decision and her life had not been the same since.

No one—besides Jack, of course—knew that. But not even he knew that she still woke up every morning wondering how long she could carry this burden before she broke under the weight, told someone—anyone—the truth, and created an opening for both her and Jack at the nearest jail. She had not spoken to anyone about this perfect storm of threat and guilt. Not her friends, not her only sibling, not the assigned department-ordered psychologist. Not even Jack.

Not yet, anyway.

She studied his face, wondering if any of these thoughts churned in his head, whether he made the connection between their first case together and this one. Wondering if they had come full circle, wondering if her period of crazy had ended, if she might be ready to go back to being the person she'd been before.

The uniformed patrol officer interrupted her thoughts. He hadn't seen anything of any interest in either garbage can, at least not on the surface. "What's on top don't look fresh, either . . . I doubt this place gets a lot of traffic in the winter. I mean, you can check, but if you ask me, your weapon isn't buried in there."

"Duly noted," Jack said. "Thank you."

"No problem. At least I'm not in the middle of a cluster in some apartment building with psycho moms threatening to beat my ass, like, say, my shift yesterday. Much rather be out here with my nose going numb and—hey, you know who this is?"

The two cops and Maggie gave the young cop their full attention. Riley said, "What? You know our victim?"

"No, not him. Whose grave he's laing on."

Disappointed, Maggie tried to read the large stone looming up from the snow, but the elements of too many years had worn down the surface. Then she noticed, for the first time, that the slab the victim sprawled across had broken and slightly separated, with grass springing up in the cracks as if they were flagstones. "Somebody famous?" she asked, to be polite, since the two detectives showed no interest.

"Chief Joc- O-sot."

She squinted. Indeed, the raised letters of the broken slab spelled that out in a line above the victim's head.

"He was an Indian chief in the Black Hawk War."

Now Riley did show some interest. "What the hell was the Black Hawk War"

"I have no idea, but it sounds cool, don't it? He wasn't actually from Cleveland. He came here with some friend of his and became sort of a media darling. Queen Victoria had his portrait painted when he visited her in England." Now that all three of his companions stared at him, he explained, "My kid had to do a history report on this cemetery."

"Ah," Maggie said.

He spoke more quickly, recognizing short attention

spans when he found them. "Supposedly he haunts this area. The trip to England aggravated an old wound, and he was trying to get to his old home to be buried with his tribe, but only made it back to Cleveland before dying. So his spirit doesn't really want to be here. Supposedly."

"I doubt a ghost gutted this guy," Riley said.

"Doesn't have to be the Indian," the cop mused aloud. "This cemetery used to be a lot bigger, but when downtown real estate needed to expand, they moved a bunch of graves. Might have ticked off a lot of spirits. Like in *Poltergeist*."

Riley argued, "No, in the movie they built over the graves. Here, as long as they actually moved them it should be cool."

"Tell that to the ghosts."

"If you guys are finished discussing the supernatural," Jack said, "I see the ME is here."

The Medical Examiner's Office investigator, a middle-aged man with very dark skin and zero body fat, prodded the body but discovered no new insights. Maggie helped him turn the now-stiff corpse over, but the back pockets were as empty as the front. No phone, no further items, no ID. The jacket similarly held nothing of interest.

"The body snatchers are going to be a while," he told them. "They're stuck at a four-car pileup at Dead Man's Curve."

"Bunch of fatalities?" Riley asked.

"No, but traffic's backed up for two miles and they're looking for an exit."

Riley groaned as if this inefficiency were a personal affront and turned to Jack. "Why don't you see if CSU can tell us anything about that swipe card? I'll stand here and freeze my toes to Popsicles and hear more about Chief Jackspit."

"Joc-O-sot," the patrol officer corrected.

"I'll go with you," Maggie said.

Both cops stared at her.

She said, "Cleveland State's a sprawling campus. It take a half hour of wandering around to find anything if you're not familiar with it. It's only two blocks away." They didn't seem convinced, but she added firmly, "Let's go," and began to walk.

After fifteen or twenty feet, Jack glanced back to make sure they were out of earshot, "What was all that about?"

Maggie said, "We need to talk."